**Praise for *New York Times* bestselling author
Lindsay McKenna**

"McKenna provides heartbreakingly tender romantic
development that will move readers to tears. Her military
background lends authenticity to this outstanding tale,
and readers will fall in love with the upstanding hero and
his fierce determination to save the woman he loves."
—*Publishers Weekly* on *Never Surrender*

"Talented Lindsay McKenna delivers excitement and
romance in equal measure."
—*RT Book Reviews* on *Protecting His Own*

"Lindsay McKenna will have you flying with the daring
and deadly women pilots who risk their lives... Buckle in
for the ride of your life."
—*Writers Unlimited* on *Heart of Stone*

**Praise for *New York Times* bestselling author
Joan Johnston**

"A guaranteed good read."
—*New York Times* bestselling author Heather Graham

"Joan Johnston does short contemporary Westerns to
perfection."
—*Publishers Weekly*

"Joan Johnston continually gives us everything we want...
fabulous details and atmosphere, memorable characters,
a story that you wish would never end, and lots of tension
and sensuality."
—*RT Book Reviews*

NEW YORK TIMES BESTSELLING AUTHORS

LINDSAY McKENNA

& JOAN JOHNSTON

DEADLY SILENCE
&
HAWK'S WAY: FALCON

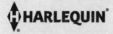 HARLEQUIN®

PLEASE RECYCLE · THIS · PRODUCT IS RECYCLABLE

Recycling programs
for this product may
not exist in your area.

ISBN-13: 978-1-335-58011-5

Deadly Silence & Hawk's Way: Falcon

Copyright © 2020 by Harlequin Books S.A.

Deadly Silence
First published in 2011. This edition published in 2020.
Copyright © 2011 by Lindsay McKenna

Hawk's Way: Falcon
First published as The Unforgiving Bride in 1994.
This edition published in 2020.
Copyright © 1994 by Joan Mertens Johnston

This edition published by arrangement with Harlequin Books S.A.

For questions and comments about the quality of this book,
please contact us at CustomerService@Harlequin.com.

Harlequin Enterprises ULC
22 Adelaide St. West, 40th Floor
Toronto, Ontario M5H 4E3, Canada
www.Harlequin.com

Printed in U.S.A.

CONTENTS

Lindsay McKenna is proud to have served her country in the US Navy as an aerographer's mate third class—also known as a weather forecaster. She was a pioneer in the military romance subgenre and loves to combine heart-pounding action with soulful and poignant romance. True to her military roots, she is the originator of the long-running and reader-favorite Morgan's Mercenaries series. She does extensive hands-on research, including flying in aircraft such as a P3-B Orion sub-hunter and a B-52 bomber. She was the first romance writer to sign her books in the Pentagon bookstore. Visit her online at lindsaymckenna.com.

Visit the Author Profile page
at Harlequin.com for more titles.

DEADLY SILENCE

Lindsay McKenna

To the men I worked with as a volunteer firefighter in 1981–1983, West Point Volunteer Fire Department, West Point, Ohio. Chief Wayne Chamberlain, who was open to the first woman joining a twenty-man station. Lieutenant Gary Amato, former US Air Force firefighter, who supported me and taught me so much about the business. Paul LaNeve, volunteer, who saved my life when a floor collapsed out from beneath me at a structure fire. And last but not least, my husband, David, who was the one who convinced me that I could be a firefighter. And this is dedicated to all men *and* women volunteer firefighters who would give their lives to save others. Nowadays, women are welcomed into fire ranks across the USA. You are all heroes in my eyes, regardless of gender.

CHAPTER ONE

MEGAN JERKED OUT OF A deep sleep. The six-year-old had heard a sound—"pop." It momentarily startled her. She heard nothing else. Snuggling down in her bed with Elmo, her red Muppet, she closed her eyes once more.

And then she smelled smoke. Was she dreaming? The Muppet clock with Big Bird on it read 3:00 a.m. Sitting up, Megan suddenly felt alarm. *Smoke!* She wasn't dreaming! Her daddy was a firefighter. He and Mommy had taught her that if she smelled smoke she should run to the window and escape to safety. Their home was one story. Daddy had taught her how to open the window and climb out.

Maybe she was dreaming. Megan slipped out of bed and clutched Elmo to her red-flannel-nightgowned chest. A small night-light gave enough radiance to see her partially opened door. There was a haze of whitish smoke filtering into her room. Blinking, Megan stood in shock, gripping Elmo to her chest and staring at the silent and deadly smoke.

What was wrong? Daddy had gone to a special school in Cheyenne over the weekend. She and Mommy were here alone. *Mommy!* Running out of the room, Megan raced down the hall toward the bedroom at the other end of the home. As she did, she began to cough violently. The purling smoke became thicker. She couldn't see.

Megan was disoriented, and her eyes watered badly. Coughing violently, she tried to breathe. It was impossible!

There was a dull orange glow pulsating through the thick wall of smoke. Megan heard a window breaking somewhere beyond the smoke.

"Mommy!" she shrilled. "Mommy! Mommy! Wake up! There's fire!" and then Megan's voice cracked and she started coughing violently. She couldn't breathe!

Turning, Megan raced out of the smoke now tunneling down the long, wide hall. It was March; there had been a huge blizzard last night. At least two feet of snow had fallen. Megan ran back to her room, which now was filled with smoke. *Mommy! Where is Mommy?*

Grabbing her robe, Megan put her toy on her bed and thrust her small arms through the sleeves. Wrapping the red sash of her flannel robe around her, she grabbed Elmo to her chest. Pushing her feet into her fluffy red Elmo-headed slippers, Megan ran out of the room. The smoke was so thick, she couldn't see anything. Oh, if only Daddy were here! He'd know what to do.

Megan coughed continuously, tears streaming down her face. She hurried down to the other end of the hall that led to the kitchen. There was a phone there. She couldn't reach Mommy! Sobbing, she picked up the phone and dialed 911. Both her parents had worked with her since age four to teach her how to call for help.

"Nine-one-one. What's your emergency?"

Megan recognized Claudia, one of the dispatchers at the fire station in Jackson Hole. "Claudia, this is Megan Sinclaire…" She coughed. "Our house is on fire! My mommy… I can't get to my mommy! She's trapped in her bedroom! I need help…help…"

The smoke stole silently into the kitchen. Alarmed, Megan saw it billowing in thickly. As soon as she'd got Megan's information, Claudia told her to get out of the house. She was to put on a coat and warm headgear, if possible. And then she was to stand far away, outside the burning home. Megan said she understood and put the phone back down.

Gripping Elmo, she hurried to the front porch. Breathing was difficult. Mouth open, saliva trickling out the corners of her mouth, Megan shakily pulled on her heavy parka, slid her feet into warm fleece boots and donned her thick knit cap, scarf and mittens. She unlocked the door. The snow had piled up, and though she pushed on it, the door wouldn't budge.

Fear gripped Megan. She saw the red and orange lurid colors now coming down the hall toward the kitchen. Knowing they were flames, she realized in panic that the whole house was on fire. Crying out, one arm around Elmo, Megan pushed again and again against the door. No use!

Turning, she ran from the porch to the kitchen door. The only light she had to see with was from the flames licking rapidly toward her. With shaking hands, Megan unlocked the door and slammed her fifty-pound body against it—it barely moved. There was ice build-up on the concrete steps. Again, Megan thrust herself and Elmo against the door and felt cold air suddenly filter through the edge.

Heat was rapidly building up in the kitchen. Her skin smarted and she sobbed. Megan screamed out for her parents as she hurled herself again and again into the stubborn door. There was no movement. The thick, accumulating smoke combined with that awful orange color to stalk her like a fire-breathing dragon. She hit the door with her bruised shoulder and felt it move a few inches more against the snow build-up. *I have to get out!*

Coughing, Megan dropped Elmo at her feet and used both her hands against the oak door. This time, it gave way. It opened just enough to allow her to squeeze through. Somehow, she had to get to Mommy! Leaning over, Megan grabbed Elmo, pushed herself through the door and out into the bitterly cold night air.

She stood on the icy steps, the stars bright and close. It was so cold her breath shot out of her mouth like a white flashlight. As she turned to look back at the house, Megan's eyes widened enormously. The roof over her parents' bedroom was on fire! Gasping, Megan ran down the steps. Earlier that night, her mother had cleared the path around the ranch-style home. Now, slipping and sliding, Megan awkwardly ran around to the front of the house.

As she rounded the corner, Megan saw a dark-colored pickup spinning its tires and racing down the dirt road. A yellow streak of lightning was painted horizontally across the tailgate. The truck sloughed drunkenly through the unplowed freshly fallen snow that blocked the road. It weaved back and forth through the drifts, the tires spinning and screaming. Megan didn't know who it was, and it was too far away to call for help. Racing around the corner of the garage, she headed for the front door of their home. As she reached it, Megan skidded to a halt. Where her parents' bedroom was located, the house was fully consumed in flames.

With a cry of alarm, Megan ran forward and was instantly surrounded by a noxious odor. It smelled like gasoline! Why would there be the smell of gas out here?

Megan slipped and slid on the sidewalk to get to her mommy's bedroom. Fire licked out in bright, shooting red-and-yellow flames through the only bedroom window. Megan screamed again and again for her mother. There was no answer! The popping and snapping of wood burning, the explosion of other windows breaking filled the night around her.

Panicked, Megan dropped Elmo on the sidewalk. She had to get to Mommy! She ran up to the window, gasping and choking. The flames were breathing as though a dragon was inside that room.

"Mommy! Mommy!" Megan shrilled, as she approached the window. "Wake up! Wake up! You have to get out of there!" Megan leaped up to the window, her small hands on the window sill for a second. She screamed and dropped back into the snow—both her hands burned. Megan struggled out of the snowbank sobbing and confused and backed off.

Turning, she looked down the one-mile-long dirt road. The truck was gone. The bright stars in the night sky blinked overhead. The temperature was at least ten below, and her breath shot out in ragged clouds from her contorted mouth.

Megan ran over and grasped Elmo to her chest. She stood looking anxiously at the window. It would be impossible to get into the bedroom. But there was another way! Sliding and falling on the icy sidewalk, Megan got to her feet and made it around to the back door. All she wanted was her mommy. As she struggled through the build-up of snow on the concrete porch, she saw the flames consuming the rest of the house. The fire raced along the roof with a roar.

Looking out toward the road, Megan whimpered.

She knew it would take the fire trucks a long time to
get out here—three miles from the center of Jackson
Hole. They lived on a dirt road that wouldn't be plowed
until dawn came. Crushing Elmo to her chest, she stood
crying and staring at the back door. The snow was too
thick and she couldn't reach the doorknob. And then, the
window in the door blew out toward Megan. Shards of
hot glass showered around her as the build-up of gases
within the home punched out the window like a fist on
the other side.

Crying, Megan threw up her hand. *Too late!* The entire door blew outward. Wood struck the little girl. In
seconds, she was flung off the porch and into a nearby
snowbank.

That was how the paramedics found Megan when
they arrived: stuck in a snowdrift, nearly hypothermic,
hands with second-degree burns, her face pockmarked
by the shards of glass embedded in her flesh.

MEGAN JERKED AWAKE AND sat up. She was gripping
Elmo hard to her heaving chest. *The fire! The fire!*
Looking wildly around, Megan saw that the small lamp
nearby was on. Anxiously, she looked toward her partly
opened door. She saw no smoke. But she could smell
it! Scrambling out of bed, sobbing, she ran to the door.
There was a night-light in the hall. There was no smoke
visible yet. Hurrying down the hall, her green flannel
nightgown flying around her bare feet, she headed for
her daddy's bedroom.

Matt Sinclaire heard his bedroom door fly open. His
eight-year-old daughter, Megan, stood in the doorway,
sobbing and clutching Elmo to her. Groaning, he slipped
out of bed.

"Megan, it's okay. There's no fire," he whispered. He quickly moved to his trembling daughter. Her long blond hair was in wild disarray around her small oval face, her blue eyes wide with shock. Matt crouched down and brought his daughter into his arms to hold her tightly against him. "It's okay, okay, Meggie. There's no fire," he whispered, his fingers moving across her tangled hair and her shoulders. She was trembling. Sounds, strangulated and without meaning, came from her mouth.

Tightly shutting his eyes, Matt held and rocked his daughter. "It's okay, Meggie. It was just a dream. I'm okay and so are you. There's no fire, no fire…." His voice cracked with emotion that threatened to engulf him. When would this nightmare end? Matt knew his daughter had post-traumatic stress disorder. As he rocked her, he felt her small, stick-thin body tremble less and less. At least once a week, Megan would relive the horrors from two years ago. Matt had never slept well since the fire had taken Beverly, his wife. Now, it was just him and his daughter, Megan.

"Elmo isn't afraid," Matt whispered. "Is he? Have you seen if he's shaking?"

Megan eased out of Matt's arms just enough to look down at her doll. Looking up at her daddy's shadowed face, she shook her head.

"See? Elmo would know if there was a real fire," Matt soothed. He stood up and brought Megan against him. He was six foot two and his daughter was only just over four feet tall. She huddled against his thigh, head resting against his hip. Keeping a protective hand around her hunched shoulders, Matt said, "There's no

fire anywhere in this house, Megan. Do you want to go
back to your room to go to sleep?"

Matt always hoped in these moments that his daughter would rediscover her voice. The paramedics had
found Megan unconscious in the snowdrift. She'd become conscious in the ambulance on the way to the
hospital, and from that moment on, she'd never spoken
another word. The psychiatrist in Idaho Falls, Idaho,
who had endlessly tested her, told Matt it was "hysterical muteness," and that someday, Megan would
start talking again. Grimacing, Matt knew his daughter would have to get through the trauma of seeing her
mother burned to death in an arson fire.

Heart breaking all over again, Matt saw Megan dip
her head forward in answer to his question. Leaning
down, Matt lifted her into his arms and carried her
down the hall. Since the fire, Matt always made sure
there was plenty of light so that Megan could see that
her room and the hall were not on fire. He always kept
his bedroom door partly ajar. Holding his daughter
close, he whispered soothing words to her. Megan laid
her head on his broad shoulder, Elmo squeezed in between them.

In a way, Matt was glad the little red Muppet was
there for his daughter. He could talk to Elmo in order
to reach her. Since the murder of his wife, the loss of
their home, his world focused only on Megan and her
ongoing trauma. His child had never spoken a word in
two years. Would she ever find her voice again? Inhaling raggedly, Matt kept his guilt and grief to himself.
He didn't want Megan to know how devastating it had
been for him to lose his Beverly, and worse, to com-

pound the tragedy, to have his daughter so affected by the arson attack.

Pushing open the door to her bedroom, Matt gently slid his daughter back into her bed. He tucked Elmo, who was looking terribly ratty and old, next to her. Kneeling down, he gently covered Megan back up. "Listen, Elmo would tell you if there was anything wrong. But there's nothing wrong, Meggie. The house is fine. I'm here. If there was a fire, I'd know it in a heartbeat and I'd rescue you." He smoothed several golden strands off her furrowed brow. The worry and anxiety was clearly written in her eyes as she searched his face for some kind of reassurance.

"You know I would smell the smoke, don't you?" he asked softly, continuing to move his hand across her mussed hair. At times like this Matt knew Megan needed not only physical reassurance, she needed him as security against the nightmare. Even to this day, there were burn scars on her small beautiful hands. Matt's heart twisted in anguish knowing that his little six-year-old had valiantly tried to climb through the window to rescue her mother. Her courage shook him as nothing else ever would. He saw her eyelids begin to drift closed.

"Let me tell you a story about Elmo and Big Bird," Matt whispered as he knelt at her bedside. Meggie loved his made-up stories. They always had happy endings and magically diverted Megan so she'd fall back to sleep. She loved the little red Muppet. Matt silently thanked Jim Henson, the creator of the Muppets, for bringing them into existence. Elmo was the only way he could reach Megan. She would respond if he talked to Elmo about her.

In ten minutes, just as he finished the made-up story about Elmo's latest adventure, Megan's eyes had drifted closed. Her breathing became shallow and softened. Matt fought the tears that burned his eyes and gulped several times. His daughter couldn't be allowed to realize how much he was affected by the tragedy. Slowly getting to his feet, Matt made sure the flannel quilt Bev had made for Megan, which had been in the car during the fire, was drawn up snugly to keep her warm and feeling secure. Bev had made the nine-patch quilt from colorful fabrics Megan had chosen three years earlier. Megan loved bright colors, especially red. Elmo was the same color. Reaching out, Matt briefly touched the soft quilt, as if to touch Bev. At least Megan had this quilt, like arms of her mother around her as she slept.

Matt trod silently across the pine floor, the wood stabilizing his torn emotions. He eased through the door and made sure it was opened enough that Megan could see light from the hallway cascading into her room. Awake now, he went back to his lonely bedroom, picked up his plaid flannel robe and pulled it on. Wrapping the sash around his waist, he walked down the hall to the kitchen at the other end of the one-story home.

Looking out the window, Matt saw the stars hanging like white, shimmering jewels in the blackness of the sky. There was no moon tonight. It was late April and the spring thaw was finally starting to take hold. Snow still covered the half-acre lot that surrounded his new home. He rested his hands on the counter, his fingers curving into the aluminum double sinks. God, how he missed Beverly. Closing his eyes and hanging his head, Matt felt his heart tearing apart a little more. When his firefighter friends had found Beverly, she was charred beyond recognition. They'd placed her into a body bag. The coroner, Dr. Jason Armitage of Jackson Hole, later told him Beverly had been shot once, in the head.

Opening his eyes, Matt scowled. He needed a stiff drink, but that wouldn't solve the mystery of who had murdered his wife and deliberately set his house on fire to kill his daughter. Matt opened the cabinet door and drew out the canister of ground coffee. The coffee was soon perking, and, while he waited, he leaned against the counter, arms wrapped against his chest.

Who had murdered Bev? Matt remembered being in Cheyenne and getting the call at 4:00 a.m. from Captain Doug Stanley, his boss. He'd broken the shocking news as gently as he could. Matt had set off that early morning, fighting snowdrifts and nearly skidding off the interstate many times to get home. He'd gone straight to the hospital in Jackson Hole where his daughter was in good condition. That whole morning had been a nightmare to Matt. He'd lost the love of his life. Bev and he had grown up together, gone through school here in Jackson Hole. They'd always loved one another. He'd gone into the Marine Corps for four years after graduating from high school, taken courses and, by the time he'd finished his service, he had a degree in Fire Science. He'd come home to join the Jackson Hole fire department and marry his sweetheart.

"Where did I go wrong?" he muttered, frowning into the darkness of the kitchen. "Where?" And who had killed Bev and set his house on fire?

The coffee now ready, Matt automatically poured himself a cup and stood in the silence of the kitchen. Mentally, as he sipped the hot, black brew, he went over the cold case. As badly as the local police and the county sheriff's department had tried, they couldn't find the killer or the reason for such a shocking attack. Jackson Hole was the Palm Springs of the Rocky Mountain states. It was filled with corporate millionaires, oil tycoons, politicians, Hollywood stars, ranchers, overseas tycoons and national tour operators. The middle class lived on the outskirts or in Driggs, Idaho, across the Grand Tetons or fifty miles south in Star Valley, Wyoming.

Who would want to do this to him? Who had a vendetta against him? Matt had lived here all his life. He made friends, not enemies. The sheriff's department had gone out of their way to work hand-in-hand with the Jackson Hole police department. They'd found nothing. *Nothing.* Matt's mouth was a grim line as he considered the possibilities. There were none. And Matt lived in silent terror of this home and his daughter being attacked once again.

Matt didn't taste the coffee. He never did at this time of morning. When Megan had her nightmares, his mind would churn with so many unanswered questions. His good friend, Cade Garner, a deputy sheriff, had gone above and beyond the call of duty to try and find out who had done this. Cade had come up empty-handed. The deputy felt the arsonist might have been an itinerant who had wandered through the area, but Matt's gut told him otherwise.

At thirty, Matt had been a firefighter for four years. He knew fire. He knew its ways. And yes, as Cade had informed him, he knew they had a few amateur arsonists in the valley. But none of them had killed anyone. And the county sheriff had personally confided in him that Bev had been killed by a professional. One shot to the head. That bothered him more than anything else. The coroner, Jason Armitage, had told him his wife had not been molested or harmed in any other way, and that gave Matt some relief. He didn't think he could stand the thought of Bev being raped and then murdered. Dr. Armitage had postulated that someone had hired a hit man to come in and do the killing.

Shaking his head in frustration, Matt moved restlessly around the large, airy kitchen. The coolness of the pine floor felt good against the soles of his feet. It grounded him, kept him here. Who would hire a hit man to kill his wife? And why hadn't the hit man walked down the hall to kill Megan, too? It just didn't make sense!

Growling an obscenity beneath his breath, Matt stopped, turned and stared out the large window above the kitchen sink. It was dark and quiet outside this house. His gut churned. He'd gotten heartburn a lot since Bev's death. It always kicked up when Megan would run down the hall and wake him, sobbing and clinging to him as if a monster were chasing her.

Megan knew something. Matt sensed it. What had she seen? She couldn't speak, and a host of child psychologists over the last two years had tried to spring open that door and get her to talk, but all Megan would do was cling to Elmo and stare up at them with huge, terrified blue eyes, her mouth open, lips trembling—but no sound other than animal-like cries would issue forth. Rubbing his wrinkled brow, Matt paced around the island in the kitchen. What could he do to get Meggie to talk again? *What?*

Guilt that he was gone when this had happened ate daily at Matt. If he'd been here, he'd have heard someone breaking into their house. Bev had always been a deep, hard sleeper. An earthquake could have shaken the place and she wouldn't wake up. Matt, on the other hand, had always been a light sleeper. The least noise and he sprang awake in a millisecond. He knew he'd have heard the murderous intruder. If only he'd been here and not away at fire school in Cheyenne. He could have saved Bev's life, stopped his daughter from being utterly traumatized and saved the house he'd built with his own two hands from being burned to the ground.

Halting, Matt sipped the last of the coffee. It was scaldingly hot, but he wasn't aware of that. His heart and mind were centered on Megan. He would be taking her to school at 7:00 a.m. She would sit in the back of Mrs. Harrington's class, mute, attentive and taking notes. Sherry Harrington, Megan's second-grade teacher, was wonderful with his daughter. Matt thanked God for that. Megan was intelligent and caught on quickly. She could read and comprehend, but she never uttered a word out loud. Sherry had even tried getting the children to read from Muppet stories in hopes that Megan would want to take part, but she did not.

And so, Megan would sit mutely in class. Mrs. Harrington was sensitive and attentive, even though she had a class of thirty second-graders. She went out of her way to create unique teaching content for Megan. Matt was forever grateful to the teacher.

What now? Dawn was crawling up the horizon, and the Grand Tetons looked like sharpened dragon's teeth slowly congealing out of the darkness. Matt placed the cup in the sink. Sherry Harrington had written him a note yesterday. She was going to try something new in hopes of reaching Megan. This morning, Katie

Bergstrom, a raptor rehabilitator, was bringing several birds in to the class and would give a talk about them. With her would be a ranger from the Grand Teton National Park, ten miles outside Jackson Hole. Sherry had written that she hoped this might catch Megan's attention and maybe, fingers crossed, it might inspire her finally to talk.

CHAPTER TWO

CASEY CANTRELL TRIED to shore up her sagging spirits. She'd been assigned to help Katie Bergstrom, a raptor rehabilitator who had her business on the outskirts of Jackson Hole, Wyoming. They stood in front of Sherry Harrington's rapt second-grade class. This was her first official duty for the U.S. Forest Service. She had been hired straight after graduation from Colorado State University at Fort Collins. She looked at Katie, who was relaxed and smiling, with a red-tailed hawk named Hank on her leather glove. The eyes of the thirty children were huge with anticipation. She had their full, undivided attention.

"First," Katie told the children with a smile, "let's hear from Ranger Cantrell. She's going to tell us why it's so important to have raptors in our area. Ranger Cantrell?"

Clearing her throat, Casey gave the reasons for the importance of raptors to the ecological balance of life in the area. She was serious and low-key compared to bubbly Katie Bergstrom. As she spoke, Hank would lift and flap his wings every now and again, much to the children's delight. She kept her explanation short, understanding that second-graders had an attention span of about two seconds. Glancing over at Katie, Casey said, "It's all yours, Katie," and stepped to one side to position herself near Sherry.

"Thank you, Ranger Cantrell," Katie said, grinning and carrying Hank, who wore soft kangaroo-leather jesses around his yellow legs, closer to the children. Their desks formed a huge semicircle facing the front of the room. Casey thought it looked like a crowded amphitheater. The glow of excitement on the children's faces lifted the anxiety she felt.

Earlier, Sherry had met them outside the door for a quick chat. She was concerned about Megan Sinclaire, and gave them the story of her being mute. Casey's heart broke when she heard about the little girl's tragedy. Sure enough, Megan was at the back of the group. Sherry Harrington was afraid that Megan might be frightened of a hawk flying around the room, so it would be Casey's job to stand near the little girl when Mrs. Harrington donned the other leather glove on the other side of the room and Hank flew to her from Katie's glove.

Casey felt comfortable working with the little blond-haired girl. She moved quietly to the rear, her back to the windows. Megan was only three feet away, and she seemed absolutely enraptured over the hawk, just as all the other children were. Megan clasped her hands, smitten by Hank, and Casey tried to relax.

Casey's boss, Charley Davidson, believed in educating the children from the ground up about nature. He said such programs would serve to keep all species safer. He often had Katie come and give talks with her hawks and owls at the visitor's center just inside Grand Teton National Park.

"Okay," Katie sang out now, "how many of you would like to see Mrs. Harrington put on this glove?"

She held it up so the children could see it. "And then, we'll let Hank fly to her. Raise your hands!"

Every hand shot up, the children wriggling like excited puppies in their seats. Casey saw Megan's hand shoot up, too. She was so excited that she stood up, jumping up and down. Casey heard excited rasps coming from her. But no words.

"Okay, okay!" Katie laughed, handing the teacher the glove. "You've voted for Mrs. Harrington to do this. Let's quiet down now. Hank doesn't like a lot of noise. It bothers his flying concentration."

Instantly, everyone sat down. All except Megan, who remained standing, her small hands clasped to her chest, all eyes.

Casey did nothing. Megan was clear of the flight path, and though Katie saw her, she didn't direct her to sit down. The child's cheeks were a bright red, her blue eyes now bright with excitement. Mrs. Harrington pulled on the glove, held it high for the children to see and then walked to the other corner of the classroom.

Casey's focus was on Megan. Clearly, she loved what was going on. She knew little of the child's trauma other than that her mother had been murdered and the house set on fire and that she had barely escaped. Casey's heart bled for Megan.

Everyone ooohhed as Hank flapped and took off from Katie's glove. He flew low across the classroom to Mrs. Harrington's outstretched glove. The delight and awe were clearly written on every child's face.

Mrs. Harrington had a look of pleasure as Hank settled on her arm, his yellow feet and curved talons delicately grasping the leather gauntlet. He settled down, folding his wings and looking around at the thrilled class.

"Wow!" Katie called, laughing. "Wasn't that something?"

The children whooped, shouted and clapped. Pandemonium reigned for a moment. They could hardly sit still in their seats.

"Okay," Katie said, raising her voice and holding up her hands. "If you'll sit quietly, I'll put a little rabbit meat on my glove and we'll call Hank back to my glove. Can you do that? Do you want to see him fly again?"

Casey chuckled softly. Every child except Megan sat squirming in anticipation. Katie said nothing about Megan continuing to stand and nor did Sherry. Casey remained where she was. When Hank swooped low across the diagonal breadth of the classroom once more, everyone collectively gasped. Casey saw the awe burning brightly in Megan's eyes. She was enthralled, as if magically swept away on a carpet to Disneyland. The sounds issuing from her were soft cries of joy. But no words. Just sounds.

Heart breaking for the father of this child, Casey tried to understand his terrible tragedy. This child had not talked since the incident. *Two years.* How had he been able to deal with it? With his daughter's psychological scar? Casey remembered her own tragedy in the spring of her sophomore year at university. She had blundered onto a huge marijuana-growing area up near Red Lake in northern Colorado. The growers had jumped her, beaten her nearly to death, tied her up and dumped her unconscious body far away from their drug fields. She was sure they hoped she would be eaten by hungry grizzly bears coming out of winter hibernation.

But she hadn't died; luckily, she'd been rescued by a group of hikers. Casey touched her left temple where a scar still reminded her of that savage day when she'd nearly lost her life.

Looking at Megan, who was clearly enthralled with Hank, Casey wondered if the little girl's PTSD was the wall that stopped her from speaking again. Casey had spent ten days in a Fort Collins hospital in a coma. She couldn't remember the incident for nearly a year. Then her brain had downloaded the whole scenario one morning when she was sitting in a wildlife biology seminar. Casey recalled that day, the power of the deed done against her. She saw the five men's faces. Saw their rage and their desire to kill her. Shivering inwardly, Casey pulled her thoughts back to the present.

Studying Megan's rapt features, Casey understood as few could how the brain protected someone from such a life-changing trauma. Only when the person was well enough, strong enough, would the brain give up those horrible memories. Casey sensed Megan was not ready to talk yet, because what would come out of that child's mouth was just too terrible for her to comprehend, understand or accept. She felt deep compassion for Megan.

"Okay," Katie called, smiling at the group, Hank on her glove, "I'm going to bring out Susie, the barn owl, now. Ranger Cantrell? Would you like to come and assist me?"

"Of course," Casey murmured. She had trained with Katie for several days before this show so she knew what to do. The bird boxes were large and made of green cardboard. Casey moved to the front of the class and picked up Hank's box. She placed it on Mrs. Harrington's desk and opened it up. Inside was a perch wrapped with Astro Turf so Hank could grasp it firmly with his claws and not slip or fall off it.

The children watched with burning silent curiosity. Casey stood to one side after the box door was opened. Hank jumped off Katie's glove and eagerly went into his box. Katie gave him one last bit of rabbit meat and gently closed and locked the door. She handed the box to Casey. Then, a second box was brought up to the desk by Katie.

"Now, kids, this is a barn owl. We have lots of them here in Wyoming. Do you know where they live?" She turned and smiled at the class.

"Barns!" a boy shouted.

"Yes!" Katie said, grinning. "Barn owls love barns. That's why they're called barn owls. Now, Susie here," she opened the box to show the small, delicate barn owl sitting on her perch, her black, luminous eyes surrounded with white feathers, "was found in the bottom of a rancher's barn a year ago. She was a baby and had tried to fly out of her parents' nest when she was too young. The rancher found her flopping around on the floor when he went in to feed his horses one morning. He picked her up and found she had a badly broken leg. So, he called the Game and Fish Department, and then they called me." Katie put her gloved hand into the box and Susie hopped onto the glove.

Bringing Susie out, Katie held her up on the glove so the children could see the barn owl. "The rancher wanted the barn owls in his barn. Do you know why?"

"They eat mice and rats!" a little girl cried. "They're good!"

"That's right," Katie said, laughing. Susie fluttered

her wings, showing the white and soft-caramel coloring beneath her wings. The children oohed and aahed. "The rancher wanted to save Susie. He'd seen the mice and rat population dwindle to nothing because these barn owls were around. They keep a natural check and balance."

"Do they eat gophers?" another boy asked.

"You bet they do!"

"Good, because my daddy lost his best horse when he was herding cattle last year. His horse stuck a foot into a gopher hole and broke his leg. My daddy cried over it."

Nodding, Katie said, "I'm so sorry to hear that. But yes, hawks and owls will eat any four-legged critter. The hawks hunt them during the daylight hours and the owls hunt them at night. Did you know that your daddy can call me and if I have a barn owl that is healing up I may be able to put one in his barn?"

The boy gasped. "Really?"

"Sure," Katie said. "Tell your parents about this to-night. I have a barn owl who is ready to be placed. I'd be happy to talk to them about it."

The boy rubbed his hands together, glee in his face. "This is *rad!*" he shouted.

Everyone laughed, the energy of the room amping up.

Casey took her place once more at the back of the room near Megan. The child continued to stand. No one admonished her. The other children were too enthralled with Susie the barn owl to look to the rear of the class to see her standing.

"Now, I need a volunteer," Katie called out. "Some-one who would like to put on a glove and have Susie climb from my glove to their glove."

Megan shrieked and ran to the front of the class, eagerly waving her hand to take the glove. Casey saw Sherry Harrington's face go blank with surprise. Katie smiled and handed Megan the glove. Could the raptors be a doorway to Megan's healing? Casey wondered.

"Okay, we have a volunteer. Megan, right?"

Megan nodded her head and excitedly pulled the child-size falconer's glove onto her right hand. She could hardly stand still, her gaze rapt on Susie.

"Okay, Megan," Katie soothed, "the first thing you need to do is stand very quietly. A raptor gets upset if it's being jostled around. Do you understand?"

Megan instantly quieted and nodded her head, suddenly becoming very serious.

Casey took a small camera out of her pocket. She wanted photos of Megan and Susie for the child's sake. She would download the photos into her computer tonight and make sure that Megan got copies of them in the mail. Just as Susie was transferred to Megan's outstretched glove, Casey took several photos.

Megan stood there, her blue eyes huge as she stared wonderingly into Susie's black, unblinking eyes. The barn owl was relaxed on her glove. The rest of the class gave a collective "ooohhh…"

Katie had Megan turn to the class. "Now, Megan, how does it feel to have Susie on your glove?"

Casey held her breath. The little girl struggled. She opened her mouth, closed it. Frowned. And then tears tracked down her reddened cheeks. Katie gently patted her shoulder. "It's okay, Megan. Many of us have no words for how wonderful a raptor feels on our glove. Isn't that right, kids?"

Casey's heart burst open with sympathy for Megan.

The girl nodded briskly and quickly wiped her tears away with her other hand. Susie blinked and seemed to understand what was going on, quietly sitting on Megan's glove. Casey took several more photos before Susie was transferred back to Katie's glove.

Just as Katie's demonstrations were complete, the noon bell rang; it was time for lunch. All the children went to the cafeteria, leaving the three women alone.

Sherry Harrington's face was filled with excitement. "Katie, Casey, this is a first! Megan Sinclaire has been a ghost throughout the first and second grades. You don't realize how wonderful this is!"

"Raptors are magical," Katie murmured, closing Susie's box. "They can reach in and touch our hearts in a way nothing else can. I thought for sure Megan was going to speak."

"She tried," Casey murmured.

"Oh, I know!" Sherry sighed. "Katie, I honestly believe you've provided an important breakthrough for Megan. This afternoon I'm going to have the children draw their favorite raptor, and then we're going to the library computers and they're going to do research on their raptor."

"I have photos of Megan with Susie," Casey told her. "Do you think that it will be helpful to send them to her father?"

"I think so. In fact," Sherry touched Casey's arm, "would you do something for me?"

"Sure."

"I'm going to call Matt Sinclaire tonight and tell him what happened today. Would you have time to drive over to his house with the photos? You saw Megan here in class. She knows and she trusts you. Maybe if you take the photos over to Megan, he can see for his own eyes the effect it had on her. This could be a way to get her to speak again. Oh, I'm so excited! We owe both of you so much! I was so worried for Megan. I was anxious that the birds would scare her or traumatize her even more. But they didn't. They opened her up as nothing else has!" Sherry quickly wiped away tears. She took out a tissue and blew her nose.

Katie touched the teacher's shoulder. "I had heard of Megan's situation before this. Jackson Hole is a small town and we all knew what happened to the Sinclaires. I was over at Quilter's Haven when I heard about it from Gwen Garner, the owner."

Sniffing and laughing, Sherry said, "Oh, yes, our quilting store! If you want to know anything about what's going on, you go there."

"You know that Bev Sinclaire was a quilter before she was murdered?" Katie asked.

Casey said, "I'm new here, and I haven't gotten to know this area yet."

"Do you quilt, Casey?" Katie asked.

"I sew my own clothes. I don't have any quilting skills."

"Well," Sherry said, "since you're stationed here for the next five years as a ranger at the Teton National Park, make yourself known to Gwen at the quilting store. The women all gather over there. They know everything that's going on in the area. It might do you some good to go there for a visit with Gwen before you see Matt Sinclaire and his daughter."

Nodding, Casey said, "I've just rented an apartment in town with a woman firefighter, Cat Edwin."

"Oh, I know her!" Sherry said. "She's the only

woman on the fire department. And she's a quilter. Did you know that?"

Shaking her head, Casey murmured, "I just got the apartment with her because she'd advertised for a roommate. I knew she was with the fire department, but I haven't had time to get to know her much at all."

Katie grinned and picked up the two raptor boxes. "Go visit Gwen. She's the wife of a rancher. The Garner family has been in this valley since the fur trappers came here a hundred and fifty years ago. I think it's a great idea to take the photos over to Megan, but get the scoop from Gwen first. That way, you can be educated and handle the situation with the father and daughter even better."

Casey nodded. "Okay, sounds like a plan. I'll do that."

Sherry gave them a warm look. "Thank you, ladies. Casey, give me your phone number. I'll call Mr. Sinclaire tonight and fill him in. He can call you and you two can set a day and time to exchange those photos of Megan holding Susie on her glove." She clasped her hands. "I just pray to God this is the breakthrough Megan needs. Her father, Matt, is so filled with guilt over his daughter's condition. It just tears my heart up."

Casey nodded. She understood tragedy, suffering, grief and guilt. "Sounds like a plan to me. She's a sweet child. I'd like to see her work through her trauma and start talking again."

Katie walked to the door and waited for Casey to open it for her. "It's known as hysterical muteness, Casey. Megan has been through a battery of shrinks and they've all told Matt Sinclaire the same thing—it's hysterical. A little six-year-old doesn't realize that, of course. And now, two years later, Megan is still mute, which tells you the power of the trauma she experienced."

Casey opened the door. "Yes," she murmured, "it does."

Sherry followed Kate and Casey out into the empty hall and walked with them. The children were all in the lunchroom, but Sherry kept her voice low. "Listen," she told Casey, "Mr. Sinclaire has his problems, too. I mean, Bev Sinclaire and he were childhood sweethearts from the moment they met in the first grade. She was the love of his life. He's not over her death. He's filled with guilt and remorse from what I can see."

Katie nodded and they turned down the hall toward the exit doors. "He's blaming himself for what happened. He was in Cheyenne at fire school when it occurred. But look, go to the quilting store. You'll find out everything you ever needed to know about Matt Sinclaire from Gwen."

Casey opened the door, the cool April breeze hitting them. There was snow on the ground, but the sky was a bright blue. The sun warmed her a bit. "Okay, I'll do that." Casey gave Sherry Harrington her business card. "Call me, Sherry, when you know something."

"Oh, I will, Casey. Bless you! Thank you!"

Casey didn't feel very blessed. She walked with Katie out to her SUV and opened the rear door so Katie could put the bird boxes in and strap them down. The asphalt parking area had been cleared of snow and was wet and gleaming under the midday sunlight.

"Do you know anything about Matt Sinclaire?" Casey asked, shutting the door.

Katie fished the keys out of the pocket of her red jacket. "He's a hunk."

Casey laughed. "Okay."

Grinning, Katie said, "He's thirty years old, black hair, green eyes, square face and about six foot two inches in height. He's been on the fire department eight years, and he's a lieutenant. Before Bev was murdered, Matt was a pretty outgoing dude. But now—" Katie opened the driver's-side door "—he's pretty serious, unreadable and just about as mute as his daughter."

"Sounds pretty grim," Casey muttered, frowning.

Katie nodded and frowned. "How do you get over your wife suddenly being torn from you? And on top of that, your child goes mute and is trapped inside her own trauma? Matt can't fathom what she has endured. No one can."

"Really bad stuff," Casey mumbled, frowning. She shoved her hands into the pockets of her brown nylon Forest Service jacket. Her mint-green USFS truck was parked next to Katie's vehicle.

"Gwen has said repeatedly that Matt needs psychological help, but he's refused. He's gummed up tighter than Fort Knox when it comes to his own grief. All we see is his guilt. He just hasn't been able to open up and let out all that toxic grief," Katie said. She climbed into her truck. "Maybe, Casey, you're a ray of sunlight into his dark world. That was smart of you to take those photos." She grinned and slipped the key into the ignition. The engine growled to life. "Who knows? Maybe those photos will not only help Megan, but Matt, too. Good luck!"

CHAPTER THREE

CASEY'S HANDS WERE DAMP as she stood at the door of a white, one-story, ranch-style house with green trim. Flexing her fingers, she couldn't stop the tension that thrummed through her. Nervously, she smoothed her shoulder-length brown hair. The April morning was sunny with a cobalt-blue sky—a rare event for this time of year, she'd been told by her supervisor, Charley, who had given her two hours off to run over to Matt Sinclaire's home.

Knocking a couple of times, Casey stood back and waited. In her left hand, she held her beat-up brown leather briefcase that had seen her through her university years. What was Matthew Sinclaire like? And how would Megan receive the photos of Hank, the red-tailed hawk?

The door opened.

Automatically, Casey held her breath for a moment. Her eyes widened as a man in a red T-shirt and jeans appeared. Instantly, her heart began a wild, unfamiliar beat. She looked up into his green eyes and felt consumed by his intent gaze upon her. To say that Matthew Sinclaire was a hunk was understating the obvious. The red T-shirt emblazoned with the words *Jackson Hole Fire Department* emphasized his broad, deep chest. His shoulders were powerful. He stood relaxed, body at a slight slouch; a man who was comfortable with who he was.

"You must be Ranger Casey Cantrell?" he asked in a deep voice.

Giving a nod, Casey rasped, "Yes, sir, I am. Are you Lieutenant Matthew Sinclaire?" She felt, suddenly, like a teenager in front of this guy. Clearly, Sinclaire was a man's man, and it triggered something deep and hungering within her. Fingers tightening around the handle of her briefcase, Casey tried to appear just as relaxed as he seemed to be.

"Call me Matt. Come on in. Meggie is waiting for you." He smiled a little and gestured for her to step into the brightly lit home.

Casey walked past him and into the house. It was near freezing on this April morning and she welcomed the warmth inside. She waited on a red and gray Navajo rug. Megan was standing at the other end of the foyer. The girl was dressed in a pair of dark green corduroy pants, a white blouse with long sleeves, her hair in a pair of cute pigtails. In her arms was Elmo, looking pretty bedraggled from a lot of care over the years. Casey smiled at her. She took off her ranger's hat, which she hated wearing anyway, and quickly ran her fingers through her flattened hair.

"Hi, Megan. Do you remember me? I'm Casey."

Megan broke into a welcoming smile and waved shyly at her.

Matt turned after closing the door. He saw Megan's reaction to the woman ranger. Having a strong reaction to her himself, Matt tried to brush it aside. "I want to thank you for coming over on a Saturday morning, Ranger Cantrell."

"Call me Casey," she asked. Looking up at Matt, she felt her heart spring open like a flower in bloom. Sinclaire's face was oval with a strong chin, broad forehead and crinkles at the corners of his eyes. Casey knew he was thirty years old from the gossip she'd gotten down at Quilter's Haven, where Gwen Garner had filled her in on this handsome firefighter. It was so easy to drown in the dark green of his intent eyes. He seemed to Casey to be an eagle, his pupils huge and black as he studied her, a slight tilt to his head. She was only five foot seven inches tall compared to his six foot two, but she was built with good, strong bones, no wilting lily of a sticklike woman. Still, Casey felt overshadowed by Matt Sinclaire's powerful presence. There was an unspoken care that radiated from him toward her. Casey could see why this man, when in his firefighter gear, would ooze a sense of protection toward anyone in his safekeeping.

Matt gave her a tentative smile. "My friends call me Matt. Come on in. I've got coffee waiting for us in the kitchen."

"Oh…" Casey murmured, "I was just going to drop these photos off, Mr. Sinc—I mean, Matt. I'm on duty today and Charley gave me some time off to deliver these to Megan. I don't want to intrude on your weekend."

"You're not." Matt held out his hand. "Give me your jacket, Casey. I know your boss, Charley. We're good friends. I know he won't care if you have a cup of coffee or two with me and Meggie."

Hesitantly, Casey slid out of her warm brown nylon jacket and handed it to him. She saw Megan watching her, her eyes shining as much as they had in class five days earlier. "I've brought the photos of Megan holding

Susie," she offered. Dressed in her ranger uniform—a tan long-sleeved blouse and dark green trousers—Casey felt very unfeminine. She watched Sinclaire move. He possessed a cougar's grace, bred from being an athlete. Casey knew firefighters lifted weights and jogged daily to stay in tip-top shape for the demands of their dangerous job. Still, she had to tear her gaze from his powerful back and narrow hips as he hung her coat up on a wooden peg next to the door. She gulped, and her mouth went dry. What kind of reaction was she having around this stranger?

"Come on in," Matt invited her warmly, reaching down to take his daughter's small hand that was swallowed up in his.

Quickly looking around, Casey saw a huge woodstove in one corner with flames dancing behind the glass window. The red-and-yellow cedar floor was waxed and gleaming. There were Navajo rugs here and there. The room was painted a pale yellow; the drapes at the main window were brown with red flowers and green vines woven into the fabric. To her, this was a man's home. There were no photos or pictures up on the walls. There were no green, living plants anywhere, either. It felt like a shell to Casey, not exactly alive or nurturing. She wondered if their home had exuded more of a woman's touch when Bev was alive.

Following father and daughter into the kitchen, Casey saw Megan sit in a chair with Elmo in her lap. Her father had given her a glass of orange juice. "I feel badly for interrupting your breakfast," Casey murmured, standing uncertainly in the doorway. The kitchen was white with blue curtains over the window. The smell of frying bacon filled the air.

"Don't worry about it," Matt murmured. "Just take a seat opposite Meggie here at the kitchen table. Have you eaten breakfast yet?"

"No… I don't eat breakfast." Not anymore, at least. Casey saw him frown and then saw the question in his eyes. She hoped he wouldn't ask it. Gripping the wooden chair, Casey pulled it out and sat down. "But if you have a cup of black coffee, that would be fine," she added.

Matt opened his mouth to say something, but shut it. He saw sudden fear come to Casey's huge, very readable gray eyes. "Sure," he murmured, going to the counter and pulling down a mug. The last thing he'd expected was a beautiful woman in a ranger's uniform to be at his door this morning. Oh, Matt knew Charley was sending someone down who had attended Megan's class last Monday, but he'd had no idea Casey was so stunning. Out of habit, he looked at her left hand. She had long, beautiful fingers, her fingernails blunt-cut and without polish. No ring on her left hand. Of course, nowadays, there usually wasn't any surefire way to tell if a woman was hitched or not.

Pouring the coffee, Matt found his body responding fiercely to her as a woman. What was *this* all about? He'd felt numbed from the inside out since Bev's murder. In fact, he had plenty of opportunity to meet the women of Jackson Hole on a regular basis, but none of them had stirred him. Until Casey Cantrell had shown up at his door just now. He took the mug and set it down in front of her. She had soft sable bangs across her broad brow, her hair shot through with reddish and gold strands beneath the kitchen light. Although she had straight hair, it was softly curled around her proud shoulders. "There you go," he murmured. Turning, he had to pay attention to the bacon frying in a skillet on the gas stove.

"Thank you," Casey murmured. She smiled across the pine table. "How are you this morning, Megan?"

Megan shrugged shyly, smiled and gripped Elmo tightly to her chest. She took a sip of her orange juice.

Matt twisted a look over his shoulder. "Did Mrs. Harrington fill you in on my daughter?" he asked, trepidation in his voice. It was always painful to speak about Megan in the third person. Guilt wound through Matt as it always did when a stranger came into their lives. He would have to tell the story of Megan's muteness all over again, and he dreaded it.

"Yes, she did." Seeing the anxiety in Matt's face, Casey also read guilt in his narrowing green eyes. Trying to put herself in his shoes was impossible but she saw he loved his daughter with a fierce protectiveness that made her heart open to him even more. This man was clearly a modern-day warrior. Oh, he might not wear chain mail, carry a sword on his hip or have a war horse nearby, but Casey clearly felt his protectiveness toward his daughter.

Casey added, "She told me everything," as a hint to Matt to relax. He wouldn't have to say anything in front of Megan. Relief instantly came to his features.

"Oh…good…good." Matt turned back to finish frying the bacon. Clearing his throat, he said, "Charley said you'd just been assigned to the Teton's station. Where were you before that?"

Suddenly, Casey felt as though she was on a hot plate. "Uh… I just graduated. This is my first assignment."

"Oh? Where did you graduate from?"

"I received a degree in wildlife biology from Colorado State University." She felt like running. Casey wanted no one to know of her horrific past. She gripped the mug of coffee in both hands and tried to sound as if she didn't want to speak on the topic anymore.

"I see," Matt murmured. He lifted the bacon out of the skillet and transferred it to a plate covered in paper towel to soak up the extra grease. "I graduated from there, too," he said, walking over to the table to put the bacon near his plate. "I took my firefighting courses there." He looked into her eyes. They were fraught with fear. Why fear? Was she afraid of him? Matt figured because she was new to the Forest Service, Casey was probably worried she might say the wrong thing. Turning, he went back to the counter and cracked four eggs into the skillet.

"Are you from Colorado?" Casey asked. She'd seen the curiosity in his eyes and didn't want to answer any more of his questions. The best defense was a good offense. If Casey wanted her past to remain buried and unavailable to anyone, she needed to ask the questions instead.

"No," Matt murmured, adding salt and pepper to the eggs now frying in the skillet. "I was born here in Jackson Hole. I went there for my training."

"Did you always want to be a firefighter?"

Nodding, Matt said, "Yes, my father was one. He was the fire chief here for twenty years before." He turned and gave her a slight smile meant to reassure her. "You're new to Jackson Hole. We're a pretty interesting town. If you haven't been over to Quilter's Haven and talked with Gwen Garner, then you probably don't know all the stuff there is to know about all of us." He chuckled.

"I met Gwen," Casey admitted softly. She couldn't stop looking at the firefighter. He was tall, sinewy, the muscles thick and hard in his upper arms. There was dark hair sprinkled across his lower arms. And she'd seen that hair peeking out above the T-shirt he wore, too. His hair was cut military-short and there was no wasted motion about Matt Sinclaire.

Laughing a little, Matt said, "Then you'll know all the stories about the residents. Do you sew or quilt?" He lifted the eggs out and put them on a plate. Turning off the gas stove, he removed the skillet and set it aside. Scooping up the blue-and-white plates, he walked to the long, rectangular table and sat down at the end of it. On his left was Megan and on his right, beautiful Casey Cantrell. He gave his daughter a plate and put one down in front of himself. Going to the fridge, he poured Meggie a glass of milk and came over and set it down in front of her.

"Sure you don't want breakfast?" he asked, sitting down. Opening up his dark green linen napkin, Matt spread it across his lap. He leaned over and helped Meggie arrange the large napkin across her small lap.

"No…no, thank you."

Shaking his head, he murmured, "I could not move without a big breakfast." He smiled over at his daughter. "Hey, you're chowing down today, Meggie. Must be hungry, huh?"

His daughter vigorously dipped her head, her little pigtails moving back and forth across her small shoulders. She relished the scrambled eggs and bacon. Matt had put apricot jam across her toasted spelt bread earlier, and Meggie was dividing her attention between the toast and her bacon right now.

Casey grinned. "Megan looks like she did the day Katie Bergstrom brought the raptor program to Mrs. Harrington's class."

Matt ate his eggs and bacon. Between bites he said, "I've never seen Megan that excited before."

"Her teacher noticed that, too," Casey said, knowing full well Megan probably understood every word they spoke.

"Mrs. Harrington said you had a minor in Education?"

Raising her brows, Casey realized everything was passed around. She'd have to be very careful in the future. "Yes."

"Did you, at some point," Matt asked, "want to be a teacher instead of a forest ranger?"

His insight into her was startling. Ever since the trauma she'd endured, Casey had to keep herself hidden from prying eyes. This man, however, seemed to have X-ray vision. Or maybe he could read people's minds? Moving uncomfortably in the chair, Casey said, "Yes, at one time I wanted to teach first- and second-graders."

"You love children."

The statement was filled with curiosity. Casey avoided his momentary burning gaze. Looking down at the mug she had gripped between her hands, she said, "Yes, I love kids…."

Nodding, Matt said, "Megan seemed to really take to you. Her teacher noticed that, too."

"All I did was stand near her," Casey protested. And yet, Megan's blue eyes were always filled with warmth for Casey.

Nodding, Matt quickly finished off his breakfast. "I'd like to speak to you more about that later," he said, getting up. Picking up his plate and flatware, he carried them over to the sink.

"Of course," Casey said, fully aware that Matt wanted to talk to her when Megan wasn't around. "I'd love to give Megan the photos. Are we at a point where I can do that? Charley's given me two hours off."

"Right, I know you're on a deadline," Matt said, coming back to the table. He put his hand on his daughter's shoulder. His hand was huge in comparison to the child, and Casey found herself wondering what it would be like to have Matt's hand on *her* shoulder. The thought was so foreign, so shocking to Casey that she nearly choked on a sip of coffee.

"All done?" Matt asked Megan.

Nodding, Megan held up her emptied plate to her father. She picked up her glass of milk and sipped from it.

Casey's heart gave a twinge. What would it be like never to hear your child's voice again? Only grunts, sighs and unintelligible sounds? If it hurt Matt, he didn't show it. He quickly cleaned the table so that it shone beneath the lamp above it. Casey pulled open her briefcase and withdrew the photos after he'd sat down.

Megan laughed as Casey handed her the four photos. She had made colored eight-by-tens. The joy in the little girl's eyes made Casey smile. Megan reverently touched them with her fingers, awe in her expression. She would make sounds and hold each of them up for her father to see.

Casey was shocked when Megan scooted out of her chair, left Elmo in it and ran around the table. The little girl threw her arms around Casey's waist and buried her head against her breasts.

Caught off guard, Casey automatically closed her arms around Megan. She felt the strength of Megan's thin arms around her. She was surprisingly strong. Leaning down, Casey whispered her name, pressed a kiss to her soft blond hair and gently squeezed her. When she gazed in Matt's direction, she saw the stunned look on his face. Unsure what his reaction meant, Casey gently untwined Megan's arms and looked down at her. Megan was crying. Rasping sounds were escaping her contorted mouth.

Heart twisting, Casey whispered, "Come here…" to Megan and brought her back into her arms. Megan instantly crushed herself against Casey, head buried against her. As Megan clung to her, she behaved like a child who was drowning and grasping for a life raft. Casey's instincts took over. She absorbed the child's neediness, her hunger to be nurtured and simply cradled. Mind spinning, Casey wondered if Matt had a relationship with another woman who could provide Megan with some maternal care. Obviously, Megan needed to be held by a woman. And probably any woman would do. Gently running her hand across Megan's flyaway hair, she smoothed the strands down across her head. Rocking her gently, Casey simply allowed the child to stay as long as she wanted in her arms.

Five minutes later, Megan withdrew. Her cheeks were a fiery red and her eyes danced with excitement as she ran around the table, grabbed the photos and then brought them back to Casey. "What is this?" she asked Megan, hoping that she would talk.

Megan made more guttural sounds, like a puppy

that was yelping and happy as she waved the photos in front of Casey's face.

"I think," Matt said, his voice sounding strangled, "Meggie wants you to help her draw them." He gave Casey a look that pleaded with her to stay a bit longer.

Casey read his look. "Sure, no problem. Does Megan have crayons and paper in her bedroom?"

Swallowing hard, Matt nodded. His mouth flattened and he tried to hide his shock over Megan clinging to Casey. She'd never done that before. "Yeah...come on," he said, scraping the chair back and standing.

Casey followed suit. Megan wouldn't leave her side. Taking the child's hand, Megan pulled her down a hall and into her bedroom behind her father. Megan's room was painted a soft pink with ruffled white curtains embroidered with red strawberries. It was a beautiful room that had been painted and decorated with a great deal of care and thought. Matt was standing by the desk getting the crayons out of the drawer for Megan.

Megan dragged Casey over to the desk. She released her hand and sat down, grabbing a black crayon. Matt laid the paper in front of her. Megan then set the pictures next to the paper and rapidly began to draw. As she did, she made excited yelps of happiness.

Casey's brows rose. She stood inches away from Matt. He looked grave. His mouth was thinned and flexed, as if holding back words or emotions that he couldn't express right now. Casey could feel the heat of his masculine body and the scent of pine around him. Was it an aftershave lotion he wore? The shampoo he used on his hair? She couldn't be sure. Dizzied by his nearness, Casey couldn't move because Megan wanted her at her side.

"Look at that," Casey whispered, leaning down, her hand resting lightly on Megan's shoulder. "You're a wonderful artist!" And indeed, she was. Drawing the barn owl came easily to Megan. She missed nothing, the crayons scattered as she worked feverishly to get the right color of eyes, the tan and creamy feathers on the owl and her bright yellow legs. Looking up at Matt, Casey said, "Wow, your daughter is a real artist. This is amazing!"

Matt took a step back. His gut knotted. Guilt soared through him along with unparalleled joy. Nodding, he didn't dare try to speak. Swallowing the lump of tears stuck in his throat, he finally managed to say, "Let's leave Megan alone. She loves to draw. I think she'll be in here for at least an hour. She'll draw each of those photos for you. Would you like another cup of coffee?" Matt was desperate to talk with Casey. She had to realize what had just taken place. It was a miracle he'd never dared hoped for. *A miracle.*

Getting the hint, Casey said, "Yes, I'd love another cup." Turning to Megan, she patted the child's shoulder. "You're doing wonderfully, Megan. Why not draw each photo? I know your dad would love to see them when you're done. If you need us, we'll be out in the kitchen."

Megan was focused on her work. There were no sounds, no recognition, and Casey quietly left the room and followed Matt to the kitchen. There, she found him scowling, a mixture of emotions clearly written on his face. He was leaning against the sink, hands on either side, staring darkly in her direction as she emerged from the hall.

Heart speeding up, Casey walked over to the counter and stood in front of him. She saw he was in a quandary, his mouth working to hold back something, either words or feelings. "Tell me, has Megan ever done this before?"

Matt shook his head. He saw the intelligence burning in Casey's gray eyes. Hell, if he could, he'd run into her arms just to be held, too. His daughter could do it, but he couldn't. He whispered, "I guess there's something special about you, Casey. Megan needed you. I've *never* seen her do this to any other woman." He didn't mention there weren't that many other women who came here. "We go to church every Sunday and there are plenty of opportunities for Megan to run to any woman if she wanted to be embraced and held. But she never has. Not until now…"

He searched Casey's upturned face. She was beautiful in an arresting way. Her face was broad, oval and she had high cheekbones. He saw a scar on her left temple and realized her nose had been broken. It was no longer straight, but had a bump at the top of it. Her brows reminded him of a bird on the wing. Lashes, dark and thick, framed her glorious gray eyes that reminded him of diamonds softly sparkling.

"I see," Casey said. She retrieved her coffee cup and filled it. Sitting down at the table, Casey said, "Do you think something good is happening here? Maybe the raptor program broke something loose in Megan? I don't know her. What do you feel?"

Matt remained leaning against the sink. The coolness of the granite counter calmed him to a degree. His heart was racing. His mind churned. "For whatever reason," he rasped, keeping his voice purposely low so it wouldn't carry to Megan's opened door at the end of the hall, "Megan has finally bonded with someone. Every shrink I took her to said that before she would speak, she'd have to form a bond with another woman. They said at some point, she'd reach out and find a substitute mother. I guess that's you, Casey...."

CHAPTER FOUR

SHOCKED BY MATT'S STATEMENT, Casey whispered, "I'm not sure I can be that for Megan. I'd like to help her where and when I can, though."

Rubbing his brow, Matt nodded. There was nothing to dislike about Casey. "Thanks, I realize this is an odd request. I *really* appreciate anything you can do." He knew he was asking a lot of her. After all, Casey was a stranger to them, for all intents and purposes. He'd been so startled by Megan's reaction to Casey, that he'd blurted his request out. Silently chastising himself, Matt realized belatedly he shouldn't have asked that of Casey. She was a newcomer to the town and this was her first job after college. What a fool he'd been. How to fix it?

Biting down on her lower lip, Casey remained silent. Gwen Garner had told her everything about Matt's tragedy. It wasn't up to her to bring it up. She could see the pain in his eyes and had no wish to cause him more.

"I'm sure you know what happened to us," Matt said without preamble. He automatically looked toward the hall to Megan's room. Keeping his voice low, he said, "Mrs. Harrington saw such a change in Megan with the owl on her glove that she suggested I call the pediatric psychiatrist in Idaho Falls." Matt added, "Barbara Ward has been the most help to me in understanding what's happened to Megan." He stared darkly down at the mug of coffee in his hands. "And you need to understand what happened, too."

"Of course," Casey murmured. Oh, how badly she wanted to reach out and give Matt some sort of solace! She could see his eyes alive with hope and fraught with guilt mingled with fear. His mouth, she was discovering, thinned whenever he was tense. It relaxed when he was not. He had a very kissable mouth. Casey was surprised at her reaction to him. Since her own near-death experience four years ago, she'd lost all interest in men. Until now.

Matt began, "Barbara told me that someday, when Megan's memory of that night was ready to become conscious, *something* would trigger it." He gave Casey a glance. The sympathy written across her features made Matt want to reach out and embrace her. He had no idea where all of that came from and savagely tamped down the unexpected desire. "I believe that the owl incident was a trigger, but I'm not sure. I have a call in to Dr. Ward to discuss it with her."

"That sounds hopeful," Casey said.

"Dr. Ward also said that Megan, at some point, might bond with another woman who she perceives as motherlike. A nurturing woman. She felt it would eventually happen." Matt stared over at Casey and saw surprise flare in her eyes.

Raising her brows, Casey murmured, "Are you thinking Megan has bonded with me?"

Nodding, Matt whispered rawly, "I've never seen Megan throw her arms around another woman since her mother's death. This is a big first, Casey." Seeing the turmoil and hesitation in Casey's features, he asked, "How do you feel about that?" He understood not every woman wanted to have children or to be a nurturing mother type. He'd seen other women take career paths where they showered their natural nurturing upon their employees or choosing service work to help others. All women were maternal, he felt, it was just a question of how they expressed it.

"I come from a large family," Casey explained. "My parents were U.S. Navy pilots for twenty years until they retired from the military. There's five girls in our family. And two sets of twins." Casey smiled a little and said, "I'm from the second set of twins and the youngest—I'm twenty-four. My three older sisters say that Selene, my twin, and I were spoiled rotten because we were the 'babies' of our family. I grew up happy in San Francisco. Not all my sisters want a big family." She smiled fondly. "Selene and I were the ones who played with dolls. The other sisters loved Lego and geek stuff. Someday, I hope to have a family myself, but I'm too young to do that right now. I want to get some roots into my Forest Service career."

Nodding, Matt noticed the softness of her full mouth. "I see. Can I keep in touch with you about Megan after Dr. Ward calls me? I'm in limbo on this, Casey." He had to give her options. It wasn't fair to pin her down and insist she had to work with Megan.

Casey felt his desperation. This was a straw to grab at, she realized. His love for his daughter was clearly etched in Matt's narrow eyes. Despite being a powerful and masculine man, he was being vulnerable with her. She remembered all too clearly her five attackers, big, strapping men in their late twenties, who were Matt's size and height. There had been no vulnerability in them; they had nearly beaten her to death. Casey remembered some of her attack, but not all of it. She understood as few could about the memories of the trauma being locked away in her brain, too virulent and potentially threatening to her mental stability to be released. That was the way her shrink, Wanda Haversham, had described it to her while she was still in the hospital.

"I understand your position on this," Casey told him quietly. She glanced over her shoulder toward the hall to make sure Megan couldn't hear what she was going to say. She handed Matt her business card. "Call me when you hear something from Dr. Ward. I'll be happy to help Megan if I can." She saw instant relief come to his rugged features. His mouth suddenly relaxed. His hands released their grip around the coffee mug.

"Thank you," Matt said, his voice echoing his relief.

SENATOR CARTER PEYTON sat in the rear of the black limo with his red-haired wife, Clarissa. He was continually on his cell phone with his assistants in Washington, D.C. Barely looking out the darkly tinted windows as the driver slowly made his way through the melting slush and traffic on the Easter weekend in Jackson Hole, he continued making his calls. Clarissa looked bored. But when didn't she? At thirty-five, Carter knew everyone in Wyoming thought he had it made. He didn't think so.

His life had taken a terrible, twisted turn three years earlier when his first wife, Gloria, and his two young children, Buck and Tracy, had died in a house fire just outside Jackson Hole. Anger grew in him as he thought about it again. And Matt Sinclaire was to blame. The lieutenant had been on duty that night when Gloria had called 911 in a panic. Their multimillion-dollar home that sat perched high on a hill, two miles off the main asphalt road, was on fire. He was stuck in Cody, Wyoming, because of a blizzard, after having attended a meeting of townspeople. The interstates had been shut down and no flights were available. Carter blamed himself for not being at home when it happened. If he had been, he knew his first wife and their children would be alive today. As it was, Sinclaire's ineptness at getting that fire truck stuck on the muddy dirt road had doomed his family.

"Let's eat here in town," Clarissa said. She touched her lacquered red hair to ensure it was in place.

"The housekeeper will have lunch waiting for us," he growled, flipping his cell phone closed. The limo crawled along. The sky was cloudy and it looked like it was going to snow again. Carter hated going through town because he saw the fire station where Sinclaire worked. It always compounded the rage that was never far beneath the surface.

Pouting, Clarissa said, "All right then, drop me off at the Aspens restaurant on your way home. Bob can pick me up when I'm finished eating."

Carter felt torn. He'd married Clarissa a year after Gloria's death. As a senator, he needed a wife at his side. She was a tall, lissome woman who came from a rich banking and ranching family in Cheyenne. She was only twenty-nine to his thirty-five years of age, but astute and selfish as hell. Still, Clarissa was the ideal Washington, D.C., wife. She was cultured, a true political animal like him, and she desired power. Carter felt she had married him because he was a second-term senator for the state of Wyoming. She had her own agenda she wanted to pursue.

"All right," he murmured. "I know you have quilting friends here you want to chat with over lunch," he murmured. Tapping Bob on his thin shoulder, he asked his long-time driver to turn and drop his wife off at the Aspens. The driver nodded and turned down another street in the center of town.

Pleased, Clarissa gathered up the snakeskin purse that matched her heels. She was dressed in a black wool pantsuit, white silk blouse and red silk scarf. The red of the silk matched her shoulder-length hair. "Good. After lunch, I'm going to walk over to Quilter's Haven. I want to see what new fabrics Gwen has gotten in for spring."

He managed a wry smile. "I imagined you would do that." In some ways, Carter thanked God for his wife's passion for embroidery and for her cousin, Julie Neustedder, who was a famous quilting teacher over in Cheyenne. That was how they'd met: there was a quilting fest at the local high school, with two hundred quilts hung for the public to appreciate. Clarissa had been there with her famous cousin. Carter had come because, as a senator, he always went to big events where he could press the flesh and mingle. That was part of the political game. He had found Clarissa a beautiful jewel among the ranching and mining middle class at the quilt festival.

After dropping Clarissa off in front of a restaurant bedecked with a red-and-white-striped awning, Carter climbed back into the car. His wife was happy now. And so was he.

"Home, Bob."

"Yes, sir," the fifty-year-old balding, bespectacled man murmured.

Sitting back, Carter felt his stomach knot and unknot. When he was alone and there was nothing to do, the memories of what he'd done always came back to him. He blamed it on guilt. Carter didn't feel he should feel guilt about a damned thing. The limo sped up as they left the plaza area and headed up the hill toward his home on Moose Road, near the Teton National Forest, and Carter sighed.

When he'd been able to get back from Cody to Jackson Hole, knowing his family had died in that fire, he'd gone straight to the fire chief, Doug Stanley, a forty-five-year-old of German-English descent. Carter had stormed into Stanley's office to find out why his family had been left to burn alive, and the chief had defended the man at the tip of that spear: Matt Sinclaire.

Carter snorted softly. Firefighters, like lawmen, stuck together and were thick as thieves. Stanley had argued that Sinclaire had done everything humanly possible to save the lives of Carter's family. There was the blizzard of the century howling through at the time, the roads were not plowed, the county trucks had been ordered to stay off them due to the danger. Snow was piling up so fast and furiously it was impossible to clear the roads. And then, because the spring thaw was underway, Carter's muddy two-mile-long road was a mire. Sinclaire had ordered the two trucks up the hill and they had both got stuck a mile away from the burning home.

Smiling a little, Carter tapped his fingers on the leg of his expensive black pin-striped suit pants. He'd waited a year after his family's deaths and then he'd gotten even. Everyone thought a senator was clean, but Carter wasn't. He knew how to grease the wheels politically and how to manipulate to get whatever it was he wanted. Through Gerald Vern, his most trusted office staffer, Carter had hired a professional arsonist and hit man. Frank Benson, who lived in Driggs, Idaho, about fifty miles from Jackson Hole was paid a hundred thousand dollars and he'd partially fulfilled his contract.

Carter was unhappy when he found out Sinclaire's daughter had managed to escape the flames; he was very pleased when he found out Megan Sinclaire had gone mute. That was some payback, but not enough.

Flexing his fist, Carter looked to his right to the elk range. The elk always came out of the mountains to be fed and to winter over near Jackson Hole in a range thousands of acres long and fenced. He saw that about half the thousands of animals had already gone back to the mountains. It was, after all, April. The snow wouldn't melt until early June and the elk were going to the higher elevations to calve.

Rubbing his jaw, he thought about contacting Benson again. It had been two years since Bev Sinclaire had been shot in the head. Carter still wanted Megan dead. He wanted Sinclaire to feel all the anguish and loss he'd felt. Since the fire chief had staunchly defended his employee's actions, Carter knew a civil trial to sue Sinclaire would do no good. Rubbing his hands together, Carter gloated over the surprise hit on Sinclaire's family. He smiled a little. Benson was so good at his job that the police had never found the culprit. And he wanted it to stay that way.

"Soon…" he murmured to no one in particular. Peyton had found that timing was everything. Two years had passed and Sinclaire had moved into town and lived in a one-story ranch house a couple of blocks away from the fire station. Things had settled down in this backwater town. Most people now gossiped and talked about other things rather than Bev Sinclaire's unsolved murder. It was time to strike again. One final, last time…

"I KNOW LIEUTENANT SINCLAIRE is going to be happy about all this," Cat Edwin said, sitting at the table eating dinner with Casey.

Sighing, Casey shrugged. "I feel ambivalent about it, Cat." She picked at the romaine and tomato salad Cat had made for them. She'd gotten home an hour earlier, climbed out of her ranger uniform and gotten into a pair of jeans and a green long-sleeved cotton pullover.

"Why?" Cat asked, eating hungrily. She'd been on duty for twelve hours and had the next two days off.

Casey really didn't know Cat that well; they were new roommates. "It's just me," she murmured, chewing on a tomato. She liked the black-haired woman with intense blue eyes. Her square face went with her solid, large-boned build. Cat was no shrinking violet insofar as women went. She was five foot eleven inches tall, weighed a hundred and sixty pounds and was pure muscle. In one room of their large apartment was a complete gym where Cat worked out religiously for at least an hour a day. Casey knew that firefighting was physical and Cat had to be in top shape to work alongside her male compatriots.

"That guy," Cat said between bites, "is a good dude. What happened to him is a crime—literally." She wiped her mouth with the yellow linen napkin and settled it back onto her lap. "I'm not assigned to his watch, but all the guys talk favorably about Matt." She grinned a little and said teasingly, "You know he's single."

Casey cringed inwardly; she wanted nothing to do with men. She was still working through the devastation of nearly being beaten to death by five potheads. "My focus isn't on relationships right now, Cat. I just graduated and I need to do well here at my first assignment."

Nodding, Cat got up and walked to the kitchen. She'd made spaghetti and meatballs as a main dish. The air was filled with the aromas of tomato, basil and garlic. Coming back with plates piled high with food, Cat handed Casey hers and sat down. "In my job at the fire department there's no fraternization between me and the guys." Cat smiled a crooked smile. "That's okay with me. I'm only twenty-two and frankly, I don't want to get married young." She sliced open a huge meatball. "I come from an abusive family. I got out of it as soon as I could. My father beat us with a belt and my mother never stopped him."

Casey gave her new roommate a sympathetic look. Cat was beautiful in an arresting way. She had slightly tilted blue eyes that gave her broad, square face a subtle exotic look. With her short, dark curls Casey thought she looked like the mythical Greek huntress Artemis. That goddess was a warrior and a hunter and was just as capable as any man.

Casey frowned, thinking that Artemis had never endured hardship like Cat. "I'm sorry to hear of your hardship. I find that among my friends at the university, if any had a father who beat them up or was verbally abusive to them, they didn't want to get involved in a male relationship any too soon, either."

Cat held up her hand. "That's me. Not that I don't like men, I do." She frowned. "But in here, in my gut—" she touched her stomach region "—I don't trust them. I know it stems from my father. I try to work it out in my head and tell myself that not all men are like my father." Frowning, she twirled the marinara sauce and spaghetti onto a huge spoon with her fork. "So far, I haven't achieved it. I wish I could. I've met some decent men, but my emotions are still stuck back when I was an eight-year-old."

"Hmm, I understand," Casey said, sympathetic. She had the same problem, only her distrust of men had started in her sophomore year of college. "Have you seen any progress with yourself as the years go by?" she wondered.

"No," Cat murmured unhappily. "I look at guys, but don't touch. My head is stuck in PTSD symptoms, according to what my therapist told me years ago. Until I can grow up emotionally and lose my fear of men, there's not much I can do."

"Do you date?"

Cat's mouth twisted. "I have friends who are men. I do go to dances with them, I share a beer at a local bar sometimes, and I go hiking with them. But real intimacy? No… I'm just not there. Yet."

Hearing the determination in her roommate's lowered voice, Casey hoped she wouldn't have to live her life in that PTSD cage. Someday, after she got to know Cat a lot better, she'd share her story. Truly, they were two peas from the same pod. "You're pretty, Cat. I don't know of a guy who wouldn't give you a second look."

Laughing sharply, Cat said, "Listen, my looks and my body act as a guy magnet for every man around. Isn't it sad?" She patted her hip. "I got this fab body and face and I'm scared to death of men! How's that for pure irony?"

Finishing her salad, Casey nodded. "It is ironic."

"So? Are you going to work with Lieutenant Sinclaire on behalf of his daughter?" Cat wondered, giving Casey an assessing look.

"I probably will," Casey slowly admitted. "If I do, it's for Megan."

"You're not interested in him, huh?"

"No." Casey thought she must be a liar. Matt Sinclaire made her feel things she'd never felt before. He was terribly good-looking, like a rugged model on a magazine cover. There was nothing to dislike about him from what she'd observed so far. "He's terribly conflicted and guilty over Megan's condition. He felt that if he'd been home at the time of his wife's murder, Megan's muteness wouldn't have happened."

Cat snorted. "Listen, you have to attend fire school a couple of times a year. It's mandatory for all of us. You have to keep up with the evolution of fire suppression and the new equipment coming out. Matt had to go to that school in Cheyenne, Casey. As an officer he can't just up and decide differently."

"I understand that," Casey said. "I wouldn't be surprised if he didn't have ulcers over all of this."

Nodding, Cat savored the meal she'd made for them. She was proud of her culinary abilities. "He doesn't from what I know, but I see him with dark circles under his eyes from time to time. His men who are on watch with him told me once he has bad insomnia."

Casey knew that symptom really well. She had restless, sleepless nights, too, particularly around a full moon. She got so she hated that time of the month. Before her concussion and beating, she had always slept soundly and deeply. But no more.

"You know, there's a new doctor in town," Cat said,

almost to herself, "that I'm thinking of seeing. She's called a functional medicine specialist."

"What is that?" Casey asked.

"They deal with PTSD symptoms, from what I understand. And they have a good track record of getting rid of the symptoms from a hormonal level. Her name is Jordana Lawton. I've been diagnosed with PTSD, and I thought if there's a prayer of a chance that she could help me get rid of the symptoms caused by high cortisol levels, I'd give her a try."

"Let me know what happens?" Casey asked. She'd love to get rid of her PTSD symptoms, too, but no one knew she had them. And no one knew what had happened to her, not even her employer, the USFS. And she wanted to keep it that way. It was a private skeleton in the closet of her life. Casey lived in fear of anyone finding out and then going to her supervisor, Ranger Charley Davidson. There was no telling what the USFS might do. They could fire her because she'd not put down all her medical history on her employment form, for starters. It was a risk Casey had to take.

"Oh," Cat chortled, "I will." She smiled over at Casey. "This is the first time I've had a roommate. I think it's going to be nice to share with a sister. I don't usually share much about myself. We had the elephant of abuse in our family's living room and I never told anyone at school what was going on. I was so afraid." Cat reached over and touched Casey's arm for a moment. "So, if I'm being too talkative and sharing, rein me in, okay? I'm not good at this sharing stuff." She chortled.

Smiling gently at her roommate, Casey realized how fortunate she'd been to grow up in a safe, loving family.

She had four sisters who loved her. "I'm pretty good at chatting myself, so I think we'll get along fine, Cat." She saw the woman look a little more relaxed over that admission.

"Great, I think we're a good pair to be sharing this condo," Cat said, meaning it. "I know my social graces aren't the best. I trust women. They aren't my problem. It's the men."

Casey nodded and loaded her spoon with spaghetti. "We share a lot in common, Cat. I think we're going to get along just fine."

"Sisters in the battle of life," Cat said, grinning widely.

Indeed, Casey thought. Right now she had a couple of battles she'd never envisioned: Megan's unexpected affection and being drawn to Megan's father, Matt Sinclaire. Casey knew she couldn't separate one from another. There was a driving force in her to help the eight-year-old. Megan didn't know it, but they shared much more in common than anyone would ever know.

CHAPTER FIVE

MATT TRIED TO CONTAIN his excitement as he walked from the parking lot toward the beautifully constructed visitor's center just inside the gates of the Grand Teton National Park. Behind him rose the majestic and snow-covered Tetons. Thrusting his hands in the pockets of his red nylon fire department jacket, he hurried down the sidewalk.

It was 10:00 a.m. and so much had happened since Megan had seen the hawk and owl in her class. Hope warred with terror within him. Matt struggled to keep all his emotions in check. He'd found out from Charley, the chief ranger, that Casey would be on duty at the visitor's center all day. Her job was to answer people's questions. Should he have called Casey first? Something told him to show up in person. How would she take what he had to say? Would she see him as pressuring her to help his daughter? Was she at all interested in helping? Matt knew she was a stranger who had plummeted into their life out of the blue. He knew he had no right to expect anything from Casey.

Yet, as he pulled opened the glass door that led into the huge, airy center, his intuition told him Casey was a compassionate person and cared deeply for others. Would she care about the news he had?

Because he was a firefighter, Matt had been to the

visitor's center many times. If there was ever a fire here, he had to know the entrance and exit points. He had to be aware of everything so that a team sent into this place would be made aware of the structure and its inherent challenges. Charley had said Casey would be at the map desk. Not that many visitors in late April were interested in hiking trails still covered with anywhere between two and ten feet of snow. Still, a hardy few were up for cross-country skiing on these mountain trails.

He spotted Casey talking to a male visitor over a map. He slowed his pace. The center was pretty deserted at this time of the morning. Over in the gift shop he spotted Cindy McLaughlin. She smiled and waved to Matt. He returned her smile and lifted his hand. Cindy had lost her husband, Steve, to prostate cancer a year ago. Their two children were in college. She managed the gift-shop concession for the company who had won the bid to run it. The black-haired, brown-eyed woman always had a smile for everyone, despite her personal tragedy. Matt knew she wasn't making enough money to keep her two children in college.

Steve had been a civil engineer with a local company. He'd made very good money. Now, Cindy was losing her financial base. Matt felt bad for her. He turned away and saw that Casey had just handed the young man a map. Good, she was no longer busy. Taking a deep breath, Matt headed in her direction.

Casey felt her heart bang once to underscore the surprise of seeing ruggedly handsome Matt Sinclaire walking toward her. He wore a bright red jacket, his hands stuffed into the pockets. A pair of jeans on him made her appreciate how tall and in shape he was. It was the narrowed look in his forest-green eyes that made her mouth go dry. Casey had the distinct feeling he was like a wolf on the prowl. His black hair was short but a few rebellious strands dipped across his furrowed brow. No woman in her right mind wouldn't be drawn to this heroic man, Casey told herself. She saw all men and women in the businesses of law enforcement and firefighting as bona fide modern-day heroes. Matt Sinclaire embodied that concept in warm flesh and blood.

"Good morning," Matt greeted as he came up to the desk. "I hope you don't mind me dropping by unexpectedly? I have some news about Megan that I'd like to share with you."

Relief shot through Casey. This was about Megan. For a moment her silly mind had fantasized that Matt was here for her. It had been almost a week since she'd seen him. Her dreams, for once, had taken a pleasant turn and she'd dreamed of him and of kissing him. Feeling heat tunnel up her neck and into her cheeks, Casey grabbed the stool and sat down opposite him. "Of course not." She gave him a wry smile as he folded his large hands on the counter in front of her. "As you can see, we're not exactly busy."

Dipping his head, Matt drowned in her warm gray eyes. Casey's ranger uniform was spotless and ironed, and she looked sharp in the long-sleeved tan blouse and dark green trousers. The mannish clothes couldn't hide her femininity from him, however. She was tall and curvy. Most of all, he liked the softness of her lips as they pulled into a self-deprecating smile. "Thanks, I really appreciate you giving me a few minutes of your time." He cleared his throat, nervous.

"I talked to Meggie's psychiatrist over in Idaho Falls

earlier this week," he confided to her in a low voice. "And she, like me, felt Meggie was having a break-through."

"Wonderful," Casey said. She saw the anxious look in his eyes although it wasn't broadcast in his low, husky tone. Inhaling, she smelled the cold air and scent of pine around Matt. He was clean-shaven, no trace of a dark beard. There was a white T-shirt beneath his jacket. Black hair peeked out from beneath it. He was so male that it made her dizzy for a moment. Never had Casey had such a powerful response to any man! It scared her silly.

Opening his hands, Matt rasped, "Here's what you might possibly do to help Megan." He didn't say, "help me," but that was implicit.

"Sure, what can I do to help her?" Casey saw Matt's eyes were fraught with so many emotions it was impossible to accurately read them. She understood how much he loved his daughter and how guilt hounded him, much as the PTSD stalked her daily from her own near-death experience.

Relieved, Matt saw sincerity in Casey's large, intelligent gray eyes. It gave him the courage to speak. "Barbara, Meggie's therapist, feels strongly that for whatever reasons, the owl experience and you, as a woman, have opened some doors that have been closed in my daughter since that night she lost her mother."

How badly Casey wanted to reach out and touch Matt's hand. She saw the white lines of many scars upon them. Had he gotten all of them firefighting? She knew it was always dangerous work. "What else?" Casey probed gently. There was such hesitation in Matt's face at that moment, as if he were unsure he should say the rest of what the therapist told him.

"Barbara Ward is a fine therapist. Megan bonded with her as much as she can." He moved his shoulders as if to get rid of the accumulated, invisible weight he carried. "I always hoped Meggie would bond more deeply with Barbara and open up, but she didn't. Barbara said that my daughter running into your arms to be held was an incredibly positive breakthrough." Matt's voice cracked. "She said that finally Meggie is starting to move out of the paralyzing PTSD. She's reaching out to you, Casey." He stared hard into her widening eyes. Praying that she would not rebuff his daughter's chances for help, he added quickly, "And she feels that some kind of weekly contact with Meggie would be very, very helpful to her."

Shocked, Casey sat there digesting his words. She could see how needy he was about this situation. But wouldn't she be, too, if it were her daughter in dire straits? Of course. Without thinking, Casey reached out and lightly touched his clenched hand on the desk. "Of course I'll help you, Matt. Megan is a wonderful child. She's been dealt a bad hand. I'd love to work with Dr. Ward and you to help her open up."

Something old and hard shattered in Matt's heart. He closed his eyes. Casey's hand was warm and it sent tingles of reaction up his arm and surging into his pounding heart. Casey's touch had been brief. It seemed to him the moment she'd reached out and caressed the back of his hand, she'd jerked back, as if burned. Joy soared through Matt and he opened his eyes and clung to her gray gaze. "You will?"

Casey's heart broke for the father. "Of course I will.

Now, we need to work around my schedule. I get two days off a week, but not necessarily on weekends, which is our busiest time here at the park. I know firefighters have weird work schedules, too. We'll just have to dance around those obstacles and make it work for Megan." In that moment, Casey felt her heart widening like a flower opening to full, direct sunlight. The happiness in Matt's eyes made them burn like green fire. His look was startling, wonderful, and she felt heat funnel from her face down to her lower body where she grew warm and achy with need—for him—as a man. Shocked, Casey quickly tamped down her unexpected feelings toward him.

Matt blindly opened his arms and leaned across the desk and gave her a quick hug. The unexpected action on his part was pure spontaneity. "Thank you," he rasped brokenly against her ear. "Thank you so much… I owe you more than I can ever repay you, Casey…" He choked back a sob. Releasing Casey, he felt embarrassed by his own actions. Looking around, he saw the other four rangers staring at them. Mouth quirking, he gave Casey an apologetic look. "Sorry, I didn't mean…"

Laughing breathlessly, Casey held up her hand and said, "I understand. Don't worry about it." She felt her shoulders tingling wildly in the wake of his powerful and unexpected embrace. Casey knew his action was based on the joy and relief of her agreeing to be Megan's mentor of sorts. So much of the anxiety and guilt had disappeared from his green eyes. Her heart soared with the knowledge that she had been of help to two people who desperately needed a third person to catalyze them. Casey understood it on a deep level. She hadn't healed from her trauma, either, and wondered if she was doomed to a life where she felt this huge, black stain would continue to ruin her daily existence. Since nearly dying, Casey had felt no real desire to live life again. Not until this seminal, unexpected moment. What was happening?

"I have my schedule with me," Matt said, digging into his pocket and producing a neatly folded piece of paper. Opening it up, he flattened it out on the desk before her. "Do you have yours?" Matt tried to slow down. He tried to recapture his escaping emotions. Everyone called him stoic. No one would believe him in this electric moment with Casey. Matt knew that before he reached the fire station Gwen Garner would know everything, including his embracing Casey. Somehow, he didn't care. Gwen wasn't a gossiper. She verified things first before telling her clientele anything. Smiling to himself, Matt felt relieved that for once, good news would be ladled out by the quilting queen of the town.

Sympathetic for Matt, Casey pulled the rangers' schedule from the desk drawer. "Okay, let's compare," she said lightly, hoping to ease the tension between them. Her softly spoken words had a profound effect on him, she realized. Casey had always heard that people who loved one another could soothe their loved one's fractious state with voice alone. She'd seen it often between her parents, Clay and Alyssa. And now, Emma, her oldest sister, had emailed her last night telling her that she was falling in love with U.S. Army Captain Khalid Shaheen, a fellow Apache gunship pilot, who was in Afghanistan with her. Funnily enough, as Casey moved through the sheets of paper to find her schedule, Emma's words echoed in her head: *All Khalid has to do is speak to me and I feel like this warm velvet energy surrounds me. I feel his love, his care. I've never felt anything like it in my life. This must be love. Have you ever had this experience, Casey?*

Casey could now email her back after work and tell her that yes, she not only understood, but had experienced this herself. But love? Giving an internal shake of her head, Casey decided she was not ready for love. She wasn't ready for a man—any man—in her life, either. She was still too wounded to reach out and trust any of them right now.

As Matt leaned forward, their heads bare inches from one another as they studied their respective schedules, Casey felt suddenly joyous. The emotion was so foreign to her since her own tragedy, that it caught her completely off guard. Taking in a deep, shaky breath, she tried to quell the feeling. The sensation she felt was like a hawk flying free after a long imprisonment. She gave Matt a confused look; he didn't realize what was happening, his gaze locked on the papers laid out before them. Maybe that was just as well. Casey knew she couldn't handle his full attention. Better that he was focused on Megan. That little girl was a safe haven for Casey at this moment. Casey was still in a raw state of vulnerability. Megan was safe; Matt was not. She could easily concentrate on the child, and, right now, that was all Casey could handle.

"It looks like this Friday is good for us," Matt murmured, looking up. Casey was so close that he could smell her feminine scent, jasmine in bloom. He wondered obliquely if she washed her shining brown hair with a jasmine shampoo. The fragrance intoxicated him and his gaze dropped to her mouth. Her lips were parted and Casey was so close…so close that all he had to do

was move three inches forward and he could kiss her
senseless. Electrified by the awareness, Matt suddenly
straightened so they weren't so close. He saw so much in
Casey's eyes. Her pupils were dilated, huge and black,
and were centered on him. Feeling as if he were spinning out of emotional control, as if someone had lifted
the gate on so many of his suppressed feelings, Matt
gulped and tried to appear unaffected by her nearness.

"Uh…yes, Friday is good," Casey stammered. She
sat upright on the stool, wanting as much room between
herself and him as she could get. Matt was simply too
raw and male. He appealed to her feminine senses on
a visceral and primal level. There was a raw neediness now clamoring deep in her body, something Casey
had never felt before. As if she were hungry for Matt
in every possible way a woman could want her man.
Shaken, Casey managed in a hoarse tone, "What time
on Friday? And does Dr. Ward have any suggestions
on how I'm to interface with Megan?"

Matt blinked, feeling as though he was coming out of
the deep freeze insofar as his emotions were concerned.
Giving himself a stern, internal lecture, he said, "Yes.
She suggested we take Megan after school over to the
raptor rehabilitation center that Katie runs. I've already
cleared a visit from us and Katie is excited. She feels
that Hank will continue his magic on Megan."

"Oh, good," Casey said. The raptor center was a
safe place. Right now, Casey did not want to be feeling
trapped inside Matt's beautiful home with him. "And
after the visit? Is there more?"

"Katie has a coloring book that she uses with children. She thought if all goes well, that Megan can sit in
her office and use crayons to draw Hank. And there's

other raptors in the book, too. We're just supposed to be in the background at this point. Barbara said we just have to play it by ear. If Megan wants to do the coloring project, Barbara is interested whether she'll give one of us the drawing."

"And if she does?"

"It shows bonding," Matt said. "If Megan asks for your help, or wants you near or wants some kind of connection with you while she colors, Barbara feels that's a good sign, too."

"Of what? Bonding?"

Nodding, Matt said, "Yes." He bit back the rest of his comment. Wanting that bonding to happen so badly he could taste it, he saw the uncertainty in Casey's face. "You have concerns?"

Shrugging, Casey placed her schedule beneath the counter. "I don't know what *bonding* means to Dr. Ward. I mean, I've never been put in a position like this before, Matt, and I'm worried I'll say or do the wrong thing. I have fears of making your daughter regress instead of progress."

Without thinking, Matt reached out and touched her hand for a brief moment. "Look, you can't do anything wrong, Casey. I did the wrong thing. I was gone when I should have been home." He quickly removed his hand. Her flesh was warm and supple.

There was nothing wimpy about Casey. He could tell she was an avid hiker, her legs long, curved and hidden in those dark green trousers. She was an outdoors person like himself.

Shocked by his touch, Casey withdrew her hand. Feeling panicky now, she quickly tucked her hands into her lap where he couldn't reach them. Yet, she had thrilled to his touch. She had felt how roughened and work-worn his fingers were when they had grazed her flesh. "You can't blame yourself for what happened," Casey protested. "You have to go on courses just like I do. You can't mind-read that something awful will happen to your family when you are away, Matt."

"I know you're right," he said in apology. His fingers ached to touch Casey again. How easy would it be to slide them up her arm, across her proud shoulder and caress her clean, strong jaw? And then, to lean down and brush her lips with his? Shaken to his core, Matt wondered what was going on with him. Barbara Ward had said about six months ago that at some point he would come out of that tunnel of grief and guilt and want to start living again. Was he waking up from that long sleep as a man with desires and sexual needs once more? Had it finally started to happen? Was Casey the trigger?

"I was told that time heals all." Casey didn't want to say any more than that. Her parents had flown in to Colorado when she had gone missing on her hike. And they were there at her bedside when she came out of the coma a week later. They had all cried for different reasons. And it had been her parents who told her what had happened because her mind was blank about the attack. One of the last things her mother Alyssa had whispered to her as she leaned over and pressed a kiss to her bandaged brow was, "Time will heal everything, Casey. Everything. You're going to be fine. I just know it...."

Giving her a wry look now, Matt refolded his schedule and shoved it back into his pocket. "That's what Barbara tells me all the time. I believe her, but it's been a long haul with Megan. I guess I was losing hope.

Until…well…you came along." He lowered his voice and said, "Casey, I'm so relieved that you're here for Megan. I'm grateful beyond words that you'll do this for her. I know we're strangers and we have sort of crashed into one another's lives. It's heroic of you to take this on. Most people wouldn't." He grimaced. "There's a lot of people out there in the world today who don't feel they're responsible to anyone but themselves. The whole fabric of being a human has changed since about 1970. There's a segment of our population that just doesn't care anymore. But here, in this valley of ranchers, cowboys, trappers, miners, oil men and rugged individualists, that extended care never got destroyed. Neighbors do rely on one another. Friends help where and when they can. We're a tight-knit community from that standpoint and you sure fit into it." Matt gave her a warm smile meant to make her feel good about her volunteering to help Megan.

"I grew up in a large family, Matt. We were taught reliance on one another, and that our neighborhood was everyone's responsibility." Casey smiled a little, feeling her heart opening even wider as Matt stood relaxed, a happy glint in his green eyes. "I'm finding that Jackson Hole isn't like the rest of the world. Gwen Garner told me the same thing you just did. I like being with people who care, with people who are their neighbors' keepers. It takes a village, as Hillary Clinton wrote in her book. We're all connected. We all have to work together or we perish together, as I see it." Casey had experienced amazing support not only from her friends at the university, but from the faculty, as well, after she left the hospital. For a moment, she wanted to share that very special and private experience with Matt. She felt he would understand. And right now, he looked achingly vulnerable despite being the rugged, heroic man he was. Casey could see on his face and in his eyes his emotions and concern for his daughter and her welfare. His whole life was focused on Megan.

"I'm in this for your daughter," Casey assured him. "Megan needs a village right now. We all come together like the warp and weft of the village fabric to cradle and support her getting better. That's how I see it, Matt—we're fabric. Each strand is a person. We overlap, we touch and we are connected. And to sit here and turn you down or say no to helping Megan isn't something I could ever do." Casey opened her hands. "I just pray to God that I don't make her worse."

"You can't possibly do more harm to her," Matt said with fierce emotion in his deep tone. "Megan reached out to you, Casey. Not the other way around. I was shocked when she threw herself into your arms." Hell, *he* wanted to be in Casey's arms! But that desire would never see the light of day and Matt swallowed those words. "There's just something unique about you, Casey. Megan saw it. I see it. I can't put it into words, either. There's just this feeling around you and because of it, Megan gravitated to you like the moon wanting to orbit Earth. I feel on a gut level that Megan sees you as someone not only to be trusted, but someone she feels safe with. She's never felt safe since the fire." And then he added hoarsely, "I no longer make her feel safe, either."

His words tore at Casey's heart. "Stop being so hard on yourself, Matt. Time heals all. I believe that." Not for her, but at least in Megan's world, it appeared to be happening. As Casey sat absorbing Matt's tall, powerful frame, his rugged face and his eyes burning with care, she stifled the urge to hold him. That's exactly what he needed, Casey realized. Matt needed to be held. She was sure he hadn't let anyone help him through all of this from what Gwen had told her. He was an iconic battle-weary knight fighting the dragons to save his daughter's precious life. He'd ignored his own needs and healing for hers, instead. In her eyes—and heart— Matt Sinclaire was a true hero.

CHAPTER SIX

FRIDAY WAS BLUSTERY WITH chilling rain off and on. It was near freezing as Casey made her way to the converted greenhouse where Katie Bergstrom kept her raptors. Katie met her at the door and smiled.

"Hi, Casey! Come on in! Matt and Megan are already here."

Friday was her day off, so Casey was bundled up in civilian clothes. She pulled off her purple knit cap and quickly moved into the large, airy greenhouse. It was warm and she gladly began to unwind her purple muffler and open her bright red squall jacket. She saw Matt with Megan standing at the opened office door halfway down the long expanse. As she lifted her hand to greet them, Casey felt her heart take off once more.

"Hey, Katie, how are you?" Casey asked, shrugging out of her jacket and hanging it on a nearby hook.

"I'm fine. How do you like our late-April weather? Sucks, doesn't it?"

"A lot of mud out there," Casey agreed. She lowered her voice. "How long have they been here?"

"Oh, about ten minutes," Katie said. "Come on…"

This was the first time Casey had seen Katie's headquarters. There were mews—cages—on both sides of the huge greenhouse. It was spotlessly clean. Every hawk, falcon and owl had several large perches plus a warm "house" to go into when chilled. The cages were huge, about twelve feet by twelve feet, giving each raptor room to fly a little bit. Huge shallow pottery bowls of water in the bottom of each cage were large enough so that if the raptor wanted to wash itself, it could. Raptor rehabilitators had to be licensed by the state with frequent inspections of their facilities and Casey was sure that Katie's operation passed on all counts.

Katie smiled as she and Casey drew up to Matt and Megan. "Okay, we're all here."

Casey nodded to Matt, whose gaze burned through her, making her pulse quicken. Today he wore a pair of jeans and a dark green long-sleeved polo shirt. His clothes did nothing but emphasize the breadth of his powerful chest and the masculinity that throbbed like sunlight around him. Casey stood within the circle of Matt's invisible sunshine. He smiled.

"Thanks for making it out on this rainy, cold day," Matt said. He looked down at Megan. "Meggie was coming no matter what the weather was like." He laughed a little.

Casey laughed with him. She crouched down in front of Megan. The child's eyes were bright and filled with excitement. "Hi, Megan. How are you today?" Casey wasn't going to treat her as if she were mute. She would speak to her as she would anyone else.

Megan pulled her hand out of her father's hand and began flapping her arms for Casey.

Grinning, Casey said, "Ah, you're going to take off today, are you?"

Raspy, excited sounds came out of Megan.

Standing, Casey turned to Katie. "Okay, what do we do next?"

Katie said, "I thought I'd take Megan from one end of the rehab center to the other and explain things as I go. You two can follow me. If you have questions, just pipe up." Katie opened her hand and Megan instantly slipped her hand into hers.

Casey fell back as Katie took Megan to the front of the greenhouse. Matt fell in beside her. The aisle was a good four feet wide, but when two people walked side by side, it became very intimate. Casey railed inwardly. She put her hands behind her back, but even that did not stop them from occasionally touching one another. It couldn't be helped.

As Katie took Megan to the work area where there were jesses, feathers picked up from the cleaning of the mews and other items, Casey tried to focus. It was impossible. She felt Matt's gaze on her from time to time. What to talk about? Certainly not last night's torrid dreams of Matt kissing her! Feeling her cheeks grow warm, Casey cleared her throat.

"How is the firefighting business going?" she asked.

"We always have a lot of wood-fire calls this time of year," he said in a low voice, not wanting to disturb Katie's talk with Megan.

"I was over at Quilter's Haven yesterday," Casey confided to him, "and Gwen said there was a bad fire out on Cox Road."

Grimacing, Matt said, "Yeah, I was on that call. We had our tanker that carries about twenty-two hundred gallons of water sink down to its axles in the mud. We were half a mile away from the home when it happened."

"Gwen said the house burned to the ground."

"Yes, it did." He scowled. "You'll find that a lot of

the ranches out in the valley are situated one to five miles off the main asphalt road that goes north to south through Jackson Hole. No one has the money to asphalt that kind of road. It would cost millions and most ranchers don't have that kind of money. So, every year, spring and fall, their roads turn to a mire. This isn't the first time our trucks have sunk down to their axles and been unable to make it to the fire in time to save the structure. It's hard on the people who called us and it's hard on us."

"Heartbreaking," Casey agreed, seeing the turmoil in his green eyes. "Gwen said they saved the dog and cat and family, but everything else went up in flames."

"At least they have their lives," he murmured in agreement, thinking back to the time three years ago when the same thing had happened with Senator Peyton's home. Only then, his wife and two children had burned to death. Matt would never forget that horrible night.

"Gwen said you had to call two eighteen-wheeler wreckers in to get you unstuck."

Nodding, Matt said, "That's right. Won't be the last time, either."

"Isn't there something the people can do to their roads to make them passable?" Casey wondered. Katie was finished showing Megan the soft kangaroo-leather jesses that fitted around the raptor's legs.

"We work with the land owners and the county," Matt said, following Katie and Megan to the first mew. "Tax money is spent on putting gravel on these roads, but that's expensive. The gravel gives the soil some purchase. Over the last two decades the fire department has sent men and equipment to gravel these roads to help the ranchers. It's not a perfect system."

"Gwen said about three years ago Senator Peyton, who lived two miles up on a steep hill, refused to upgrade his road. And then his house burned down and his family died. I find that mind-blowing. Here's a guy who is a millionaire fifty times over and he refuses to help pay for gravel on his dirt road? What was he thinking?" Casey shook her head.

Squirming inwardly, Matt knew he had to be careful what he said. Senator Peyton had sued the fire department after the loss of his family. The lawsuit was decided in the fire department's favor, and the senator had decided not to sue Matt in civil court. "I don't know what he was thinking" was all Matt said.

Looking up at him, Casey saw darkness in his narrowed eyes. His mouth was thinned. Realizing he wasn't saying all he could, she added, "Gwen said he sued the fire department and lost. And he was really pissed about the verdict."

"It was a messy lawsuit," Matt agreed quietly. "It was sad. I couldn't be angry with the senator. He lost his wife and two children. That's a terrible price for anyone to pay."

Studying Matt's rugged face, Casey sensed the tight emotional reactions he wasn't going to divulge. There was so much to Matt. He didn't give up anything about himself easily. But how could he? Casey had had a lot of time to think through Matt's situation. His wife Bev had been murdered. His child had nearly died in an arson fire. He'd lost a home he'd built with his own two hands. He'd had to start all over again. Casey realized that in some ways, she faced a similar path, only her loved ones had not been lost. She had lost a huge part of her happy-go-lucky self, though, to the beating by the druggies. Once, before the near-death experience, she had been an ebullient, outgoing person. Afterward, she became tight-lipped, conservative, distrustful of men, and she rarely gave any of herself to anyone. Casey saw the parallels.

Did people who had suffered through terrible trauma attract one another? Casey didn't have an answer except to know that she had looked forward to this day more than she should have. And for all the wrong reasons. She cared deeply for Megan's plight, but what made her heart beat with excitement was realizing Matt would be here. It gave her another chance to absorb him without his knowledge. In some ways, Casey felt like a thief. Matt didn't know she liked him. What did that make her?

"I don't know how you live with all of that," Casey confided in a lowered tone. "I mean…being stuck in mud and watching a house go up with people inside it." She lifted her chin and stared into his eyes. "How *do* you live with that, Matt?" Maybe her question was too personal because she saw him flinch. His mouth tightened and then it relaxed. Matt's gaze went from surprise to sadness and then bleakness.

"I have a tough time with it even now, Casey." He shrugged. "I try to forget it, but I can't. I have thought about that call a thousand times and replayed it as many times in my mind. Did I do something wrong? What could I have done differently? The elements were against us. When your tanker and engine sink to their axles in mud, there's nothing else you can do. We didn't even know if Senator Peyton's family was in there.

Word was that they'd all flown back to Washington, D.C. That didn't stop me from ordering my men up to the residence, however. We did what we could, but by that time, his family had died of smoke inhalation. We had no idea they were in there until the fire chief called Senator Peyton's office in D.C. and found out his family was home. When the 911 call came in, I thought it was a neighbor calling it in. Everyone assumed the senator and his family weren't here."

"That must have hammered you emotionally," Casey said. She kept her gaze on Megan, who was staring into a mew that had an injured red-tailed hawk in it. Katie was crouched next to the little girl explaining about the hawk being shot by a rancher and losing part of its left wing.

Matt, under ordinary circumstances, would have shut these kinds of questions down. But this was different for him. The softness of Casey's lips, the burning care in her gaze all conspired against him. Because of the lawsuit, Matt had swallowed his comments and feelings about the situation. Senator Peyton had sworn that if anyone talked about the loss of his family, he'd sue them. Matt didn't want to go through a second lawsuit with the angry senator. Once was enough. Swallowing, he rasped, "We're charged with saving lives. It was hard on everyone, Casey. No one has forgotten it happened. There isn't a day that goes by even now that I don't run the scenario through my head."

"Mud up to the axles is your answer," Casey said. "It's pretty black-and-white. What I don't understand is, with the senator's millions, why he didn't fix the road?"

"Well, therein lies the seeds of debate," Matt told her. "The senator's road was the next that was to be graveled by the county that coming summer. He felt the county should bear the entire burden of upgrading his road because he was a senator. Our county commissioners told him that on all the other roads, the ranchers pitched in as much money as they could to help. Why shouldn't Peyton ante up? If our ranchers, who are always struggling with the bottom line and eking out a living, can do it, why didn't he?" Matt felt old anger stirring within him. He felt the senator was trying to bleed the county dry. Like many of the rich, he wanted to hang on to his money and let the others be damned.

Shaking her head, Casey muttered, "Wow, that is beyond beyond—"

Wasn't it, though? But Matt didn't speak the words. Bad blood still ran deep in Jackson Hole because of that night and the senator's loss. It was worse because Peyton had a home here in Jackson Hole—his favorite. He also had a residence at the state capital in Cheyenne. Matt hated running into the senator, although truth be known, the places Peyton frequented weren't on Matt's itinerary. Except for the gym. There, he had run into the senator more than he wanted to. And every time they met, the hatred was alive in Peyton's eyes and was always aimed at him. He made Matt feel as if he were a criminal. And he knew he wasn't.

Megan screeched with joy and they both returned their focus to her. Katie had fitted her with a leather glove and she was in front of Hank's mew. Matt moved down the walk and pulled a small camera out of his pocket. Casey followed. For the next ten minutes, Megan learned not only how to get Hank to move from his perch to her glove, but also how to fly him.

Katie came over to Casey and offered her a leather

glove. "Put it on. You stand down at the other end of the walk. I'll stay with Megan and we'll fly Hank back and forth. This is what we do on awful days outside. Hawks won't fly in rain or snow. They're grounded. So we use the flyway here to give them daily exercise. You game?" She grinned.

"Of course," Casey said, relieved to be away from Matt's powerful masculine presence. She fitted the glove and Katie gave her instructions.

Turning at the end of the walk, Casey's heart melted with joy as she saw Megan with Hank perched proudly on her thin little arm. The child-size glove was too large for her. Her eyes glimmered with excitement. Katie had soothingly told Megan she couldn't make noises, laugh or jerk her hand around. All those things would upset Hank. The girl quickly understood. She was a model pupil. In Casey's eyes, Megan was as smart as her handsome father. The only difference was, she couldn't talk.

Casey had been given some rabbit meat in a pouch that she had belted around her waist. She placed a small bit of the meat between the thumb and index finger of the glove. Hank saw that and launched himself off Megan's glove to fly straight toward Casey. She was surprised at the power of Hank's "pounce" as his claws gripped the glove and he quickly gobbled down the red meat. The hawk turned and looked toward Megan and Katie. Smiling, Casey saw Katie place a bit of meat on Megan's glove. Instantly, with surprising power, Hank opened his wings and flapped through the air to land on Megan's glove.

It was a joy to watch Megan's face light up with incredible happiness as Hank landed on her glove. Matt was busy taking photos about halfway down the aisle where he could get good shots of Hank and his over-joyed daughter. Katie was all smiles and praised Megan. Casey put more meat on her glove. Hank missed nothing and launched off Megan's glove with a powerful flap of his wings.

For the next ten minutes, they flew Hank. Casey was caught up in the child's joy. From time to time, she would glance at Matt, who was crouched down by a mew taking photos. He was smiling. And what a change in his demeanor! Casey found herself gawking at Matt the way an awkward teenager would at her idol. Gone were the wrinkles in his broad brow. His laughter was deep and rolling. It filled the greenhouse and made her heart beat a little harder in her breast. She couldn't believe the difference. It was as if she were seeing two different Matt Sinclaires.

All Casey had known was the dark, pensive, brooding firefighter. But now, he was lighthearted, laughing, smiling, his cheeks flushed. To Casey, he looked like a little boy out doing something he loved. Indeed, he looked years younger. It was then that she realized the invisible load Matt had carried since Senator Peyton's family had died in that blaze. Did Matt accept Megan's muteness as a curse for what had happened that night at Peyton's home? It was a ridiculous thought, but Casey couldn't otherwise explain the surprising difference in Matt's demeanor.

Casey held her glove up with meat and Hank swiftly flew to it. Was Matt feeling this guilt and wearing the cloak of it? Casey held her arm steady as Hank turned, spotted the meat being put on Megan's glove and took off in a flurry of swift beats of his wings. Casey frowned, not wanting to let go of what was bothering

Matt. Was it guilt he carried over his wife's demise? The case remained cold and unsolved. Or was he worrying constantly that the killer was at large and possibly still stalking him and Megan? Casey decided Matt had enough worries, concerns and grief to kill an elephant, much less a man. He was carrying a horrible load.

Feeling nothing but compassion for him, Casey began to realize Matt Sinclaire's strong moral fiber. He was trying to do the right thing by his daughter. And in these precious moments, he seemed to step outside all the responsibility he carried and be in sync with his smiling child. Her heart opened wide and Casey felt intense emotions sweep through her. She gasped softly. What was she feeling?

Casting around like a fish out of water, Casey decided to call her mother tonight. Alyssa was wise in ways that always made Casey admire her. At fifty, she was worldly. Even more, her mother had raised her five daughters always to have lines of communication open. Casey was grateful her parents weren't like those who made their children feel unable to talk with them. When she'd made blunders and mistakes, her parents had never chewed her out. Instead, they talked and asked her what she'd learned from the experience. Casey loved them fiercely. And, since the beating, they'd drawn even closer to one another. Yes, a phone call to her mom was in order.

Matt looked toward Casey, his camera poised as Hank flew to her outstretched glove. It was an excuse to photograph her. Little did Casey know he simply wanted a photo of her smiling. Just being around her lifted his dark, hobbled spirit. Did she realize how positively she affected him? Matt didn't think so because he'd given her no indication. Right now, his focus was on Megan. And Casey was now a part of that focus. Matt felt good about that. Casey was stable and grounded. She had common sense and cared for others. She wasn't one of those narcissistic victim types that seemed so pervasive nowadays. No, Casey was considerate, caring and insightful. Her questions to him earlier had startled Matt. Few people were as perceptive as she was.

Megan laughed. He turned, hearing new sounds coming from his daughter. Hank had flown to Megan's glove and she'd allowed her joy to explode into a rich, high laughter. He felt a bolt of hope dance through him. Megan was really laughing. Not the rasping sounds she usually made.

Turning, he saw Casey walking up to him and removing her glove. "Did you hear that?" he asked, amazement in his tone.

"What?" Casey tilted her head and saw the shock in Matt's face. "What happened?"

"Megan laughed. She really laughed. That's new…"

Hearing his stunned words, Casey gripped his upper arm for a brief moment. "That's wonderful! Barbara was right—bringing Megan out here to work with Hank is helping her!"

Wildly aware of Casey's firm grip on his muscled upper arm, Matt felt the wild electricity flowing through him. Her touch galvanized his desires. Matt looked down at her and smiled, and she quickly released his arm. Casey's cheeks went bright red. She liked him. In that moment, Matt saw it clearly for the first time.

"Come on, let's go celebrate Megan's first breakthrough in two years!"

CHAPTER SEVEN

ON THE WAY OUT OF THE raptor habitat, Megan gripping both their hands, Matt asked Casey, "Do you have time for a hot fudge sundae at Mo's Café?"

How could Casey say no? The look of happiness on Matt's face made her feel as if she were walking on air. Even better, Megan was laughing. She was gripping Casey's hand as if to let go would mean never to see her again. Grinning, Casey said, "Sure. I love hot fudge sundaes." Looking down at Megan, she asked, "What do you like, Megan?" Casey used every opportunity to put Megan into the situation where she was forced to speak.

Megan's rasps and laughter were the response.

"Okay, off to Mo's," Matt said, smiling. He felt as if a part of the invisible load he'd carried for so long was dissolving from his shoulders. Literally, he could feel the weight leaving him. Was it because there'd been a breakthrough with Megan today? Since starting to laugh she had practiced it over and over again, as if tasting and testing the sounds that came from within her. And Casey, he knew, was no small part of this tiny step forward with his daughter. He felt the sunlight against his flesh and reveled in the moment. All the darkness that haunted him had momentarily evaporated because of this special time.

At Mo's Café, which sat on the main square of Jackson Hole, a red-haired waitress came to take their order. Mo's was always busy. The owner made her own ice cream and was known throughout the state for the thick, rich fudge that was slathered over any kind of ice cream that was ordered.

"Hey, Jody," Matt greeted the waitress, "how are you?"

Jody, who wore a tan Stetson on her shoulder-length blond hair, smiled. "Hiya, Lieutenant Sinclaire. Hi, Megan. How are you?"

Megan glowed. She had chosen to sit next to Casey and opposite Matt in the roomy red leather booth. She lifted her hands and laughed.

"Wow," Jody said, "she's laughing! That's wonderful!"

"It is," Matt said, and gestured toward Casey. "Jody, Casey Cantrell is new to our town. She's a ranger stationed out at the national park. Casey, Jody is a fixture here, she's Mo's daughter."

Casey smiled up at the woman in a brown leather skirt, cowboy boots, and a vest over a bright red shirt. "Nice to meet you, Jody. I've heard so much about Mo's, but just haven't had the chance to get over here yet to check it out."

"My mom makes the best ice cream and toppings in the state," Jody crowed. "Isn't that right, Megan?"

More laughter.

Casey joined in.

"Jody, the bill's mine. Give the ladies what they want," Matt said.

"Thank you," Casey said, smiling over at Matt. She couldn't get over how happy he looked. The darkness that usually marked his demeanor was gone! He had beautiful forest-green eyes and Casey had to stop herself from staring like a starstruck teen at him. How ruggedly handsome Matt truly was when the depression lifted.

Later, as they slurped through huge hot fudge sundaes topped with thick whipped cream and a red cherry, Matt felt he wanted to know more about Casey. She was an enigma to him. He sensed she was hiding something. That evasiveness and wariness was always there with Casey, he'd discovered. Further, he would see fear or maybe anxiety every now and again in her eyes. Why? Would she share with him? For the first time in two years, Matt found himself attracted to another woman. Guilt ate at him, however, and because Megan was enthralled with Casey, Matt told himself it was only curiosity on his part to get to know her better.

"Where do you originally come from?" he asked her.

Casey tasted the rich fudge and then licked her spoon. "I'm from San Francisco."

"Ah, a real Westerner," Matt teased, wanting to keep the conversation light.

Shrugging, Casey said, "Californians are different."

"They are, but that's nothing to hold against you."

"Thank you."

Matt smiled a little. "What do your parents do?"

"They met each other as pilots in the U.S. Navy. My mother was one of the first women allowed to fly a P3 sub-hunter aircraft. That's a submarine hunter plane. That's where she met my dad, Clay Cantrell."

"Did the sparks fly?" Matt wondered. He saw the happiness sparkling in Casey's eyes as she talked about her family and sensed that because it was a good family, not a dysfunctional one, this was a good way to get to understand who she was.

Chuckling, Casey dug into the vanilla ice cream with her spoon. "Oh, you could say that. My mom, Alyssa, has red hair and she's got the personality to go with it. When my dad tried to get rid of her as a copilot, all heck broke loose. My mom didn't stand for his neanderthal tactics and took him to task." She grinned a little. "In the end, my mom proved herself just as good or better than any other P3 pilot."

"And how many sisters? You said there are five of you?"

"Yes. Mom loved the Greek myths, and we were each named after a goddess."

He liked that idea. "What is yours?"

"My real name is Castalia. She was a nymph goddess of fountains. I hated the name and I got everyone to call me Casey instead."

Matt met her smile. "Castalia… I have to bone up on the Greek classics, I think. And a fountain goddess?"

"You have to know Greece in order to understand. It's a very dry, desertlike place and water is very valuable. If a person wanted to find water, they prayed to Castalia to show them where they could find a fountain. Back then, she was a very important goddess."

"Amazing," Matt murmured. He savored their conversation. "Was Castalia an outdoor girl like you?"

Grinning, Casey said, "I haven't thought of her in that way, but yes, she was. The nymphs were part of the fabric of nature."

"Why do you think your parents named you after that specific goddess?"

She liked his insight and question. "I asked my mom

about that and she said I was born under the sign Pisces, the two fish. It's a water sign. She told me that Pisces people are very sensitive, emotional and easily touched by nature. And—" she licked her spoon again "—that nature is always healing and revitalizing to us. So, she chose the name Castalia for me."

"But you hated the name."

"Well," Casey drawled, "try that name in the first and second grade. Kids made fun of me. They couldn't pronounce it, so they slaughtered it. I came up with Casey and from then on, I stopped being teased."

"The teasing bothered you?"

"Yes. My mom was right—I'm a Pisces. I often feel like a piece of raw meat thrown out into the big, bad world of life."

"What would you rather be doing, then?" Matt stared deeply into her eyes.

"What I'm doing now. I went for a degree in wild-life biology in order to be close to nature. I'm always happiest when I'm out hiking in the woods and I'm one with everything around me."

Nodding, Matt asked, "Your mom sounds like a Renaissance woman to me. She knows a lot about the ancient world and their beliefs."

"Oh, she's pretty futuristic, too," Casey said, smiling. It was so easy to drown in Matt's interested gaze. She told herself that he was interested in her because of his daughter, Megan. The child was happily eating her smaller sundae, paying no attention to their conversation. "My mother paved the way for other women pilots to fly in the U.S. Navy. She put in her twenty years and was always opening doors for other women to follow. I think it was that indomitable Trayhern spirit that made her such a leader of women's rights in the military."

"Your mom sounds courageous," Matt said, meaning it.

"I have heroic roots," Casey told him. "My uncle, Morgan Trayhern, is a real military hero. And nearly all of our family has served in the military for over two hundred years. I'm one of the few in the family who didn't choose military service. Emma, my oldest sister, is over in Afghanistan right now. She's a pilot and flies Apache combat helicopters. My older twin sisters, Athena and Juno, are graduating this year from the naval academy. Athena is a marine and Juno is in the navy. Athena wants to fly helos like Emma, and Juno is pushing to allow women into black-ops combat. Selene, who is my twin, is in the naval academy, too. She's two years behind but wants to fly also."

"That's impressive," Matt said. "A military dynasty of sorts?"

"You could say that," Casey murmured. "My uncle Noah and his wife Kit have five girls, too. Women and twins run in the Trayhern family. Although Uncle Morgan has one son and four daughters. His wife, my aunt Laura, is wonderful. I'm lucky that we have such a close-knit family." *For more than one reason,* Casey thought. They'd all rallied to her side when she was in a coma and no one was sure she'd come out of it. Casey didn't dwell on that. It was her secret. Her shame. She wanted Matt to think highly of her and not know about her past.

"You're fortunate," Matt agreed. Jody came over and filled their emptied coffee cups once more.

"What about you?" Casey asked, going on the offensive. "Do you have family here?"

"I do. I was born here," Matt said. He leaned across the table and took a swipe with his napkin at Megan's mouth where some fudge had gathered. "I have a younger sister, Jessie, who is twenty-five years old. My dad, Lou, owns a small ranch below Jackson Hole. It's a beef ranch of about three hundred acres. My mother, Val, died five years ago. Jessie, who is a registered nurse at the hospital here, babysits Megan when I have my shifts at the fire department." Matt added, "I don't know what I'd do without her help."

"But your schedules must overlap sometimes. Then who takes care of Megan?"

"My dad does. I drive her out to the ranch when I have weekend duty."

"I'll bet your dad enjoys having that time with Megan."

"He does. Without my family, I'd be in dire straits. After the...well, after I lost Bev and the house we'd built, I just didn't want to leave Megan with strangers. We have a great day-care center here, but I wanted to protect her. She was just too vulnerable and open after the fire. Jessie came to me and offered her help."

"You have a great family, too," Casey murmured. She saw Matt struggling to avoid words like *murder* in front of his daughter. Megan was coloring on the table mat.

"It works," Matt said. "Of course, Jessie has put much of her life on hold to help us. I feel badly about that because she's sacrificing so much for us..." His voice trailed off. "So much has been given up by so many people for our sakes."

Seeing the pain linger in his eyes, Casey began to

realize that Matt was not egotistical. He cared about others. He realized the sacrifices his family had made since Bev's murder. And he took it personally. *Maybe too much so?* she wondered.

"That's what family is for," Casey parried. She tipped her long spoon into the bottom of her emptied sundae glass. And then, the words just leaped out of her mouth, unedited, not thought through— "When I was in a coma…" She abruptly stopped. Her heart raced. She looked tensely across the table at Matt. Instantly, he reacted.

"Coma? You were in a coma? When did this happen?"

Groaning inwardly, Casey sat back, closed her eyes and mentally called herself stupid, among other names. Opening her eyes, she saw sincere concern on Matt's face. It wasn't made up.

"I—er… I didn't mean to bring it up," she managed in an apologetic voice.

"I wondered about that scar on your left temple."

Casey automatically touched it. The flesh was indented from the blow that had sent her into the coma. "Yes…well…" She moved nervously. Right now, all she wanted to do was run away. "It was just a slip of the tongue."

Matt gave her a tender smile he hoped would allay her sudden tension. He realized she had made a mistake. Yet, what she had said now sat like an uninvited guest between them. It was as if each of them had a dark, unhappy side that could appear without effort on their parts. "Sometimes slips of the tongue are things that need to be given some air time."

Matt's quietly spoken words broke through Casey's

terror. "I'm worried that if I tell you, it will get all over town. I can't afford that to happen, Matt. I don't want my past ruining my career."

Holding up his hand, Matt murmured, "I promise you, Casey, I won't breathe a word of anything you share with me."

The sincerity in his eyes made Casey hesitate. "I haven't told anyone. Not even my best friends…"

"I'd like to be your friend. You can trust me." Matt realized he really wanted Casey to do just that. He saw the wariness in her expression, but yes, he wanted to be her friend because he was consumed with wanting to discover who she was. She was like a multifaceted gemstone, she had so many sides to her. He wanted to know all of her, not just a part.

"I believe you," Casey uttered, all the life going out of her voice. She checked on Megan, who was now busy with the crayons that Jody had given her earlier. She was rapidly coloring a mountain lion sitting on a rock in the forest. Turning her attention to Matt, she told him the story. As she dove into it, she saw real fear in his eyes— for her. There was a powerful, unspoken connection between them that Casey couldn't explain. Just as she finished the short version of her ordeal, Jody came over.

"Anything else, Matt?" she asked, putting the bill next to his hand.

"Maybe some more coffee?" he asked.

Casey nodded. "I could use another cup, please." Actually, she needed a stiff belt of whiskey. Inwardly, she was trembling. Just talking about it made her blood pressure rise and the adrenaline pour into her bloodstream once more.

"You got it," Jody sang, turning away to retrieve the coffeepot.

Casey gave Matt a helpless look. "Will this conversation upset Megan? I'm worried."

Matt shook his head. "Megan has an amazing ability to focus on what she's doing and blot out the world around her." He gave his daughter a warm look as she worked hard to keep the coloring inside the dark lines of the picture. "It's okay."

Jody poured fresh coffee into their cups and left.

Matt took a sip and watched Casey over the rim of his mug. She looked out of sorts, fingers trembling as she picked up the coffee. His heart turned in his chest. All he wanted to do was hold Casey. Hold her and protect her somehow from her dark past. But he couldn't do that. Setting his cup down, he said, "I recognize PTSD when I see it. Have you been diagnosed?" He knew she must have been, but would she fess up and be honest with him?

Grimacing, Casey held on to her cup. "Yes. I guess it shows?"

"Only to me," he soothed. "In the firefighting business everyone gets PTSD sooner or later. It's something you live with. And it's easy to spot it in another person."

"Phew, I was worried. I try to hide my symptoms from everyone."

"Well, you had me fooled, Casey, until just now." He managed a crooked smile of understanding.

"Good, I'm glad," she whispered, staring down at the cup. "I'm worried that if anyone where I work knows about this, it will hurt my career."

"So you didn't put any of that incident down on your résumé?"

"None of it." Casey gave him a searching look. "I really needed to be a ranger. I need the forest. Mom was so right about me—nature is where I feel safe, where I recharge. I love being a wildlife biologist and I hope to use my skills for the U.S. Forest Service. If they knew about this…well… I just can't risk it, Matt."

"Not to worry. Your secret is safe with me." God knew, he had his own secrets.

Touching her left temple, Casey said, "And isn't it funny that nature is where I almost got killed? The very place I thought was safe really isn't."

Hearing the wryness in her voice, he said, "Well, I thought I was in a safe marriage. I never thought I'd lose Bev like that. I'm still reeling from it, if the truth be known."

Realizing Matt was giving her very personal information, Casey gulped. "I'm so sorry that happened to you and Megan. I've tried to put myself in your shoes and ask what I would do? How would I feel about it? I tried to see it happening in my own family and it's so devastating I can't put words to it, Matt. I don't know how you're surviving as well as you are. I know I wouldn't. I'd be so crippled by it I wouldn't be able to function."

Matt gave her a tender look. "In the past, shortly after it happened, I wasn't too functional at times. It's better than before, though. Everyone tells me it will take time, and it has. Most of my focus has been on Meggie, not myself." Shrugging, Matt added, "My family and friends tell me I need to take care of myself, too, but I just can't get there. At least…not yet."

"Guilt?"

"Yeah, something like that." Matt ran his fingers through his short hair.

"You look normal to an outsider," Casey assured him.

"And so do you." Matt laughed a little. "And here we are—both with major loss and trauma in our lives. We're both crippled. It's just to what extent, how we wrestle with it on a daily basis and how we try to get well even if we don't feel like we'll ever make it there."

Casey agreed. "In my short life I'm aware that everyone gets wounded, Matt. It's just a question of when and wounded by what. Tragedy is always lurking around. My family was shaken to its roots by what happened to me. The doctors were telling them I wouldn't make it."

Nodding, Matt said, "It's a tough place to be if you're a family member. I'm glad you decided to live, Casey. You're a bright spot in our lives."

His words touched her as nothing else ever had, and she gave him a warm look, then touched Megan's hair and whispered, "Thanks, I appreciate that."

Studying her in the silence, Matt began to realize just how sensitive Casey really was. Megan looked up and laughed as Casey grazed her hair. The smile she gave his daughter melted his heart. It was true, Casey was a highly emotional person. Matt was now privy to the real woman, not the one hiding with a painful secret from the past she carried around with her daily. And his daughter obviously loved Casey's touch. Megan's eyes sparkled. She impulsively dropped her crayons on the table and threw her arms around Casey's waist.

Casey drew her near, held her gently and placed a kiss on her hair.

Matt wanted to cry in that moment, but he didn't.

Casey's mothering instincts were right there in front of him. She had closed her eyes, pressed her cheek against Megan's small head and gently rocked her in her arms. His daughter was like a small puppy simply absorbing all that love and maternal nurturing she was giving her. What would it be like to be in Casey's loving arms?

The thought was like a thunderbolt out of the blue to Matt. He sat there stunned in the aftermath of the unexpected thought. Yet, as he allowed himself to think in those terms, red hot guilt ate at him. He'd loved Bev like no other woman he'd ever met. They'd been a couple since first grade. He and Bev were a team. They'd loved one another with a fierceness Matt rarely saw in marriages nowadays. Bev had been ripped from him. He'd not protected her. Or Megan. And those were the walls that surrounded Matt: his inability to protect those he loved. And they'd given their lives instead. He could never do that to another person.

Sitting there staring at Casey as she rocked Megan in her arms, a cold terror worked through Matt. It was a warning. It was impossible to love again. He'd end up putting Casey and his daughter in jeopardy again. There was a killer still on the loose and he swore never to put another loved one in the gun sights of his wife's unknown killer until he was found. Not ever.

CHAPTER EIGHT

CASEY SLOGGED DOWN A TRAIL carrying a heavy pack. She gloried in the early-morning fog that lay across a meadow. In the center of it was a thick stand of willows. She was on Moose Trail, the Tetons still clothed in heavy snow above her. Breath white, because it was below freezing at this time of year, she slid her gloved hands along the straps of her pack. Finally! Her boss had released her from the deadly boring visitor's center to go into the field.

Today she was to check out several trails used by the tourists who would be flocking to this area come early June. From then through the end of August, the Tetons would see over a million visitors who loved this rugged and beautiful landscape. In her pack was a map, a digital camera, pad and pen. Crews would be coming in to remove trees that had fallen beneath the heavy snows of the long winter. Sometimes rocks fell on the trail or melting snow would course across a flat trail and cut a groove into it. Her job was to note these conditions and, with her GPS, pinpoint where the crews should come in to repair the trails.

Breathing in the morning air, she watched the sun crest and shoot powerful rays across the valley. The Tetons were on the western side of the valley. In the middle of it was the mighty Snake River. As she

tramped down the trail, Casey's mind moved back to
Matt Sinclaire. Had a month flown by since she'd met
him? Every week now, she arrived at his home to work
with Megan. The little girl was opening up like a proverbial flower. Matt took Megan to the rehab center to
work with Hank twice a month. Birds had a magical effect upon her. She was doing better at school and even
becoming more involved in class activities. She didn't
talk, but she was wanting to. It all looked so hopeful.

A large pine-tree trunk was across her path. Shedding her pack, Casey pulled out her GPS, pad and pen.
For the next five minutes she typed in the info that
would go to her boss's computer back at the visitor's
center. The actual USFS headquarters was across the
street from the center. Charley would get the data and
then figure up a route for his men and women who
would be making the repairs. She idly wondered if Matt
had had something to do with her being chosen for this
unexpected assignment. Everyone wanted this plum
assignment in the spring, and usually the most senior
rangers got it. Not this time. Casey, who was the least
senior ranger, had been chosen instead. She felt as if
there was an invisible pipeline of communication that
went through this town.

Turning off her GPS, Casey gazed around. Near the
willows she saw a reddish grizzly bear, her nose up
in the air testing the breeze. Taking her small camera
out of her coat pocket, Casey took several photos. The
bear wore a collar and that meant it was a denizen of
the area. Right now, that grizzly was sniffing the air to
catch the scent of elk. The elk were calving right now
and their favorite place to birth was in stands of willow
just like this one. Casey stood quietly, the grizzly no

more than two hundred feet away from where she stood. Every ranger wore a quart-size can of "bear spray" on their belt. It was mainly red pepper, and if the grizzly decided to charge, it would be pulled out and used to stop the attack. This time of year, grizzlies were starving, having just come out of hibernation.

For Casey, being this close to a female grizzly was a thrill. She wasn't afraid of the huge, eight-hundred-pound animal. Respectful? Yes, always. Grizzlies roamed the Tetons and Yellowstone at the top of the food chain.

Suddenly, there was a roar of a rifle behind her. Jerking around, she saw the mud erupt two feet in front of her.

The grizzly woofed and stood up on her hind legs, staring angrily at Casey.

It was against the law to shoot within the boundaries of any national park. Heart pounding, Casey tried to see who was firing the rifle, but there were so many trees and bushes that she couldn't see far. Frustrated, she heard movement to her right, and saw the grizzly running down the meadow just outside of the willows. Frightened by the shooter and his closeness to her, Casey moved back against a huge pine tree, her pack pressed up against it.

She fumbled for her radio in her belt, hands shaking, and finally got hold of it. Radioing in, she told the ranger at the other end what had just happened.

"You okay, Casey?"

"Yes, I'm fine." Breathing hard, she twisted and looked around the tree.

"Just one shot?"

"Yes. Two feet in front of where I was standing. What the hell is this?"

"Take it easy. I'm sending two rangers down to your area immediately. Just wait there."

Fuming, Casey saw the cinnamon-colored grizzly hightailing it out of the meadow area. She turned and went west and disappeared into the thick, ten-foot-tall underbrush.

Who was firing a rifle? Anxious and angry, Casey had never entertained something like this. Oh, she'd heard from other rangers about out-of-season hunters. It was common knowledge that outside the park boundaries, many ranchers hunted elk year-round, whether it was legal or not. The people of this valley had been raised on wild meat; they ignored the laws many times. And Casey knew there just weren't enough law-enforcement officers—or rangers—to stop the illegal hunting. And the ranchers knew that, too. Usually, they killed elk and deer on their own property and it was hard to prove.

Her breathing began to steady. Moose Trail was just off the main highway and about a mile down the muddy, rutted dirt road. She knew it wouldn't take long. Briefly touching her own pistol in the holster on her left side, Casey knew she didn't want to have to draw her weapon, because to draw it meant she was going to use it. This was the part of her job she hated.

She heard the crunching of gravel and narrowed her eyes as a mint-green pickup sped toward her. That was a USFS vehicle. Moving away from the tree, Casey wondered: was it a hunter shooting at the grizzly and missing? Who would kill such a beautiful animal? Frowning, she moved back onto the trail and tried to ferret out any movement from the direction of the shot. Nothing.

Within minutes, two male rangers were huffing down the trail, guns drawn. Casey met them on the trail. She recognized Charley and one of his subordinates.

Charley was looking fierce and angry, his sixty-year-old, heavily lined face puckered. Casey tried to smile.

"It's okay," she called to them. "No more shots."

Breathing hard, Charley looked around. "You said the bullet hit two feet from where you stood on the trail?" He holstered his gun and continued to survey the area.

"Yes," Casey said, "here." She pointed down to the hole in the mud on the trail.

"Johnson, dig for it," the supervisor told the younger ranger.

"Yes, sir," he murmured and knelt down and began digging with his Buck knife into the soft mud.

Casey watched her wary supervisor take his binoculars and scan the area to the west of them. "Has this happened before?" she wondered.

Charley's mouth moved into a tight line. He dropped his binoculars on the green parka he wore. Turning to Casey, he said, "Indoctrination alerted you to the fact there's a couple of roving teenage gangs that come into the park. Did you forget that?"

Uncomfortable beneath her supervisor's narrowed blue gaze, Casey said, "No, sir, I've not forgotten." She lifted a hand. "I just thought it might be an out-of-season hunter was all."

Snorting, Charley looked around some more. "That's not it, Ranger Cantrell." He watched the younger male ranger who had found the bullet and was pulling it out with his gloved fingers. "We've had an escalating problem here for the last year, Cantrell. We've got a bunch of Jackson Hole teens who think it's 'radical' to come into the park and kill animals." Frowning, he added, "They usually take a limb, a rock or some weapon like a baseball bat and chase down a rabbit, a raccoon or something like that."

"But this was a rifle."

"Yeah, I know." Charley scratched his head.

"Here you go, sir," the ranger said, handing the bullet to the supervisor.

Peering down at it, Charley grunted. Handing it back to the man, he said, "Take it to the Jackson Hole police. Have forensics run a test on it and compare it to the other one."

"Other one?" Casey asked. "This has happened before?"

"Yes. Last year. I want to see if it's from the same weapon. My gut tells me it is."

"Last year?" she echoed, frowning. "Did another ranger get shot at?"

Nostrils flaring, Charley looked down at her. "Yes. We weren't sure if it was aimed at the ranger or the elk herd he was counting."

"Same area?" Casey demanded. Why hadn't someone told her about this? She felt anger surge through her. They had sent her out without preparing her. Without knowledge. What else hadn't her supervisor told her? Casey bit down on her lower lip to stop the words. Now was not the time to speak about it; she'd wait until things calmed down.

"Yes." Scowling, Charley looked around. "There are two gangs of young men, ages twelve through seventeen, that the police say are doing these killings."

"But do they have rifles, too?"

Shrugging, Charley muttered, "I hope not. We were worried about this—an escalation from beating animals to death to shooting them."

"Why would anyone do this?" Casey demanded, opening her hands, frustration clearly in her tone.

"You've got a bunch of rich kids with a lot of time on their hands," Charley said. He gestured for her to walk back with them. As Casey fell into step with her supervisor, he added, "Look, this is a recent problem. We're doing all we can to catch these spoiled brats who are bored with life. They get a high from chasing down a wild animal, cornering it and then beating it to death. It's like some kind of tribal initiation to those punks."

"Have you caught any of them?" Casey felt fear; she'd been attacked by a gang of young men. To realize these teens were roving around in a pack frightened her. Oh, she'd been told about it in her indoctrination lecture, but the speaker had made little of it—and so had she. Until now.

"Nope, we haven't."

"Then how do you know it's them?"

"Word gets around, Cantrell. In case you didn't know yet, there's a really fine gossip pipeline in Jackson Hole, and if you want to know what's really going on, you get hooked into it. Right now, we have an undercover ranger who looks like a male teenager trying to break into these rings. That's secret and you talk to no one about it."

"I won't say a word," she promised, choking. Alarm spread through Casey. Suddenly, she felt shaky. And her sense of safety here in the Tetons shattered. Two male gangs were roving with impunity through the beautiful Tetons intent upon killing. She wondered when they would stop looking at animals as their focus and choose a two-legged human being. Or would they? Was this only teen pranks? Or was it something more sinister and dangerous?

Back at the start of the trail, Casey climbed into the USFS pickup and drove back to headquarters. The supervisor drove into Jackson Hole with the bullet round. She couldn't shake the terror that was now rising up within her. What would a band of irresponsible, savage teens who found it fun to beat and kill an animal to death do if they found a lone woman hiker somewhere out on one of those trails? There weren't that many hikers on a given trail and noise was muted because of brush and thick stands of trees. How easy would it be for this neanderthal group of teens to decide to rape and then beat the woman hiker to death? All those possibilities ran through Casey's mind as she put her coat and other gear into her locker at headquarters. Suddenly her dream of being a ranger shattered. No place was safe. No place…

"WHERE HAVE YOU BEEN?" Clarissa Peyton scolded her sixteen-year-old son, Bradley.

The teen halted at the door of his mother's sewing room. Hands in the pockets of his low-slung jeans, he said, "Just out hiking, Mom. Why?"

Clarissa was working on a quilt top. She stopped what she was doing and peered at her acne-faced son by her first husband, whom she had divorced. Her son had been rebellious for years about the breakup. And his father, Jared Bourne, a Wall Street banker, was still very much involved in his son's life, much to Clarissa's discontent. Brad had never warmed up to her second husband, Senator Carter Peyton. They hated one another. And Brad hated having to live with his mother and her new husband. In the divorce settlement, Clarissa had gained custody. Jared saw his son on major holidays, but not all of them. And, until Bradley was eighteen, he had to live with Clarissa.

She spied his muddy boots. Wrinkling her nose, she said, "The least you could have done, Brad, is taken your boots off in the mud porch."

Shrugging, he muttered, "Maria will clean it up."

Scowling, Clarissa snapped, "You should do it yourself! You're not going to have a maid who will follow you around to clean up your dirt the rest of your life, Brad."

Smiling a little, he shrugged again. "Hey, she needs a job. I'm giving it to her."

"Why aren't you at school? Are you skipping again?"

"Yeah, me and some of my friends went for a hike. I hate school. It's boring."

Putting down the quilt top, Clarissa felt helpless. "You can't do this, son. You need an education." Brad always had a chip on his shoulder. He hated coming to Wyoming when Carter needed to work with his constituents. He much preferred the wild life of Washington, D.C., where he had rich friends. He ran with the Costa Rican ambassador's son, a well-known Formula 1 racer. Brad always liked dangerous things and that scared Clarissa. She hoped it was only teenage hormones and that her six-foot-tall son would grow out of the need for risky behavior.

"Ah," he said, perking up, "I'll make up for it, Mom. I'm smart. I'll get the assignment and finish it in no time. I'm a straight-A student. Don't worry." Turning away, he slouched down the pine hall to his room. He didn't want to hear the rest of his mother's diatribe, which he could repeat verbatim. Shutting the door, Brad sat on his queen-size bed decked in a brown, green and blue quilt that his mother had made for him on his last birthday.

Shoving off his muddy hiking boots, he left them in the middle of the floor. Maria could take care of them. His adrenaline was still running high. He and his gang, the Cougars, had trapped a raccoon up a tree, which he had climbed to force the terrified animal out of. As it hit the ground, the other six teens were there to beat it to death with clubs. Brad had missed the killing as he'd inched down the tree. The raccoon was a bloody pulp by the time he'd landed on the ground. They'd been celebrating their kill by taking meth when someone nearby had fired a rifle. It was close and it scared the hell out of all of them. They took off running for their SUVs parked about a mile down the trail.

Bradley shucked out of his dirty clothes and left them wherever they fell on the pine floor. He needed a shower before meeting the Cougars at their local hangout, Brick's Café. Still feeling the buzz of the meth, Brad sauntered into his huge, well-appointed bathroom to take a long, hot shower. Life was good.

MATT WAS TALKING WITH Deputy Cade Garner at the counter of the sheriff's department when Ranger Charley Davidson arrived. What caught Matt's interest was the shell casing in the ranger's gloved hand.

"Morning, Cade," Charley greeted, handing the deputy the bullet casing. "Got another one."

Matt stared down at it. "Morning, Charley."

"Hi, Matt." Charley nodded in his direction. "Busy morning?"

"Yes," Matt said. He was on duty and was discussing a suspicious structure fire that appeared to be arson. Cade Garner was taking the report. "What you got there, Charley?" he asked, pointing at the casing that Garner was studying.

"Someone shot at one of my rangers this morning," he grunted. "This is the second time. Happened last year, too. I want Cade here to compare the bullet casing with the other one. I want to know if it's comin' from the same rifle."

The hair on the back of Matt's neck stood up. "Who was shot at?" he demanded.

"Ranger Cantrell."

"What?" The word exploded out of Matt in disbelief. "Is she all right?"

"Yes, she's fine. Bullet was fired from the west and onto the trail she was on. It landed two feet away from her. She's fine."

Heart pounding, Matt felt alarm. He glanced over at Cade, who was scowling.

"Do you think she was being targeted?" Garner demanded of the supervisor.

Shrugging, Charley said, "I don't know. I wasn't there. Ranger Cantrell said she saw no one. The Moose Trail has a lot of thick brush and there's woods surrounding it, so it would be hard to see anyone." He jabbed his finger down at Cade's opened hand. "Just see if this one matches the other one from last year?"

"I will," Cade said.

Matt struggled to remain silent. He felt dizzied by the information. "We're aware of two gangs of teens that have been killing animals inside your park, Charley. Do you think it might be them?"

"Better hope not, Matt. That would mean those brats have graduated from the caveman tactics of beating animals to death with clubs to using rifles and killing two-legged creatures instead. That's not a happy thing for me to contemplate. If I've got two gangs roving in my park with rifles and pistols, well...that's a whole different scenario." His mouth turned downward. "And it ain't one I seriously want to contemplate."

Wiping his mouth, Matt said, "This is serious."

"Yes," Cade murmured, "it is." He turned to Charley. "I'll get our gal in forensics to check this bullet against the other one we're holding. I'll call you as soon as we get an answer."

Nodding, Charley said, "Fine, thanks, Cade."

"If those kids have guns," Matt said, "they're taking their parents' firearms, then."

"Maybe, maybe not," Cade said. "We have a black market on drugs and guns here in the valley. And you know Westerners by nature are independent and believe in carrying firearms. If those parents are unknowingly supplying them, that's one thing. And that's what I'd think. No parent is going to let his teen take a rifle out to shoot wildlife around here. There's just too much respect for the parks in most people who live here to do that."

"Oh," Charley groused, "there's some real fanatic gun enthusiasts around here, Cade. You know they're capable of just about anything."

"Yes, and we know who they are," Garner parried. He held up the shell casing. "Let me get to work on this. I'll be in touch."

Wagging his finger at the deputy, Charley warned, "My gut tells me things are escalating. I don't know who or how, but this ain't a good sign. We all need to change our tactics and find out just who the hell is behind it. I'm not having my rangers shot at. I just won't." He stared hard at the deputy. "You tell your commander that if he don't put some of his people into busting those two teen gangs, then I'm going to change my tactics."

Matt heard the warning in the supervisor's growling tone. He saw his friend Cade nod.

"I hear you, Charley. We'll do what we can and I know our commander will be in touch with you shortly."

"Come June first, Cade, you know the world lands in Jackson Hole. We got six million tourists coming from June through the end of August. If those teen gangs are running rampant, unchecked and undiscovered as they have been thus far, we're in a world of hurt. Can't you just see the headlines now?" He held up his hands and spread his arms. "'Tourists gunned down in national park.'" Allowing his hands to fall to his sides, he said, "That ain't happenin' on my watch, Cade. The Tetons are my responsibility. I ain't gonna have some juiced-up teens running like wild cavemen through the trails with rifles and pistols. That's a recipe for disaster."

"It is," Cade soothed, trying to ramp down the ranger's escalating anger. "One step at a time, Charley. We're with you, not against you on this problem."

Rubbing his strong chin, Charley stared hard at the deputy. "Look, I got a young, green ranger who is shaken to her roots. Over the decades, we've been forced to carry weapons on us. Now, we're more like law enforcement in these parks than what we used to be—caretakers of some of the most beautiful and pristine land in this country. Everything's changed since I entered the Forest Service. I don't like my people are out there on the line as targets for these punks."

"I hear you," Cade said. He glanced over at Matt and then back at the supervisor. "We'll work with you."

"I'd better hear from your commander on this," Matt warned. "You know we have to make runs out within the Tetons." There were several ranches within the boundaries of the park. "I sure wouldn't want someone firing a rifle at my teams if they're trying to fight a structure fire."

"We'll gather everyone," Cade promised. "There needs to be coordination on this."

"Humph," Charley groused. He turned on his heel and left.

Matt watched Garner push through the door into the rear where the offices were located. Becky, the receptionist at the desk, looked up at him. "You look pale, Matt. You okay?"

"I'm okay," he assured the forty-year-old brunette as he left. Outside, the warmth of the sunshine mixed with the barely-above-freezing cool breeze. He wanted to contact Casey. Was she really all right? He recalled her sharing her story of nearly being beaten to death by five drug runners out in the forest. Running his fingers through his hair, he headed for his bright-red-and-white SUV with the light bar on top of it. First, he had to get back and let Captain Doug Stanley know what had happened. His next phone call would be to Casey.

CHAPTER NINE

CASEY HAD JUST FINISHED writing out a report of what had happened to her out on the trail when her cell phone rang. "Hello?"

"Casey, this is Matt. Are you all right?"

Sitting back in the chair at her desk, she said, "Yes, I'm fine." He sounded raw and worried. It was then that she realized he cared for her. A lot. Compressing her lips, she laughed a little. "Honestly, everyone around here probably thinks I'm the dumbest ranger on the block. When the shot was fired the last thing I thought of was being fired at. I thought it was a hunter trying to shoot a bear this morning."

"I was at the sheriff's department when Charley came in. I overheard the conversation with Deputy Cade Garner. He's an old school friend of mine. We grew up together. They seem to think it was not a hunter."

Brows rising, Casey murmured, "Charley said none of that to me. Who would want to shoot at me? I'm a nobody."

"Maybe you are somebody," he said grimly. "Are you free for lunch today? I don't start my shift until 6:00 p.m. We could eat over at Dorman's restaurant in the park?"

Dorman's was on one of the ranches enclosed by

Grand Teton National Park. "I'd like that. Dorman's has great food."

"I'll see you at noon over there, then?"

Her heart expanded with silent joy. "Yes, see you then."

The USFS headquarters building was a teeming hive of activity. Everyone was gearing up for June first when visitors from around the world would begin to descend upon this valley. Frowning, Casey looked over her report. Had she been stupid? Why hadn't she thought about someone shooting at *her?* Shaking her head, Casey decided she just couldn't go there. She'd barely been here for two months. In that time, she'd gotten along with everyone. And most of the time she was over at the visitor's center, not out on the trails. Casey had written no tickets on people in the park. So, who had it out for her?

THE SENATOR SEETHED. He was in Idaho Falls, incognito, at a seedy motel on the outskirts of the city. Wearing dark glasses, a sporty gray hat and the clothes of someone with a helluva lot less money than he had, he hoped no one would recognize him. It was chilly as he sat out in front of the yellow cabins of the rundown motel. Where the hell was Benson? Peyton was always on edge with these meetings. Things had gone wrong.

The door of one of the cabins opened. Benson, in his late forties, hopped in through the passenger door of the Chevy truck. "Hey, Senator, how's it going?" He took off his red knit cap, grinning and showing the gap between his upper front teeth.

Turning, Carter glared at him. "You screwed up,

dammit! I paid you good money to take out that ranger. What the hell happened?"

Chuckling, Frank Benson sat back, a lopsided grin on his unshaven square face. "Well, it's a good one, Senator. I had set up for the shot, had my finger on the trigger, when a mama grizzly bear and her two cubs found me in that willow thicket." He glanced at the livid senator. "I never heard them coming. When I focus on a shot, I block the world out. I hear nothing. And I didn't hear the sow and her cubs coming. I was so damned surprised, I jerked off the shot and missed the ranger by two feet."

Fuming, Carter said, "That's just great."

"You could say something like, 'Hey, Frank, how'd you get from between that rock and a hard place?'" He laughed to himself, rubbing his long, large hands across the knees of his jeans. "I guess I shouldn't expect human compassion or kindness or concern to really enter into our relationship, should I?" Frank gloated as he saw the senator's face become a dull red. He didn't like Peyton, but he liked his money. And he had plenty of other buyers for his sniper skills, so he didn't mind tweaking the arrogant bastard a little.

"A grizzly bear?" Peyton snarled.

"It happens, Senator."

Biting back more epithets, Peyton switched gears. "Okay, here's what is happening. My town spies have seen this ranger, Casey Cantrell, getting close to Sinclaire. I asked you to take her out. I told you years ago, I'm taking everything Sinclaire ever loved away from him. He took my wife and children." His mouth thinned. "I'm going to make this bastard pay..."

"Then why not cut to the chase?" Frank asked. "Forget the girlfriend. Let me set fire to his new home when he and his daughter are asleep."

Rubbing his chin, Carter said, "No. I can't have two houses in a row burned. That sends up a huge red flag for the police. I have to get him and his daughter in other ways. Besides, fire is too unpredictable."

Snickering, Frank said, "Too bad they weren't with me when that sow and cubs found me. That's what you need—some kind of situation where they're out in the woods and their deaths look to be from natural causes. Lots of people get killed by grizzly bears every year. Even here in Wyoming there's always one or two. Why not them?"

"It'd be damned hard to lure a grizzly bear somewhere that they're hiking."

"But they hike a lot."

"No. It's too time-consuming and you can't control where a grizzly goes."

"You heard anything about my shot from local authorities?" Benson asked.

"I haven't nosed into it. And I'm not going to."

"That bullet went into soft mud. It's probably going to be seen as a sniper special. We use only a certain type of bullet to do the job. I don't think the police in Jackson Hole are stupid."

"They'll never pin it to you, so stop worrying about it." Flexing his hands on the steering wheel of his pickup truck, Carter added, "I need a new plan. Something different. We can't try killing her with the same tactic."

"I think what needs to happen here," Frank said, "is to let me tag along and follow them. I need to find out their schedules. I can do this if you rent me a nice log cabin somewhere around Jackson Hole. I'll use an alias, I'll shave my beard, get cleaned up and look like a tourist in town. That way, the next time around, I won't miss. And who knows, Senator? I might be able to get all three of them at once, should the god of snipers decree it." Benson grinned unevenly.

Carter knew that Benson was a master of disguises. What he didn't want was to be associated with him in any way. "I'll give you a month."

"Okay," Frank said, smiling. He held out his hand.

Glaring at him, Carter opened the glove compartment. In it there was a brown envelope filled with money—cash on the barrelhead. "Is ten grand enough?" he demanded, quickly flipping through the one-thousand-dollar bills.

"For now," Benson said. "That gives me nice digs, allows me to eat at restaurants they may frequent and things like that. I'm going to pose as a photographer. The Tetons and Yellowstone are a photographer's paradise and I won't raise suspicion if I'm carrying around a tripod with a camera attached to it."

Nodding, Carter gave him the money. "It's a good disguise." Frank Benson had a weathered, deeply lined face. He loved the outdoors and most of his assassination work was performed outside.

"Who knows?" he chuckled. "I may get *very* close to one of 'em. We'll see. The more I know, the better the ambush I can set up."

"Agreed," Carter muttered. "Get going." He looked at his Rolex watch hidden by the gray sweatshirt sleeve. "I gotta get back to Jackson Hole." His wife was holding a gala at the local museum to raise money for wildlife preservation this evening and it was already noon. Clarissa had no idea where he was and he wanted to make damn sure she never found out, either.

Tucking the money into the pocket of his green nylon jacket and zipping it shut, Benson opened the door. "I'll be in touch, boss."

The truck door slammed shut. Benson walked away. In some ways, Carter admired the sniper. He was utterly confident, needed no one and kept his secrets. Still, as he backed the truck out of the parking lot, Peyton knew that Benson could turn on him at any time and black-mail him. After all, he was a senator and worth nearly half a billion dollars. He was an easy target.

Pulling the Chevy truck on the road and heading back toward the freeway entrance that would take him south to Driggs, Idaho, Peyton was thankful that, thus far, Benson had not tried that ploy with him. Hands on the wheel, he smiled thinly. If the sniper ever tried it, Carter would up the ante on him. What Benson didn't know was that he had other criminal resources who would gladly put a single bullet into his head, should he get out of line.

Focusing on the future, he looked forward to to-night's gala at the museum. It would be all rich Repub-licans there. No paltry, middle-class Democrats, for sure. This gala was done yearly and had been a smash-ing success last year. He was pleased with how Clarissa was using her money, power and name to help him raise money for his next senate run in two years. She didn't love him. No, theirs was a marriage of convenience: she wanted the power and prestige and he wanted her beauty, brains and drive.

The sky was threatening either rain, sleet or snow. As he moved onto the highway, Carter relaxed. He was the scion of a family that included some of the most powerful financiers in Wyoming. He felt the power of that knowledge flowing through him. It was an aphrodisiac that Carter absorbed like an addict. Money was power. Greed was good. The whole country was reeling from a depression that was being touted as a recession. Chuckling, Carter indulged himself in some irony: his own family's banking system had relied heavily on derivatives and in the end, would have failed. However, the feds had pumped it up with billions of dollars to rescue it. Now he was richer than ever, thanks to the taxpayers of America. Yes, life was good. *Damn good.*

"CASEY," CHARLEY SAID, coming into her cubicle at the USFS headquarters, "I want you to represent us tonight at Senator Peyton's fete over at the museum. You interested?"

Surprised, Casey said, "Of course. It would give me a chance to meet some more of the people who live here in Jackson Hole."

Charley nodded and said, "I know Matt Sinclaire has just been ordered by his chief to attend. You got any problems hooking up with him? The fire department always sends a representative to this fete, too."

Swallowing, Casey asked, "Do I go officially? In my uniform?"

Chuckling, Charley said, "No. Those highbrows don't like mingling with us poor folk. You are there officially to represent us. No need to make yourself obvious. If you get drawn into conversations about us, then you can contribute. You strike me as a diplomat and this is what this fete requires. Besides, it will make you aware of the big money floating around this town, the kingpins, the politicos, the Hollywood stars and anyone else who lusts after pure power."

Grinning, Casey said, "Sounds like fun."

"It can be," he said. "Just don't get drunk and make a fool of yourself. The fete starts at 8:00 p.m. I'd arrive about 8:30 p.m.—fashionably late. If you happen to eavesdrop and hear anything of interest, drop by my office first thing tomorrow morning and let me know."

"But you're the supervisor, sir. Why wouldn't you and your wife go?"

Charley grinned and rubbed his chin. "Oh, let's say I've made a bad name for myself by taking on some of the big shots around here. I'm not on their A-list anymore because I'm not diplomatic or political enough." His grin widened into a full smile, showing his large teeth.

Nodding, Casey said, "And they are expecting us?"

"Yep. You and Matt *are* on their A-list. Just give your names to the doorman after you've hung up your coats in the coatroom."

"I got it. Be discreet, diplomatic, ears and eyes open and saying little."

He gave her a nod. "That's it, in a nutshell."

"What do they wear at this fete?" Casey was beginning to panic. She knew already that Jackson Hole was considered the Palm Springs of the Rocky Mountain states. Indeed, Hollywood had a hefty presence here, as did most billionaire corporate heads, and millionaires were as common as robins on a spring lawn.

Waving his hand, Charley said, "My wife, Judy, always wore a fancy pantsuit. Now, you're gonna find some decked-out women there, but don't worry about it. Clarissa Peyton is a real blue blood. She's the senator's new wife. Nice lady, actually, and her heart's in the right place. She's high end, and you'll find most of 'em in cocktail attire with enough rocks around their neck to pay off the national debt."

Liking Charley's laid-back country ways, Casey said, "Yes, sir, I think I can handle this assignment."

Charley got more serious and lowered his voice. "Now, as to this bullet. I just heard back from forensics and the shell casing does not match the other one from last year." He refrained from telling her it was a sniper's bullet.

"What do you think it means?"

"I don't know. I'm sending out two of my rangers tomorrow to start combing the area to see if we can find any footprints or anything else."

Alarmed, Casey said, "Sir, I just can't believe this person was shooting at me."

"I can't, either. You're new here." Rubbing his chin, Charley said, "In the past we've had some really pissed-off ranchers who were used to taking down deer and elk as they pleased, no matter what time of year it was. When I got here twenty years ago, I made a lot of enemies. There were a couple of times when I or some of my rangers would be shot at. No one was killed, but it was meant as a warning for us to back off and leave them alone. We didn't. Eventually, I ended up putting a couple of big-time ranchers around here in prison for five to ten years. That really put the lid on out-of-season deer- and elk-killing. There's a lot of history around here, Ranger Cantrell, as you can tell."

"Yes, sir. I never realized…" She frowned. "But who would want to take a shot at me? I haven't arrested anyone yet to get them riled up. This doesn't make sense, sir."

"No," Charley agreed, "it doesn't." His gray-and-white brows fell. "But we have to take this seriously. For all we know, we might have a mentally unbalanced person running around out there taking pot shots at tourists." He grimaced. "I'm hoping we can find some evidence, maybe some other hikers who were out there at that time, and ask them some questions."

It seemed hopeless to Casey. "Do you want me to change my habits at all? Or is it safe for me to be outside?"

"No, you go about your business. Right now, I want you close to HQ. I'm assigning you permanently to the visitor's center until we can get a handle on what went down. I don't want your life in jeopardy."

"But," Casey protested, "I was promised some work with the river otters in the Snake River. I need to—"

Holding up his hand, Charley Davidson said, "Whoa, Ranger Cantrell. You got a whole career ahead of you. I worry more for you than you do yourself. Those river otters will be there today, tomorrow and the next season, so pull on the reins a little here."

Chastised, Casey nodded, swallowing her disappointment. "Yes, sir, you're right, of course."

Brightening, Charley said, "What I would like you to do is divide your time between the center and the field station next to HQ here. Team up with Jackie Gifford, the head of our wildlife biology department. She needs some help over there."

Maybe her supervisor wasn't completely insensitive to Casey's need to be out in nature. "Thank you, sir. That's wonderful."

"Yeah," Charley chuckled, "you'll get to go through otter scat and check its DNA through a microscope."

He sauntered out of her cubicle. "That would make my day." He laughed as he disappeared down the hall.

Casey turned and tapped her pencil against the report she was working on. *A fete.* She knew from her mother's many big charity activities in San Francisco that a fete was more or less just a reason to get monied people together to donate to a good cause. Casey had been at many of them and knew how to conduct herself. Charley didn't know that, but she felt he'd made a good choice.

And then, her heart turned to Matt Sinclaire. He would be there. Suddenly, the night looked promising.

CHAPTER TEN

"KAM!" CASEY CALLED OUT. Her cousin Kamaria Trayhern was with her fiancé, Wes Sheridan. Casey was just waiting at the coat check when they walked in. She saw Kam's face light up and she grinned.

"Hey, cuz! I didn't know you'd be here." Kam rushed forward and embraced Casey. Turning, she introduced Wes to her.

"Casey, good to meet you. I know you and Kam are thicker than thieves." Wes grinned and shook her hand. He took off his black Stetson and handed it to the woman in the coatroom.

Casey thought they looked wonderful together. Kam's left hand bore the engagement ring that Wes had recently given her. "Nice to meet you finally, Wes. Kam is always going on about how wonderful you are." She saw Kam flush as she handed the woman her long, black wool coat.

"Oh, cuz, now don't embarrass us!" Kam said, linking her arm through Casey's. How did you manage to get an invite?"

"My boss asked me to attend," Casey told her. Wes caught up with them and they presented their invitations to the man at the entrance. "I didn't have time to call you to find out if you would be here."

Kam released Casey's arm and held hands with her

fiancé. "Oh, I don't think anyone is going to ignore the Elk Horn Ranch. It's the largest spread in the valley."

The man at the door smiled and handed back their gold engraved invitations and gestured for them to enter the huge round room. The walls were sheathed in glowing gold and red cedar. The museum had hung western wildlife art on the walls. Casey hadn't yet had time to come to the wildlife museum. Now, looking at the world-class art on the walls and the bronze statues placed here and there, she could see why this was a sportsman's jewel in Jackson Hole.

"What's the protocol here?" Casey asked as they took glasses of champagne from a waiter.

Sipping the champagne, Kam said, "My father said just to mingle. We've brought the ranch donation check to give to Clarissa, who is the fundraiser. My father likes supporting her charity work." She turned to look up at Wes. "Wes, do you want to do the honors and give this to Clarissa?"

He took the check. "Yep, be right back."

Casey waited until he was out of earshot and leaned over toward to her cousin. She sighed. "Wes is a hunk, cousin."

"Oh, yes." Kam sighed. "He's an incredible person. Did you know that his mother signed over the Bar S Ranch to him? After his dad died of a heart attack recently, she didn't want to run it by herself. Now he's the owner."

"What do you do? Divide your time between here and Cody?" She knew Wes's ranch was in Cody, Wyoming. There were at least a hundred other people in the rotunda and the chatting was constant, like a hive of bees connecting with one another. Most of the men were in business suits and the women looked like glittering jungle birds in their cocktail dresses. Charley had been right about the jewelry. As Casey scanned the well-coifed women, the gemstones glittered like flashes of fire and light. Casey had plenty of experience with charity events like this because she helped her mother put them on all over San Francisco. Truly, this was a very rich and powerful crowd.

Kam shrugged. She tugged at her black wool jacket and smoothed down her wool pants. "We do. My father has already put in his will that I'm to get the Elk Horn when he's ready to sign off on it. Iris, my grandmother, is all for it."

"How can you run two huge ranches?"

"We can't. Wes is actively looking for a great manager that he can assign to the Bar S and he'll remain here at the Elk Horn with me."

"And right now he's splitting time between Jackson Hole and Cody?" Casey knew that was a long trip for anyone. They had to drive through Yellowstone in order to get to Cody, east of the national park.

Rolling her eyes, Kam said, "Yes. Not the best of situations, is it?" And then she smiled and pushed her black hair off her brow. "But, this, too, shall pass."

"What I'd give to love someone like Wes. He's so nice, Kam." Casey gripped her cousin's arm and squeezed it gently. "You deserve someone like him."

"Thanks, but so do you," Kam whispered. "All you've gone through... I never prayed so hard as when you were in that coma. I'm glad all our prayers were answered. You look as if nothing had ever happened to you."

Frowning, Casey whispered back, "My scars and

wounds are worn on the inside of me, not the outside."
She touched the scar on her left temple. "Most people
don't even see this."

Wes came back. "Hey, Clarissa wants to see us.
Ready?"

Casey followed the happy couple. She was glad to
be with them because everyone looked up to see who
they were. That's the way fetes were in Casey's experience. The richest always looked to check out who was
present. Was it someone they should know? How rich
were they? Make a connection with them or not? She
could literally feel the energy of the powerful and rich
in the room jockeying for unseen positions. Class consciousness was alive and well at this level, she thought.

"Welcome," Clarissa sang out. She stepped forward
and offered a quick air kiss to Kam's cheek. "And thank
your dad for his generous donation, Kam."

Casey stood back and took in Clarissa. Her red hair
was held up by a gold tiara with diamonds. She wore a
bright red svelte Vera Wang cocktail dress with matching Jimmy Choo high heels. Casey noticed the simple but sparkling single strand of diamonds and rubies
around her throat. She was beautiful and Casey liked
the woman. Clarissa, she had discovered at Quilter's
Haven, had a cousin who was a famous quilt designer.
And the senator's wife was always over there buying
the latest fabric that came in for her. That was a nice
and thoughtful thing to do in Casey's world.

"This is my cousin, Casey Cantrell, Clarissa. She
works for the Forest Service out at the national park.
Casey, meet Clarissa Peyton."

Casey gently shook Clarissa's red-fingernailed hand.

There wasn't one callus on her palm as there were on her own. "Nice to meet you, Clarissa."

Raising her finely arched brows, Clarissa tilted her head as she released Casey's hand. "Hmm, you look familiar. By any chance are you related to Alyssa Trayhern-Cantrell of San Francisco?"

Grinning, Casey said, "I'm one of her daughters."

Instantly, Clarissa's demeanor changed from cool casual to enthusiastic. "Oh, my! Truly, you *are* her daughter? Why, Alyssa is famous for her charity work in San Francisco!" Reaching out, Clarissa gave Casey's cheeks air kisses, too. Casey had now moved up to a higher echelon of importance here. She was sure others noted it, too. That's how it went in high society: the powerful and important versus those who wanted to be in that heady sphere.

Casey smiled and remained low-key. "Yes, I am her daughter. I remember my mother talking very highly of your work here in Jackson Hole. She said you were a major fundraiser for the poor."

"Oh." Clarissa sighed, smiling warmly. "I'm nothing compared to your mother. She's raised millions for the poor and needy around the world. I've got a long way to go to catch up with her."

That was all true. Casey loved her mother fiercely for all her hard work and her focus on those who had much less than they did. Casey had grown up working in soup kitchens on Thanksgiving and Christmas and helping to build homes for Habitat for Humanity during her summer breaks. Alyssa's passion was always education for those who had less. She had built a global network of Fortune 500 corporations and could raise millions by simply going to them with her latest project—drilling wells for clean water or building schools to educate the children. Casey thought she saw a bit of jealousy in Clarissa's large green eyes along with admiration for her mother.

"Well," Casey said soothingly, "my mother thinks you rock, Clarissa. She admires all you do out here in Wyoming."

Coloring, Clarissa touched her cheek and smiled. "Really? She has mentioned me? That's incredible!" And then she turned to Kam and Wes and whispered, "Alyssa Cantrell is *the* fundraiser in the U.S.A.! We all aspire to do as much as she does." Turning, Clarissa reached out and lightly touched Casey's shoulder. "My dear, we *must* do lunch! And soon. I'll have my secretary call you and we'll set up an appointment…"

"I'd like that," Casey lied. She hated small talk, even though her mother had schooled her to be diplomatic when necessary. "I understand you have a cousin who is a quilt designer?"

"Yes, yes, I do." Clarissa preened a bit. "Are you a quilter?"

"I'm a seamstress of sorts. I'd like to learn quilting and I've visited Quilter's Haven. I think I'll take a beginning quilting class from Gwen Garner one of these days."

"Gwen's just the best!" Clarissa gushed. And then she looked around. "Oh, I must welcome more of my guests. Do excuse me, please." She gestured toward the food table at the rear of the rotunda. "Help yourself to snacks and more champagne!" And with that, she flew off like a beautiful red bird to more arriving guests.

Casey smiled a little. Kam and Wes looked at one another, their expressions unreadable. Gripping Kam's arm, Casey said, "Okay, cuz, I purposely didn't eat dinner and I'm starved!"

"Oh, there's the senator," Kam said, looking toward the door.

Casey halted at the buffet table and picked up a white china plate. She glanced in the direction of the door. Never having met Senator Carter Peyton, she was curious about the man. Clarissa was fluttering like a crimson tropical bird and he was somber-looking, handsome in his black tux and starched white shirt and crisp black bow tie, his gaze perusing the crowd like a predator. "I see," she murmured, turning away. She was hungry, and Casey had seen her share of senators and congressmen over the years at her mother's extravaganzas in San Francisco. She saw that Kam was properly in awe of the striking senator, who strode into the room as though he owned it and everyone in it.

"Wow, that's one powerful dude," Kam murmured, standing next to Casey and picking up a plate. "I've heard a lot about him but had never seen him in person until just now. Charisma to burn, eh? Kind of reminds me of Caesar entering Rome after conquering the known world."

Shrugging, Casey murmured, "Don't go gaga on me, cousin. He's just a senator. People give politicians way too much power, in my opinion."

"That's right," Kam said, "you grew up at your mother's side meeting and shaking hands with all kinds of politicians from around the world."

Nodding, Casey added some more food to her plate. "You have to remember, Kam, they all put on their pants the same way as we do." She grinned. "It levels the playing field."

Chuckling, Kam and Wes nodded.

CARTER PEYTON WENT THROUGH the motions of meeting and greeting the heavy-hitting monied couples in the room. He worked the room with his fluttering wife at his side. There was a secret joy in watching Joseph and Barbara Elsworth suddenly simper like beta wolves as he strode over to them. Peyton knew that with monied people you either were the commander in charge or nothing at all. With his shoulders squared, chin slightly up and an air of disdained authority, he presented forty-year-old Barbara with an air kiss and gave Joe a strong, solid handshake.

"Nice party," Joe said, releasing his hand.

"Thank you," Carter murmured, turning to his wife, who was all smiles. "Clarissa, as you know, deserves all the credit."

"Tell me, Carter," Barbara said in a conspiratorial tone, "who is that young woman over there with Kam Trayhern? She's new. I don't recognize her. Should we know her?"

Peyton turned. Instantly he froze. It was a momentary twinge on his part. Did they see his gut reaction? *Damn!* That was Casey Cantrell, the woman Matt Sinclaire was interested in! Opening his mouth and then shutting it, Carter was at a loss for words.

"Oh," Clarissa wheedled, "that's someone you should know, Barbara." She went on to tell the couple all about Casey's famous mother, Alyssa Trayhern-Cantrell, who had raised millions for charity. Instantly, the couple was focused on the woman, who was now sitting down and eating.

Carter tasted panic and it had a burnt taste. He'd had no realization of any of Casey Cantrell's background. Cursing silently, he glared in her direction and then quickly masked it. Suddenly, he wanted to escape this cloying, suffocating gala. Carter hated them. The amount of money raised depended upon how you simpered and begged for it from all those who had it to give. Feeling diminished by the expectations of the powerful group, Carter wished for the thousandth time that Gloria was still alive. She had been the perfect politician's wife: neither seen nor heard from. Clarissa, on the other hand, was like a bright butterfly flitting from one event to another. She loved getting the newspapers and internet to talk about her fetes and charity work. The only time she was happy was when she was on the evening news or on the front page of a newspaper. That was his job, not hers. Still, Clarissa had used her abilities to spring him into national news, too.

"I wonder," Barbara said with a smile, "if Charley Davidson knows who she is?"

Shrugging, Clarissa said, "I don't know. I do know he sent her here tonight, so I suspect he knows something of her background."

Nodding, Barbara said, "She's very pretty. And Kam is her cousin? She's monied, no doubt."

Peyton wanted to puke. He kept the forced smile on his face. Knowing that monied individuals always decided where an individual was by their bottom line, he began to wonder himself if Casey Cantrell was rich. If she was, why the hell was she eking out a living as a forest ranger? They didn't get paid very much at all. Cursing again to himself, Carter knew he was in a pickle with Casey Cantrell. If she was found murdered, all hell would break loose because her family had the money to hire anyone they wanted to find the killer. He couldn't have that. No, some kind of "accident" would have to be devised, instead. They had been right to plan for that. Peyton felt even better now about such a plan. If Casey Cantrell was killed by a grizzly bear, no one would suspect foul play. People got killed by bears every year. It wouldn't raise an eyebrow.

"Oh," Clarissa gushed, "Alyssa Trayhern-Cantrell is the queen of charities! I'm surprised you haven't heard of her, Barbara." Clarissa knew that the woman, who looked like a shrew with a pinched face and small, close-set eyes, was still a backwoods hick from Cheyenne, Wyoming. It was her brain that enamored Joseph, not her looks, body or upbringing. Barbara was trash from the wrong side of the tracks. Clarissa knew the woman, who put on all kinds of airs because her husband was worth a billion dollars, had no idea of how to conduct herself in high society.

"Oh," Barbara parried, "I'm sure I've heard the name. I don't travel much and I hate San Francisco. Way too liberal a place for me." She wrinkled her sharp, thin nose, and that made her eyes look even beadier.

Clarissa smiled faintly, nodded and said nothing. The Shrew, as she referred to the five-foot-tall, skinny woman, really didn't know Alyssa at all. Many in Wyoming were conservative by nature and, although Clarissa came from this state, she was far more moderate in her outlook than Barbara. She loved San Francisco, liberal city or not. It was one of the finest examples of glittering high society melding with the arts. It wasn't something she wanted to share with Barbara. One didn't argue with a donor. Not ever.

"Dear," Carter said warmly, "I need to make a cell phone call." He excused himself and quickly exited the rotunda. Moving up the stairs, to where he knew the private level of the museum was located, he pulled out a throwaway cell phone and called Benson. He would leave a message for him, then destroy the cell and throw it into the Snake River, never to be found. This would ensure that he could not be traced or tracked.

CASEY WAS GLAD TO LEAVE the fete after two hours. She'd seen all the players. And Matt had never arrived, much to her regret. No wonder her boss hadn't wanted to come. Without a Ph.D in small talk, a person would go down in flames in a heartbeat. Her head was aching when she left the museum. Above, the stars were bright in a wide canopy across the dark sky.

"Casey?"

Jerking to a halt, she turned toward the male voice. Matt Sinclaire stood there in his red fire-department jacket, hands in the pockets. His eyes were filled with concern.

"Matt!"

He gave her an apologetic smile. "The chief told me you were ordered to this fete. I thought I'd try and meet you afterward." His voice lowered. "Are you all right?"

Her skin prickled pleasantly as his gaze moved from her eyes to linger on her parted lips. In the overhead lights just outside the doors to the museum, his face took on a deeply rugged appearance. "Yes, I'm fine."

Walking up to her, Matt said, "Let me escort you to your truck. Someone's shot at you, they're loose out there and you should have some kind of protection."

His hand cupping her elbow sent warmth through her. "How long have you been waiting out here?"

"Oh, maybe half an hour," he murmured, checking his stride for hers. The parking lot was filled with high-

end SUVs—Mercedes and BMWs; vehicles belonging
to the cream of Jackson Hole. "How'd it go in there?"

Casey was grateful for his presence. Protection
poured from him to her like a warm, embracing blanket. She told him about the fete. By the time she reached
her truck, she added, "Senator Peyton appeared and
then disappeared. Funny thing, Matt," she said, turning
to him after opening the truck door, "I saw him look
over at me with the strangest expression on his face."

"What do you mean?" Matt peered down into her
darkened eyes. Starlight became Casey. Her shoulder-
length brown hair was slightly curled and framed her
oval face beautifully. She was not model-pretty but
that didn't matter to him. The gleam of life in her gray
eyes, the softness of her mouth, all conspired to make
him ache. The memory of what it was like to ache for
a woman had been foreign to him until she'd stepped
into his life.

Shrugging, Casey threw her purse into the passenger-
side seat and said, "It was the oddest look. As though
he was seeing a ghost or something. Really bizarre, if
you ask me. I mean, I don't know the man, never seen
him before, but he was looking at me like he knew me,
Matt. Truly weird."

"Your mother works in those circles. Has he met her?
Do you and Alyssa look a lot alike, maybe?" The wind
was picking up, cool and chilling.

"I don't know," Casey murmured, pulling her coat
tighter around her. Looking up into his face, his eyes
gleaming with intelligence and care, how badly Casey
wanted to lean up on tiptoe and kiss this heroic man's
mouth. She found herself shocked at that desire. There
was nothing not to like about Matt, but her past was

still melded to her present. "Next time I talk with my mother, I'll ask her. I look more like my father than I do my mother. Emma, the oldest, has red hair like my mom." She touched her brown tresses. "I have my dad's hair." She smiled warmly, thinking how much Matt was like her dad—the strong, silent type.

Matt looked around the parking lot, at the snow pushed to the sides of the area, the asphalt gleaming beneath the sulfur lights, noting that there were few people outside the museum right now before returning his attention to Casey to share today's earlier events at the sheriff's department with her. When he finished, her eyes had widened considerably.

"Charley felt the shot was aimed at me," Casey said. "He discussed it with me earlier today."

Holding up his hand, Matt said, "Don't go there just yet. There's a lot of conjecture here, Casey. Charley sent out a team today to search for the shooter's spot. You might ask him tomorrow morning if they found anything."

Casey muttered, "I will." She frowned. "I just do not want to tell my parents about this, Matt. They've already gone through hell with me once over the Red Lake incident. I don't want them worrying about me again." She sighed. "I just can't believe there is an assassin hired by someone out there gunning for me. I'm a nobody." She lifted her gloved hands upward. "No one!"

"You're too nice a person to have any enemies," Matt agreed, trying to soothe her. He saw the worry banked in Casey's eyes, the darkness and fear. She was remembering her beating in the past. Without thinking, he slid his hand against her cheek and jaw. Leaning forward, their mouths only inches apart, he whispered, "You have friends here, Casey. I'm one of them. I'll make sure you're protected." How badly Matt ached to kiss her. Watching her pupils grow huge and black, Matt nearly dipped his head to capture her mouth. She was so close…so close…

"I've got to go," Casey whispered raggedly. She pulled away, afraid of herself more than him. Matt was so masculine, confident and virile. All the things she'd ever dreamed of in a man were standing right in front of her, Matt's hand cupping her jaw as he looked deeply into her eyes. Easing away, Casey climbed into the truck. Her hand shook as she slid the key into the ignition. Giving Matt a quick glance, she saw he was neither disappointed nor angry. The hunger burning in his eyes made her sorry she hadn't kissed him after all.

Matt nodded. "See you tomorrow," he said and gently shut the door to the USFS pickup. Standing back, he watched the truck pull out. Casey lifted her hand in farewell and slowly drove by him. Matt sauntered down the hill toward the lower parking lot. He knew Senator Peyton was inside the museum pressing the flesh. The man hated him to this day. There was no way Matt had been going to go to the fete. The old saying that you let sleeping dogs lie was, in this case, wise advice. Although the chief had offered him the invitation to the fete, Matt knew he was not expected to show up because of his sordid past with Peyton. He had come because he knew Casey was attending. Seeing her had made his night.

The cold, brisk breeze made Matt feel alive. Because he'd nearly kissed Casey? Her mouth was so soft. He hungered to feel it beneath his. Would she be burning with passion? Or soft, like a pink dusk dissolving out of the darkness of the night? Or…? His mouth pulled into a sad smile. As he neared his vehicle, Matt felt his life was turning toward chaos once more. Casey had entered his and Megan's life like an unexpected rainbow of promise and hope. She had infused them with joy in a way Matt had never thought possible.

Opening the door, he slid into his truck. His heart felt warm and mushy in his chest. Shaking his head, Matt sat there after closing the door. Why hadn't he leaned those few inches and kissed Casey? He'd seen the approval in her eyes. But something fleeting had stopped him. What else had he seen in her eyes? Fear? Matt tried to put himself into her place. She'd been nearly beaten to death by five men. Her trust with men was broken. Matt knew his would be, too, under those very circumstances.

Gripping the steering wheel, he tried to ferret deeper into Casey's expression as she drowned in his gaze. Her lips had parted, she was ready to be kissed by him. Why had he hesitated? Was he afraid to try and love again?

"What the hell?" Matt rasped tightly, looking out the window of the pickup at the shadows and parked cars. Was it really him? No woman had interested him since his wife's death. Not one. Until now. Two years had passed. Was that when grief stopped and life began again? Matt had no idea. What he couldn't afford to do was put his selfish needs in front of Megan's.

No…he had to restrain himself for his daughter's sake. Megan adored Casey. Better to be friends right now, because Matt didn't want to take the chance of damaging Megan's connection with Casey in any way. Shaking his head, Matt slipped the key into the ignition. As he drove out of the lot, the lights stabbing into the darkness down the long, winding road, Matt felt torn. He was protective by nature, and Casey had been shot at. He didn't care what the sheriff or Charley thought. Someone was after her and he could taste it. And he was damned if Casey was going to die. There was just no way…

CHAPTER ELEVEN

CASEY MARVELED AT THE changes in the Tetons on June first. Just as her supervisor, Charley, had said, the world shifted and changed. Working at the visitor's center, she saw a tremendous increase in tourists. She had gone from being bored out of her mind three of the five days a week she was at the desk, to being engaged with enthusiastic people from around the world. The other two days were spent in wildlife biology and she always looked forward to the change of pace.

The sun was slanting through the floor-to-ceiling glass in the west side of the visitor's center as Casey got ready to quit her shift for the day. As she turned, she saw Matt and Megan enter. Smiling, she waved at them. In the last two months they'd tried to get together once a week, but that didn't always work with their crazy schedules. Her heart pulsed warmly as she saw Matt's normally serious expression break into a warm smile meant only for her.

Megan waved enthusiastically and smiled her toothy smile.

Casey said goodbye to her other three ranger friends and slipped out from behind the counter. Megan tore out of Matt's grasp and ran across the shining waxed floor, her arms open wide, her hair flying behind her. Laughing, Casey knelt down and opened her arms. The eight-year-old flew into her embrace, hugging her hard and laughing.

Megan nestled her head against the crook of Casey's shoulder. She kissed the girl's hair. "And how was your day, Megan?" Casey asked.

Making unintelligible sounds, Megan simply clung to Casey. She was highly affectionate every time Casey saw her. It was as if Megan was sure she would disappear. Casey understood the girl's reaction. Megan had lost her mother and she didn't want to lose another woman with whom she was bonding.

"Hi," Matt greeted. He shoved his hands into the pockets of his jeans. "We thought we'd catch you at quitting time and take you home with us. Megan loves spaghetti and she's been helping me make the sauce for it today. I asked her if she'd like to have you over for dinner and her head's been bobbing ever since." Matt looked inquiringly down at Casey. Megan was so happy in her embrace. Guilt conflicted with desire within him. He couldn't shake the past, his love for Bev and how she had filled his life with joy. Yet his heart pined to be with Casey. It was terrible to be emotionally strung between, Matt decided. The past anchored him and another part of himself wanted to be free of it in order to begin to live again.

Casey lifted Megan into her arms. The girl squealed with delight, her small arms tight around her neck. "Hey, this is a nice surprise." Casey asked, "Did you cut up the onions?"

Nodding eagerly, Megan twisted around and looked at her father. She babbled on in sounds, not words. Matt grinned and tousled his daughter's hair.

"I think that is, yes, I helped cut up the onions and

yes, I cried as I did it." He met Casey's warm gray gaze. "She had a box of tissues next to the cutting board. Half the time she was fighting the onion with the paring knife. The other half she was wiping her eyes and blowing her nose. And then, she'd be washing her hands in between."

Chuckling, Casey gently placed Megan's tennis-shoed feet on the floor and straightened. Megan's hand found hers and Casey squeezed it gently to reassure the child. "Hey, that's how I cut up onions, too! A paring knife in one hand and a tissue in the other." She grinned down at Megan. "Isn't that how everyone does it, Megan?"

Nodding, Megan laughed and jumped up and down like a fractious colt who wanted to run.

Matt felt whole in that moment. The three of them stood close to one another trading something so simple and yet so profound as cutting an onion. He recalled similar conversations with Bev as they absorbed Megan's discoveries about life. Each one was precious. And each was a new step into his daughter's awareness of who she was as a person. Matt never wanted to miss any of those moments, but he knew he did. Though he was grateful that his sister could babysit Megan, he more than once wished that he was married so that Megan's stepmother could be there to see these moments. Sadness swept through him because Matt knew that was not to be. Forcing himself to stop thinking along those lines, he walked with Megan and Casey to the door.

"We make a pretty mean spaghetti," he told Casey. "I learned to make this at the firehouse."

"Oh, no," Casey teased, walking through the opened

door Matt held open for them. She glanced down at Megan. "And you survived this spaghetti?"

Laughing, Megan nodded. She skipped happily between them. There were less tourists at 5:00 p.m. Everyone was going to dinner. The June sky was a light blue with some puffy white clouds. The snow had mostly melted from the slopes of the Tetons, except at the tops of their sharp granite peaks.

"Hey, we've got lots of news," Matt said as they turned off the sidewalk to the parking lot. "Do you want to ride home with us? I can drive you back afterward?"

Casey liked the idea of a few quiet, private moments with Matt. She knew Megan was all ears and that some discussions couldn't be shared with her. "Sure, sounds good."

"CAT'S RECOMMENDATION was that I take Megan to see Dr. Jordana Lawton, the functional medicine specialist, and I did." Matt sat in front of his emptied plate. Casey was opposite him finishing off the last of her spaghetti. Megan was on her second piece of garlic bread, her plate shining clean.

"I know you took Megan to see her. What were the results of that saliva test?" Casey asked. She saw a new light in Matt's eyes and couldn't interpret it.

"The saliva test shows Megan's cortisol levels. Shows whether they're outside the normal limits." Matt got up and took all the plates into the kitchen. When he came back, he retrieved seven pages of test results and handed them to Casey. "The one I want you to look at," he said, leaning down near her and helping her thumb through the results, "is this one…" He inhaled Casey's sweet scent. The fragrance of pine was still lingering in her shining brown hair. "This is the box diagram that shows the normal cortisol levels and the peaks outside of it are Megan's results."

Matt was so close it dizzied Casey's senses. She automatically absorbed his power and masculinity. Looking where he placed his thumb, she flattened the papers on the table. "Look at this. Three out of the four are outside the normal limits of where her cortisol levels should be." She turned, Matt's face inches from hers. Gulping, Casey tried to suppress her feminine reaction to him. His face was dark with beard growth. It made the planes and angles of his features give him a dangerous look. One that beckoned to her.

Smiling, Matt nodded and tapped the box. "Dr. Lawton said that the Diagnos-Tech test would show if Megan's cortisol was in or out of normal. She said it's out the most at night and, of course, that's when the fire happened."

Casey looked over at Megan, but she seemed completely absorbed in the garlic bread. Still, she chose her words carefully. "And so when the cortisol is outside the normal lines this causes those symptoms of anxiety, tension and restlessness that she has?"

"Exactly!" Matt grew excited as he traced the three peaks. "Dr. Lawton said that at 9:00 a.m., 3:00 p.m. and late in the evening around 10:00 p.m., were Megan's high-cortisol periods."

Worriedly, Casey looked at the illustration. "So, what can be done to force the cortisol back into normal levels for her, Matt?"

Matt walked over to the kitchen counter and picked up a bottle. Setting it down in front of Casey, he said, "This is the adaptogen. Dr. Lawton prescribed it for

Megan. It's designed to block the cortisol receptors. The trauma Megan survived has shut down her pituitary gland's ability to order the adrenal glands to stop making cortisol." He tapped this bottle. "By plugging the receptors at the peak times when her cortisol is abnormally high, this medicine, she says, will bring them back inside normal bounds. And then," Matt smiled a little and caught Casey's gaze, "it means that all those symptoms Megan has will go away. Permanently."

"Wow," Casey murmured, impressed. "And what about Megan's broken sleep? And her nightmares?"

Standing, Matt allowed his hands to rest on his hips. "Dr. Lawton says that a thirty-day regime of this medication is going to handle all of that, Casey. Megan will finally sleep through the night instead of waking up two or three times."

Marveling over the good news, Casey picked up the bottle. "This is fantastic! Who knew this medicine was out there?"

"I know. If not for Cat, we'd still be looking at other alternatives to help Megan." Frowning, Matt walked back over to his chair and sat down. "I've really resisted giving Megan anti-anxiety medication and sleeping pills. Her pediatrician has really pushed me on this and I've balked. Dr. Lawton was saying that traditional medicine handles high cortisol but it doesn't address the core issue. And it doesn't lower the person's cortisol levels, either. All you're doing is covering it up with other drugs."

"I remember Cat going on this adaptogen, too." Casey held the bottle up to him. "This was about a month ago."

"Yes, she was telling me that her background had a

lot of trauma." His voice faltered. "I guess she was severely abused as a child."

Nodding, Casey said, "Yes, we've had long talks until after midnight sometimes about her family upbringing. But I noticed that when she started taking this medicine she wasn't so skittish, restless or anxious. And now, she's really calm, centered and doesn't overreact to everything. This is amazing stuff, Matt." Casey gave Megan a warm look, the girl happily focused on chewing her bread with gusto. "I'm going to look forward to seeing the changes in Megan."

"Yes." Matt sighed. "I pray that this is what we need to unlock so much…so much…"

Feeling his worry and guilt, Casey knew he'd been looking for a breakthrough like this. "Has Dr. Lawton handled other children in her practice who had trauma?"

Nodding, Matt said, "Yes, she has a lot of experience with children as well as adults. She's an amazing person. After talking with her about Megan's condition, I left her office so full of hope." He scowled. "She didn't throw drugs at Megan. She offered something very specific to bring the cortisol back to normal, functioning levels. She focused on the root cause, Casey, not the plethora of symptoms that high cortisol can give a person."

"I wonder," she said softly, "if I should see Dr. Lawton?" Casey didn't want to speak of her own incident in the world of trauma in front of Megan. The girl had been through enough. She saw Matt's eyes gleam and his very male mouth draw into a smile.

"I think you should see her, Casey." He shrugged. "There's nothing to lose. It can address your cortisol and I'm sure after talking to Dr. Lawton, that your levels are out of the normal range, too."

"And Dr. Lawton feels it will take how long to see a difference in Megan?"

"She said it takes about seventy-two hours for it to kick in and to start seeing differences. She said I should observe Megan and keep a daily journal of her actions and reactions." Matt held up his hand, his fingers crossed. "Let's hope this works."

Sighing, Casey said, "That makes three of us. Before I leave tonight, give me Dr. Lawton's phone number. I want to see her."

"Great," Matt said. He felt a deluge of emotions as Casey's face glowed with renewed hope. "This stuff," he pointed at the bottle, "could help so many people, Casey. Dr. Lawton said soldiers who have PTSD can get rid of their symptoms by taking this adaptogen. She said abused children will stop their patterns of negative behavior. And adults who have been abused as children or who have suffered any kind of severe trauma in their life can all benefit from this very same regime. Can you believe, it only takes one inexpensive saliva test to find out?" He shook his head, some anger in his voice. "Do you know that the last two years I've searched high and low in the medical field to find Megan relief from her symptoms?"

"I know you've tried a lot of things," Casey said, giving him a tender look. She saw the strife in Matt's expression, the frustration and hopelessness. "But it sounds like functional medicine is a new branch. And maybe that's why you didn't find it before this."

"Yes," Matt muttered, pushing his fingers through his short hair. "Dr. Lawton said it is a brand-new branch and until it gets known, there's a lot of PTSD people out there still suffering and trying to suppress their symptoms with other anti-depressant drugs. As soon as they go off the drugs, all their symptoms come back. And that's not a cure. That's suppression."

"At least with this method," Casey said, feeling hopeful, "there is a cure. Did Dr. Lawton say that once Megan goes through this thirty-day cycle her levels will be normal?"

"Dr. Lawton said she'll give her a second test about three months from now to make sure. And she said most people only need it once, for a month. In severe PTSD and trauma cases, though, the person might need a second month of taking this adaptogen."

"Still," Casey said, brightening, "this is so hopeful." She wanted to get up and dance around. "Cat said she no longer has those horrid nightmares that would wake both of us up at night. Literally, Matt, I'd hear Cat scream and our bedrooms are opposite one another with a hall between us. And our doors are closed. That is how loud she was yelling."

Grimacing, Matt said, "Cat is an excellent firefighter but I could see she had a lot of problems she wasn't sharing with any of us."

"Well," Casey murmured, "Cat is the only woman in an all-man fire department, so she's gun-shy of sharing anything for fear some of the guys will use it against her."

Sad, Matt nodded. "Yes, there's a good ol' boy attitude that the chief is trying to change. And to be fair, Cat is taking a lot of lumps because there's some men in there who don't want to see a woman doing their job. It's discrimination, pure and simple, but until we catch these dudes doing it, there's not much we can do."

"I get discrimination over at my job, too. There's guys in there who think being a ranger is a job for men only. I just hate that kind of mentality."

"Women get it every time," Matt agreed. "In my family, my two younger brothers assume they'll take over the ranching when my father, Lou, retires."

"Did your sister Jessie ever want to do it, though?" Casey wondered. She'd met Jessie several times and liked the red-haired twenty-five-year-old with blue eyes. Unlike Matt, she was perky and outgoing. Casey wondered if Matt had been that way before the tragedy and the loss of Bev, his wife.

"No," Matt said, "Jessie always wanted to be a nurse. She took four years of college in Cheyenne and then came back here to work. Right now, she's trying to talk her boss into letting her be part of the medical flight team. He's balking and she told me he's prejudiced against women doing a job like that. So, she's bucking the traces on it but not getting anywhere fast."

"Yes, but she has red hair," Casey said, smiling a little. She knew there were strong Irish genes in his family. "True or not, I think people with red hair get their way sooner or later."

Chuckling, Matt nodded. "Listen, the more you get to know Jess, the more you'll realize that she will get her way. The guy who's her boss doesn't know it, but he will." Getting up, he said, "Time for dessert?"

Groaning, Casey held up her hands. "Listen, I have to maintain my weight. Dessert is off my list. Until Charley figures out he can send me on outdoor assignments again, this desk work is making me fat." She patted her hip.

"You aren't fat," Matt said. "And what's the latest on that gun incident that happened a couple of months ago?"

Casey got up and walked with Matt to the kitchen. "Well, maybe not fat, but I've gained five pounds sitting behind that darned counter. And there are no new leads on that rifle incident. Charley hasn't let it go but he's more relaxed. Now, he's letting me go out on trail again, thank goodness." As a firefighter, Matt faced tremendous physical demands and they kept him lean and hard. It was a treat for Casey to watch him saunter ahead of her. Today, his white polo shirt and jeans outlined his muscular body to perfection. She especially liked his hands. They were large, the fingers long with calluses on the palms. Matt was an outdoors person. Even in the snow and ice, he liked working outside when he could.

Matt brought out a cherry pie he'd made earlier in the day. "Sure you won't have a little piece? I won't put vanilla ice cream on it." He grinned over at her.

Pulling down two plates from above, Casey laughed. "No, you can't bribe me. As if only ice cream has the calories and the pie doesn't. Shame on you, Matt."

Chuckling with her, he absorbed the easy familiarity of Casey being with him in the kitchen. For a moment out of time, Matt tried to imagine that they were married. Is this what it would be like? This happy camaraderie? This gentle teasing? He ached to have his life whole again, realizing once more that he was the kind of man who needed marriage in order to feel complete. Tearing his thoughts away from that, he said, "Guilty as charged."

"I'll make us fresh coffee," Casey offered.

Nodding, he said, "Go for it."

For the next few minutes a warm blanket of peace fell over the kitchen. Casey felt happy. It was a rare thing, she realized as she brought the coffee down from the cupboard. Happiness had stopped being an emotion when she'd experienced the trauma.

"Matt?"

"Yes?"

"What are some of the other symptoms of high cortisol levels?"

"Dr. Lawton said people can have a very broad range of symptoms."

"Humor me. What are they?" She poured the grounds into the machine.

"A lot of people feel only two emotions—fear and anger. No other human emotions are there. You have to understand that when you feel that your life is being threatened, fear is a good thing to have. It spurs you into action. And the anger is a natural component of survival—it's you or the other guy. It makes sense to me. Does it to you?" He glanced over at Casey. She looked pensive as she made the coffee.

"Yes. You've hit the nail on the head. Those are the only two emotions I have. Fear and anger. I always feel on guard. Apprehensive. Wondering when the next bad thing is going to happen."

Nodding, he hurt for Casey. Matt knew she didn't deserve what had happened to her. "Dr. Lawton would probably say you're in the fight-or-flight survival mode. Most people who suffer from PTSD get imprisoned between these two emotions because the high cortisol always makes them feel as if the next threat is right around the corner and going to jump out at them."

Flipping the switch on the coffeemaker, Casey nodded. "Are there other symptoms?"

"She mentioned heartburn, swelling of your stomach shortly after eating a meal and ulcers."

"I don't have any of those symptoms."

"She said that there's a cascade effect and that these other symptoms will slowly show up over the years. Your incident wasn't that long ago. Maybe, if it isn't treated, in another five or so years you could start having these symptoms."

Nodding, Casey said, "It makes sense to me. I do have the waking up two or three times a night. I hate broken sleep. I never had it before my…well…that time in my life." She didn't even like to talk about it. Matt gave her a warm, understanding look.

"So, there's anxiety, feeling anxious, restlessness, inability to sit still very long and a sense of foreboding."

Matt nodded. "Yes."

"It sure sounds like a lot of ADHD symptoms to me. Does it to you?" Casey turned and rested her hips against the kitchen counter as Matt cut the pie and put two slices on the plates. For Megan, it was a very thin piece and for him, it was a quarter of the pie. Casey smiled and said nothing. There was something incredibly endearing about Matt.

"When the person who has the trauma has gone further into it, Dr. Lawton mentioned allergy symptoms start coming on. All kinds of allergies. She said the immune system is getting depleted by the high cortisol so it leaves the person wide open to a myriad of allergy symptoms."

"Hmm," Casey said. "I have an allergy I just got in the last year. I've suddenly become allergic to cat hair, of all things. At home," she looked over at him, "my parents have four Abyssinian cats and I was never allergic to them. What else?"

He placed the plastic lid back over the pie and put the container up against the wall of the counter. "She mentioned the thyroid could get hit by it over time, citing that a lot of women go hypothyroid and start putting on unwanted weight."

Touching her hip, Casey frowned. "I wonder if it's because of that or my sitting behind a desk eight hours a day?"

"Only one way to find out," Matt said, handing her one of the plates. "Go see Dr. Lawton."

"I think it's a great idea," Casey agreed. She walked into the dining room. Megan looked up, her eyes widening when she saw the dessert. She began making sounds and reached out for it as Casey placed it down in front of her. Oh, how Casey wanted Megan to talk again! Sitting down, Casey wanted to ask Matt about that, but this was the wrong place and time to do it. Maybe when he took her home, she could speak with him. And truth be known, Casey looked forward to that ten-minute trip from his home to the condo. It was a special time when she could fully absorb him. They didn't have to edit their conversations with one another. And when her gaze fell to his very male, wide mouth, Casey felt herself go hot and shaky inside. No man had ever affected her like this. What was she going to do?

CHAPTER TWELVE

"CASEY!" KAM GREETED her cousin as she walked into Iris Mason's greenhouse on the Elk Horn Ranch. She scooted off her stool and ran to her cousin. Hugging her, Kam grinned. "I'm so glad you had the day off! Isn't it gorgeous this morning?"

Casey smiled and released her tall, black-haired relative. Kam looked so happy. Her wedding to Wes would take place in less than a week. Casey liked the cowboy. He was a perfect match for her professional-photographer cousin. "Yes, a wonderful day for a ride." She craned her neck and waved to Iris Mason, the matriarch of the ranch. At eighty years old, Iris was vital, fit and full of fire. Around Jackson Hole, she was sometimes lovingly called "Dragon Lady." The only enemy she'd had had been Rudd Mason's wife, Allison. Now, Allison was in jail awaiting trial for trying to kill Iris and Kam. Rudd, Kam's recently found father, was in the midst of divorcing Allison. Their two children, Zach and Reagan, had moved into town. Zach was doing drugs, Reagan was deeply involved in her mother's court case, having completely thrown away her scholarship to a university in California where she would have learned film-making and directing. The children had blatantly ignored Rudd and Iris and that had hurt them deeply. Life had so many twists and turns, Casey realized.

"Hey, Casey!" Iris lifted her hand. "Time for a ride! I'm going out shortly to gather some flower essences up in the hills. Want to go with us?" She cackled and rubbed her hands together.

"You bet I do, Iris," Casey sang back. "I love to ride on a sunny morning like this."

Kam smiled, and gripped her cousin's arm and whispered, "Grams has a suitor!"

Brows raising, Casey said, "Are you serious?"

"Humph," Iris called from her desk, where she was finishing off a violet flower essence for an order. "Why can't an eighty-something fall in love? You think we don't have hearts that feel? You younguns make me laugh."

Turning, Casey walked with Kam over to the long wooden desk where Iris sat primly on her three-legged wooden stool. She had a green apron draped over her pink long-sleeved blouse and jeans. Her silver hair was piled on top of her head with several tortoiseshell combs. "Hey, I think that's great," Casey said.

"He's coming with us," Kam said in a conspiratorial whisper.

"Now," Iris chided her granddaughter, wagging her finger in her face, "you just behave yourself, Missy! Professor Timothy Varden is a Harvard wildlife biologist." Preening a little as she set the one-ounce eyedropper bottle into a nest of paper to protect it during shipment, she added saucily, "And he's absolutely enamored with what I do. Making flower essences. He had no idea that they are an alternative medicine. Before, he just looked at a flower and could reel off its Latin name and tell me all about its anatomy."

Casey saw the elder's eyes flash and gleam. Iris reminded her of an impish elf from Ireland just about ready to play a trick on some unsuspecting human. Iris was like that all the time: cagey and the sharpest knife in the drawer. "And what did you tell him?" Casey asked with a chuckle. Knowing full well Iris always told everyone what was on her mind without preamble, Casey waited. Of course, Iris had the richest and most powerful cattle ranch in Wyoming, and here in the valley, she and Rudd Mason, her adopted son, were the king and queen of the cattle ranches, so to speak. Best of all, they were nice people, unlike some of the power snobs Casey had met at Clarissa Peyton's fete.

Arching her thin brows, Iris said, "I knocked him off his feet!" She grinned like a coyote as the two young women stood near her hanging on her every word. Placing tape on the box, Iris found a label and pen. "Little did Tim know that violet here, for instance, is for a wounded heart. It helps a person get through their grieving. It doesn't remove the grief, it just helps a person work through it better than they would without this dainty little flower's energy." She quickly wrote out the name on the label that she placed on the small, square cardboard box. Handing it to Kam, whose job it was to mail them every afternoon at the post office, Iris sighed. "He's the first man I've met—except for my Trevor—who was sincerely fascinated by this discovery."

"I know he's sweet on you," Kam teased.

"Oh, maybe."

Chortling, Kam said, "Grams, he absolutely dotes on your every word. Yesterday, when you told him at lunch you were going to make some flower essences out there in the hills, he was beside himself. He wants to learn what you do."

"Actually," Casey said, "it sounds like kismet. He's a plant lover. Why wouldn't he be interested in what you know, Iris?"

Giving a nod, Iris said, "That's right, Casey. Like a good academician, Harvard-trained no less, he's open-minded and curious about the plant world. He's not one of these idiot men who thinks he knows everything and, therefore, is blind, deaf and dumb!" She scooted off her stool, pulled off her apron and dropped it on the desk. Standing barely five feet tall and slightly over-weight, she rubbed her hands briskly together once more. "Okay, girls, let's go a-flowering! Our horses await us over at the stable. Wes said he'd make sure all the flower-essence-making supplies would be in our saddlebags."

Kam picked up her tan Stetson from her desk and settled it on her head. She wore jeans, a red T-shirt and a denim jacket, because it was still chilly in the morning. "I'm ready, Grams!"

Casey walked with the two women to the huge red barn. The Elk Horn Ranch was part dude ranch, but the greater part of it was devoted to raising organic buffalo and cattle meat for a growing market across the world. It had been Iris's idea to start selling organic buffalo meat because it was so lean and could lower the cho-lesterol of a meat-eating person. Her idea, way ahead of her time, had taken off in 2000 and she had never looked back. It was a multimillion-dollar business now with half the ranch reserved for the shaggy buffalo and the other half to raising Hereford cattle.

Wes, who was now the manager of the Elk Horn, stood with the reins of four horses in hand, smiling as they approached. The sun had just risen above the hills; a chill was still in the air, but the morning was fresh and promising. Casey saw a very tall, thin, bearded man in a floppy green canvas hat wearing gold wire-rimmed glasses hurrying toward them. On his back was a green knapsack. He was, she guessed, the wildlife biologist. His hair was shaggy and shone as silver as his neatly trimmed beard. Casey saw his blue eyes light up as he spotted Iris. There was no question this eighty-year-old man was interested in feisty Iris. When Casey looked toward Iris, she was glowing, her cheeks suddenly pink and her eyes dancing with happiness.

Wes helped Iris into the saddle of her favorite horse, a small mustang. Fred, also a mustang, was Kam's mount. For Casey, he'd chosen a black quarter horse gelding named Frank.

"Iris, yoo-hoo," Tim called, waving his hand as he hurried toward the group. "Don't leave without me!"

Kam traded a look with Casey. They moved their horses to one side as Wes held a tall, rangy half-thoroughbred quarter horse for the professor. "Is he always late?"

Chuckling, Kam said, "Always. Maybe it has to do with him being the absentminded professor?" They both giggled. Iris, hearing the comment, raised one eyebrow as if to warn them to be kind to the professor who flapped toward them like a gangling bird on stilted legs ready to take off.

"At eighty we are not absentminded!" Iris huffed. She pulled her horse around and scowled at them. "Now, I agree, our minds aren't the same as you twentysomethings, but we have eighty years of experience under our belts which you do not have!" She lifted her chin to an imperious angle, just daring them to refute her statement. "And because of that, we deserve your undying and continual respect."

"Guilty as charged." Casey laughed. Kam joined her.

"You're right, Grams."

"You bet your boots I am!" She turned, her focus to Tim, who was all smiles as he approached. He pulled some bedraggled flowers from the huge pocket of his green canvas coat.

"Iris, these are for you," he said, handing them to her. "I was on a walk before the sun came up and I saw these wonderful daisies and I just couldn't resist them."

Touched, Iris took them. They were decidedly the worse for wear, their white-petaled heads drooping in her hand. "Tim, couldn't you at least put them in some water? Why, these poor children are half-dead!"

Chastened, Tim rubbed his hand across his bearded chin. "Why, Iris, you're so right." Then he gave her a boyish smile that made her glow. "You need to teach me about our plant neighbors. As a biologist, I pick them, I pull them apart to count petals, count stamens and such."

"Well," she huffed, giving him a hard look, "these are my children, Professor. They are not to be treated as throwaways." She waved the droopy flowers in his face.

"Quite right," Tim agreed apologetically. "Next time, I shall walk with a vase in my pocket and use the water from my bottle to give them sustenance."

"Still," Iris murmured, pleased, "it's a very thoughtful gift. Thank you, Tim."

Flushing, the biologist took off his floppy cap and bowed to her. "Anything for the Queen of Flowers…"

Casey sighed inwardly. Tim was so knightly, a throwback to Victorian times. There was no question he absolutely idolized the matriarch of the valley. And glancing over at Iris, who sat proudly on her mount looking down at him, she could see she *was* the queen. And he worshipped her.

Sighing, Casey smiled over at Kam. Wes, too, was grinning. He helped the professor climb on board Lucky, a very quiet bay gelding who handled people who had never ridden a horse before. Tim was like a flapping crow, legs and arms akimbo as he struggled into the Western saddle. That endeared him to Casey.

"Tim, you need riding lessons!" Iris rapped out smartly. "Wes, you need to get him in the riding ring or he's gonna fall off sooner rather than later."

Wes tucked his smile away and said, "Yes, ma'am, I'll do just that."

Straightening, his hat slipping over his glasses, Tim finally sat up with his boots thrust into the stirrups. "There, Iris! I'm aboard!" He pushed his beaten old hat up on his head and beamed over at her. "Do I not look like a knight in shining armor to you, now?" He raised his long arm in a flourish, taking a proud posture in the saddle.

"You look more like Don Quixote to me," Iris fumed, giving him a sad look and shaking her head. "Just try to stay on Lucky, okay? I don't want to have to pick you up off the ground."

Chuckling, Tim moved his gelding next to Iris's horse. "You just tell me what to do, my lady, and I'll do it. How I love this country! Why, I've never felt so full of life as when I came here to your dude ranch. I'm glad my children pushed me into coming. You know," he leaned over toward her and whispered, "this is their fault!"

Iris said, "Fault? How is it a fault to come to the best dude ranch in the West?"

Grinning and showing the gaps between his large front teeth, Tim said, "Oh, Iris, I'm not against dude ranches. It's just that I was unhappy being in my Harvard office day in and day out. They know how much I love and revere nature." He waved his hand around his head with a flourish as Iris led them past the corrals and onto one of the main trails that led to the hills about two miles away. "I just get soggy when I'm inside too much."

"Soggy?" Iris quipped, a devilish look in her eyes.

"Well…er…you know." Tim shrugged helplessly. "Soggy, as in depressed or sad. If I spend too many days inside, I just fall apart. Only nature can put me back together." He suddenly grinned and swept his arm grandly across the vista in front of them. "This revives my spirit." Then he became very sincere and added in a courtly manner, "But you feed my soul, Miss Iris."

"Humph."

Snickering, riding six feet behind the oldsters, Casey and Kam shared knowing looks. Casey leaned sideways to whisper to Kam, "We might be twenty-somethings but we can still identify love, can't we?"

Giggling, Kam nodded.

Iris turned in her saddle and gave them a merry look and then turned back to continue her conversation with Tim, who hung on her every word.

Kam rolled her eyes and said nothing, her mouth

wide in a smile of happiness. Casey shared her joy. They pulled back from the couple so they could talk to one another.

"So, when did the professor get here?" Casey wondered.

"Last week. He saw Grams and he fell all over himself. He was like a happy puppy dog around her. He's like an ungainly bird flapping to take off, but he needs a long runway to do it."

Giggling, Casey nodded. Indeed, the coat the professor wore was sizes too large for him, so the corners of it flapped right along with his effusive use of his long, gangly arms. And the canvas hat that was probably like an old friend to him was equally floppy around his head. Between all these, Professor Timothy Varden reminded Casey of a great blue heron who was certainly awkward on the ground. Once in the air, however, the great blue heron was all grace, and Casey didn't see that quality in the professor, which made him even more endearing. The man was not an egomaniac or a snob. Instead, he was like a curious little boy about everything. He constantly plied Iris with wonderful questions about her flower essences.

"How do you know what they are good for?" Tim wondered.

Iris gave him a flat, frustrated look. "I talk to them!"

"Oh…er…you…talk to them, Miss Iris?"

"Yes, don't you hear them when you're workin' with 'em?"

Tim sat up in the saddle contemplating her hurled question. Stroking his beard thoughtfully for a long moment, he finally admitted, "Why, I don't believe I have ever heard a flower speak to me, Miss Iris. What does one sound like?"

"Oh, for heaven's sake, Timothy!" Iris spouted in disbelief. "Here you are, a world authority on plants, and you've never heard one speak to you? What kind of biologist are you?" She leered challengingly at him.

His thick gray-and-black brows flew upward. "Why... Miss Iris... I guess I'm not a good biologist at all, then. How do you talk to them? I'm absolutely mesmerized by your skills."

Iris colored and preened in the saddle. "Well, there is a way to do it."

"Will you teach me? Please? I would give anything to hear a plant speak to me. Why, that would be earth-shaking!"

"You got any Indian blood in you, Professor?" Iris demanded in a severe, assessing tone.

"Er...why, no...no I don't." He gave her a puppy-dog look of surrender. "I'm afraid I'm boringly Irish and English is all. Does that mean I can't talk with a plant?"

Waving her hand, Iris said, "Oh, it's a hurdle to be jumped but anyone can learn to communicate with a plant."

Lively in his saddle and barely able to sit still, Tim said, "That's wonderful news, Miss Iris! What language do they speak? Is it English? Or do they have their own secret language that I must learn?"

"Humph! Professor, if you don't sit quietly in that saddle, you're gonna make Lucky think he wants you to run him. Now, I suggest you sit still for starters."

Chastened, Tim stopped flapping his arms and legs. "Of course, Miss Iris."

She gave him a long, steely look. "And just for your

information, plants do not speak English! How could they?" She patted her heart beneath her coat. "Plants speak from the heart, Professor. That is the only language they know."

Giving her a crestfallen look, Tim stammered, "But what is the language of the heart, Miss Iris?"

Groaning and shaking her head, Iris muttered, "Professor, you're such a greenhorn! You've lived your whole life in the plant world and you don't have a clue about them!"

"But," he rallied, giving her a warm smile, "you will fill in that gap for me, won't you?"

Casey squelched a laugh. Kam gave her a merry look. They weren't hanging far enough back that they couldn't hear the spirited conversation in front of them as the horses clip-clopped along the muddy trail. Turning to her cousin, Casey said, "When does the professor leave?" She knew the dude-ranch programs were five days long.

"Oh, he's signed up for a second week to hang around Grams," Kam said. "He called Harvard and is now on sabbatical. I think he's looking to rent a condo in Jackson Hole so he can stay here to be with her."

Casey nodded. The two elders were having a wonderful, spirited conversation. They were animated, engaged, and their attraction was palpable to anyone who had a pair of eyes in their head. "Well, Iris could let him rent one of the cabins here on the ranch."

Kam smiled. "I think what will happen is, since our wedding is a week away, Iris will invite the professor to stay on. She can easily rent him one of the dude cabins."

Pressing her hand to her heart, Casey said, "Isn't love wonderful?"

Nodding, Kam said, "Yes. A rocky road to get to it," she murmured, remembering her own hurdles and challenges when she'd first come here to the ranch to find her father, Rudd Mason. "Love has a strange way of showing up just when you don't expect it." Motioning to the twosome in front of them, Kam added, "And look at Grams. Her husband, Trevor, died five years ago of a sudden heart attack. She was absolutely lost without him. And when I got here, she could do nothing but bring up his name, and I could see her loneliness."

"Yes, but things have taken a turn," Casey said, gesturing to floppy Tim. "Iris really likes him, don't you think?"

"I've never seen her so animated. Or so happy." Tears came to Kam's eyes for a moment. "Iris truly deserves this. I know my dad is thrilled pink. This takes away some of the grief and guilt he's feeling about his two stepchildren, who have sided with his wife, Allison, who is in jail. The children refuse to come out here or have anything to do with him, yet Rudd has given them everything. Right now, Zach is into drugs. He's hooked on cocaine, according to the police. He's been in and out of jail twice, and to rehab twice. It hasn't done any good. And Reagan…well, I don't know what's going on with her. She's walked away from a rare directing scholarship with a California university to stay here with her mother."

"I heard Reagan is viciously gossiping about you, your dad and Iris."

Mouth turning thin, Kam nodded. "Reagan is spreading all kinds of vile lies about us. She blames all of us for her mother's problems."

Snorting, Casey said, "Allison put out a contract on

you and Iris. If Wes hadn't stopped the hit man in time, you would all be dead. She got what she deserved."

"My father is twisted in knots over it, Casey. I wish… I wish I could take away some of his pain he's feeling."

"You do," Casey whispered, giving her cousin a warm look. "He's found his daughter and I know he's happy that you're in his life."

Kam tried to smile but failed. "I feel the same about him, Casey. I guess they're going to stick with their mother through thick or thin, even if she doesn't deserve their blind loyalty."

"You can't blame them," Casey agreed, "but the gossip they're spreading is awful."

Grimly, Kam said, "Neither of them are up to any good. Zach, who's a geek, is spending all his time at Brick's Game Room. I don't know if you know it or not, but there's a lot of drug traffic in that place. Rudd's worried about Zach. The police have been trying for years to catch Brick's employees dealing drugs, but so far, they haven't been able to. If they could, they would shut that nest of drug dealers down for good."

"Gwen Garner was telling me the other day that Brick's is a bad place, and yet it draws all the teens who are bored and want something to do. And she knows drugs are over there and that a lot of the kids are using meth, cocaine and marijuana."

"Yeah, it's a gaming spot for sure," Kam said, frowning. "And Zach is so naive. He never learned social skills. He was always in his room addicted to his video games. Now he shares an apartment with Reagan, and she doesn't ride herd on him like Iris did when he lived out here."

"Sounds like trouble is brewing for all of you," Casey

murmured. She knew that sooner or later, when Allison's children found out she was in town, gossip would stain her, as well. After all, Kam was her cousin.

Shrugging, Kam uttered, "Reagan used to be an A student and won that scholarship to go to Hollywood, but she threw it all away when Allison was caught and charged with attempted murder. Now she's spiraling down, too. They're angry at Rudd, me and Iris. What an utter waste of their lives."

"I am so sorry," Casey murmured, reaching over and touching Kam's arm. "This is painful for everyone. I wonder if Allison ever considered her actions would hurt so many?"

"Allison can only think of herself," Kam said grimly. "And Reagan is particularly nasty. She's her mother's daughter, believe me. She's intelligent, and she's got a mouth on her and she can cut you into two million pieces in a millisecond."

"What's she doing in town?"

"She works for Jason's Cameras. Certainly not working up to her potential. She had the world on a platter—her film at the Sedona Film Festival took third place. It's sad. Reagan has thrown away a very promising career to support her mother. And, her real father, who is a director in Hollywood, won't have anything to do with her. He's refusing to acknowledge her as his daughter, even though the paternity test shows that she is his legitimate daughter."

"It's a rough time for Reagan, too," Casey agreed. She wondered what she would feel like if her father would not acknowledge her as his daughter. Casey always tried to put herself in other people's situations to try and understand their behavior. This time, it wasn't a pleasant place to be. "Everyone needs a mom and dad."

"Yes," Kam murmured, "and Zach is in the same situation as Reagan. His father is a famous director. But in Zach's case, he seems not to care one way or another. Maybe because he's escaped into computer games and drugs. I found my real dad. It's meant the world to me, Casey. I had this huge hole in my heart." Kam touched her chest. "And finding Rudd and having him acknowledge me as his daughter healed up that wound."

"Gwen has nothing but good things to say about Rudd and Iris."

Smiling, Kam nodded. "Gwen is fair and honest in her appraisal of people. I really like her. She won't pass on gossip for gossip's sake. She demands proof before she'll speak to others. I give her credit because if you want the down and dirty on someone, you go to Quilter's Haven." Laughing, Kam said, "Even the police go to Gwen. That's how much she knows about the underbelly of our cow town."

"Well," Casey muttered, "maybe I need to talk to Gwen, then."

"About someone shooting at you?" Kam wondered.

"Yes, because no one else has a clue. I'm tired of being pigeon-holed in the visitor's center. My supervisor is so afraid that if I walk outside, I'll get shot at. I think it's wrong." Moving the leather reins to her other hand, Casey said, "I just don't have the sense someone is after me, Kam. I hate being cooped up inside."

"Have a talk with Charley," Kam suggested. "Or, better yet, go see Gwen Garner and ask her what to do about the situation. She was born and bred here in Jackson Hole, and her son, Cade, is a deputy sheriff. If anyone knows what to do to get you sprung out of that prison, Gwen will."

That was good advice. Casey decided that this afternoon after the ride was over, she'd drive into town and do just that. Gwen Garner, the gossip maven of Jackson Hole, might shed some light on her predicament. Crossing her fingers, Casey prayed that the woman would have some positive counsel for her.

CHAPTER THIRTEEN

MATT ENJOYED THE GAIETY, laughter and happiness at the Elk Horn Ranch. At 3:00 p.m. in the afternoon, the June sun was warm, the sky a soft blue. All was perfect for Kam and Wes to be married. He sat one row back from the front where the couple stood beneath a bower of flowers that Iris Mason had gathered earlier in the day. Each bouquet of wildflowers had its own plastic container with water so they looked bright and beautiful. Kam looked beautiful in a strapless silk dress with a corset-seamed bodice adorned with Venice lace. The ivory dress had a tulip skirt that came to her knees, and she carried a wildflower bouquet made by Iris, as well as wearing a garland of wildflowers in her black hair. Wes wore a black Stetson and a conservative gray Western-style suit. The bolo tie he wore with the white shirt had the Elk Horn Ranch logo on it. It had been specially made by a jeweler friend of the family and the logo was carved out of turquoise.

Megan sat between Matt and Casey. He watched the members of the huge Trayhern family who had flown in for the occasion. Morgan Trayhern, Kam's adopted father, and her real father, Rudd Mason, led her down the aisle together. Both were smiling. Kam hadn't wanted bridesmaids. Instead, she simply wanted the whole family here to take part in the happiest day of her life. Everyone sat in a semicircle of chairs raised up on six different levels beneath a huge white tent as bride and groom joined hands and faced their smiling minister.

Matt was moved by the Trayhern clan. Morgan and Laura had traveled from Montana, Noah and Kat came from Florida, and Alyssa and Clay flew in from San Francisco to be here.

Kam had been adopted by Morgan and Laura after a terrible earthquake in Los Angeles, California. Kam's journey to find her real father had led her here, to Wyoming.

Smiling over at Casey, who was crying and dabbing her eyes with a handkerchief, Matt felt the powerful love of the entire family. Truth be told, Matt could barely keep his eyes off Casey, who was wearing a tasteful lavender dress with a necklace of amethysts and pink opals around her slender neck. Rarely did he see her in a dress, and this one certainly outlined her sleek, curvy features to perfection. The silk dress had a boatneck, puffed sleeves, and hung to her knees. Casey glanced over at him and smiled. Matt felt his heart swell with such need for her that he wasn't sure he could keep up the charade of not letting her know he desired a closer relationship with her.

Megan smiled as the minister, dressed in a light pink robe, raised her hands. The crowd of onlookers quieted in anticipation. All gazes were on the smiling couple who stood holding hands and looking into one another's eyes.

Casey felt Megan's hand tighten around hers. Anytime they were together, Megan wanted close contact with her. The eight-year-old looked cute in pigtails, a purple dress with white lace down the front of it and

a silver sash around her waist. Matt had gone to great
lengths, with Casey's help, to make sure Megan looked
beautiful. It was Megan's first wedding and Matt wanted
to make it a happy experience for her.

Reverend Ariel Saunders launched into the words
that Kam and Wes had written, and Casey felt thrilled
for her cousin. In the audience were not only Kam's
family of origin, but the entire Trayhern clan, including most of the grown children of each family. Some
couldn't make it because they were in the military and
on overseas assignment. Casey's mother and father,
Alyssa and Clay, sat to her right. Not only was this a
celebratory day for Kam and Wes, but it was a wonderful get-together of the entire Trayhern clan. The only
sad part was that Chase Trayhern, her grandfather, had
broken his leg in a water-skiing accident, and he and his
wife, Rachel, couldn't attend. Casey loved her grand-
parents fiercely because they loved visits from all the
grandchildren.

Casey felt teary-eyed as Reverend Saunders pro-
nounced Kam and Wes husband and wife after the short
dissertation. When Wes drew Kam into his arms and
kissed her, Casey felt her own heart break. Since her
traumatic incident, she'd been afraid of men. Oh, she
knew they weren't all like the five thugs who'd beaten
her up, but the wound had created a rift in her trust.
How Casey wished that wasn't so!

Gulping, she stole a look out of the corner of her
eye at Matt. The happiness mirrored in his face shook
her. What would it be like to be his wife and partner?
Quickly averting her glance, Casey looked at the happy
couple in front of them as they broke their kiss and
smiled tenderly into one another's eyes. Was such hap-

piness possible for her? Casey wasn't sure and sadness enveloped her for a moment. As Wes and Kam Sheridan turned to face the audience, thunderous applause and shouts of joy filled the air. There were cheers and clapping. Kam's two fathers congratulated each other afterward and stood grinning proudly, tears in their eyes.

Ariel, who was five foot eleven inches tall and a rabid basketball player, placed a hand on each of them. She called out, "The bride will now throw her bouquet to all of you ladies! And then it's time for us to eat and celebrate!"

Casey saw about fifteen young single women rush over to the designated area to try and catch the bouquet that Kam would toss.

"Why don't you go over there?" Matt asked, smiling. "You're single."

"Yes, but I don't want to get married just yet," Casey said. Seeing disappointment in his eyes, she felt bad—and a little guilty. "Well," she amended, "I guess I can. She's my cousin and she'd want me over there."

"Good," Matt murmured.

Walking over to the area between the tent where the food preparation was under way and the dance floor where a local band was getting ready to play, Casey felt out of place. The women around her were like excited children as they waited for Kam to arrive and toss her beautiful bouquet of wildflowers that Iris had picked and wrapped in a rainbow of ribbons.

Putting herself at the back of the crowd of jostling women eager to catch the bouquet, Casey felt that she really wanted nothing to do with it all. But she also didn't want to disappoint her cousin, whom she loved like a sister. There was a good six feet between her and the knot of milling and expectant women.

Kam took her place on a small wooden dais while her new husband smiled up at her. Kam's face glowed with happiness as she turned her back to the waiting crowd. With a heave, she threw the bouquet over her head toward the shrieking crowd of single women.

No one was more surprised than Casey when the bouquet seemed to arc as though it had wings and landed in her hands! Gasping, Casey gripped the colorful wildflower bouquet. All the women who had wanted it turned and gave cries of disappointment. Standing there, Casey felt heat rush into her cheeks. She gave the women an apologetic look. If it hadn't been Kam's bouquet, she'd have gladly pawned it off to any one of them. One look into her cousin's joyful expression and Casey forced a smile, held up the bouquet and tried to be graceful about it.

"You're next!" Kam cried, clapping her hands.

The crowd around the group broke into applause.

Casey wanted to sink into the ground. By accident, as her gaze swept across the well-meaning crowd, she caught Matt's gaze. He had a tender look in his expression, a warmth that shook her to her soul and made her heart speed up. What would it be like to be married to him? Casey sensed he'd be a wonderful partner. Someone who would love her for who she was, not what he wanted to mold her into. She came from a family of strong women and her mother had taught all five of her girls from the time they could walk that they had rights equal to everyone, man or woman.

"Thanks, cousin," Casey called, waving the bouquet above her head.

The crowd clapped again and everyone began to break up to go to the food tent.

Instantly, a cowboy band struck up a peppy tune. There was a wooden floor laid out so that everyone who wanted to dance could do so. The air was filled with accordion, violin, harmonica and the angelic voice of a young woman called Crystal Wyatt. Casey stood, bouquet in hand, and watched the nineteen-year-old sensation sing.

Matt and Megan approached her. Casey leaned down and gave Megan the bouquet. The little girl's eyes grew huge as she accepted the gift.

"Everyone should get flowers," she told Megan, smiling at her.

Megan crushed the bouquet to her chest, her eyes shining with joy.

Matt smiled at Casey as she straightened. "Thank you," he mouthed without saying the words.

Nodding, Casey was more than happy to give Megan the bouquet. It would stop people from teasing her about being next to get married. "Let's eat. I'm starved," she told them. Anything to avoid the topic of marriage!

Everyone was ushered toward the white tents decorated with pink, green and white ribbons. Everything was catered from Mo's Café, with the owner personally serving the happy affair. She had hired several other people and was moving from one table to another making sure everything was ready for the partying crowd of over two hundred guests. Casey liked energetic and tireless Matty. Her husband had died of cancer at age twenty-five, leaving her with a growing restaurant business and a small daughter, Jody. Casey saw Jody smiling and following her black-haired mother around, an ice cream scoop in hand. No one worked harder than Matty, and Casey loved going to eat at her restaurant.

Matt smiled over at her. "You've got quite a family. I didn't realize how large it was."

Casey grinned. "Yes, we're a clan. My mom and dad like you."

Nodding, he said, "I like them. They're heroic—your mother broke through the men-only glass ceiling to fly that sub-hunting airplane. And your father supported her."

"Well, after a fashion." Casey laughed. She got in line and handed Megan a plate. "My father wasn't exactly happy about having her in the cockpit at first."

"Yes, but your mother has red hair," Matt pointed out. "Red-haired women are valkyries. Cat Edwin has red hair. She's breaking down the barriers in that all-male fire department," he said, picking up his plate.

"Yes, and, like my mother, Cat's paying a price for hanging in there and showing the men she's just as good—if not better—than they are at firefighting."

Frowning, Matt had to agree. "There's a couple of guys in there that are still clinging to the men-only mentality. The rest of them, though, completely support Cat."

As they approached the trays filled with tantalizing choices of food, Casey picked up her flatware and got ready to choose from the many delicious items that Matty had created. "It's hard on her, though, Matt. Isn't it enough that she can do a credible job? Why can't those guys get over their prejudice?"

"I hear you," Matt murmured. He picked Megan up so that she could see the food in each tray. "And I agree."

"Nothing in life is fair," Casey said. She saw Megan point to a tray of chicken enchiladas and scooped one up and put it on the plate Matt held.

Matt had to agree with Casey. After they went through the line, they were asked to sit beneath another huge, airy tent where tables and chairs were awaiting them. They found a table near the wedding party, who sat at a long, long table in front of everyone. Matt remembered his own wedding to Bev, how stressful and yet how much fun it had been. This brought back a lot of bittersweet memories. As he got Megan in her chair and put the plate of food before her, Matt couldn't shake the past as much as he wanted to.

After the meal, the toasts and speeches were given. Then, all the children moved to another tent that was filled with all kinds of fun things for them to do. Matt walked at Casey's side as they headed toward the dance floor. "Want to dance?" he asked her.

"I'm not the greatest," Casey protested. What would it be like to have Matt hold her? She'd ached in her dreams to have his strong arms around her. And Casey wasn't about to tell him of her dreams of him kissing her until they melted into one another.

Matt smiled and led her onto the crowded dance floor. Crystal was singing a slow song, her voice strong and clear over the huge crowd. He slid his hand around Casey's back, palm resting lightly against it. Watching her expression, he saw she really wanted him near her. That made his wary heart take off in a heavy beat. As their hands met and entwined, Matt made sure he gave her ample opportunity to either draw away or draw near to him.

Her skin tingled as Matt's hand hovered over the

small of her back. Casey looked up and drowned in the warmth of his forest green eyes. For a moment, all the noise, the music, the laughter, dissolved as she drowned in his huge black pupils surrounded by that dark green color. Shaken, Casey pulled back inwardly, her pulse racing maddeningly whether she wanted it to or not. How long had she dreamed of this moment, unsure it would ever happen? Mouth dry, she pulled her gaze from Matt's relaxed and darkly tanned face. Wanting to move those scant inches and lay her head on his chest, Casey didn't dare. This was enough for now. Since her trauma she'd avoided personal interaction with men, frightened by the emotional wounds that the beating had created. Casey felt safer with Matt than she had with anyone since then. It was a positive step for her, although Casey couldn't share that with him. What would he think of her? Would he tell her she was imagining things? That he would never lift a hand to hurt her? That he was to be trusted?

Matt saw a lot of unspoken emotions in Casey's shadowed eyes. She was stiff and tense in his arms. Was it him? Or her? Was she doing this only because she had to in front of her family? Was it all just a show for their benefit? Or did she really want to dance with him? They glided around the floor without stepping on one another's feet. Matt felt her beginning to relax a little as he guided her expertly between the many other laughing, chatting couples.

"Crystal's got an incredible voice," he said, hoping to make Casey feel at ease.

Glancing toward the blonde, blue-eyed singer who wore a tasteful blue dress that fell to her knees, Casey agreed. "I heard Gwen Garner say she had the voice of an angel. She's right, she does." ⎯ ⎯

Matt wanted to move Casey to a topic that was safe for her. Already he could see some of the fear beginning to recede in her eyes. Okay, if it took social talk to put Casey at ease, he'd do that. Above all, Matt cared for this woman in his arms.

"Crystal had a tough start in life," he confided to her in a low voice. This wasn't something he wanted spread around, even though he suspected nearly everyone knew about the singer's past. "Something happened in her family and she was put into three years of juvenile detention. The court records are sealed, and I feel Crystal's trying to get a new start in life on the right track."

"Oh?" Casey was relieved that the talk wasn't about her. "I haven't heard anything about Crystal."

Giving her a wry smile, Matt said, "You haven't lived here long enough. In time, you'll know about the good, the bad and the ugly of our town."

Nodding, Casey said, "Well, as long as she didn't kill someone, I hope she makes it as a singer. I know Gwen said Crystal had dreams of breaking into the music industry and making it big. She's talked of going to the *American Idol* tryouts next year."

"She's got the looks, the voice and the timing's right for her," Matt agreed.

"Don't you think we all have some kind of past that can haunt us, Matt?"

Startled by her serious question, he locked gazes with her. "No one is perfect, Casey. And we all have baggage of one sort or another to carry." He squeezed her hand for a moment, as if to reassure her because he sensed deep emotion behind the question. "The town's people, or most of them, at least in Crystal's case, have treated her well despite her unknown past and being in juvie hall for three years. There's been a lot of nasty gossip about her and why she was put in juvie hall. She's not talking about it, either."

"It's none of anyone's business," Casey muttered. She felt sorry for the beautiful Crystal with the angelic voice.

Matt heard deep pain in Casey's comment. He wanted to protect Casey and give her a calm bay from the storm she'd endured. And it seemed to him that the past was following her around like a good friend. Of course, he told himself, if he'd nearly been beaten to death, gone into a coma and then woken up afterward, he might see the world a lot differently, too. Casey struggled with her past. Matt saw it in her eyes and in her voice every time they were together. He wished he could give her solace. An ache built in him and without thinking, as they danced in one another's arms, he leaned down and kissed her.

Casey had seen the kiss coming. A part of her wanted to tear out of his arms, but the larger part of her heart wanted Matt's kiss. Suddenly, she didn't care if the whole world saw them kissing. Certainly, there were many couples on the dance floor. A wedding always brought out romance and love in everyone. When his mouth met hers, she felt her entire world anchor to a halt. Even though they were still dancing, their feet moving in tune with the slow music, Casey was no longer aware.

Matt's mouth slid across her parting lips. She tasted the cherry pie on them, felt his power as a man monitoring his strength as he met her awaiting lips. There was nothing shy about his mouth as he slid it provocatively against hers. His breath was warm and moist against her cheek as she closed her eyes and sank fully into his embrace. For once, Casey trusted a man—fully and without reserve. He held her gently, as if she were some fragile, rare being that would shatter should he allow his masculine power to overwhelm her.

Matt felt Casey's soft mouth open and allow him to kiss her fully. She tasted sweet, her hair fragrant with the scent of pine, her flesh soft and satiny against his skin. At first he was shocked over the unexpected and spontaneous kiss. As soon as Casey stepped forward and moved more deeply into his embrace, her breasts brushing his chest, Matt knew. He knew that this was the right thing to do. How long had he wanted to help Casey? To support her as she wrestled through the darkness of her past? And now, as he met her lips, tasted her and absorbed her like the starving thief he was, Matt felt their worlds collide and change in that split second.

The music slowly ended. Crystal's voice whispered away with it. Matt tore his mouth from Casey's and opened his eyes. He clung to her tender gray gaze. He read so much in Casey's widening eyes. There was need there. Real hunger. That shocked Matt. Casey had never given him any signal about that. They stood there in one another's arms, both stunned by the unexpected kiss.

"Casey… I'm sorry… I don't know what happened," Matt began, apology in his tone. Would she get angry? Walk out on him? Matt now began to have fears that squashed the euphoria soaring through him.

Opening her mouth and then closing it, Casey whispered, "I—I didn't expect it…" But she had partaken of it like a woman starving for life instead of stasis.

Her brows fell and she pulled out of Matt's arms, more than a little aware of the curious gazes in their direction. Casey felt his strong, callused hands resting gently around her upper arms. It was as if he knew she'd take flight. Would she? Casey did want to run. But she couldn't. Her mom and dad were here. The whole Trayhern clan would expect her to remain for all the after-wedding festivities.

Gulping, Casey stammered, "Matt, I'm afraid."

Giving her a tender look of understanding, he rasped, "If it makes you feel better, so am I, Casey." His hands fell from her arms. "Let's just take this a day at a time. Okay? I promise, I won't do it again unless you ask me first." He gazed deeply into her glistening eyes that spoke eloquently of her desire and fear. It occurred to Matt for the first time that Casey might be afraid of all men because of her trauma. That thought struck him like a lightning bolt. Now it all made sense! Staggered by his stupid inability to understand what was fueling Casey's detachment, Matt added, "First of all, I want you as a friend. Friendship is the basis for any relationship. The ball is in your court, Casey. You just tell me what you want, what you feel comfortable with. All right?"

His rasping words were like his work-worn fingers lightly grazing her flesh. Did Matt realize the power and sway he had over her? Casey wasn't sure, but his words of understanding made her heart swell with a new emotion: hope. "Yes, that's fine. That's what I need, Matt."

Giving her a slight, one-cornered smile, he asked, "How about a glass of wine?"

Casey wanted to say she'd like something stronger,

but she knew alcohol didn't solve a thing. "Right now, I think some iced tea is about all I can handle."

Cupping her elbow, Matt led her off the dance floor. He saw her father, Clay Cantrell, watching them. Not seeing censure in her father's face, Matt exhaled. What he didn't want was Casey's parents to be upset with what had unexpectedly happened. Matt wouldn't be able to explain it away. Clay barely tipped his head. Relief poured through Matt as he acknowledged the airline pilot's barely discernible nod. Above all, Matt knew they wanted only the best for their daughter and maybe Clay Cantrell had just given him a thumbs-up to his courting of Casey.

As they walked to the refreshment line to get iced tea, Matt stood behind Casey. He kept plenty of room between them. Off in the distance, he kept an eye on Megan who was happily playing with a bunch of other children in the tent that had hundreds of colorful balls that they could jump into. Returning his attention to Casey, he found her, once more, withdrawn.

How badly Matt wanted to pull Casey aside, take her for a walk and simply talk to find out what was going on inside that head of hers. His mouth tingled wildly in memory of her soft, returning kiss. Matt ached to make a deeper connection with her. This kiss had shown him that he was more ready than he'd originally thought to leave the past behind and start living in the present once more. The bigger question was Casey. When she'd caught the bouquet, she'd looked shocked by it. Matt felt that if she could have thrown it to someone else, she would have. The situation kept Casey from doing anything except sheepishly accepting the bouquet—the last thing she wanted to do.

In a quandary, Matt felt a volcano of giddy, unfettered feelings loosen within him. It was as if something had startled a herd of mustangs and they'd scattered in ten different directions. He couldn't get the kiss out of his heart or mind. He didn't want to. Just looking at Casey's profile, Matt swore he could feel what she was thinking—that this was the last place she wanted to be right now. That his kiss had broken through an unspoken wall she had erected against the world. The real question was: what was Casey going to do now?

CHAPTER FOURTEEN

"DAMMIT, BENSON, I want action!" Carter whispered harshly into the throwaway cell phone. He stood looking out the huge picture window at the craggy Tetons that rose up out of the plain. "It's July! You keep telling me you're still strategizing, but I want this job wrapped up *now!*" His nostrils flared and he began to stalk back and forth, glaring out the window at the July Fourth weather. It was a perfect holiday with a deep turquoise sky, long strands of cirrus high above that reminded Peyton of a horse's mane flying as he galloped along.

For a moment, Peyton hesitated, glancing toward the open door of his office in his home. Everyone was gone. The maid was out shopping. Usually he didn't make such calls from his home simply because it was too dangerous. This time, he was running late. He wanted to squeeze in the call to the sniper and arsonist before he had to go to the town square and give a rousing patriotic and political speech about freedom in this country.

CLARISSA HURRIED INTO the house. When she closed the door, she heard her husband shouting. Startled, she hurried toward his office. She'd come home early from a luncheon with her best friends at the posh Aspens restaurant. What was Carter yelling about? She rarely heard him lose his temper.

Halting just outside the door where she couldn't be seen, Clarissa heard him.

"Benson, I paid for this contract, dammit. Now I want it done! Do you hear me? Time's up! You hear me? Get rid of Sinclaire!"

Gulping, Clarissa automatically placed her hand on her long throat. Her brows dipped. Get rid of Sinclaire? The Sinclaire family of Jackson Hole? Her mind spun with questions. She heard her husband snap the cell phone shut. Whirling around, Clarissa hurried silently down the pine hall.

Once in the kitchen, Clarissa made sure she opened and shut the door loudly so that Carter would hear it. Dressed in a white sundress with pink, yellow and white daisies splashed across it, Clarissa called out, "Carter? I'm home!" Her husky voice carried strongly down the hall. She waited and then she heard her husband's footsteps coming her way. Gulping, she grabbed her white leather purse and rushed to meet him.

"Hi, doll," Carter murmured, kissing his wife's cheek.

"I just got home," Clarissa said breathlessly, giving him the customary peck on his cheek. "Are you about ready to leave? I thought you had an appointment at the town square?" She looked at the gold Rolex watch on her thin wrist. "You're late, Carter."

His mouth turned down and he walked into their master bedroom. "I know, I know. Seems like every-thing is jammed up today," he muttered, grabbing the dark brown suit coat that went with the trousers he wore. Picking up a red-white-and-blue tie, he quickly wrapped it around his neck.

Clarissa stood in the doorway. Her husband's normally genial face was tense and she saw anger lurking in his dark brown eyes. *Washington?* she wondered. Her mind focused on part of the phone call she'd heard. Was there a Sinclaire in the senate? No. Maybe a congressman or woman? No. Surely, he couldn't have meant the Sinclaires of Wyoming. She knew Matt was a firefighter and that his family owned a ranch outside of Jackson Hole.

Carter drew a deep inner breath. Thank God Clarissa hadn't heard his phone call. That had been close! Trying to stop his hands from trembling as he shifted the tie into place around his neck, he managed a grimace. "You'd think on the day of our country's birthday that everyone inside the Beltway back in D.C. would be on their best behavior."

"Mmm," Clarissa said, trying to sound sympathetic. She wondered about the cell phone he'd used. Something bothered her about his angry, shouting words about Sinclaire. Knowing Carter was hurrying around, Clarissa decided that after he left, she'd search his office for the cell. It would have the phone number of whom he called. That way, she would be assured that his angry words were probably just letting off steam about a D.C. colleague. "Bob is downstairs with our limo."

"I know, I know," Carter rasped, grabbing his suit coat and rushing out of the room.

"You have your speech?" she wondered.

"Yes…yes." He'd nearly forgotten it! Angry at himself for being scattered, Carter ran back into his office and scooped up the papers. "I'll be back in an hour." He gave her a tight, stressed smile. "Gotta go press the flesh…"

"I'm glad it's you and not me," Clarissa sang out as

he moved into the kitchen, jerked open the door that led to the underground garage and disappeared.

Clarissa waited for a moment, then changed into a pair of fashionable pale pink slacks and a colorful Hawaiian silk blouse. Going to the master bathroom, she made sure her coifed hair was in place. In the walk-in closet, she chose a pair of pink leather sandals and opened her huge hundred-drawer wall jewelry chest. Clarissa loved jewelry and she moved to the pink section and chose a strand of tasteful freshwater pearls that had faceted pink tourmaline spacers between them.

Feeling properly dressed, Clarissa clicked down the pine hall to her husband's office. The sunlight spilled brightly into the large rectangular room. Spotting the cell phone on his desk, she went over and picked it up. Frowning, she realized this wasn't the cell he carried on him all the time. *That's odd.* Turning it over, Clarissa flipped it open. Recognizing this was a cheap throw-away phone, Clarissa grimaced. What on earth was Carter doing with this cheap, shoddy-looking thing?

Punching a few keys, she saw the phone number he'd just called. She was familiar with all the important numbers he used. This wasn't one of them. And when she scrolled through the rest of the phone's addresses, there were none. Just this one number. She was stymied; this didn't make sense to her. Writing down the number, Clarissa turned off the cell and flipped the case down. She placed it on the desk where she'd found it.

Part of her job was to keep Carter's list of donors and this might be a new one. If so, the person needed to be added to the database. That, she could do. But what was his or her name? Carter was always good about giving her the info on a donor. His political life depended upon these people.

Something didn't feel right to Clarissa. Tucking the piece of paper into her pocket, she turned her attention to the barbecue party they would be giving for their supporters at 5:00 p.m. today on their large, beautiful patio. Her chef, Sadie Parker, would be arriving at any moment now. Maria, the maid, would be coming back with all the food that Sadie had asked her to buy for tonight's celebration. Forgetting about the incident, Clarissa hurried down the hall toward the kitchen. There was plenty to do. An army of trucks and men from Cheyenne would be arriving to set up the fifty chairs and tables and umbrellas. The circular flagstone patio in the backyard would be turned into a red-white-and-blue extravaganza that Clarissa had planned with this company months earlier. Now, under her direction, the huge backyard that looked upon the grandeur of the mighty Tetons would be the perfect backdrop for the monied guests who were Carter's top donors.

Still, as she walked out the back door to the patio, Clarissa couldn't shake the name *Sinclaire*. Who in D.C. had Carter been yelling at? Was something going on that she didn't know about? A slight, warm breeze moved strands of her hair across her brow and Clarissa pushed them back into place. Usually she knew Carter's enemies and friends. She'd become the bulwark of his new senate campaign. Something cautioned her not to talk to Carter about this incident right now. She decided to set the incident aside. She wanted her husband to focus on getting these fifty donors to fork over more cash for his war chest. That was the focus. No money, no senate seat.

MEGAN RAN DOWN THE GRASSY knoll after the red ball that Matt had thrown to her. She'd missed it and it had bounced on the slope. Casey stood at the top with Matt's father, Lou. They had driven to Cheyenne to the family Bar V Ranch where Matt had his roots. His father was a strapping man—six foot three inches of towering strength and hard muscle. At fifty years old, Lou Sinclaire looked like the proverbial cowboy from the Old West. He wore a black Stetson and a white cotton shirt with the sleeves rolled up to the elbows that showed off his lean, hard forearms and hands. Casey saw a lot of scars on his hands and knew they were from his ranching life.

"Megan's just so purty," Lou drawled. "Val, my wife, always said she'd grow up to be a beauty. She was right," he said, draping his hands over his narrow hips.

Casey smiled faintly. Lou Sinclaire was a mountain of a man, lean and carved out of the elements of the tough Wyoming landscape. "She's getting more and more vocal. Matt's hoping that one day soon, she'll start talking again," Casey confided to him. She watched daughter and father running down the slope after the escaping red ball. Their laughter was infectious as Matt allowed Megan to beat him to the ball as it rolled to a stop at the bottom of the hill.

Grunting, Lou muttered, "Yeah, I certainly hope so. This has been hard on my son. He lost Bev and then his child goes mute." Shaking his head, his green eyes narrowed, he added, "Just ain't right. Matt's suffered enough."

Silently, Casey agreed. This was the first time she'd met Matt's father. The Bar V was a sprawling three-hundred-acre ranch outside the capital of Wyoming. Lou ran five thousand head of cattle. He had seven wranglers who worked under him. Matt was the spitting image of him. Both men were terribly handsome in a raw, natural way. Both were practical and common-sensed about everything in life.

Megan stood out like a bright butterfly in comparison to the two hardened men of the West. Casey looked over her shoulder. The two-story family home was made out of logs and was over a hundred years old. There were several large pipe corrals that held horses and cattle. Megan's favorite corral, a much smaller one, held the family pet llama called Gus. Lou had bought him as a baby two years ago, shortly after Megan had gone mute after losing her mother. He had hoped the baby llama would somehow ease Megan's pain and help her.

Gus was a white llama from Peru and he had turned into quite an affectionate character. He loved Megan and that was clear when she'd run to the corral after they'd arrived yesterday. The love affair between little girl and big, white Gus cheered everyone. Gus would follow her around like a lovesick puppy.

Casey gave Lou a warm look. As hard as this man with the square jaw looked, he had a soft heart just like his son. She saw the pain etched in Lou's face, his mouth thinned to hold back a lot of grief. Five years earlier, his wife Val had died of breast cancer. Three years after that, Matt had lost Bev.

"I'm going to lend you a hand with the barbecue, Lou."

"Mighty fine of you, Casey. You're a hard-workin' young lady."

"It's my nature to work," she said, laughing. Walking back toward the family homestead, the whinny of horses, the lowing of cattle made her feel happy. Since that life-affirming kiss at the wedding, Casey wasn't sure about much of anything. Matt's kiss had been warm, loving and caring. She'd not only tasted his mouth on her, but felt how much he cared for her as a person.

Casey joined Andy, the sixty-year-old camp cook, who was busy barbecuing the chicken and steaks. Ever since that kiss, it seemed to Casey she and Matt had had no time to sit and talk about what had happened. Matt's schedule was crazy because one of the firefighters had been injured. And then there were planned vacations. He had been working nonstop until yesterday. For the next three days, he had a break in his hectic schedule. Matt had wanted her to meet his father and see their family ranch. Casey had agreed with some reluctance. Luckily, their schedules meshed and she could get the time off. All she wanted was some time alone with Matt.

"COME ON," MATT COAXED, taking Casey's hand and leading her around the house. They'd just finished their Fourth of July meal near 4:00 p.m. Lou had taken Megan over to talk to Gus. Other friends who had come were happy discussing politics, the weather and cattle-breeding over cold beers on the patio. He smiled and led her around the corner of the log home.

Casey laughed and followed him. This was the first time Matt had touched her since their kiss that had rocked her world. She squeezed Matt's hand in return because she could see questions in his eyes as to whether his advance was welcomed. His green eyes glistened with tenderness toward her. Heart pounding over that silent look, Casey followed him across the wide yard to the bright red two-story barn with a steeply sloped tin roof.

"When I was a kid, I had a hideaway in the hayloft up there," Matt said, pointing to the large, flat area that was piled high with bales of alfalfa hay.

"Is that where we're going?" she ask breathlessly. Once they were in the shade and coolness of the barn, Matt released her hand.

"Yes. My old haunt. Don't you want to know what I did as a kid?"

Casey nodded. "I always envisioned you as a hard-working kid helping your father with cranky tractors and trucks."

Chuckling, Matt halted at the wide wooden ladder that led up to the loft. "Oh, I did that, too." He stepped aside. "Do heights bother you?"

Shaking her head, Casey said, "No." She climbed up to the sweet fragrance of the baled alfalfa on the platform. Standing aside she watched Matt quickly climb the ladder.

"What do you think?" he asked, gesturing around after joining her. "Is this a great kid's hideaway or what?"

Nodding, Casey said, "And is this where you escaped to when you were tired of working?"

Matt sauntered over to a couple of bales of hay and sat down. He patted the one next to him. "I got to come up here *after* my work was done." He laughed. "Come on, sit down with me."

Heart pounding, Casey knew what was coming. She sat and left a good amount of space between them. Resting her elbows on her jeans-clad thighs, her hands clasped between her legs, she held Matt's gaze. "A lot has happened to us," she murmured. Matt assumed the same position she had taken and became serious.

"Yes, and I'm sorry we haven't had time to just sit and talk, Casey." He compressed his lips for a moment and then said, "You have to know I did want to kiss you. I like you a lot and I'd been wanting to somehow deepen our relationship." He gave her an apologetic look. "I was afraid of being rejected. Maybe some part of me decided to risk it all that day?"

Casey felt him trying to understand how she felt. "Well," she said, "I haven't exactly been forthcoming, either, Matt." Straightening, she said in a low tone, "Ever since I nearly got beaten to death, I've been afraid of men. I know it's crazy-sounding. Not you." Her brows fell as she considered her next words. "I— just can't find it in me to trust any man. At least," she murmured, "not yet."

Nodding, Matt saw the frustration and pain in her gaze. "I thought that might be it…"

Wanting to reach out and grip his arm, Casey couldn't do it. "Your kiss was wonderful, Matt. And truth be known, I'd been wanting to kiss you for a long time, too." She gave him a hopeful look and he brightened considerably. More than anything, Casey saw relief in his expression. "You didn't do anything wrong. It's just that…well… I'm in a tug of war with myself. I want to have a deeper relationship with you. Every time I think that, I get scared."

"Look," he whispered, "I know what trauma does to people who have terrible auto accidents or their home burns down. I figured you were in that same place."

Giving a bitter laugh, Casey said, "Yes, it's called post-traumatic stress disorder. My doctor diagnosed me with PTSD. It makes me afraid, Matt. Up here, my head screams that all men can hurt me at any time they want." She pressed her hand to her heart. "But here, I know the difference. My heart tells me not all men are out to hurt me again." Her mouth curled. "But I cannot, for the life of me, get my head to stop that litany and listen to my heart. I'm so frustrated, Matt. You have no idea…"

"Look at my daughter," Matt whispered, understanding all too well. "She has PTSD. It stole her voice…" Matt felt pain move through his chest over that admission. "I wish… I wish I could do something to help her heal. But nothing has worked so far."

Casey felt his despair and grief. "And here I am. I'm no different than Megan. The only difference between us is I didn't lose my voice. But I lost other things."

"I feel like we're at a stalemate, Casey. Not only with my daughter, but with you."

"Don't give up on either of us," she counseled. "Healing takes time. More time than I ever realized. Megan is making progress. Even you can see that." Casey knew the desperation and guilt Matt felt over his daughter's condition. She saw positive changes in Megan but maybe he didn't.

With a sigh, Matt looked at her and gave her a pained smile. "Maybe you're right. Any more, I don't know."

"Life's burdens aren't fun," she agreed quietly. Aching to reach out and simply hold Matt, because that was what he needed, nearly drove Casey to do just that. Would he misinterpret her actions? That was what Casey was afraid of, so she quelled her reaction and sat there staring down at her clasped hands.

"What about us?" he asked finally.

Shrugging, Casey said, "I don't know, Matt. When

I get up in the morning, I may feel one way. But something happens during my day, and it's destroyed. I move from fear to anger and back to fear in minutes. I'm not good company most of the time. Oh, I can put on a face and be pleasant with tourists and all, but I have to let down. I have to be myself and be honest with how I'm feeling at a given time."

"Have you seen Dr. Jordana Lawton yet?" he asked, hope in his voice.

"Not yet," Casey admitted. "I talked to my doctor back in Colorado about it and he pooh-poohed a cure for PTSD. He said it was just a gimmick, that there was nothing to lower cortisol levels in someone who had PTSD."

"Doctors don't know everything," Matt growled.

"I'm going to see Dr. Lawton," Casey murmured, agreeing with him. "I've heard so much good about her. The other day I was talking to Charley about her. He said she was someone to be trusted. He told me about one of his rangers. He said the ranger went to Jordana, got tested and treated. Now, he doesn't have his PTSD symptoms. That's pretty strong validation that Jordana knows something that might help me."

Whistling, Matt said, "Yes, it is." He sat up and rubbed his hands on his upper legs, the denim material outlining his strong, muscular thighs. "That's good to hear. Charley's to be trusted. I'm crossing my fingers that something can be done to help Megan." He frowned and his voice lowered with feeling. "I'd give anything to hear Megan talk again. I really would. I don't care if other physicians think this cortisol testing and treatment is gimmicky."

Casey stood up. "Based on what Charley told me, I'd

already made a decision to see her, Matt." She looked down and gave him a tender look. "I want my life back. I don't want to keep living like this—swinging back and forth between fear and anger. I'm tired of feeling threatened by stupid things all the time. Before this, I loved life. I loved living. Now, I feel like I've been smashed into a little box and life sucks."

Matt stood and walked to the ladder. "I hear you."

Casey wanted to reach up, embrace Matt and kiss him. The need was so strong that she took a step away from him. It wasn't fair to Matt or herself to be on this crazy emotional roller coaster. "I'm holding out hope against hope that Jordana can perform a miracle for me. I'll be seeing her next week."

"Good, and I'll keep you updated on what she finds about Megan's cortisol levels," Matt whispered. He forced himself not to graze her pink cheek. "I'm there for you, Casey. I like what we have. Let's keep on being friends?"

Nodding, Casey climbed down the ladder. Friendship was better than nothing, but then, Casey wanted Matt far beyond that point. Her torrid dreams at night confirmed that as nothing else could. Could Jordana really give her back her life?

CHAPTER FIFTEEN

"MATT?" CASEY FOUND HIM sitting with his turnout gear in the bay where the fire trucks were kept. The huge garage doors were open to allow a breeze to circulate in the mid-August heat wave being experienced by the valley.

Matt's head snapped up, and his eyes widened appreciably as Casey walked around the red-and-white fire truck to where he was sitting on the rear bumper. He was cleaning the visor on his helmet. "Hey," he greeted, smiling as he stood up, "this is a surprise." Indeed, it was. After their heart-to-heart talk up in the hayloft, Casey had seemed less tense and on guard toward him. Today, she looked beautiful in her jeans, a dark green T-shirt and her USFS baseball cap. The gleam in her eyes made him curious. She looked like bubbly champagne about to spill over. Going to the wall where the turnout gear was hung, he settled his hardened plastic helmet on a hook.

"I've got some good news I couldn't wait to share with you," she murmured, looking around the quiet, cavernous bay. "Is it okay to be here with you? I know you're on duty for the next eight hours."

"Sure," he said. "Want a fresh cup of coffee? I just made some in our kitchen."

"I won't be underfoot?" Casey wondered. How handsome and virile Matt looked in his dark blue T-shirt with the fire department's symbol emblazoned in white across it. The dark blue serge trousers he wore and his black leather shoes all conspired to make him look like a modern-day hero in her eyes. And wasn't he? Just last week Matt had saved a baby from being burned to death in a house fire. The mother, who had been sleeping downstairs, awoke to thick smoke throughout her small house. Her baby daughter was upstairs and she couldn't reach her. At Matt's direction, his team put up a ladder. He climbed up, broke the window and climbed into the baby's room. Casey would never figure out how Matt had found the infant before it died of smoke inhalation. She'd heard from others over at Quilter's Haven that the smoke was so thick a person couldn't see their hand in front of their face. Her heart swelled with growing love for him.

"The guys are all napping up on the second floor," he assured her, opening the door to the kitchen.

Nodding, Casey passed him and moved into the brightly lit, large kitchen where there was a rectangular table with six chairs. It looked like a normal kitchen one would find in an upscale home. "I smell something cooking," she murmured.

"Yeah," he chuckled, bringing down two white mugs from the cabinet. "Today's my turn to cook for the crew. I'm making chicken enchiladas."

Sitting down at the table, Casey thanked him as he brought over her coffee and sat next to her. Opening her tan leather purse, she pulled out a bunch of papers and spread them before him. "Pay dirt, Matt. Look at this." She tapped them with her index finger.

Glancing at them, he said, "Hey…these are your cortisol results from Dr. Jordana."

"They are." She gave him a tentative smile. "I just came from her office." Casey pulled a bottle from her purse and sat it in front of him. "The doc confirmed my cortisol is high. And she's prescribed an adaptogen to plug the hormone's receptors so my cortisol will drop back into normal function. Just like Megan's has."

Matt studied the results. He knew that in the past month, since Megan had been on the same prescription, his daughter's behavior had shown amazing and positive changes. "Same medicine," he murmured, looking at the bottle. "But you're taking it at different times than when Megan took hers."

Nodding, Casey said, "Dr. J said she'd rarely seen cortisol results that were this far out of normal limits."

Setting the papers down, Matt held Casey's sparkling gaze. There was hope in her eyes. "It goes to show how traumatic the beating was for you," he murmured. Wanting to touch her hand that curved around the mug, Matt fought himself. He allowed his gaze to drop fleetingly to her smiling mouth. He'd dreamed about that tender, gentle kiss they'd shared nearly every night since then.

"No one really knows the effects of trauma except the person who has suffered it," Casey quietly agreed. Tapping the bottle, she said, "I take the medication when my cortisol has peaked outside its normal limits. That means I'm taking it at noon, three in the afternoon and at bedtime. I can hardly wait to see if I can finally sleep without waking up two or three times a night."

"Megan's sleep has changed completely," Matt told her. "Not only is she sleeping soundly through the night, there are no more nightmares." He rolled his eyes. "I can't tell you how many nights I'd hear her scream and it would jolt me out of a deep sleep. The only time she'd go back to sleep was if I was in her room, sitting in the rocking chair near her bed."

"She wanted to be reassured that she'd be safe," Casey murmured. "I know that one. I never slept with a night-light on until… Now I refuse to go in any room that's dark. It scares me." She tapped her head and gave him a silly smile. "I know there's nothing in the room, but emotionally, my feelings haven't grown into my logic."

"Don't be hard on yourself," Matt said. Casey tended to be that way, always unhappy that her mind couldn't just heal up her wounded emotions. He understood that trauma stained her emotions and, until they healed, she would always be wary.

"I have such hope," Casey told him. "I see how much Megan has changed since taking that medication for thirty days. It's a miracle, Matt." She saw him nod but also saw the sadness deep in his eyes. "I know she's still not talking, but she's so much more engaged with life, with school and her friends. She has enthusiasm now."

"Yes," he said, sipping his coffee and looking out the window. Summer was the most wonderful time of year in Jackson Hole, but way too short for him. The Wyoming town spent eight months of the year with snow on the ground. The green leaves shining and dancing on the cottonwood trees now made him feel happy. Turning his attention to Casey, he offered, "Megan is continuing to change. Dr. Jordana tested her a second time and we're waiting for the results. She said it usually only takes one thirty-day prescription to get most people's cortisol back to normal."

Casey smiled and sat back in the chair. Matt was eye candy. She always looked forward to the times when she could share time and space with him. "Dr. J said I might have to take this stuff for one or two months in order to bring my cortisol down. She said the worse the PTSD, the more time it takes to normalize it."

Nodding, Matt said, "It makes sense. I wondered how it made Megan feel, but she doesn't talk, so I don't know what else she felt from taking the medicine. Maybe you can share?" He grinned. Casey's cheeks were pink, her eyes sparkling. Without the baseball cap on, her straight, shoulder-length hair was a frame bringing out all her lovely features.

"You'll be the first to know," Casey promised. She had talked to Dr. J about her sex life, which was nil. That was all part of the PTSD. And Casey had finally confessed in tears about being unable to trust men. Dr. J had patted her gently on the shoulder and told her it was all part of the trauma and high cortisol levels. How could she trust anyone when her levels were so high? Her traumatized mind and body saw everything as a threat. It made sense to Casey but she ached to cross that threshold of distrust and connect emotionally with Matt.

"I like the necklace you're wearing," Matt said. "Is that new?" It was a single strand of lavender and green gemstones in a choker style that emphasized her slender neck.

"Oh." Casey laughed a little. "Well, you know Lannie Wilson? She's the jewelry designer who has a little shop on the main plaza in town?"

Nodding, Matt said, "Yes, I know her. She's a struggling jewelry artist making a name for herself." He didn't go into Lannie's background: Her father was in prison and her mother had died when Lannie was only two years old. Hank Wilson was a mean son of a bitch of a drunk. When Lannie had been taken to the hospital with a broken leg at age five, the doctor on the case had said it was abuse. Lannie's relatives in Cheyenne had refused to take her on, so she'd ended up in a number of foster homes here in Jackson Hole. Lannie had turned angry and rebellious. She'd gotten into a lot of trouble off and on as a teen. And then her lifestyle had caught up with her and, at fifteen, Lannie had nearly died. Matt had watched the young woman's life play out across the fabric of the town. Though there were people who hated her, Lannie had her supporters, too. Only her creativity and love of making jewelry had saved her from a life on addictive drugs.

Touching the necklace, Casey said, "Ever since I came here, I've gone over to Jewels of Terra and drooled over Lannie's creations. They're expensive and I've wanted one for so long."

"And so you bought it today as a celebration that you're going to get well?" Matt guessed. He'd suspected Casey loved jewelry, but she never wore any. Maybe it had to do with her PTSD?

"How did you know?" Amazed, Casey laughed. Matt had a lot of insight into people's actions. "Lannie doesn't just make pretty jewelry. She knows about the energy of the stones, too. There's purple lepidolite beads on my choker. Did you know lepidolite contains natural lithium? And that lithium calms a person who has anxiety or restlessness?"

"No, I didn't."

"Yes, and there's amethyst on here, as well. Lannie made this especially for me, Matt, based upon all my symptoms. She calls them 'working' necklaces. The gems she chooses are just right for a particular person." Patting it gently, Casey said, "I love this necklace, Matt. When I put it on this morning after my doctor's appointment, I just felt so good!"

Warmed by her enthusiasm, something he rarely saw in Casey, he said, "Now I wish I'd known you loved jewelry so much. I've never seen you wearing any."

Frowning, Casey said, "I guess I'm coming back to life, Matt. Charley finally released me from the visitor's center and I'm working in the back country on several wildlife biology projects. He seems to think that maybe he was wrong about me being targeted. I was so relieved! And, of course, getting help with my PTSD… I just wanted to celebrate it all by purchasing this necklace."

Smiling fully, Matt fought the urge to lean over and kiss Casey's smiling, soft lips. "Maybe we should take Megan over to see Lannie? My daughter loves jewelry."

"What a wonderful idea," Casey said. "Lannie says making working necklaces for children is tough because they are hard on them and sometimes, they swallow beads and choke on them. We can always ask Lannie and see what she says."

"We will. Megan loves jewelry," Matt said. "She was constantly digging into Bev's jewelry box. I think she'll be okay wearing a necklace."

Nodding, Casey felt her heart swell with such hope that all she could do was burst into a smile. Without thinking, she reached over and gripped Matt's hand that rested near his coffee mug. "Listen, I want my whole life back, Matt. I want to be my old self. You never got to meet the original Casey Cantrell." She felt his fingers move to curve around hers. Feeling the monitored strength in them, the work-worn flesh tingling against her smoother skin, she added in a whisper that only he could hear, "I want you, Matt. All of you. I deserve happiness and so do you. We make each other happy. Just think what could happen if my cortisol levels go back to normal! Dr. J said I would be my old self, just like before the attack happened. Because, back then, my cortisol was within normal ranges."

Hearing the urgency, the hope in her huskily spoken words, Matt yearned to kiss Casey. He didn't dare do it here in the firehouse. Being on duty meant exactly that. Releasing her hand, Matt rasped, "I'm going to enjoy getting to know the old Casey Cantrell. A new chapter in our lives?"

Nodding, Casey felt the prick of tears and fought them back. Oh, to stand up, frame his face in her hands and kiss him until they melted together! That was what Casey wanted more than anything. Matt had been patient and understanding. She'd seen the yearning to kiss her in his eyes, but he respected her needs and never made a move to do anything but support her. In her eyes, he was a true hero. "I can hardly wait for this month to be over!"

"Makes two of us." Matt shared an intimate look with Casey. She immediately colored.

"Well, speaking of that, Charley has asked me to work with Gwen Garner on the Arts Committee. They're holding their Fall Arts Festival in mid-September." She patted her necklace again. "Lannie actually got me involved in that in one of our conversations earlier this year. She's going to enter several of her working necklaces. And I love art, anyway, even if I can't draw a straight line."

Grinning, Matt could see there was a nice relationship between rebellious Lannie Wilson and Casey. Both women had certain qualities of independence that many women did not. "Charley is coordinating through you for artists who paint wildlife?" he guessed.

"Yep. I was surprised to find out Charley is a wild-duck painter. I learn something new about my supervisor every month." She grinned.

"The Fall Arts Festival draws the biggest artists in North America here. Did you know that?"

"No, but I'm finding it out. Gwen is assigning me to a group of people who take care of the entry paperwork." She held up her hands. "I'm a fast typist."

"You're a fast learner," Matt said. "I'm glad you're teaming up with Gwen. There's nothing she doesn't know about everyone." He chuckled.

"That's true," Casey murmured, finishing off the last of her coffee. She set the mug aside. "Gwen's always very careful what she doles out. Slander isn't where Gwen is at."

"I agree," Matt said. "Hey, I heard the other day over at the sheriff's department that Cade and Susan Donovan are finally going to get hitched. He told me September twenty-first is their wedding day."

"That's wonderful!" Casey said, clapping her hands together. "I was wondering when they'd get hitched! Gwen told me about her future daughter-in-law. She was in the FBI witness protection program and they moved her here to Jackson Hole to hide. Gwen told me Susan's ex-husband escaped from prison back east and he was hellbent on finding and killing her." Shivering, Casey said, "Now that, to me, would be a horrible and chilling threat. I've met Susan several times and she's a wonderful person, Matt. And Cade's adopted daughter has taken to her and calls her Mommy now."

"Cade told me that his mother is running around like a one-armed paperhanger balancing all the wedding plans along with this arts festival."

"Oh," Casey said, laughing, "if anyone can balance two events like that, it's Gwen Garner! She knows how to ask people for help and gets them whipped into team formation to do the work." Her eyes sparkled. "I ought to know. I walked in to buy some material for a fall blouse I wanted to make, and before I knew it, she'd roped and hog-tied me into volunteering on the arts festival."

"That's Gwen," Matt agreed. The change in Casey already was stunning. Matt hungered to simply sit here and pass the hours away talking with her. Dr. Jordana had offered her help—and more importantly, hope. That was what had been missing in Casey, he realized. All those times he'd seen sadness lingering in her gaze and had been unable to interpret it accurately. Matt had no doubt this medicine would work and give Casey back her life. He could hardly wait.

Rising, Casey looked at her watch and said, "I've got a meeting with the Arts Festival people in twenty minutes."

Matt stood. "Careful—if Gwen sees you have volunteeritis, she'll take advantage of you." He grinned.

Walking to the door, Casey said, "No, I'm not going to let that happen." She turned. Matt was less than two feet away. Silently, Casey appreciated his broad, strong shoulders. The navy-blue T-shirt stretched tantalizingly across his deep chest. She stopped the urge to step into his arms and kiss him. Casey imagined running her exploring fingers across his hard, powerful body. She ached to feel safe again with a man. But not just any man. Just Matt Sinclaire. Moving her gaze to his eyes, she absorbed the predatory hunger lurking there. There was a magical connection between them, and Casey swore she could read his mind and his desires.

There was a new gleam in Casey's large gray eyes, Matt discovered. She had just started her treatment with the adaptogen, but he swore he already saw a difference. He lifted his hand and gently curved his fingers along the line of her shining brown hair. Matt barely grazed the shining strands and he saw Casey react in the most wonderful of ways. Instead of seeing the fear and caution in her eyes that he'd always seen before, he saw something new. As his hand fell to his side and he gave her a sheepish grin, Matt saw desire burning there. Desire for him. For a moment, it stunned him. He'd wanted Casey for so long, hungered for her, dreamed of her nightly. Now he was seeing it returned in her eyes. And it was real. It was no longer a figment of his imagination. Swallowing, he whispered, "Only good things for you from now on, Casey. You're like Persephone who was stolen by the Greek god, Hades, and dragged into his dark Underworld within the Earth. Now, you're being released and you're seeing daylight and your hope has started to come back."

"I love the Greek myths." Casey sighed. "And yes, you pegged me right on that one. I'm like Persephone who was abducted by Hades and forced to live with him in his underground world. No sunlight, no warm breezes, no moonlight, just the darkness of his cave-like existence." Her scalp tingled where Matt's fingers had barely grazed her hair. How much more she wanted from him! Cautioning herself, Casey knew that one day on the medicine wouldn't cure her distrust and wariness, but she recognized that hope had replaced her depression. And Matt had accurately read her expression, and he'd known she wanted him to touch her. And he had. Her heart bubbled with such excruciating joy Casey wondered if she could die from happiness.

Pushing open the door that led out into the bay where the fire trucks sat, Casey said, "I'll be in touch, Matt. Stay safe, okay?"

CHAPTER SIXTEEN

"I'M SO GLAD WE COULD meet here at the Aspens and finally have lunch," Clarissa said to Casey. As the senator's wife, she had the best seat in the small, exclusive, five-star restaurant. The U-shaped blue leather booth was situated along the wall where she could see anyone who was coming in or leaving the posh place.

Casey smiled. "Me, too. I don't get out to places like this too often, and it's a treat." Clarissa was dressed in a white linen pantsuit perfect for the August weather. Casey was sure that her multicolored silk scarf covered with butterflies was hand-dyed. The opal drop earrings enhanced the tasteful ensemble.

"Oh," Clarissa said, "I'm sure your mother took you to many places like this in San Francisco."

"She did," Casey acknowledged, spreading the white napkin out across her lap. The maître d' arrived and, with a flourish, presented them with the gold-lettered menus. And then the waiter, a young, thin man in his twenties, delivered Clarissa her favorite drink, a glass of Sofia Riesling, from the Coppola Winery in California. She had persuaded Casey to try it, as well.

"My husband is in Washington, D.C., but I wanted to take a break from all the inside-the-Beltway insanity and get back out here where real people live." Clarissa smiled, lifted the glass and they clinked them together.

Taking a sip, Clarissa closed her eyes. "I just love this wine! What do you think?"

Casey tasted it. "Wow, this is really nice. Many flavor levels to it."

Beaming, Clarissa nodded. She wore her red hair up and swept back into a tortoiseshell comb set with small opals. On her wrist she wore a similar bracelet. "I'm so glad you like it!"

Casey set the wineglass down as the waiter came over to take their order. She knew without any doubt that if her mother weren't one of the most successful fundraisers in the U.S. Clarissa would completely ignore her. People like Clarissa sought out power, wherever it was, and orbited the powerful individual's structure to see what they could get out of it. No, Casey didn't treat this luncheon as anything but Clarissa poking around to see if Casey Cantrell was really worth her time and focus. The shallowness was always there behind the smile papered across her full mouth. Casey never saw the smile reach Clarissa's mascaraed eyes with the pale green shadow emphasizing their emerald irises.

After ordering, Clarissa happily focused on Casey. "You look very fetching in your pantsuit," she said.

"Thank you. It's nice to get out of my Forest Service uniform," Casey murmured.

"I don't recognize the designer who made it for you." She barely touched the soft blue linen jacket with her bright red fingernails.

"Oh," Casey demurred with a teasing grin, "it's a very famous designer." She knew that in Clarissa's world, everyone wore designer clothes. It was just a question of which designer. And the more expensive the creation, the higher up that woman was seen on the pedestal of power.

"Tell me," she pleaded, smiling. "I especially like the thread work on the lapels. Really well-done."

Touching the lapel, Casey said, "My mother made it for me."

Brows flying upward, Clarissa sat back in amazement. "Really? Because the design on your clothes speaks of top-seamstress work you'd find in a French couture house."

Hiding her smile over Clarissa's gushing and taking it in stride, Casey said, "My grandmother, Rachel Trayhern, taught my mother how to sew. My grandmother, to this day, makes clothes for all the kids. Even though she's in her eighties, she manages to make something for all of us girls on our birthdays."

"Amazing," Clarissa murmured, again touching Casey's lapel. "This is just the best work. Well, when I meet your mother at another charity I must tell her that her work is superior. The fact that this isn't made by a designer tells me her skill level."

"Yes, if she wasn't so good at raising millions for charity," Casey said, "I guess she could find a job at a fashion house."

"Oh, my," Clarissa said, waving her elegant hand in Casey's direction, "she's far too good for that!"

Their salads were brought and Casey was glad for the diversion. This kind of small talk was always stressful for her. Granted, her mother made it a high art, but Casey had never liked the shallowness of it. She didn't like shallow people. She preferred people like the Garners and Matt Sinclaire, who were the salt of the earth.

And what they told her would be honest and backed with integrity.

"So tell me," Clarissa said as she delicately moved her fork through the baby Bibb lettuce and croutons, "I hear all kinds of gossip over at Quilter's Haven. Why, just the other day I was over there getting some new summer fabric for my cousin when I overheard some quilters whispering about Matt Sinclaire."

Keeping her face unreadable, Casey said, "Oh?"

Smiling, Clarissa said, "You're sweet on him!"

Groaning inwardly, Casey said, "He's my friend, Clarissa. That's all." *Liar.* Casey wasn't ready to go there with this woman. Gwen Garner had the good sense to know when not to spread gossip. Clarissa did not.

"I hear that his mute daughter, Megan, just dotes on you. I think that's so wonderful of you to volunteer to help that poor child. It just broke my heart when we heard that Matt had lost his wife, Bev, in that arson fire. I felt so sorry for Megan." She frowned and stopped eating for a moment. "No child should go through that kind of trauma. Gwen was telling me that you are having a positive influence on Megan."

Nodding, Casey focused on her salad. The less said, the better. But Clarissa wasn't detoured.

"She said that the new doctor in town, Jordana Lawton, is treating her." Wrinkling her long, fine nose, Clarissa whispered across the table, "You do know about Dr. Lawton, don't you?"

Looking up, Casey said, "No."

"She's got a very checkered past, you know." Raising her chin to an imperious level, Clarissa said, "Frankly, I would never let her touch me."

"Why is that?"

"She's trailer trash."

"Umm."

Tilting her head, Clarissa said, "She just doesn't belong here in Jackson Hole. Only the finest people live here."

Translated, Casey knew this meant the snobbish woman would like to see all hardworking people thrown out, leaving the town to the rich and famous. "I like Dr. Lawton."

Giving Casey a guarded look, Clarissa pushed her mostly uneaten salad aside. A busboy quickly picked it up and took it away. "Why do you say that?"

"Because Megan is improving under her care."

"Oh... I didn't know that."

"No, it was obvious you didn't. I guess that didn't get to Quilter's Haven yet?" Casey gave her hostess a dripping smile that spoke volumes. Clarissa's carefully made-up face twitched as she considered the veiled warning.

"Oh...well... I'm glad Megan is responding."

The waiter came over with a fresh wineglass of Sofia Riesling. Clarissa was silent for a moment. More patrons were filling the restaurant and she eyed each one. Some of them came over to speak to her, others placed air kisses on her cheeks and still others shook her hand.

Casey said nothing and wasn't introduced to any of the millionaires coming in for lunch. That was fine by her. They would all be shallow intros and she would be passed over in favor of the powerful senator's wife, Clarissa. It was a world Casey wanted nothing to do with. She swore silently that there would be no more lunches with Clarissa. She wanted the simplicity and honesty of

Matt and Megan. She often wondered how her mother was able to tolerate this world, and figured she had some genes that didn't get passed on to her daughter.

After the small talk with the new visitors, Clarissa returned her attention to Casey. "I like your necklace. What designer made it for you?"

Casey smiled a little. "Another piece of trailer trash here in Jackson Hole, Lannie Wilson."

Brows dipping, Clarissa's mouth turned downward for a moment. She looked at the tortoiseshell and opal bracelet on her thin left wrist. "I see, well, it's very nice despite that."

"Thank you," Casey murmured, laughing inwardly. She was sure Clarissa wanted her to ask about the expensive opal bracelet but she wasn't about to. The rich always liked to compare. How much did the bracelet cost? Who designed it? Again, it was part of the unspoken competition between those with money to burn to figure out just where they each stood on the monied ladder of power.

"Those aren't real amethysts, are they?"

Casey smiled. "Yes, they are. Grade-A amethysts, as I'm sure you know. The darker purple they are, the higher the grade."

"You do know your gemstones."

"Actually, Lannie taught me. Amazing that trailer trash could be so educated, isn't it? Lannie has a degree from the Gemological Institute of America, GIA." Casey knew about gemstones because of her mother. And GIA graduates were considered the most knowledgeable in the world when it came to pearls, diamonds and colored stones.

"I didn't realize Lannie had upgraded herself," Clarissa sniffed. "She was such a problem teen here in the town. I understand from my husband that she was in and out of juvie hall all the time."

"Well," Casey said, allowing some of her emotion to come through, "if you'd had the stuffing beat out of you by an abusive and drunk father, you might not be whole, either. Trauma changes people, Clarissa. It's nice that you've never had to experience that part of life, but many others have."

"Oh, I didn't know it was her father," Clarissa began lamely. "I just heard from Carter that she was a hellion and always causing trouble."

"Yes, well, too bad the rest of Lannie's terrible childhood didn't reach you. She's pulling herself up by her bootstraps and trying to better her life. I admire people like that." Casey touched her amethyst necklace, a single strand set on a silver chain with silver spacers. "I like to support people who are struggling to make it in life."

Their main courses came. Clarissa looked relieved for the interruption. For a few minutes, she ate in silence. By now, the restaurant was bulging with well-heeled diners. The classical music was low and unobtrusive. The fine paintings along the wall were all originals by some of the American West's finest artists.

"So how long are you here?" Casey wanted to know.

"Oh, I hate D.C. in the summer," Clarissa murmured. "I much prefer the dry heat of Wyoming." She held up her manicured hand for a moment. "I blow up like a balloon in the dog days of July and August back on the east coast. Carter understands. We're always out here to celebrate the Fourth of July, and then he heads back to Washington and I remain here or at my parents' ranch over in Cheyenne until September first. Then I fly back to D.C."

Casey thought it must be nice. Knowing Clarissa would be here for several more weeks, she was going to make sure that she wasn't available for another power lunch with this woman. "Gwen said you grew up on a cattle ranch in Cheyenne?" Casey said.

"Yes, I did. In fact, my family's lineage goes back to the first trappers that came into this area." She preened a bit. "My family created one of the first huge cattle ranches here long before barbed wire was created."

"What's the name of your parents' ranch?" Casey saw Clarissa frown. She supposed she thought everyone should know that without having to ask.

"The Triple R. Our ancestors who first started our ranch were Renards from Canada. I guess they got tired of trapping and saw cattle as the latest fad and decided to settle down. Lucky for us they did. Our ranch is the largest in the Cheyenne area."

"And you have brothers? Sisters?" Casey knew the rich loved to talk about themselves. This was a far better tactic for her because she didn't want to reveal that much of herself to this gossip queen from D.C.

Smiling fondly, Clarissa said, "My older brother, Frank Renard, works with my father. Eventually, Frank will inherit the ranch, but, of course, the money will be split evenly between the three of us."

"There's a third sibling?"

Making a face, Clarissa said, "Please keep this private?"

"Sure," Casey murmured, enjoying her hamburger. For once, the facade that Clarissa wore dissolved. She saw real pain in the woman's green eyes. It wasn't made up.

"My younger sister, Nicole is…well… I'm ashamed of her." Cupping her hand near her red lips, she said, "Nicky is the youngest. She always hated being the last born. In school she got into trouble with drugs."

"I'm sorry to hear that," Casey said, and she meant it. The pain continued to linger in Clarissa's eyes.

"Nicky was in and out of trouble her whole life. Mama said she inherited the bad genes from one of our French relatives, who was a murderer and was eventually hanged. Of course, that was a long time ago," she said, waving her hand as if to make the truth go away. "Nicky is jealous of me. She hated that my father favored Frank and ignored us girls. Nicky wanted to learn to run the ranch just like Frank, but Daddy forbade it. She has *such* a temper." Touching her red hair, Clarissa added, "And she's got our famous red hair, too. And anything you've heard about red hair holds true for Nicky. She's got a hair-trigger temper, has a smart mouth on her that won't quit and she's always confrontational."

"Those aren't necessarily bad traits," Casey said, trying to ease the pain she saw in Clarissa's face.

"That's true," she said, rearranging the napkin on her lap. "In Daddy's view, he doesn't have a second daughter."

Casey grimaced. She came from a five-daughter family and couldn't imagine her parents banishing one of them. "So Nicky can't be at the ranch or visit your mother?"

Mouth turning down at the corners, Clarissa nodded. "She's not allowed to. My mom has to meet her outside ranch property. It's a very, very sad, ongoing situation."

"Where's Nicky now?"

"In Cheyenne. She wants to move here." Clarissa sighed. "I mean, she *is* my sister, Casey. I feel guilty and want to help her."

"Nothing wrong with that," Casey murmured. "I think it's nice you'll support her. What does she do for a living?"

"Nicky managed to get an MBA in Business Administration from Harvard University. She's got a wonderful mind if she could just tame those raw, wild emotions of hers," Clarissa murmured, frowning.

"Those are impressive credentials."

"Yes, but Nicky hated every moment of it. Daddy wanted her to get a degree so she could take care of herself. When she graduated and returned to the ranch, she demanded that Daddy take her on so she could help learn the business of cattle-ranching. He refused."

"And that's when he disowned her?" Casey wondered. She saw Clarissa pull a silk handkerchief from her purse and dab the corners of her eyes. Her heart went out to Clarissa. For all her money, power and fame, there was nothing she could do to fix a sad family situation. It made her human in Casey's eyes. And the tears were real, not the crocodile tears that some could create on demand. She could see worry and love for Nicky in the woman's drawn features.

"Yes, I'm afraid Daddy is like a caveman. He believes there's man's work and there's woman's work. My mother put up with it and so did I. Nicky never did. She fought him tooth and nail to be allowed to learn how a ranch of that size was run and made money."

"Ouch," Casey said. "I'm really sorry to hear this, Clarissa. It must be painful for everyone concerned."

Sniffing, Clarissa shored up, tucked the handkerchief away and forced a smile she didn't feel. "Everyone's in pain except Daddy. He's hardened his heart against my baby sister. I begged her to come out here where she could start all over. There's plenty of ranches in this area that could hire her. She's a fast learner and she loves riding and roping. Nicky has always been a tomboy while I was the lady."

Nodding, Casey could see that. Clarissa dug into her purse and produced a picture of her younger sister.

"You can see, she's beautiful. She's only twenty-five and has the whole world in front of her with her Harvard degree."

The pride in Clarissa's voice was genuine and filled with hope. Nicky looked very different from Clarissa. In fact, she would not have believed they were sisters except for the red hair they shared. "She is pretty," she offered. "Is she going to use your help?" Casey was sure that with Clarissa's powerful statewide ties in ranching, she could get her baby sister a good job as a business manager.

"I've put in a few calls on her behalf," Clarissa said, sliding the picture back in her purse.

"She wants to live here to be near you?"

"I think so. Nicky and I were always close. We didn't get along very well because I liked doing girlie things and she hung out with the boys." She laughed a little. "Well, I hung out with the boys, too, but I was very popular in high school and always had dates."

Casey nodded. "Nicky ran with the guys because she wanted to?"

"She loved baseball versus softball, loved touch football and joined the fencing club and fenced with the best of them. Nicky always felt like she had something to prove to Daddy, I guess." Clarissa sighed. "One way to do it was to run with the boys and show them up. Show them that she was better than they were."

"And was she?"

"Absolutely. But Daddy said it wasn't right for a young woman to be showing up men. They each had their place in life. He was never happy she was out roughhousing with them."

Casey kept her mouth shut. There were still a lot of the men of the Baby Boom generation against women being their equals. "I hope Nicky finds something she'll be happy doing around here."

"Oh," Clarissa said, hope in her tone, "I've sent her some leads. The one I hope she does not take is a run-down ranch, the Flying R. You know about it? The story?"

Shaking her head, Casey said, "I guess I haven't lived here long enough to know all the stories circulating around this pot-boiler of a valley."

With a grimace, Clarissa said, "It's a sad story, re-ally. And I hope Nicky does not take the job that's open there. The Flying R used to be a well-run cattle ranch." Her mouth quirked. "Life is sorrowful for so many. Li-anna Royden died of leukemia two years ago. Her hus-band, Mick, drank himself to death a year later. In the meantime, their only son, Lieutenant Pete Royden, was in the U.S. Army. He was over in Afghanistan fighting when his mother died and was unable to come home for the funeral. And then, his father went on a drinking binge shortly afterward." With a shrug, her voice softer with sympathy, Clarissa murmured, "Pete left the army after his six-year tour was up and returned home to a ranch that has pretty much spiraled into a mess. It used to be profitable, but now it's not. The wranglers left, and Pete walked back into a disaster. Now he's trying to save his family's legacy. He placed a want ad in the local paper for a business manager."

"Sounds like Nicky could be of help to him," Casey said.

Shrugging, Clarissa asked, "You ever met Pete?"

"No. Why?"

"He's a mean son of a bitch," Clarissa whispered. "Pardon my language, but there's no secrets here in the valley. He's irritable, angry all the time, impatient and won't tolerate anyone. He's out at his ranch right now trying to do it all himself. I just don't want Nicky getting involved with the likes of him, is all. The war has changed him."

Casey looked at her watch. "This has been a nice lunch with you, Clarissa, but I've got to run." She pulled out money to pay.

"No, no," Clarissa said, holding up her hand. "I'll buy. Let's do this again?"

Getting up, Casey laid the linen napkin on the table. "Sure," she lied. "Thank you for lunch."

"Please give your mother my regards?"

"Right. I will." Casey wanted to leave. An hour of Clarissa was enough, even though, in the end, the woman wasn't the heartless bitch she had first thought. Clarissa had feelings, had sympathy, and that was good to know. Swinging out the door, Casey decided to walk around the plaza to Quilter's Haven. Gwen Garner was holding some material for a blouse she wanted to make.

She walked down the crowded wooden-plank walk, threading through the hundreds of tourists ambling along and peering into the picture windows of different stores. She heard the fire siren go off. Matt was on duty. Worry descended upon Casey. The more she allowed herself to like Matt, the more his job worried her. Firefighting was equally as dangerous as being a law-enforcement officer. With a sigh, she crossed the street and halted at the pale yellow two-story brick building. Quilter's Haven looked busy inside. When wasn't it?

The siren continued to scream over the town. As Casey pulled open the door, she automatically prayed that Matt and his team would be safe.

CHAPTER SEVENTEEN

CASEY MADE HER way through the crowd of women. Gwen was holding her sale on the latest Christmas fabrics and now was the time to buy. She went to the desk near the rear of the store and Gwen greeted her.

"Hey, how are you, Casey?" Gwen reached down and pulled out the fabric she'd kept for her.

"Fine, Gwen. And you?"

The woman smiled. "Keeping my eyes and ears open as usual," she chuckled. "I saw Clarissa drive up earlier. You have lunch with her over at the Aspens?"

Shaking her head, Casey said, "Nothing misses you, does it?" Pulling open her purse, she paid for the fabric, a Hoffman batik that had purples, blues and reds in it. Casey wanted a nice long-sleeved blouse in one-hundred-percent cotton for fall, and this would be a beautiful choice.

"Nope," Gwen said, smiling as she rang up the purchase on her cash register. "She's not as bad as you thought, eh?"

Startled, Casey sometimes wondered if Gwen Garner read people's minds. Taking the change, she placed the coins in a small leather purse. "No, she's got worries and problems just like the rest of us."

Gwen nodded. "She's not such a bad egg. Her little

sister, Nicky, is acting out for the whole toxic family dynamic."

Again, Casey was amazed at Gwen's insights. "You should run for mayor, Gwen. Or become a psychologist. Your insights are always correct and you know everything about everyone!"

Laughing a little, Gwen moved some graying curls off her broad forehead. "Come with me," she said, gesturing for her to follow. "I've got some new Hoffman batiks in and I know that's your favorite fabric."

Casey took her purchase and walked to the corner of the store. Gwen had special sections of some of the most popular fabrics desired by quilters. Hoffman was the best of the batiks. They were made by hand in Indonesia and they were always Casey's first choice.

The fabric stands held roughly a hundred bolts of cloth. The Hoffman stand was in the corner and Gwen rounded it to where they were alone. Casey had a distinct feeling this wasn't about seeing new fabric. Coming to a halt, Gwen once more checked around to ensure there were no ears to hear what she was going to impart to Casey.

"Listen, word has it that there's a man in town that no one knows. I saw him yesterday, and I got a bad feeling." Gwen was short and so she stepped closer so only Casey could hear her. "Normally, with all the tourists who come here, I don't pay much attention. But this guy, whoever he was, came in here." She pointed her index finger down at the floor. "He looked to me like the least likely person to be interested in quilting, much less sewing. I didn't like the look in his eyes, either."

Frowning, Casey said, "What does this have to do with me?"

"He asked for you. By name."

"Oh?" Casey gave Gwen a helpless look. "Can you give me a description of him?"

Gwen gave it to her. "Now, does that ring a bell?"

"No. Not at all."

Rubbing her chin, Gwen said, "I told my girls who work here that if they see him again to try to get a photo of him. I keep a small digital camera at the cash register."

Giving her a partial smile, Casey said, "You take photos of people, Gwen?"

"When I think it's warranted, yes." Giving Casey a steely-eyed look she said, "You know, no one's solved that bullet being fired at you last spring. I know Charley, your super, has released you back to working outdoors again because he can't keep you locked up forever at the visitor's center. And my son said it's a dead end—no one found the shooter. And no one was hiking in that area to tell him anything. This guy reminded me of a predator, pure and simple. He just had that look about him."

"Who talked to him at the counter about me?" Casey asked.

"Donna did. She told me he asked if you came in here. Now, I train my girls to be closemouthed, especially when the situation seems to warrant it. Donna said she didn't know and played dumb. He got angry with her, asked her some more questions. It's obvious to me he's been watching you, Casey, because he let slip that you'd been in here two days ago."

A chill worked up Casey's spine. "That doesn't sound good."

"No, no, it doesn't." Reaching out, Gwen placed her hand on Casey's arm. "Listen, I've already told my son about it. I've given him a description of the man. He can't do much at this point, but he did ask the other deputies to stay alert. They're watching for him now."

Grimacing, Casey murmured, "Gosh, Gwen, I just don't have a clue. I don't know anyone by that description."

"Did Clarissa talk to you about her donor list?"

Startled by the question, Casey said, "No. Why?"

"Well, Clarissa was in here yesterday buying Christmas fabric for her cousin over in Cheyenne and she told me about this man on the donor list. You know that Clarissa is in charge of it?"

"No, but it makes sense she would be since she's always putting on fetes to raise money for her husband's senate bid next year."

Nodding, Gwen said, "She said she found a throwaway cell phone on her husband's desk. When she looked at the number of the person he was calling, she didn't recognize it, so she wrote it down. Then, as she does with all donors, she did a background check. Senator Peyton has to be careful who donates. He can't have criminals or other bad elements donating money to his campaign. It wouldn't look good for him. Clarissa is the clearinghouse for all of that stuff."

"Okay," Casey said, not sure where this information was going.

"She goes to a special internet site where she does criminal background checks. Anyway," Gwen said, "when she typed in the cell phone number, this guy's name came up. She didn't recognize him at all. So, she went and put his name in the background check." Her mouth flattened. "The guy's name is Frank Benson.

And he's been in and out of prison so many times it makes my head spin."

"I'm sure Clarissa took him off the donor list?"

"Well, see," Gwen said, "this is the funny thing. He's not on the senator's donation list. And it was Carter who made the call to this dude with a criminal record."

"I'm sure the senator deals with all kinds of people in his line of work," Casey said. She saw nothing out of line with that. Frequently, senators and congress people were called to help a prisoner who felt they were in prison and innocent.

"Well," Gwen said, wrinkling her nose, "I agree with you."

"So, what is out of place about this?"

Shrugging, Gwen said, "Nothing, really. But the day Clarissa came in to tell me about it was the same day this guy showed up asking about you."

"Well, you have his name. Can Cade run a check on him?"

"That's what he's doing today. I want to see the guy's face. Cade's supposed to bring me over a photo and I'm going to show it to Donna to see if it's the same guy." Tapping Casey's shoulder Gwen said grimly, "And if it is, then we all need to worry. Because Benson is a murderer, Casey. He's been out of prison for three years and has been keeping a low profile."

"But I don't understand," Casey said, slightly exasperated by Gwen's logic. "What would the senator, I and this criminal all have in common that I should be worried about?" Fear niggled at her and she tried to ignore the hammering of her heart. What if this man had been stalking her and she didn't know about it until now? Casey tried to reassure herself that it was her vivid imagination at work. Still, the fear crawled up in her throat, and she felt as though she would strangle to death. Gulping several times, she touched her neck with her fingers as if to make the fear go away.

"That's the question," Gwen said. She looked around the corner at her store. "Listen, I have to get back to the counter." She patted her arm. "I just want you to stay alert. When Cade gives me that photo and if Donna confirms it was the guy, then I'm calling you. Because, that means something is going on..."

"Do you think he might be the shooter from this past spring?" Casey wondered. Her mind whirled with questions that had no answers. If this man was hunting her, why was he doing it? She was a nobody. Unimportant in the greater scheme of things. None of it made sense to Casey but it left her feeling frightened.

"That's what I'm thinking." Gwen tapped her head. "Of course, it's only a thread in this thing. Gotta wait to see which way the fabric goes." She smiled a little. "Until then, just stay alert. Okay?"

"Okay," Casey murmured, "thanks." She glanced at her watch. Matt's sister, Jessie, was due to go on nursing duty in an hour at the hospital. Every once in a while, on Casey's day off, if Matt needed a babysitter, he would ask her to pinch-hit for Jessie. Casey was glad to do it.

"HEY," JESSIE GREETED her brightly after opening the door to her brother's home to Casey, "thanks for spelling me."

Casey came in and smiled at the five-foot-six-inch tall woman with red hair, blue eyes and freckles across her cheeks. "Anything I need to know before you go, Jessie?" She could almost be Matt's fraternal twin, they looked so much alike. Only, Jessie was curvy and looked nice in her nurse's uniform—a dark green smock and white slacks. She already had her gear parked by the door.

Jessie looked around the quiet home. "No. Megan will be dropped off down the street as usual. I know you'll be meeting her." Jessie pushed her fingers through the curly red hair that she'd tamed into a ponytail. She worked in the maternity ward and loved babies. "And it's three o'clock. Matt will be home at six." She smiled a little as she pulled the strap of her leather purse across her shoulder and picked up a briefcase. "I made Matt his favorite meal—tuna and noodles."

"Ohh," Casey said, shutting the door, "he'll like that and so will Megan."

Nodding, Jessie said, "My older brother is so spoiled by me." She chuckled. "Thanks for picking up the slack here. I don't know what we'd do without you. The woman who used to babysit at these times moved away and it really left Matt without anyone."

"No problem," Casey murmured. She placed the keys to his house on a foyer desk.

Glancing at her watch, Jessie said, "Gotta run!" Giving Casey a quick hug, she opened the door and left.

There was soft music playing in the background. Elevator music and Casey didn't particularly like it, but Megan and Matt did. She preferred passionate jazz instead. The kitchen was spotless—Jessie did a lot of housecleaning for her brother when she was here. Peeking inside the fridge she saw the huge casserole with foil on top of it ready to be popped into the oven an hour before Matt's arrival home.

Turning, Casey walked to the door and locked it behind her. Megan's school bus would drop her off at the corner in about five minutes. Casey always made a point of being there to greet the girl. She recalled that, as she was growing up, "stranger-danger" was being taught to children. As she walked down the tree-lined sidewalk, the leaves colorful against the pale blue sky, Casey lamented how the world had changed. It used to be children were safe, but no more.

As she stood on the corner, Casey could see the yellow bus slowly coming down the main avenue toward them. Absorbing the warmth of the fall sun, Casey knew that hiking days would be over soon. Wyoming always got heavy snows beginning in October. Maybe she, Megan and Matt could go on a picnic-lunch hike to a beautiful little meadow off Moose Road before that happened.

Hands on her hips, Casey smiled to herself. Tonight, she would share the evening with Matt. It didn't happen often and Casey looked forward to those unexpected times. Since being on the adaptogen to work with her cortisol levels she was discovering that she no longer felt threatened or worried by the world around her. No, if anything, this medicine was allowing her to transcend the PTSD symptoms, and she found her heart focused on Matt. And on a possible relationship with him…

CASEY WAS DRYING THE DISHES as Matt sauntered into the kitchen. He'd just put Megan to bed after her bath. The evening had been wonderful for Casey. Glancing over her shoulder she couldn't shake how powerful, how sexy and desirable Matt was to her. It was as if someone had miraculously lifted off blinders she'd been wearing. Of course, he looked incredible in his navy T-shirt emblazoned with the fire department insignia, too.

Casey was about to say something when the wineglass she was drying slipped.

"Oh!" she cried, trying to catch it. The glass shattered on the pine floor, pieces flying in all directions. Without thinking, she crouched down and picked up the largest pieces. Instantly, her finger was sliced open, blood purling up and then running down her hand.

"Casey?" Matt saw what happened. Leaning down, he captured her hand. "Are you okay?"

Grimacing, Casey muttered, "That was stupid, wasn't it?" His hand was warm and she could feel the roughness of his fingers as he gently examined the sliced finger.

"Come on," he urged, helping her stand, "let's go to the bathroom. I'll wash it out, put some antiseptic on it and bandage it up."

Casey didn't fight him. Feeling rather embarrassed, she walked with him to the large master bathroom. He placed her hand in the sink where the blood dripped and left a thin red stream in its wake. "It's not as bad as it looks."

"No," he reassured Casey, opening the medicine cabinet, "you won't need stitches." Matt met and held her gaze. Casey was clearly upset about breaking the glass. He liked the intimacy it had created. All night, Matt had tried to tame his need of her. Every time he watched her eat across the table, his eye settled on her lovely, soft mouth. He'd lost count of how many times he'd wanted to kiss her. "And hey, it's only a cheap wineglass. No big deal. It isn't like they're heirlooms." He pulled down the box of Band-Aids.

"I was always a klutz in the kitchen at home, too," Casey muttered in apology. When Matt turned on the water and slipped his hand beneath hers, his body barely grazing hers, she gulped. For such a tall, powerful man, his touch was tender as he washed the sliced finger with soap and water.

"I've lost count of how many dishes I've broken. You're in good company," he murmured, trading a quick glance and smile with her. Casey was so close… so close… Reining in his hardening desire for her, he hoped she wouldn't see how aroused he'd become. It shocked him, too. But he'd been without a woman now for two years. Taking a gauze square he gently dabbed the finger dry. Squeezing a bit of antiseptic into the injury, Matt expertly placed the Band-Aid around it.

Just from the way Matt's fingers curled protectively around her hand after it was bandaged, Casey's breath caught. He turned and now they were facing one another, bare inches between them. Lifting her lashes, Casey met and drowned in the burning green of his narrowing eyes. His mouth was relaxed. She wanted to kiss him. Nothing, in that moment, had ever seemed so right.

Without trying to analyze her actions, Casey leaned up on her toes, her mouth meeting and sliding against his. A groan escaped Matt. His mouth plundered hers. His arms automatically moved around Casey and he drew her tightly against him. Casey absorbed the stretch of the T-shirt across his well-sprung chest, felt the release of warm, moist air as their lips met and clung to one another. Her hands slid up across his broad shoulders. Beneath her fingertips, she could feel every muscle tighten in response.

Forgetting the cut, fingertips mingling with the

short strands of his hair at the base of his neck, Casey drowned in the heat and strength of his male mouth. One of his hands ranged slowly upward, as if memorizing every inch he touched, and she felt his fingers caress her spine, upper arm and, finally, her shoulder. When his hand framed her jaw and angled her so he could kiss her more deeply, Casey surrendered fully to the scorching moment.

Her breasts tightened as his fingers plunged through her hair, easing across her scalp, her skin tingling wildly in the wake of his search of her body. Casey felt the scrape of his beard across her cheek, met and responded just as wantonly as he kissed her long and hard. Their breaths were becoming short and shallow. She could feel her heart pounding in unison with his.

Slowly, ever so slowly, their searching lips separated. Casey slowly opened her eyes and looked dazedly up at Matt. He was staring down at her, his pupils huge, his eyes narrowed solely upon her. Never had Casey felt more sensual or desirable than at that moment. Matt put her in touch with her femininity in a way that no man had ever done. Stunned by her desire for him, her lips parted. No words would come. They stood in one another's arms, fused together. Her hips were against his and she could feel the bulge of his desire for her.

"I want to love you, Casey," he rasped.

"I know…" Her voice was wispy and faraway-sounding. She felt his hands move slowly up either side of her spine in a caress. If she remained in his arms, she would say yes. And why not? Her heart wanted this. Her brain wasn't sure. Realizing Matt was not a man to be afraid of, Casey said, "I didn't know this would happen…"

He gave her a wry, one-cornered smile. "Neither did I." Matt waited. He saw the indecision in her shadowed eyes. But he also saw her hunger for him alone. It made his heart soar, but he knew from experience he couldn't push Casey into anything. This kiss had been spontaneous and both of them had wanted it or it wouldn't have happened. Gazing down at Casey's glowing features, Matt realized she was just as stunned as he was by what had just happened.

Easing his hands back so that they could separate a bit, Matt said, "If this was dessert, it's all I need." He wanted to tease her a little so she wouldn't panic. When Casey took a step back, Matt released her. She had come to him of her own free will. She would again. He had to be patient.

"Yes, it was," Casey whispered, touching her throbbing lips. She could taste the power of his maleness that he'd stamped across them. And yet, he'd not hurt her. Matt stood there, shoulders back, hands at his sides— it almost hurt to absorb him in that moment. Her own body felt as if it was on fire, throbbing in the lower part like a volcano ready to explode. Matt brought out the fire in her, there was no doubt.

"I'm not sorry it happened," Matt told her in a quiet tone. "Are you?"

Shaking her head, Casey smiled a little. "No, I'm not. I didn't expect it, though."

"Me neither."

Casey turned and walked out of the bathroom. Matt followed. In the kitchen, she saw the shattered glass sparkling across the floor. "Let me help you clean this up," she said, going to the broom closet, "and then I have to get home."

Nodding, Matt respected her needs. "Listen, let me clean this up, Casey. You washed and dried the dishes for me. It's the least I can do." He stepped around the mess on the floor and met her at the door. She handed him the broom. When their fingers met, Matt nearly dragged her into his arms. But he didn't. He could see their galvanizing kiss had shaken Casey. She needed time to feel her way through it. He didn't, but his needs weren't a priority.

"Okay, thanks," she murmured. Stepping away because he was like a magnet to her own euphoric senses, Casey felt she was floating instead of walking. How could one kiss make her feel so giddy? She'd never experienced this sensation before.

Matt rested the broom against the counter and walked Casey to the front door. He turned on the light and opened it for her. She shrugged into her green nylon jacket and picked up her purse.

"I'll walk you to your car."

"You don't have to," she protested. The garage was only across the lawn of his home. There was a bright light above so she could see her way to it.

"I want to," Matt murmured, closing the door, his hand resting lightly on the small of her back.

Casey absorbed his closeness. How did Matt know she ached to have this kind of intimacy with him? Two weeks ago, she'd have stepped away. Her mind spun with questions, but Casey knew the medication that was bringing her cortisol levels down to normal was part of the reason why. At the car, she clicked the automatic door opener. Would he kiss her?

Matt moved aside as she opened the car door and placed her purse inside. Hand resting on the frame of the door, he said, "Thanks for a great evening, Casey. I hope you know how important you are to me and Megan."

Nodding, Casey slipped into the car. "It *was* a nice evening," she agreed. The fire banked in his shadowed eyes made her want to stay. Did she have the courage to get out of the car and tell him she wanted to spend the night with him? Love him? Wake up with him in the morning, his arms around her? Mouth dry, Casey was shocked by her own thoughts. She could swear she saw the same desire in Matt's eyes. But he wasn't saying anything, either.

Go slow, she cautioned herself. *We have the time....*

CHAPTER EIGHTEEN

"CARTER, I'M STUMPED by this one donor who is new to your list."

Carter was in a black limo being driven from the Capitol to a political gala in Alexandria, Virginia. He pressed the cell to his ear a bit more firmly, the connection with his wife in Wyoming weak. "Who is it?"

"Do you remember that throwaway cell phone you left on your desk?"

Scowling, Carter said, "What?" His head spun with confusion. The only throwaway cell phones he had were to speak to Frank Benson. And he never left them lying around. "I don't have any of those."

"Well, yes, you do, darling. It was the Fourth of July. You hurried out of our home for that affair at the plaza in town and you were late. I happened to go into your office and I noticed it sitting there. I picked it up, thinking you'd left in such a hurry that you'd forgotten it. And then I realized it wasn't your normal cell phone that you use."

Carter felt as though someone had grabbed his stomach and clenched it so hard he could feel the actual pain. "I'm sorry, Clarissa, I don't remember." Mind whirling, he knew he didn't dare admit to leaving it there. Carter recalled arriving back to their Jackson Hole home and seeing the cell still there in the middle of his desk. He'd picked it up, smashed it and gotten rid of it. But Clarissa had seen it. *Oh, God...*

"Well," she said, "I opened it up, thinking that it was yours. I wasn't really paying attention, Carter. And when I did, the phone came on and there was this phone number on it. At first, I thought it was someone trying to call you, so I wrote it down. I put the cell back on your desk and took the number, thinking it was probably a donor."

Closing his eyes, Carter felt adrenaline shoot into his bloodstream. His heart began to hammer. "What did you do with that number?" He kept his voice nonchalant, as if this conversation wasn't even important.

"I placed it on your new donor list, of course. And today, I was updating the list. You know I do a background check on every donor. I want to make sure no one who could cause you political embarrassment is on there."

Wiping the sweat off his upper lip, Carter felt terror. "Yes, yes, I know you do."

"Carter, this just doesn't make sense. I was hoping you could shed some light on it. That number belongs to a Frank Benson. I did the background check and, darling, he's got a criminal background a mile long."

Hearing the confusion and concern in her voice, he forced a laugh. "Oh, come now, Clarissa. How would garbage like him be a donor?"

"Well... I don't know. Do you know him, Carter?"

"Of course not! Don't be stupid, Clarissa. Why would I ever have any kind of a connection with someone like that?" Carter prayed his over-the-top reaction would stop her from any further conjecture. Clarissa always took care of his donor list. She was circumspect about who got on it. For once, her pit-bull research was re-bounding against him. Sweat popped out on his brow. He sat up, his breathing harsh. "That cell phone could belong to the maid," he muttered. "I don't have throw-away cells, Clarissa."

"I already asked our housemaid and the chef, Carter. They said it didn't belong to them, either."

He heard more hesitancy in her tone. Above all, Carter didn't want her believing he knew the sniper. Or that he had a contract out to kill Matt Sinclaire, his daughter and that woman, Casey Cantrell. Wiping his brow, he rasped, "Well, where is this mysterious phone? Do you have it?"

"Why…no… I don't know where it is. The last I saw it, Carter, it was on your desk. I completely forgot about it until recently when I was updating your donor list."

He savagely wondered why his damn wife would have taken that number off the cell and automatically put it on his new donor list. Carter knew that many people who supported his candidacy for a second term as senator called constantly. And sometimes, his cell phone would be on his desk and he would ask Clarissa to take the numbers and names of the latest callers to put on that growing list. He tried to calm himself. His wife suspected nothing. Clearing his throat, he said, "Maybe it was just a prank by someone. It wasn't my cell, Clarissa."

"This doesn't make sense, Carter. If it wasn't yours or our employees, how did it get on your desk, then? Did someone break into our home?"

He heard concealed worry in her voice. "I don't know. We have that place under Fort Knox security. I just think it's a fluke. Just forget about it. And get that

man off my donor list. I certainly want nothing to do
with a criminal."

"Of course, Carter. I just thought you should know.
This man is a murderer. He spent fifteen years in prison
for taking money to kill a woman in Idaho. He just got
out three years ago."

Groaning inwardly, Carter pulled the linen handkerchief from his pocket and blotted his sweaty brow.
"Clarissa, just forget about it! Take his name off the
donor list and let it go."

"If you want, Carter…"

Again, he heard a question in his wife's voice. He
knew she wouldn't connect him and Benson together.
"Yes, that's what I want."

"How are things in D.C.?"

Feeling a rivulet of relief as Clarissa's voice changed
and became lighter and happier, Carter said, "Missing you. I'm looking forward to seeing you come back
here."

Laughing lightly, Clarissa said, "Well, I'll be there,
but I've still got some responsibilities to the wildlife
museum and I'm going to delay returning for another
two weeks."

Frowning, Carter knew that within that two weeks,
Benson was to kill his targets. He didn't want his wife
in Jackson Hole when that happened. She might remember Benson or just the fact that he had gone to jail for
being hired to murder a person. "Can't it wait?" he demanded testily. "I need you here, Clarissa. Now. We've
already got several dinner invitations and I need you
at my side. Can't that stuff be handled long-distance?"

"I guess it could. Are the invitations that important?

You know how I like to tie up loose ends for the fall here at our summer home, Carter."

Holding on to his disintegrating patience, Carter knew this would be a balancing act with his intelligent wife. Clarissa wasn't stupid, and he was afraid she'd put Benson and the upcoming deaths together. It would be a stretch, but he never underestimated her. Besides, Carter told himself, Benson wasn't sure he could murder them within that two-week window. It depended upon so many things out of his control. Above all, Carter needed to have these three taken out in such a way that no foul play was suspected. He couldn't just have them shot in the head as Bev Sinclaire had been. The police would be crawling over everything if that occurred. No, this time Benson had to make it look natural and that meant he was dealing with a lot of unknowns. Lowering his voice, Carter said, "Clarissa, darling, if you really need that two weeks, then take it."

"Are you sure, Carter?"

"I'm sure," he said soothingly. She seemed relieved that he wasn't pushing her to leave early. With a little luck, those murders would go down after she left. Benson was watching—waiting and timing were all-important. He wanted them dead in the next two weeks, but who really knew? Peyton knew the sniper wanted the other half of his money for this gig and that made him want it done and over with. Looking out the dark, tinted window, Carter said, "Go ahead and stay there, Clarissa. It would be one thing if we got an invitation to the White House for dinner, but these aren't that important."

Laughing a little, Clarissa said, "We'd kill for a White House invite."

He managed a twisted smile. The limo was slowing down for a red light ahead, the traffic at quitting time always went at a snail's pace. "Perhaps not kill," he said, trying to sound as though he was joking a little. "I'm a Republican senator, so I don't think with the present occupants in the White House, we'll see a dinner invitation very soon."

Laughing at his teasing, Clarissa said, "Oh, you never know, Carter. I'm not willing to sit back and be left out. When I arrive there in two weeks, my first priority is to get the First Lady involved in obese children's issues. I believe exercise is part of the key. I want to meet with her because I have some good ideas. Just call it across-the-aisle goodwill."

"You never cease to amaze me," Carter said, meaning it. The limo pulled into the driveway of the hotel where the dinner was to be. "I have to go now, darling. I'll call you tonight before I go to bed. I love you."

"I love you, too, Carter. Bye…"

Snapping his cell closed and sliding it inside his dark brown pin-striped suit coat, Carter smiled a little. His wife was in the dark, right where he wanted her. God, that was a close call! He prayed that she would completely forget about his mistake. How stupid of him! Carter prided himself on being careful. Recalling that day, he remembered he'd been running late. And he'd screwed up. *Damn.*

MATT SAT WITH Casey at Mo's Café. The late-August sun shone through the windows. He was grateful that she could meet him for lunch. Although she was on duty today, she had gotten an hour and a half off for lunch. She was in her Forest Service uniform but nothing could hide her femininity from him. Remembering their kiss of two days ago, he said, "How's your finger doing?"

Casey smiled a little. She held up the bandaged finger. "It's fine." The waitress brought over two huge hamburgers with coleslaw. Casey moved her coffee cup to one side, took the platter and thanked the young waitress. Her heart beat a little harder because she hadn't spoken to Matt since their heated, unexpected kiss in his master bathroom. She felt nervous and saw that he was very serious-looking. More than usual. And it had been Matt who had called her here to Mo's for an impromptu lunch. She knew something was up. But what?

Matt put ketchup on his half-pound hamburger and placed the grilled, warm bun over it. "We need to talk," he said quietly. The music from the jukebox was in the background and Mo's was packed with tourists hungry at lunchtime. The booth where they sat was U-shaped and in a corner.

Nodding, Casey felt her heart pulse a little over his whispered words. She'd lost her appetite so she picked up her fork and pushed the spicy coleslaw around in the white bowl. "It's about our kiss?" she guessed.

Nodding, Matt saw uncertainty in Casey's gaze. He could barely keep his eyes away from that soft mouth that had singed his soul and made him burn. "I like what's happening between us," he admitted. "But I want to make sure you're feeling the same as I am. I learned a long time ago in my marriage that if I didn't talk, things could get tangled in a hurry between two people." He took a bite of his burger and set it down on the oval plate. Wiping his mouth with the paper napkin, he added, "I need to know how you feel, Casey. Is this one-way? Or not?"

Casey barely tasted the coleslaw—it had a hint of curry in it. "I like it, too, Matt. I admit, I'm changing. Before this, I avoided men because of what happened in my past. Now, being on a medication that is forcing my cortisol levels to become normal, I'm starting to feel like my old self again." She managed a slice of a smile as she held his intent gaze. "I was scared of men. I know in my head that's stupid, but as Dr. Lawton told me early on, we're all controlled by our hormones, whether we like it or not. And as long as my cortisol was high, Matt, I was on guard."

"That makes sense, Casey. And I can see the changes in you, too. You're a lot more relaxed. You used to be tense and alert. Now, you're just sitting here with me and I can see you're happy."

Nodding, Casey reached over and touched his hand briefly. "Matt, I am happy. And no one is more thrilled with the changes in me than my family. I was talking to my mom last night and she cried. They've all been worried about me since the attack."

"Dr. Lawton is incredible. I'm glad she moved here and I'm glad you've gone to her," he said, meaning it. How badly Matt wanted to make love with Casey.

"What about you?" she asked, picking up her burger.

Shrugging, Matt gave her a boyish smile and said, "I guess my grieving over Bev is pretty much worked through. Everyone told me that one day I would be looking forward, not living in the past. I didn't believe them, but now, it's really happening."

"That's good to know," she murmured. "In a way, Matt, we've both been anchored in the past by bad things that happened to us. And it seems we're slowly being freed of them."

"It's a good way to put it," he agreed.

"I worry about Megan, though."

"In what way?"

Casey grimaced. "I know Megan and I are close. I love her dearly, but I worry what she'll think if she sees us kissing one another. Or holding hands. Where is she with the grief over losing her mother?"

"I've asked myself those same questions," he slowly admitted. He took a sip of the chocolate milkshake he'd ordered. "So far, Megan has seen us together, but we've not been intimate."

"Right. And I worry what might happen if she sees us holding hands, or if you put your arms around me. Or…if we kiss…"

"I don't know," Matt said, frowning. "I don't know where Megan is with her own grief and healing process, Casey. She isn't talking. I can't read her mind." Matt sighed out his frustration. "All the child psychiatrists say that when her grieving is over, she'll probably start talking again. That's the only ruler I have with which to judge what's going on inside Megan."

Feeling deeply for Matt, Casey said, "This is a terrible, torturous place to be with your child, Matt. I feel she's happy. Does she seem happy to you?"

"Yes, when you come to our home, the lights just sparkle in her eyes, Casey. I really believe she loves you."

Warmth cascaded through Casey's heart. "There's nothing not to love about Megan. She's bright, alert and caring. She loves you, too."

"But when you come to our home, or we all meet up, Megan is super-excited. She looks forward to seeing you, Casey."

"I know she does."

"Are you okay with that? Because from where I stand, Megan is bonding deeply with you." He was worried about that, too, but said nothing further. What if he and Casey had a falling-out? What if they split up? Not that they were together, but Matt knew that Megan saw Casey at least once a week, and that was enough for his daughter to bond with her.

"If I had a daughter," Casey told him, her voice filled with sudden emotion, "I'd want one just like her."

Relief shot through Matt. His mouth softened and he clung to her tender gaze. "Thanks. It's good to hear because I know Meggie is falling hard for you." So was he, but Matt knew it was too soon to admit it to Casey. "I guess... I guess I don't want Meggie hurt—again. She lost her mother. I feel she sees you as a mother of sorts to her. Not that I can get inside her head, but everything points to that. I'm sure it has caught your attention, too."

"I agree with you," Casey said. "In some ways, I worry about that, Matt. Megan has suffered so much already." Hesitating she added in a low tone, "What if we separate? Oh, I know we're not going together, but I'm over at your home often enough that Megan could get the idea that...well, we're a couple."

Nodding, Matt respected her ability to talk about the complex issues that stood between them. "Right. My very thoughts, too."

"Megan so much wants a mother, Matt. That's my intuition talking. Not that I've had the experience of being a mother, but the way she reacts to me tells me that."

"Yes, you're right." He rested his hands on either side of his plate and stared at her. "Everything's so tentative, Casey. For me. For you. And I'm finding myself feeling trapped by a lot of circumstances out of my control. I know Megan needs a mother. But I couldn't push myself just to marry someone so that she'd have a mother again."

"No, how could you?" Casey asked, watching the strain in his eyes, the anxiety for his daughter.

"I thought about it," Matt gruffly admitted. "One child psychiatrist said marrying quickly might bring Meggie out of her muteness."

Grimacing, Casey said, "That's not very logical. Megan would know the difference, don't you think?"

"That's what I came to realize," Matt said. "I walked away from that shrink's session doing a lot of serious thinking about what he said. In the long run, I just couldn't force myself to ask any woman to be my wife so that Megan could have a replacement mother in her life."

"There are so many issues here," Casey agreed gently. "And I know you wrestle with them every day."

"I do." Matt smiled a little. "But just getting to talk it out with you helps." Matt wanted to tell her how important she was to him, to helping him. Did Casey realize she was sunlight in his dark, wintered soul?

Biting into her hamburger, Casey ate for a moment before speaking. "I feel we're all doing the best we can, Matt. The three of us are deeply wounded by different things. My mom is a very wise person. She told me after I came out of the coma that I'd heal slowly from this wound within me. She said it wouldn't be straightforward, but more like the twists and turns of a snake. My mom was right. Healing just takes time. I think what we have to do is realize that and give ourselves the space and patience to just continue what we're already doing."

"Good advice," he agreed. "Your mother is a very wise woman."

"She had a lot of wounds that my father gave her when they first flew together. There was a lot of forgiveness she had to give him and he also had to respect her as an equal. They both grew up and then love took over."

Sitting back in the booth, Matt gazed at Casey. She was young and yet, because of her traumatic past, she was much more mature than other women her own age. The way her hair curled around her face and framed it made him want to kiss her again. "I like what we have. I want to just keep muddling along with you, Casey, at a speed that's comfortable for both of us."

Nodding, she smiled gently. "We have nowhere to go but up, Matt. And somehow, Megan will grow with us. Don't worry so much about her. She's more resilient than you give her credit for."

"How about a last picnic of the year with us, then?" he challenged. "Megan and I have, for the last two years, gone out to a special meadow above Moose Creek Road just about every week in the summer. Around now, she helps me make the food for our picnic and we hike up there to see the last of the wildflowers before the serious snowing starts. Would you like to go with us?"

"I'd love to," Casey murmured. Drowning in his heated look, she found she wanted to be with him more than ever. Grateful that her PTSD symptoms were truly dissolving, Casey felt a freedom from the past that made her nearly euphoric. Matt was partly responsible for it whether he knew it or not.

"Great. I'll tell Megan. We'll plan a special meal for all of us. She'll jump up and down for joy."

CHAPTER NINETEEN

FRANK BENSON REMAINED patient as his three targets entered a familiar but little-used trail near Moose Creek Road. This road was a back door from Jackson Hole to the entrance of Grand Teton National Park. Benson had planned carefully for weeks and had watched and waited. Now that Senator Peyton had named the three of them as targets, he'd gotten busy with support activities.

Wanting a cigarette but knowing the smell could alert them, Benson sat hidden up on the brush-clad slope, undetected, looking out across the colorful valley filled with the changing leaves of fall. The mid-September sun was high in the sky. It was another perfect autumn day. There were tourists hiking everywhere, but this particular trail was rarely used because it was so steep. At the end of it there was a flower-strewn meadow, but few knew that, except for locals like Sinclaire, who visited this meadow every Friday without fail. It was a challenging trail up to the plateau above.

There was an abandoned log cabin, much of it in shambles, hidden deep in the woods just above that meadow. No one lived there, and it was a perfect spot for Benson to set up his base camp. Locals would never look into the cabin—it had been cordoned off by the county as unsafe and dangerous.

Mentally rubbing his hands, Benson sat in camouflage gear, a large knapsack with everything he'd need on his back. The senator wanted all three of them dead. And he couldn't just try to shoot them because it would create problems. Three people found, each with a single shot to the head would raise the brows of every law-enforcement goon in the state. And Peyton didn't want that kind of public focus on this assassination. And he didn't want anyone to link Bev Sinclaire's murder with this newest attempt.

No, Benson had plotted long and hard on this group killing. The senator wanted it to look natural, as if they'd gotten lost out in the thick forest, frozen to death from hypothermia at night. At this altitude—eight thousand feet—the autumn nights were well below freezing. Cold enough to kill someone—naturally.

Benson congratulated himself on his detailed research; he had found out that grizzly bear number 340, a female with two cubs, lived in the general area of the broken-down miner's cabin. He used the cabin as a central point to track her daily activities. And anyone who knew bears, knew a mother with cubs was the most dangerous of all predators. This sow, a cinnamon-colored grizzly, was particularly moody and would attack a hiker or hunter without any provocation. All the stupid hiker or hunter had to do was show up within range of her weak eyesight and she'd barrel after the human intent on killing them. She had a reputation for this and Benson smiled faintly. He'd spent a month following her, watching her through binoculars and getting used to her pattern of activities.

Best of all, her main territory was right near that old cabin hidden by the woods. She would travel ten or fifteen miles a day looking for food, but she always returned to that area, a favorite haunt of hers. The flower meadow was oval and provided plenty of grubs that she dug up from beneath the rocks to feed herself and her growing cubs. Benson had found her hibernation den up on a craggy, clifflike area two thousand feet above the meadow. At that level, snow came early and the sow would be working overtime to eat voraciously before she went up there to hibernate through the long, cold winter. He'd also discovered other caves near her den that had been created by volcanic activity millions of years ago. These caves were to the north of the grizzly's lair. And they were perfect places to hide someone so they would freeze to death.

Watching the three hikers, he saw that they were unaware of anything except enjoying their noontime hike. Getting up, he moved without sound through the brush and thick woodlands. He was at least a quarter of a mile away from them and they were too focused on themselves, not on the area around them, to hear him. Again, Benson smiled. The groves of white-barked aspen were sporting their yellow leaves. In other spots, there were trees with red and orange leaves. If he weren't intent on his job, Benson would enjoy the brilliant fall colors that came the first three weeks of September. Already, it had snowed twice, and now they were enjoying an Indian summer. Usually, winter would set in permanently by October. And that's what Benson was counting on.

Assured his targets were going to the meadow as usual, he moved swiftly up the steep slope. The land rose sharply and then descended just as sharply down to the meadow. Benson knew that at this time of day the sow and her cubs would be south of the meadow. She wouldn't hear the hikers and that's what he wanted.

His heart pounded as he pushed his toes deeply into the pine-needled ground beneath him. Now, luck would play into his hand, he hoped.

Benson arrived at the northern end of the meadow. It was filled with yellowing grass and the last of the hardy wildflowers that had managed to survive the first snows of the season and the nightly frosts in the area. The highly private area looked like a gem surrounded by the dark green forest spattered with bright fall colors. The Tetons majestically towered above it. Shedding his pack at the cabin, he made sure everything was in readiness. Double-checking that the bear was not around, Benson placed a pistol in the holster at his side. Covering it with his dark green-and-brown jacket, he mentally went over the elaborate and complex trap once again. He was ready to kidnap the kid and the woman. Smiling faintly as he headed unseen toward the meadow, Benson knew that when one of them showed up missing, it would set off a search of the area by the other two. The cabin would be a pit stop to a greater plan he had for his victims. He'd carry the unconscious woman and child up to a cave. It would be there that he'd put his victims. Benson was sure that one night alone in that cave at below-freezing temperature would kill them. Hypothermia would do the job for him. To make it look like they'd been killed by a bear, he'd put them into the grizzly bear's known path and sprinkle a trail of food so that the sow would find the unconscious victims and eat them. That would be two people killed under natural circumstances. Then, he'd wait and time the last hit on Matt Sinclaire. It might take a couple of days, even a week, but Benson had carefully planned the firefighter's demise. He would take him out and carry him to another cave and he, too, would freeze to death overnight. Grinning, Benson knew this challenge was fearsome but he felt confident he could pull it off.

Settling down behind thick brush about a thousand feet away from the meadow, Benson waited. His adrenaline was up and he savored the excitement of the hunter in stalking mode. This is what he lived for. Now who would wander nearest to where he was hiding? That was the only question that remained unanswered.

"HURRY!" CASEY CALLED breathlessly, running through the meadow, laughing. Megan was hard on her heels. Matt was bringing up the rear. Stopping, she turned and smiled down at the girl. Megan looked cute with her hair up in a ponytail. Her warm pink jacket, a red T-shirt and coveralls along with her little red day pack on her back made her look like a bright spot in the yellowed meadow.

"Help me open this up, Megan," she urged, opening the red wool blanket that Matt always used for picnics.

Megan laughed and caught hold of one corner of it. In no time, they had the bright red blanket spread across the ground. Shedding her pack, Casey set it down and opened it up. Megan helped her unload the plastic containers of food they'd made earlier in the morning for their lunch. Looking up, she saw Matt approaching. How handsome he looked to Casey. Ever since their last talk, it were as if the wall that she'd always held up to protect her from men had dissolved.

"Need some more help?" Matt called, grinning. His heart swelled with love for his daughter, who was completely focused on helping Casey pull out the plastic plates, flatware and napkins. Of late, Megan had become much more engaged with life, happier and wanting Casey around as much as possible.

"Nope," Casey called. "I think Megan and I have it taken care of."

Nodding, Matt pulled off his day pack and set it on the grass near the blanket. The sun was warm, but there was a chill in the air because they were high on the slopes of the Tetons. It never got really warm up at this altitude. Leaning over, Matt pulled out a thermos of coffee for the adults and some orange juice for Megan. Handing them to his daughter, Matt felt at peace for the first time in a long time.

Settling down on crossed legs at one end of the blanket, Megan in the middle distributing plates, flatware, napkins and closed food containers to him, Matt absorbed his daughter's expression. It was almost as if Megan was normal once more. She was also trying to form words. She made fewer guttural sounds and rasps, and it appeared to Matt that she was honestly trying to speak once again.

He silently thanked Dr. Jordana Lawton for prescribing the medicine for Megan's elevated cortisol levels. The last test had revealed that Megan's cortisol was finally settled within normal bounds. And her demeanor had changed remarkably as a result. Megan was happy. The shine in her eyes told Matt everything. They were all happy, if he was reading the look in Casey's eyes, too. How badly he wanted to take her into his arms, kiss her and make love with her.

As Matt helped open the containers, his heart expanded with more joy than he'd felt in a long, long time. Over the last month, Casey and he had slowly, like two orbiting planets, moved closer and closer together. If the look in her eyes was any indication, Matt knew they would kiss before this incredible day was over. "Let's see," he murmured, taking the spoons and putting them in each container, "we have grilled chicken, potato salad, olives and for dessert—chocolate cake."

"Who knew you were such a chef," Casey teased. She felt her lower body responding to Matt's heated look. On the way up the trail, they'd held hands. She was always concerned about how Megan would take their getting together. Matt had assured her a number of times that Megan doted on her and he didn't think there was an issue. Still, Casey cared deeply for the little girl. She would turn nine years old in five days and they had planned a wonderful birthday party for her. Megan knew nothing of it and that would make it all the sweeter to see when all her school friends came over to celebrate the milestone with her.

Preening, Matt said, "Hey, at the firehouse, my team salivates until I make this cake."

"I believe it," Casey murmured. Megan sat on the edge of the blanket between them. She made sure the girl was served first. Matt poured her orange juice from her thermos and set the cup down in front of her. There was such a wonderful happiness covering all of them, Casey realized. The autumn sun was warm and took the chill off the midday air temperature, hovering in the forties.

FRANK WATCHED THE FAMILY. They were genuinely happy. He could hear their laughter drifting his way from time to time. When they finished their meal and had packed it back up into their knapsacks, Matt Sinclaire brought out a Frisbee. The little girl loved chasing it, picking it up and slinging it through the air to the two adults. He watched, his heart starting a slow pound, as the woman threw it. She wasn't very adept at it. The red Frisbee waffled on the air and landed just at the edge of the meadow. He hunkered down and waited.

Running over to the Frisbee, Casey laughed. Turning with it in hand, she called back to Matt and Megan, who stood in the middle of the meadow, "I'm not very good at this, you know." She twisted and threw it as hard as she could toward them.

Megan screeched with delight and caught it as it thunked to the ground about thirty feet from where Casey stood.

"Weak throw," Matt called, cupping his hand to his mouth.

Grinning, Casey said, "Guilty as charged!" She laughed and felt buoyant. Something as simple as a Frisbee game was bonding them tightly to one another. Like a family.

Family... The word whispered through Casey's mind as she saw Megan scoop up the Frisbee, a smile on her face. Hadn't they been like a cobbled-together family since they'd met? Casey acknowledged it in her heart. What was there not to love about Megan? She was a bright, caring child, sensitive and innocent. And Matt... Casey's gaze moved to the man in the center of the meadow. In that moment, she realized how much she loved him. The sensation drenched her like a vibrant rush of wild river water.

Casey was so caught up in her revelations that she didn't see Megan toss the Frisbee in her direction. It was only Megan's shout that jerked her out of her reverie.

The Frisbee sailed high over her head and disappeared up the slope of the mountain. It tumbled into the thick brush, unseen.

"Are you asleep at the switch?" Matt hollered, laughing good-naturedly.

Embarrassed, Casey raised her hand and yelled, "I'll go get it. I'll be right back!" and she dove into the thick underbrush.

Matt watched her dive into it, her hand held near her eyes so she wouldn't get swatted by the brush. In seconds, she had disappeared.

Megan laughed gaily and ran back to her father, flapping her arms like a bird ready to take off. She threw her arms outward toward her father.

Matt picked her up and whirled her around and around until they both got so dizzy that he fell to the ground. Careful not to hurt Megan, Matt hit the ground first and absorbed the shock. His daughter squealed in delight and rolled off to one side. Over and over again, Megan purposely rolled through the grass. Her coat became damp from the dew still caught deep within the thick strands of golden grass.

Getting up to his hands and knees, breathing hard, he saw Megan scramble to her feet. Matt didn't even have time to get balanced when she flew into his arms. They both tumbled once more to the ground, laughing and giggling.

By the time Matt wrestled Megan and lost the "fight," he was winded. Happiness thrummed through him because his daughter was finally becoming more like her old self. Grateful for the roughhouse playing, he managed to get to his feet. Megan stood nearby, dusting off all the pieces of grass that clung to her coveralls and jacket. Matt did the same. Time had halted.

Lifting his head, he looked to the end of the meadow. Where was Casey? Frowning, he searched the brushy wall where she'd disappeared minutes earlier.

"Casey?" he called, "did you find the Frisbee yet?"

No answer. Maybe Megan had thrown the Frisbee a lot farther into the brush than he'd first thought? "Come on, Megan, let's go find Casey," he said, and he held out his hand to his daughter.

Megan gripped his hand and they walked toward the end of the meadow.

"Casey?" Matt called again as they reached the edge of it. "Casey?"

No answer. Frowning, Matt suddenly felt worried. Turning, he leaned down and told Megan, "Stay here. Daddy's going to find Casey. Stay on the blanket and watch our knapsacks."

Nodding, Megan galloped back out into the meadow to stay with the three day packs.

Moving into the brush, Matt protected his eyes with his hand from the many branches swatting at his face, just as he'd seen Casey doing. The brush was tough and it took everything he had to bull his way through it. As he emerged on the other side of the ten-foot-high brush, more walls of yellowed leaves met his gaze. Looking around, the brush too tall to see over, Matt called Casey again.

No answer.

What the hell had happened to her? Almost mouthing those words, Matt felt the first niggling fear. This was grizzly country. He knew bears frequented stands of brush like this precisely because smaller creatures hid within them. He knew a grizzly could silently move up behind a human and they'd never hear it coming—until it was too late.

Now, fear made him more than worried. Matt knew each grizzly bear had a territory. Had Casey run into one? Surely, he'd have heard it. Matt wasn't so sure. He'd been in the middle of the meadow with Megan. He hadn't been watching the grove Casey had disappeared into. His focus had been on playing with his daughter, instead. Running his fingers through his hair and turning around, anxiously searching for any sight or sound of Casey, his mouth turned grim. Again and again, Matt called for Casey.

She never answered him.

Worried now, Matt could see Megan standing uncertainly by the day packs, looking around, anxious now that both adults had disappeared. He called back to Megan to reassure her. Where had Casey gone? It wasn't like her not to answer him.

For the next twenty minutes, Matt tramped through the brush, struggling and falling several times. At the end of his search, he returned to the meadow, to Megan's relief. Pulling the radio off his belt that would put him in direct contact with the fire department, he made an emergency call for help. Megan was clinging to his hand. She looked scared. As scared as he felt. After reporting that Casey had disappeared, Matt waited. He heard no sounds out of the ordinary. He saw no movement up the brush and wooded slope. But hell, a thousand-pound grizzly could whisper through the area and never be seen or heard by a human.

Swallowing hard, Matt was torn. He desperately wanted to go find Casey. But he couldn't. Not with Megan in tow. He would not jeopardize his daughter's life if a grizzly was on the hunt. They always went for little children first. To a hungry bear children resembled small animals, their high-pitched voices sounding like a baby creature's crying. All of that made them serious food targets.

Oh, God, where are you? Casey? What happened? Where are you? Wiping his mouth, Matt knew he had to get Megan out of the area. Within the hour, the Forest Service would be sending in a team of rangers who would scour the area. The fire department was sending an ambulance, just in case. But it would be down at the parking lot, a thousand feet below them at the trailhead.

Mind whirling, Matt numbly put on his day pack and helped Megan on with hers. He gripped Casey's pack and then captured his daughter's hand. As he started to walk out of the meadow, Megan cried.

"What?" he demanded, his patience thin.

Pointing to where Casey had gone, Megan tugged on her father's hand to stop him. Tears splashed down her paling face as she jabbed her small index finger at the end of the meadow.

Matt shook his head. "Casey's missing, Megan. I have to get you back down the trail. There's help coming. We'll look for her soon."

Breaking into sobs, Megan jerked loose from his hand. She started running across the meadow as fast as her little legs would carry her.

Dammit! Matt whirled around. In several long strides, he caught up with Megan. Gripping her, he held her tightly in his arms. "Megan, Casey has disappeared," he rasped. "She's not here!"

Screaming, Megan tried to escape his hands. She

twisted right and then left. Her face was white now, with tears making her cheeks glisten.

"Mommy!" she screamed. *"Mommy!"* She jerked her finger toward the wall of brush where Casey had disappeared.

Shocked, Matt almost let go of his daughter. She was speaking! The word was clear and easy to understand. Feeling trapped in a hurricane of wild emotions of terror for Casey and joy over Megan suddenly speaking, Matt tried to gentle her into standing still.

"Mommy disappeared," he begged her hoarsely. "She's disappeared, Megan. I promise, I'm coming back here to find her. But you can't come with me. This is bear country. I can't risk you being hurt."

Her hands pressed to her eyes, Megan stopped trying to get away. "Mommy, Mommy," she kept sobbing.

Pulling Megan into his arms, Matt held his daughter tenderly, her head against his shoulder as she cried. Megan didn't understand what had happened. And he hadn't explained it very well, either. Glancing up, Matt stared at the brush. *What's happened to Casey? Oh, God, please let her be alive! This can't be, it just can't! You can't take her from us! You can't...*

CHAPTER TWENTY

CASEY SLOWLY AWOKE. She lay bound in a cave. Her head was pounding in pain, and memories dripped down into her awakening consciousness. She'd gone into the thickets to locate the Frisbee. A hand had shot out of nowhere and clamped over her mouth. In seconds, she was pulled back against a big man with garlic on his breath. She struggled, her scream suffocated by his hand. Casey felt the biting sting of a needle entering her upper arm through her jacket. And then...blackness.

Until now. She forced herself to look around even though the violent pain in her head made her wince. Whatever was in the needle had knocked her out cold within a minute. She recalled struggling, the man's breath fetid as he dragged her backward. The sunlight was barely on the other hill across the valley. Where was she? Who had done this? Looking around, she realized she was alone. And it was getting colder.

Looking at her hands, Casey groggily realized they were bound with duct tape. And so were her ankles. Her fingers were numb and she flexed them. The tape was so tight that it had cut off much of the blood supply to them. Frightened, Casey realized someone would come back. And then what? The last event where she'd been attacked roared back to her. And then, rage followed.

The rage was real. Casey sat up and shook her head

to clear it, determined to escape. The cave was barely ten feet in depth, about six feet wide and eight feet high. The ground was dry. After looking around, her heart pounding with fear and anger, Casey lay down on her side. Maneuvering her fingers to her right pocket, she sought and found her Buck knife that she always carried. To her relief, it was still there. Whoever had captured her hadn't done a body search.

Casey unsnapped the leather case. With uncoordinated and torturous movements over the next five minutes, she managed to pull the knife out. Groaning softly, she pushed herself into a sitting position once more. Glancing apprehensively at the cave entrance, she strained to press hard enough to pop the blade from its casing. It took several frustrating minutes but she accomplished it. The knife dropped to the dirt, a small dust cloud rising in its wake. Groaning, her head pounding with pain, Casey picked it up and anchored it between her hands. In three quick slices, her ankles were free.

It wasn't going to be as easy to get her hands free. Breathing coming in gasps, Casey was fueled by righteous rage. She was *never* going to allow any man *ever* to hurt her again! Forcing herself to her knees, she settled the Buck knife between them so that the blade lay up and available. With careful movements, she sliced through the tape after a number of attempts.

The moment her hands were free, she ripped off the sticky tape and disgustedly threw it aside. Grabbing the knife and holding it close to her side, Casey forced herself to her feet. Instantly, dizziness attacked her and her knees buckled. She fell unceremoniously to the dirt floor with an "Oomph!"

No! No! I have to get out of here! He'll be coming back! Oh, God, give me the strength to run away! Breath coming in explosions, Casey got to her hands and knees, the knife clenched in her fist. If she couldn't walk, she'd crawl!

Making it to the lip of the cave, Casey quickly looked around. This cave was at least a thousand feet higher than where she and Matt and Megan had been. Below her was a beautiful and bright coverlet of red, yellow and orange deciduous trees interspersed with the dark evergreens. She saw no humans.

Looking around, Casey felt alarm and fear. She had to leave this place! But where was she? Her mind was fuzzy. She wasn't thinking clearly and she knew it was the drug that had been given to her. Rage continued to clear her mind, though, and she lifted her chin. The Tetons were on one side of the huge valley. Casey was familiar with the other side and quickly realized that she wasn't that far from where she'd been attacked.

Grunting, Casey heaved herself to her feet. The cave sat on a talus slope of nothing but rocks, large and small. She realized she was at about the ten-thousand-foot level where no trees would grow. And, even worse, Casey realized this could be the cave home of a grizzly bear. *Not. Good.* Legs shaking, she gripped the rock wall and forced herself out of her prison.

She hadn't gone more than a few wobbling steps down the slope when she slipped and fell. With a groan, Casey rolled a good ten feet, the biting rocks striking and bruising her. Fearfully looking around, the knife still clutched in her hand, Casey watched for her attacker to reappear. She knew it was a man. The cloying smell of the garlic hung in the cave. Taking a ragged breath, she got to her feet, legs wide to try and compensate for her lack of balance.

With each step down the talus slope, Casey felt a little stronger, her head a little clearer. Looking at her watch, she realized a good hour had passed since the attack. Who had done this to her? And why? Breathing raggedly, she pushed herself. Casey wanted to get to the line of trees far below. If she could reach it, she could fade into the forest and not be seen as easily. Up here on the rocky, vertical slope, she was an obvious target to man and grizzly alike.

Where was her attacker? Why had she been targeted? Was this a man from her past? No, it couldn't be; all five of those men were in prison, each serving a ten-year sentence. Had one of them escaped? And abruptly, Casey recalled Gwen Garner warning her about Frank Benson. She'd brought her a photo of the man, a murderer who had been in prison, at a later date. Casey didn't know him. But was he the one stalking her now? His face was heavy, his eyes black and lifeless. Scared now, she threw out her arms to try and balance herself. Her feet skidded across the finer gravel and she wobbled unsteadily from side to side.

Her mind worked sporadically. One moment, she was thinking clearly, the next, her balance was gone and she couldn't think her way out of a paper bag. Frustrated, yet fueled by rage that this had happened to her again, Casey resolved to push on toward the safety of the tree line.

And then, in a moment of clarity, Casey realized that Matt and Megan must be terrified by her disappearance. Her love for Matt overwhelmed her. Casey sobbed. Just as quickly, she forced back her emotions.

Right now, she had to survive this and run away from whoever her attacker was. And she knew he had to be around. Somewhere. But where?

Her mind dove down into filmy, disparate elements again. Her balance dissolved and she fell. This time, Casey pitched forward. She threw her arms out in front of her. The knife was knocked out of her hand as her wrist hit a rock. She had fallen hard and then slid several feet before slowing to a halt. Breathing in ragged gasps, Casey scrambled to her hands and knees. She lunged up the slope and recovered her knife. There was no way she was going to be without some kind of protection. Ever since her first attack, Casey always carried this knife. Now she was so glad she had it. Grabbing it in her bloodied and bruised fingers, she turned around.

Her mind cleared again. It was as if her body was trying to purge itself of the effects of the drug. Almost in a tidelike fashion, Casey could count on thirty seconds of clarity followed by thirty seconds of feeling like a rag mop with no coordination or balance. She labored knowing this, and when she felt the drug hit her again, she slowed her descent. Each time her mind focused again, her legs were stronger and her balance more sure. Then she would rush down the slope. The rocks tumbled around her as she took advantage of those moments.

Finally, breathing explosively, Casey dove into the tree line. Leaning her back up against a huge evergreen, Casey tried to quiet her rasping gasp. The forest was silent. She heard nothing. Not even a bird, but at this time of year, there weren't many around because it was time to fly south. Realizing her eyesight was coming and going as well, Casey felt rage tunnel through her. Whoever had done this to her meant to hurt her.

Rubbing the elbow that she'd bruised in a fall, Casey kept the knife in her hand and aimed herself down the slope toward where she knew the oval meadow was located. As she moved, she tried not to step on any branches that would crack and make a noise. Her senses were so raw that she felt fear more than anger right now. Where was her attacker? Had he seen her escape? Was he on his way to recapture her? Mouth compressed for a moment, Casey knew she wasn't going to let that happen. Her hand tightened around the knife. She'd kill the son of a bitch before he'd ever touch her. The resolve was so powerful that when it flowed through Casey it gave her a surge of instant strength.

She began to trot instead of walk. The moments of clarity lengthened as she wove drunkenly in and around the trees. The pine needles made the slope slippery and sometimes she fell. Every time, Casey pushed herself back up, looked around and then continued down the steep incline.

Suddenly, Casey heard the *thump, thump, thump* of someone running behind her. Gasping, she jerked her head around and looked behind her. *There!* Her eyes widened. A cry erupted from her.

A tall man in camo gear, pistol in his hand, his eyes focused on her, was charging toward her! His narrow face was emphasized by his short, black hair, fierce-looking brown eyes filled with anger and his thin, determined mouth. Casey recognized him as Frank Benson. He was a murderer!

Digging the toes of her boots into the slippery pine needles, Casey hurtled down the slope. She wove in and out of the trees, her breath exploding. *Hurry! Hurry!* Tripping on a limb, Casey flew forward. She caught herself. Steadied. *Hurry!* She had no idea of where to go except toward the meadow. Her mind focused only on surviving. The slope began to be less steep. She ran faster. The *thump, thump, thump* was coming closer! Adrenaline shot through Casey. The memory of her last attack by a group of men gave wings to her feet as she ran to the breaking point.

And then, a shot was fired. The tree she had just passed exploded with flying bits of bark.

Casey gave a cry, and threw up her hand to protect her face from the flying debris. *Hurry!* Benson was trying to kill her! Why was he doing this to her? That question jammed into her head as she raced down the slope. Somewhere in her shattered senses, Casey knew he'd have a hard time hitting her because of the trees. She continued to weave and bob around them.

And then ahead, she saw the thickets where she'd been captured by this killer. With a scream, Casey began to call for help. Someone *had* to hear her! She launched herself into the thickets. Instantly, the brush snapped and whipped around her face and body. Casey didn't feel anything. All she wanted to do was escape and get to the meadow!

"DID YOU HEAR THAT?" sheriff's deputy Cade Garner said to Matt. They were standing near the tent that had been erected in the meadow. Right now, rangers and deputies were fanned out in teams of two in an effort to locate Casey Cantrell.

Matt was shrugging into his pack when his friend asked the question. He'd already spent a fruitless hour searching to the south with another team and had just come back for more water and supplies before he went out in another direction. "No? What did you hear?" He saw Garner's profile looking grim. And he was looking north.

"A gunshot. I'd swear it," Cade answered, unsnapping his holster and pulling out his firearm. "Come on!" He bolted toward the thickets.

Matt didn't hesitate. In a moment, they were striding toward the wall.

He heard another shot.

And a scream.

"That's Casey!" Matt roared, racing past the deputy.

No one was more surprised than Matt when Casey came bursting out of the thickets. He saw the terror in her face, her hands outspread, the knife in one, as she flew through the last of the brush.

"Stay down!" Garner shouted to her. In seconds, he was lunging into the thicket, gun held high.

Matt skidded to a halt as Casey fell and rolled into the meadow. She was bleeding from her hands. Her cheek was scratched. The terror in her eyes gripped his heart.

"Casey!" Matt shouted, and quickly dropped to his knees where she had fallen onto her stomach.

Gasping, Casey screamed, "Frank Benson's after me! He's a murderer." She rolled to a sitting position, jabbing her finger in the same direction Garner had gone.

Matt gripped her and instantly shielded her with his body. Several shots were fired. The gunfire was sharp. And then…silence.

Breathing hard, Casey gripped Matt's jacket, looking toward the thicket. "Oh, God, Matt. The man's name is Benson. He drugged me in the bushes. I woke up with my hands and feet tied in a cave about one thousand feet above the meadow. Go help Cade!"

"Stay here," Matt rasped, leaping to his feet. He ran into the thickets. When he pushed out the other side, he saw Cade Garner standing over a man in a camo suit. He was getting his handcuffs out from behind his belt. Whoever the stranger was, he was wounded and not giving Garner any trouble.

Running up to the deputy, Matt said, "Casey says this is Frank Benson. He's a murderer." He spotted the man's weapon farther up the slope where Cade had shot him. He glanced over at his friend. The sheriff's deputy was all business, his face grim, his mouth taut as he ordered the stranger to turn over on his stomach to be cuffed.

"I'll be damned—Frank Benson," Garner snarled, slipping the cuffs on the man. "We've got a rap sheet on you." Once done, he holstered his weapon. "Help me get him to his feet. I winged him."

Nodding, Matt gripped the stranger's camo jacket and together, they hauled him to his feet. Matt saw blood leaking out of the jacket near Benson's right shoulder. The convict glared at him.

"Hold him," Cade ordered. "I'm getting his weapon." He trotted up the slope to retrieve it.

Anger tunneled through Matt. Benson was still breathing hard, his thin mouth working, the air filled with a barrage of curses. He had tried to kill Casey. Why? And then, Matt felt rage so powerful and lethal that he shoved the killer toward Garner. Benson stumbled but righted himself. The deputy gripped him by the shoulder.

"Let's go, Benson, you have a date with the hospi-

tal and then jail," he snarled and read him his Miranda
rights as he shoved him down the hill.

Casey was sitting in the meadow with two other deputies. She saw Benson in custody, the grim look on
Cade Garner's face. Matt met her gaze and she saw the
banked rage in his eyes. He had his hand on the killer's
other shoulder. A paramedic quickly checked the prisoner's upper-arm wound, then, saying the wound was
superficial, she pointed down below, to the trailhead.
Together, Matt and Cade roughly forced Benson down
the trail that led to the parking lot far below. There, he
would be cared for by another paramedic and taken to
the hospital for further treatment. She pulled the radio
from her waist belt and gave a report to her partner waiting with the ambulance down at the trailhead.

Sitting there, Casey began to shake. Matt came and
knelt by her side, his hand on her shoulder. The paramedic signed off her radio, turned and focused on her,
then hurried over to where Casey sat.

"Hey, Casey, are you okay?" she asked, kneeling
down in front of her with her bag. "I'm Brenda Par-
sons. My partner, Peggy, is down at the trailhead waiting for that creep. I called her to let her know he was
slightly wounded."

Tears began to come to Casey's eyes. She felt the
protection of Matt and the gentle touch of his hand on
her arm. "I—I— Yes, I'm okay." She held up her hands.
"They're a little worse for wear, but I'm okay. Really, I
am…" She battled back more tears.

"Let me see," Brenda said gently. She began her sys-
tematic examination of Casey from head to toe. Matt
dug into his pack and brought out a thermos.

"Can she have some coffee, Brenda?" he asked.

"You bet." Brenda smiled. "Casey? You feel like a belt of good, hot, black coffee?"

"Y-yes," Casey said, giving Matt a look of thanks. He handed her the cap of the thermos filled with hot coffee. She was going to live. She had survived. Looking around as she held the cup in both hands, she whispered, "My God, that man is a convict and murderer. He drugged me, tied me up in a bear cave. When I escaped, he tried to kill me, Brenda."

"He's not going to hurt you anymore," Brenda said, opening her case. She already had her gloves on and she brought out gauze and gently wiped the blood off Casey's cheek. "Cade will take him back to the jail after his visit to the hospital." She frowned. "Do you guys know this dude?" She looked at the two deputies who flanked them.

The tall, lean deputy with black hair and green eyes standing nearby said, "We just had a photo of Benson passed around the department this morning."

Brenda gave Casey a smile. "How are you feeling? I know you said he drugged you up."

"Better every minute," Casey murmured, gratefully sipping the black coffee. As she sat there, the reality that she could now be dead hit her. The coffee burned her tongue. She was alive. *Alive!* And Matt's presence was a huge comfort.

Brenda took one of her hands and washed off the blood and expertly applied antibiotic ointment to the scratches. "As soon as I'm done we'll walk you back to the parking lot, and get you to the hospital."

"I don't need a hospital, Brenda. I'm fine. All I really want," Casey said in a trembling voice, "is to be home with Matt and Megan. That's all." Matt squeezed her arm and gave her a tender look.

"Honey," Brenda said in a husky chuckle, "they'll need a blood sample from you first, for this case."

"What about Megan?" Casey asked, beginning to look around. She realized now there were a lot of people in the meadow. One of the deputies had called off the search and she saw several knots of hikers returning. Realizing they had all been looking for her made Casey feel better.

"Right after you disappeared," Matt told her, "I looked about twenty minutes for you. Megan got scared because you'd disappeared. I was forced to take her down to the parking lot, but not before I called in your disappearance to the fire department and the sheriff's office. One of the other officers took Megan back home. My sister, Jessie, met them there and she's caring for her right now. She's okay, Casey."

Relief shot through her. "Why did this guy Benson do this? I don't understand."

Shaking his head, Matt muttered, "We don't know, either, Casey. Just thank God you're okay."

Nodding, Casey whispered, "At least Megan didn't see any of this. She's been traumatized enough."

"No kidding," Brenda murmured. She finished cleaning up Casey's hands and sat back on her heels and smiled over at her. "I don't know what drug this jerk gave you, but we really do need to get you to the hospital and draw blood. We have to find out what it is to treat you further."

"Whatever it is, it's awful," Casey muttered. Little by little, her pounding heart was beginning to slow down. The adrenaline was starting to decline in her bloodstream. More and more of the people who had been looking for her came up smiling, relief in their expressions.

Finishing off the coffee, she thanked Matt and handed the cup back to him. Turning her attention to the paramedic, she said, "I think I can stand, Matt."

"Okay, let's try." Matt stood up and held out his hands toward Casey.

When she got to her feet, Casey wavered a little. Instantly, Matt put a steadying hand under her elbow. The care nearly overwhelmed Casey and she bit down on her lip to stop from crying. "Let's go," she urged him.

All she wanted was to see home. As Casey turned, walking slowly, she searched Matt's grim face. Her heart yearned as never before for time alone with Matt. All this trauma had done one thing right for her. She now knew without any doubt that she loved Matt and Megan. And all Casey wanted was private time to tell him that.

Taking a deep, unsteady breath, Casey realized as she walked down the smooth dirt trail, that she'd just escaped death a second time. That shook her deeply.

CHAPTER TWENTY-ONE

MATT'S HEART BURST with a fierce love for Casey as she leaned on him. It was the look in her eyes, a mixture of love and relief, that made Matt finally break through and release his past. They stopped at the bottom of the trail. Sweeping Casey into his arms, he pulled her hard against him and held her. Just held her. She was soft and pliant, her head resting in the crook of his neck, her arms strong around him.

Closing his eyes, Matt steadied her and in a whisper said, "I love you so much, Casey. I love you…"

The words were fueled by overwhelming emotion as his warm breath caressed her temple and ear. Leaning back in his arms, she drowned in his gaze. "I love you, too, Matt. I'm so sorry I didn't tell you that before—before this happened. I was scared to tell you."

He lifted his hand and gently stroked her pale cheek. "We were both scared. And we had a lot of baggage from the past on our shoulders, too, Casey." He saw her gray eyes grow soft and tender with love for him alone. The last of the shackles from his past dissolved. She had a huge heart. Matt had seen that with her love toward Megan. And now, it was here, shining out of her eyes like food for his starving, lonely soul. "We've got a lot to talk about," he told her unsteadily, his hand coming to rest on the shoulder of her dirty jacket. "First, let's get you off this mountain and to the hospital for a checkup."

Wrinkling her nose, Casey released him. Matt tucked her beside his body, his arm around her waist. "I'm really okay, but I know they need to draw blood to find out what kind of drug that bastard gave me."

Nodding, Matt guided her down the trail, the rest of the entourage following behind them. "It shouldn't take long," he soothed. The sun had set and he could see the darkness coming their way. By the time they got all the official reports and medical checks out of the way, it would be dark. Leaning over, he caught her glance. "After that, you're coming home. With us."

Warmth began to filter through Casey. She was still a set of screaming nerves from her near-death experience. *Home.* The word held a powerful charge to her. Nodding, she said nothing and concentrated on where she was putting her feet. Although the trail was wide and well-maintained, there were rocks peeking up here and there. The hiker who wasn't paying attention would trip and fall. Besides, the drug was still in her system and her clarity continued to disappear briefly at times. When it did, Casey's legs became less compliant and she was grateful for Matt's stability, his arm around her waist keeping her upright.

The air was turning cold. Casey could see her breath. She felt the strength and steadiness of Matt's embrace. Like a thirsty sponge, she absorbed his quiet strength as they walked down the trail. Once her mind cleared, she asked, "How is Megan?"

"I had her taken home. Jessie is watching her until we get there. She's fine."

"Was she upset?"

"Yes. I searched about twenty minutes for you in the brush. She was getting frantic standing out in the meadow alone. I needed to get her out of there when I realized you weren't nearby."

Mouth tightening, Casey muttered, "I'm so sorry, Matt. Megan didn't need this stress on top of everything else." She looked up and caught his shadowed gaze.

Squeezing her gently, he said, "She started talking, Casey. I guess the fear of you being gone snapped something inside her."

Eyes widening, Casey gasped, "Really? She's *talking?*"

Smiling a little, he leaned down and whispered near her ear, "Her first words were 'Mommy, Mommy.'"

Lips parting, Casey almost halted on the path. Stunned, she saw the tenderness in his eyes. And she realized the implications of Megan's first words. "Oh, Matt..."

"I know."

Gulping, Casey forced herself to walk a little faster. Her mind wasn't functioning properly but well enough that she realized the little girl had bonded with her and saw her as her mother.

"Are you all right?" Matt asked, glancing over at her profile.

"Yes...it's just so much to deal with on top of my own stuff. I don't want to mess it up with her, Matt. I'm scared, in a way."

"Don't be," he coaxed, seeing her anxiety.

"Megan's talking? Really, she's talking?"

Smiling a little, Matt nodded. "I just got off a cell call with Jessie, and she's chattering up a storm just like she did before the fire."

Pressing her cut and scratched hand to her heart, Casey nearly cried. "That's wonderful, Matt. Talk about prayers being answered."

Grimly, he thought that more than that prayer had been answered. He'd never prayed so hard as when Casey disappeared. "I know. It's a good day for all of us," he told her, his voice cracking with emotion. As he shared an intimate look with Casey he thought he saw a glimmer of tears in her eyes, but couldn't be sure. "Besides," he added to make her feel less concerned, "Jessie is putting Megan to bed. By the time we get home, she'll be sound asleep. You'll have some time to work on yourself before she wakes up in the morning."

"That's good," Casey murmured with relief. "I just want to get this crap out of my body. When I have clear moments, Matt, I'm okay. But when I get fogged in by that drug, I feel very unstable and super-vulnerable in every way."

"I understand. Not to worry." He looked beyond the steep trail that led down to the parking lot. There was an ambulance waiting there along with several sheriff's cars and the volunteer hikers who had come to try and locate Casey. "First things first," he said. "Let's get you into the ambulance. I'll follow in my truck and meet you at the hospital."

CADE GARNER CAME into Casey's hospital cubicle. Matt was standing near her as the nurse drew blood from her arm.

"Cade?" she called, giving him a wan smile. "Is that guy in jail yet?"

Shaking his head, the deputy came around the gurney. "He's in the hospital right now. As soon as we can, we'll be taking him over to jail. The detectives are interrogating him as a nurse cleans out the flesh wound on his upper arm." Pulling a piece of folded paper from his pocket, he opened it up. It was a black-and-white photo of her attacker. Matt leaned forward and looked. "He's singing like the proverbial canary."

"Good," Matt said.

"What made him sing?" Casey wondered, shivering as she looked at the photo. It was a shot of the criminal with his name, *Frank Benson,* across it.

Smiling a little, Cade waited for the nurse to finish her duties with Casey. She completed drawing the blood and released the rubber tie from around Casey's arm. Giving them a nod, she left the cubicle with the vial in her hand. Now, Cade could talk.

"What none of us knew was this—Clarissa Peyton, Senator Peyton's wife, had called the commander five days ago about Benson." He jabbed a finger at the photo.

Casey said, "What? Why would she know someone like this guy?"

"Right," Cade murmured. "Clarissa, in August, found a throwaway cell phone on her husband's desk. There was a phone number in it that she thought was another donor, and so she took down the number. There was no name on it. Later, when she was working on investigating all the new donors, she ran into Benson's phone number. His name and criminal record popped up. That's when she called the commander. Clarissa told him that she was worried Benson was stalking her husband. That's why she called."

Frowning, Casey tilted her head. "How would Senator Peyton know Benson?" She rolled down the sleeve of her blouse and buttoned it.

Matt scowled, his voice low with feeling. "Peyton swore to get even with me over the loss of his wife and children in that fire five years ago."

Gasping, Casey looked over at Cade. The man's face turned as grim as Matt's voice. "Oh, my God. Don't tell me the senator *hired* this guy to go after Matt?"

"It's better than that," Cade assured them. He crooked his finger so that the three of them were in a tight circle, his voice barely above a whisper. This was information that couldn't get out to anyone yet since it was an ongoing investigation. "Benson said that the senator hired him two years ago to set fire to Matt's home." He looked over at Matt. "This is the guy who torched your place and murdered Bev."

Paling, Matt stared in shock at the deputy. A barrage of feelings overwhelmed him. Casey reached out and gripped his hand.

She looked at Matt and then at Cade. "But…you mean this killer was hired a second time by the senator to kill Matt? To finish off what he hadn't the first time around?"

Nodding, Cade said, "Yes, in a nutshell, that's it. Only this time around, the senator didn't want an arson fire. He worked with Benson on setting up what would look like a series of natural accidents for the three of you." He held Casey's gaze. "Megan and you were to be kidnapped, drugged and put in a cave. Benson would then lay out a meat trail for a local grizzly to follow up to that cave to kill and eat you. Once that was done, Benson was going to cut the duct tape off your hands and feet so that it looked like you two just had the bad luck of running into a grizzly."

Gasping, Casey said, "But, what was Benson going to do then?"

"He was going to rely on an ongoing search for you two and then take out Matt. He had the drug, Ketamine, on him. Benson would knock out Matt, fill him with this drug and it would kill him. He was going to carry his body to where you were. In the end, Benson wanted the grizzly to savage all of you. It would look like an accident."

Stunned and feeling numb over the horror of the story, Casey choked out, "What a horrible plan."

Matt felt hatred churn up through him. He automatically placed a hand on Casey's shoulder. "That bastard...the senator..."

"Yes, and Benson is writing up his statement as we speak. Once that's done, an arrest warrant will be put out on the senator."

"But, he's in Washington, D.C.," Casey said hoarsely.

Garner shrugged. "He'll be arrested there by authorities and then come back here to answer the charges."

"What about Clarissa?" Casey asked, feeling deeply for the woman. In more than one way, her detective work had helped save their lives.

Cade gave them a sad look. "I'm sure when it happens, she's going to be in shock. In a court of law, a wife can't testify against a husband. I don't know yet. We can't find the throwaway cell phone. We're getting search warrants prepared for his home here in Jackson Hole as well as his apartment in Washington, D.C. I don't know what we'll find. Clarissa's world is about to explode in her face."

Matt moved his arm around Casey's shoulders and gently squeezed her. "Peyton swore to get even with me," he choked out. Shaking his head, Matt added, "We did our best to reach his home. It was no one's fault."

"Didn't matter to Peyton," Cade muttered with a scowl. He folded the paper, tucked it in his shirt pocket and buttoned it back up. "He's always blamed you for the death of his family, right or wrong, Matt. What none of us realized was he was going to get even and take your family away from you."

"But I'm not family," Casey protested.

"Peyton saw you as someone Matt liked. The senator wanted to destroy everything that was important to Matt. That's why he went after you."

"God," Casey whispered, suddenly shaken even more. The sounds of the hospital intruded upon them. She thought for a moment and then said to the deputy, "Benson screwed up, then." She pointed to her upper arm where he'd jabbed the needle into her and knocked her out. "I didn't die."

"Benson said he thought you would die. After he grabbed you in the bushes and carried you up to that cave, your pulse was very slow. He thought for sure he'd delivered enough of the drug to kill you."

"Maybe that's why he didn't search and find my Buck knife, then," Casey whispered.

"Right," Cade said. "He had taped you up in the cave. Benson was certain you would die and become a victim of a grizzly attack."

Grimly, Matt said to the deputy, "I'll bet if you look at Casey's jacket, there's a lot of the drug that got released in the material before it struck her arm."

"That's what the commander is thinking." He picked up Casey's muddy jacket. "I have to take this in for evidence."

Nodding, Casey whispered, "That's okay." Feeling another wave of shock rolling through her, she added, "I just can't believe all of this. What a horrible plan to kill all of us."

"Peyton's going to pay for this," Matt growled. He pulled Casey protectively against him and held her. "He's a sick bastard."

Snorting, Cade said, "Beyond belief. The man is certifiable in my opinion." He smiled a little at them. "Look, it's going to be a rough month ahead for both of you. We're going to need your statements tonight. Do you feel up to it? We have to get all the paperwork done before we can issue an arrest warrant."

Looking at Matt, Casey said, "Yes, I'm up to it."

"Are you sure?" he asked, worried. Casey was still pale, her eyes unusually dull-looking.

"I'm positive," she muttered, sliding off the gurney. "Let's get to your truck, Matt, and we'll follow Cade to the sheriff's headquarters. I'll sleep better tonight knowing we've done everything in our power to get that senator behind bars."

"I'M SO TIRED I can barely think straight," Casey murmured as Matt closed the door to his home. She stood there and gave him a wan smile. It was midnight.

Matt locked the door and turned to her. His sister Jessie had just left. Megan was tucked into bed and soundly sleeping. He shrugged out of his coat and hung it on a wooden peg next to the door. "Makes two of us." He brought her into his arms and she sighed softly as she folded against him. Kissing her hair, he whispered, "Let's go check on Megan first."

Wordlessly, Casey agreed. They moved apart and

she followed Matt down the hall to his daughter's half-opened door. Both moved quietly inside. As always, Jessie had made sure the soft glow of a wall light was on. It gave Casey just enough light to see Megan's blond hair wrapped with her sheet and blanket. Only part of her face was visible. Her heart opened wide as Matt leaned down and placed a soft kiss on his daughter's unmarred brow. Straightening, he stepped aside.

Casey moved soundlessly and knelt down on one knee. She gently threaded Megan's silky hair through her fingers. The girl stirred, but remained asleep. Leaning down, Casey pressed a soft kiss against Megan's cheek. "We'll see you in the morning, Meggie. Your daddy is here and so am I. Everything's all right." Her whispered words faded into the silence. How innocent Megan looked in sleep. The horror that Senator Peyton wanted to kill this child sent revulsion through Casey. She slowly got up with Matt's help. Turning, she smiled up at him. He nodded.

Out in the kitchen, he pulled Casey back into his arms. "Let me draw you a hot bath?"

"That sounds good," she said, closing her eyes and simply holding him. "You have to be exhausted, too."

"Not like you," he murmured. Pressing small kisses to her hair, he added, "Bath and bed?"

"Yes." She looked up. "I want to be in your bed, Matt. With you."

He saw the determination in her darkened eyes. "You're sure?"

"I've never been more sure of anything in my life," she said, a catch in her voice. Stretching up, Casey met his descending mouth. It was the first time they'd been able to kiss since the whole event had erupted around them. His mouth was tender against hers, searching and moving warmly against her lips. It was a kiss of welcome into each other's life, Casey realized as she responded to him. They were too tired to do much of anything other than kiss. Emotionally, they were numbed by the enormity of what had just happened. Casey realized how close she'd come to dying. Right now, both were fragile, and all she wanted was to hold Matt and sleep with him. The rest would come later.

Easing his mouth from her wet lips, Matt smiled into Casey's eyes that now sparkled with love—for him. It helped Matt so much because he felt torn apart inwardly. He just could not fathom that one man's revenge could go so far and for so long. Peyton's misguided rage was shocking. The woman in his arms now smiling up at him could have been lost to him, too. Matt hadn't realized until today how deeply he'd fallen in love with Casey. What was even more wonderful was that his daughter clearly loved her as a mother. In a world gone so wrong, Matt saw the hope in the slats of light that shone through the blackness. He knew Casey loved Megan fiercely and would make his daughter whole after her world had been ripped away from her.

"All right," Matt murmured, kissing her brow, "let me get a bath drawn for you."

Casey moved into the kitchen. She knew Matt always kept a bottle of wine in the fridge. And then she remembered the doctor had said no alcohol with the drug still in her bloodstream. It would take twenty-four hours for it to work its way out of her system, she had been told. Grimacing, she decided on hot tea instead as she waited for the bath to be ready. Her heart sang even though she was exhausted. Matt loved her. And she loved him. And Megan was speaking. Looking around the quiet kitchen, Casey realized that it had been a day of miracles despite it being fraught with danger.

She pulled down two mugs from the cabinet and opened up a box of tea bags. Everything she did seemed to quell her anxiety. After finding out more about Benson, Casey found herself grateful to be alive. She should be dead. But she wasn't. Tomorrow morning, she would call her parents and her sisters. Casey was sure that if Peyton was arrested on murder charges, the news would be splashed across every national television program. And she wanted to get to them first to prepare them— but also to give them good news.

CHAPTER TWENTY-TWO

CASEY AWOKE SLOWLY. She was sleeping on her left side. She became aware of Matt's hairy arm resting around her waist. Her mind was clear now, not fogged with drugs as before. Lying there, feeling beneath the T-shirt fabric the slow rise and fall of Matt's chest against her back, she smiled to herself. How good it felt to be warm and to have him curved protectively around her body. Last night he'd loaned her a set of his light blue pajamas to wear. She remembered climbing into them, drunk with exhaustion. Then, she'd padded down the hall to Megan's room once more to make sure the child was sleeping. She was.

The scent of Matt entered her awakening state. The spicy pine soap along with his own unique male fragrance made her sigh inwardly. This was what she wanted. This was what she'd dreamed of so often since meeting him. Her mind ranged over how much she loved him. Casey didn't know exactly when she'd fallen for the rugged firefighter, only that she had. And Megan had bonded with her from the beginning. The realization that she was walking into an already-made family didn't bother her. She came from a large family herself and knew the benefits and support of others.

Feeling his moist breath against her neck, Casey simply absorbed the quiet, intimate moment. Her past seemed to be exactly that: in the past. A part of her life, but not controlling it any longer. Casey wondered if her latest brush with death had cleaned her slate. This time had been different. She'd been proactive and had actually saved herself. That was why she felt so strong and confident as she woke up. Today was the first day of her new life. A better one. A new chapter.

With that, Casey turned over. As she did, Matt awakened, his eyes clouded with sleep as his lashes drowsily lifted. And then his pupils grew larger and his eyes narrowed on Casey. She smiled softly and moved against him, feeling the latent strength in his strong male body flowing up against her own. Without a word, she eased up on her elbow, leaned over and captured his mouth. Putting all the tenderness and love Casey felt for this heroic man into her kiss, she felt him smile beneath her lips.

Without a word, Matt moved onto his back and pulled her up across him, his arms guiding her so that she settled fully on top of him. Their mouths clung to one another. Casey's hair tickled his face and his flesh tingled in the wake. Her mouth was hungry and he moved his in concert with it. Lifting his hands, Matt threaded his fingers through her silky, mussed hair. Groaning as Casey moved her hips provocatively against his own, he lifted his mouth from hers.

Looking deeply into her sultry gaze, Matt smiled up at her. "I love you, Casey Cantrell. You need to know that." His voice was roughened. "I was sorry I hadn't told you how I felt before Benson captured you. From now on, you're going to know every day how much I love you…" He guided her mouth down to his. He captured her with a fierce intensity, their breaths growing ragged, their hearts pounding in unison.

His words flowed through her, opening her heart. Casey drowned in Matt's mouth, as his fingers trailed along her jaw and moved like a tantalizing whisper across her shoulders. In a few deft movements, he moved her beside him and had unbuttoned the loose pajama top. The fabric brushed her awakened flesh as he pulled it off and allowed it to drop beside the bed. Casey moaned with anticipation.

Matt saw her eyes open, a gleam in them he'd never seen before, but that he liked. She was his equal in every way as her long fingers sought and found the edge of the dark blue T-shirt he was wearing. In a few moments, it had been removed. He absorbed the look in her eyes as she ran her hand slowly across his darkly haired chest intimately, memorizing him. Every grazing touch incited Matt and made him want her even more than before.

"I love you, Matt," Casey whispered, nuzzling his cheek and sending a cascade of small kisses down the side of his neck to his chest.

The graze and nip of her lips against his flesh tightened it and sent a sheet of wild flames roaring out across his chest. Groaning, Matt reveled in her courageous and bold actions. He absorbed her smile as Casey lifted her head, her lips parted and begging to be kissed. Without a word, Matt slid his hand down from her shoulder, cupped her breast and leaned down to capture the puckered nipple. As he did, she moaned and closed her eyes, joy radiating from her expression. Nothing had ever seemed so right. He suckled her, teethed her and felt her become like lava flowing and molding through his hands as he maneuvered the pajama bottoms away from her long legs. As Matt coaxed her onto her back, he took advantage and lavished attention upon her other breast.

The heat and urgency built in Casey's lower body. Her mind was reeling and she was barely coherent, so involved was she with the pleasure Matt was giving her with his hands and mouth. Somehow, she pushed off his pajama bottoms and they ended up at the bottom of the bed. Now naked, she moved up against his body as if she were more cat than human. His muscles leaped and tensed. When her hips brushed against his, he was more than ready for her. That discovery excited her as nothing before. Looking deep into his eyes, watching the way his mouth flexed, Casey felt herself being lifted and brought on top of Matt. She smiled as she leaned down, met and moved against his male mouth. She felt him tense, felt a tremor pass through him as she settled against him. Her heart flew open.

For so long, Casey had hidden from men because of her traumatic past. Meeting Matt was like meeting the sun after a dark, hellish time in Hades itself. He reminded her of Apollo, the sun god from the Greek myths. Yes, Matt was her sunlight. He fed her hope with every small kiss against her face, neck and shoulders. His body was powerful, yet he was tender with her. All of that conspired in Casey's whirling mind and scintillating emotions as she captured him within her woman's confines and loved him.

The moment Matt felt her move, he groaned and closed his eyes. He didn't know who was absorbing more pleasure in that moment—him or Casey. It didn't matter. The heat, wetness and sleekness of her moving against him erased every thought. Drowning in her strength as a woman as she moved her hips against his, her mouth wreaking fire from his lips, Matt felt the past slip away with finality. He was here, now, with a new love of his life, a woman who was incredibly courageous, giving and loving despite all that had happened to her.

The building inferno within Casey exploded and she felt bathed in rhythmic pulses that made her moan over and over again with pleasure. She could feel the unleashed power of Matt's body as he moved with her. And then, just as her orgasms were diminishing, she felt him tense, growl, and the flow of his life joined hers. Later, as she fell exhausted against him, the thought that they were one, that this mingling of love between them could create a child, didn't bother her. As she nestled her face against his cheek and jaw, her arms around his shoulders, Casey had never felt as fulfilled as she did at that moment.

"MOMMY?" MEGAN CALLED. She stood on a stool at the kitchen counter where Casey was making them a breakfast of French toast. Matt was at the stove frying the bacon.

"What?" Casey asked, whisking the eggs and milk in a bowl. She thrilled to hear Megan's high, squeaky voice. The girl was in a bright green T-shirt, jeans and matching sneakers. Megan had brushed her hair earlier in the morning and brought it into a cute ponytail, replete with a yellow and green ribbon.

"I want two." She held up her fingers. "Please?"

"Two?" Matt called, looking over his shoulder at his daughter. He smiled at Casey, her cheeks still stained red from their lovemaking. His own body glowed and pulsed in memory of their time together in the bedroom. "You've never eaten two before," he noted, teasing Megan.

"Well," she said, "I'm *really* hungry this morning!"

Chuckling, Casey leaned over and placed a kiss on Megan's head. "Eat one and then if you're not full, I can always make another. Okay?" She searched the child's upturned face for any signs of trauma. All Casey saw was a child who was completely happy. Shortly after she'd showered and dressed, Casey had met Megan out in the hall. The little girl gave a cry of delight and threw her arms around her. Casey had knelt in the hall, holding Megan and reassuring her. What made it an incredible and magic event was Megan talking to her for the first time. And since that moment, the girl had been a nonstop chatterbox, but that was fine by Casey. She would much rather hear her talk than remain mute.

"Okay," Matt called. He lifted the black iron skillet off the stove and walked to the counter. "Bacon is ready. How's the French toast gang doing?" He grinned as he put the bacon into a paper-lined basket.

"We're ready to go," Casey promised. There was such joy this morning in the kitchen. Megan was speaking. She was engaged and happy. Weren't she and Matt, too? *Oh, yes!* As Matt replaced the skillet on the stove, Casey moved the bread and bowl to it. They traded places and Matt got Megan to set the table with him.

As she made the French toast in the large skillet, Casey replayed their conversation after they'd made love to one another. Matt wanted to marry her whenever she wanted. Casey wanted her family here to be part of their wedding and that would mean next June. Until then, she would move in with Matt and they would live together. He saw no harm in that and felt Megan would really bloom because Casey would be there full-time. Casey agreed, but she also said that it would be good for the two of them, too. Matt smiled a very male smile and agreed.

The phone rang. Casey frowned for a moment. Matt went to the wall and picked it up. Just as she'd thought, it was the sheriff's department. Trying to hold on to her happiness, she knew they would both have to probably go down to the office and fill out more paperwork sometime today.

Hanging up, Matt turned. "That was Cade. He'd like to see us at 1:00 p.m. today. Any problem with that?" Above all, he didn't want his daughter to know the details of what had happened.

"Sure," Casey said. Using a spatula she put the French toast on three plates. "Come and get it."

"SENATOR PEYTON IS in custody," Cade Garner told them. He was standing next to the commander's desk. "And he'll be arraigned in Washington, D.C."

Matt sat next to Casey, her hand in his. "And Benson?"

"He's in jail. Basically, with his lawyer, he made a plea deal. He gave us the whole scenario for a shorter sentence to be determined by the court later on."

Shaking her head, Casey said, "Wow…this is just too incredible. Who would ever think a U.S. senator would do something like this?"

Matt squeezed her hand. He glanced over at her. "He lost his family, Casey. I've tried to put myself in his place a thousand times since it happened. I know how

I felt about losing Bev and almost losing Megan. Those kinds of losses do funny things to people."

Cade nodded. "That's true," he said. "But most don't go ballistic like Peyton did. You didn't," he said, looking grimly at Matt.

Nodding, Matt said, "But it ate at me, Cade." He touched his stomach. "I never knew who had killed Bev." He flexed his mouth and his voice lowered. "Now, I do. Now, I can get closure."

Squeezing his hand, Casey whispered, "It's over, Matt. Really over."

"Yes," Cade said, "for the most part, it is. You'll both be in court as witnesses and that will be rough enough, but at least you know who the killers are. And they're going to get the justice they deserve."

"I feel sorry for Clarissa Peyton," Casey murmured. "She must feel so torn up and confused. I can't imagine how I would feel if the man I married was a killer in disguise." She shivered and gave Matt a sorrowful look. "Clarissa is a victim in this, too."

Cade nodded. "What you don't know is that Clarissa is waiving spousal privilege. She's going to testify against her husband. That took real guts."

"Clarissa is a tough Wyoming-bred woman," Matt said. "Out here in the West there's an unspoken cowboy code of conduct. You don't cross those lines and her husband did. I'm not surprised by her decision."

"I thought of that, too," Cade admitted. He picked up some papers and walked over to Matt and Casey. "Still, it has to hurt her a lot. Her life, as she knew it, is over. In the blink of an eye.

"Here, I need you two to read through these papers

and then sign them if they're okay." He handed each of them a set of documents and a pen.

As Casey read the report she'd given the night before, she felt deep sadness move through her. Clarissa, for all her airs, was a decent person. She wondered, as she signed the papers, what would happen to her. She looked up at Cade. "Do you think Clarissa will divorce him?"

"Yes," Cade said. "And knowing her, she's a rancher's daughter and will grab the bull by the horns and make things right for all involved. Clarissa comes from money. And I'm sure in this divorce, she'll get half of Peyton's money, which will be considerable. She'll make out all right."

"I wonder if she's going to stay here at their home or not?" Casey mused.

Shrugging, Cade said, "That's anyone's guess. Her family's ranch is near Cheyenne."

"But she loves it here," Matt said. "All her friends, the clubs and charities she manages are here in Jackson Hole. My money is on her to stay."

"I hope she does," Casey murmured. "I'd like to get to know her as a friend. She's done so much for us." She glanced over at Matt.

"The whole town is in shock about this," Cade said, gathering up the reports and setting them on his commander's desk to be initialed.

"Yes, it's all over the news," Matt said, standing. He held out his hand and Casey took it.

"You two take it easy," Cade said. "You've been through a lot."

"The chief is giving me a week off," Matt told his friend. "And Charley is giving Casey the same amount of time off."

"Hey," Cade teased, "seven days. Make the most of them."

Grinning, Casey said, "We will, Cade. Thanks for everything."

"You're welcome. I'll be seeing you."

Walking out of the sheriff's office and into the afternoon sunlight, Casey sighed. She liked walking next to Matt, their coats against one another, their hands entwined. "What now?" she asked, gazing up into his strong, rugged features. Matt looked like a knight to her in his bright red firefighting jacket, dark blue jeans that hugged his long, powerful legs, and cowboy boots. The breeze was cool, the sky spotted with white clouds that hinted at a front coming in. It would snow tonight, the radio weather forecaster had promised.

"We need to move your stuff from the apartment you're renting with Cat over to my house." Matt walked to his truck and opened the door for her to climb in. "I think we can get most of it today before the snow storm hits tonight."

Casey waited until Matt slid into the cab and shut the driver's-side door. "Sounds good to me. I know Cat will need to get a new renter, but that will be easy. And I like the idea of being at home to meet Megan at the bus stop. I really want these seven days to cement some kind of constancy in her life."

Brushing her cheek, Matt murmured, "For all of us," he said, his voice husky with feelings.

Casey sat back after putting on the seat belt. She'd called her parents and sisters after breakfast this morning, before the news spread about Senator Carter Peyton being arrested for murder. Her parents were relieved. So was she.

Matt backed the truck out of the parking space and wheeled it around in the asphalt lot. His heart was full of happiness. Megan was speaking nonstop. He'd called her psychiatrist in Idaho Falls and told her the good news. Even better, the therapist had told Matt that the worst was over. Megan was bonding with a new mother, Casey, and by speaking, her healing was well under way.

Turning onto the tree-lined street, two-story Victorian homes on either side, Matt was stunned by the turnaround in his life. He felt like the luckiest man in the world. So much had been taken from him, his daughter and Casey. They had all lost so much. Yet, life had conspired to give it back to them in a new and wonderful way.

Reaching out, he gripped Casey's hand. "I love you," he told her. "I'm going to spend every day of my life showing you that."

* * * * *

Joan Johnston is the *New York Times* and *USA TODAY* bestselling author of more than fifty novels with more than fifteen million copies of her books in print. She has been a director of theater, drama critic, newspaper editor, college professor and attorney on her way to becoming a full-time writer. You can find out more about Joan at joanjohnston.com or on Facebook at Joan Johnston Author.

Books by Joan Johnston

Hawk's Way: Jesse
Hawk's Way: Adam
Hawk's Way: Faron
Hawk's Way: Garth
Hawk's Way: Carter
Hawk's Way: Falcon
Hawk's Way: Zach
Hawk's Way: Billy
Hawk's Way: Mac
Hawk's Way: Colt

Visit the Author Profile page
at Harlequin.com for more titles.

HAWK'S WAY: FALCON

Joan Johnston

PROLOGUE

FALCON NOTICED THE woman right away, even though she was standing in the middle of a crowded sidewalk in downtown Dallas. She was not the sort of female who usually attracted his attention, being boyishly slim and merely pretty, rather than beautiful. But there was something about her that drew his eyes and held him spellbound.

He had barely begun to admire her assets—long, silky black hair whipped by the hot summer breeze, spectacular blue eyes and a tall, supple body—when he spotted the little girl at her side. The woman was joined a moment later by a man who slipped his arm around her slender waist and captured her mouth in a hard, possessive kiss. The little girl quickly claimed the man's attention, and he leaned down to listen to her excited chatter.

Falcon felt a sharp stab of envy that he wasn't the man in the quaint family picture. Not that he wanted kids, or wanted to be married, for that matter, but he would have given anything to be on the receiving end of the warm, approving look the woman gave the man as he attended to the little girl.

He was startled to realize that he knew the man. Which meant he could easily wrangle an introduction to the woman.

She's married.

Falcon didn't dally with married women. At least, he never had in the past. He pursed his lips thoughtfully. There was no reason why he couldn't meet her. Without stopping to think, he approached the trio.

"Grant? Grant Ainsworth?" Falcon inquired, though he knew he wasn't mistaken.

"Falcon Whitelaw!" the man exclaimed. "I haven't seen you in—it must be ten years!"

"Nearly that. Guess we lost touch after graduation from Tech," Falcon said with a smile as he extended his hand to meet the one that had been thrust at him. He forced himself to keep his eyes on his old football teammate from Texas Tech. But he wanted to meet the woman. He wanted to feast his eyes on her face at close range. He wanted to figure out what it was that made her so alluring.

"What have you been doing with yourself, Grant?" Falcon asked.

"Got married," Grant replied with a smug grin. "This is my wife, Mara, and my daughter, Susannah."

Falcon turned to greet Mara Ainsworth. He was sorry she wasn't one of those progressive women who shook hands with a man. He would have liked to touch her. She nodded her head and smiled at him, and he felt his stomach do a queer turn. He lifted a finger to his Stetson in acknowledgement of her. "Ma'am."

Because he knew it was expected of him, he lowered his eyes to the little girl. She was hiding half behind her mother's full skirt. Susannah had Mara's black hair, but her eyes were hazel, rather than blue. "Howdy," he said. "You're a pretty little miss. Almost as pretty as your mother."

The little girl giggled and hid her face completely.

From the corner of his eye, Falcon caught the flush of pleasure on Mara's face. He wanted to touch her cheek, to feel the heat beneath the skin.

"How old is your daughter?" he asked Mara. He needed a reason to look at her. His eyes lingered, cataloging each exquisite feature.

"Susannah's seven," Mara replied.

Falcon heard Grant talking, but he couldn't take his eyes off Mara. For a moment he thought he saw something in her open gaze, an attraction to him as strong as the one he felt for her. But he knew that was only wishful thinking.

Her lids lowered demurely so her lashes created two coal crescents on milky white skin. Whatever she was feeling, it was hidden from him now. Her lips parted slightly, and he could just see the edges of her teeth. He had to restrain a harsh intake of breath at the overpowering desire he felt to claim her mouth with his. He had never felt a need so strong or so demanding.

Falcon was aware that Grant was asking him something, but he only caught the last half of the sentence.

"...so if you're staying the night in Dallas, maybe we could get together and have a few drinks for old times' sake," Grant finished.

Falcon saw the quick flash of annoyance on Mara's face. Obviously she would rather have Grant to herself than share him with an old friend. Falcon started to give her what she wanted but realized that if he had a few drinks with Grant he could find out more about Mara, more about the state of their marriage. It looked happy from the outside, but if there were problems, maybe there was a chance Mara would welcome his attention.

Falcon hated what he was thinking. It wasn't like him to go after some other man's woman. But there was something about Mara Ainsworth that struck a chord deep inside him. If he had found her unattached, he might even have contemplated giving up his bachelor freedom. But it was folly to let himself even think about her so long as she was another man's wife.

By the time Falcon had come to the conclusion he ought to just get the hell away from the Ainsworths, he realized he had already invited Grant to have drinks with him at a bar near the stockyards.

"What brings you to town, anyway?" Grant asked.

"I'm here to buy cattle for my ranch."

"Didn't know you had a ranch of your own," Grant said.

"I inherited the B-Bar from my grandfather, my mother's father, about five years ago," Falcon replied.

Grant whistled in appreciation. "If I remember rightly, that's quite a spread."

Falcon hadn't done anything to earn the B-Bar, but he was proud of owning it. It was a big spread. He glanced at Mara to see if she was impressed. Most women were. But she was watching Grant. She had caught her lower lip with her teeth and was chewing on it. She looked worried about something. Was his rendezvous with Grant going to interrupt some previously made plans?

Falcon had grown up in a family where strong wills were the norm. He had learned that with determination and a little charm, he could usually get what he wanted. As a result, he wasn't used to denying himself anything. That had worked out fine, because there hadn't been anyone but himself to please for the past five years since he had inherited his grandfather's ranch. Suddenly he found himself wanting to take the worry from Mara's brow, even if it meant giving up the opportunity to quiz Grant about her while they were having drinks.

"Look," Falcon said, "if you all have other plans for the evening, I don't want to intrude."

Mara had opened her mouth to respond when Grant said, "No plans. I'll meet you at eight. See you then."

Falcon watched the gentle sway of Mara's hips as Grant led her away. She glanced back at Falcon over her shoulder and caught him staring at her. He felt himself flush, something he couldn't remember doing for a long, long time. He tipped his Stetson to her one more time. It looked like she wanted to say something to him, but Grant kept walking, his arm around her, and the moment was lost.

When the three of them were gone from sight, Falcon exhaled a long, loud sigh of regret. The woman of his dreams had just walked out of his life. He debated whether he ought to do something else tonight and leave a message at the bar for Grant that he couldn't make it. His feelings for Mara Ainsworth were dangerous. If he pursued the matter, he was asking for trouble.

But when eight o'clock came, Falcon was waiting at the Longhorn Bar. Five minutes later, Grant Ainsworth came in. There was a bond between teammates that extended beyond ordinary friendship, and Falcon was reminded of all the times he and Grant had tipped a brew after winning a difficult football game. He knew nothing of what had happened to Grant after college, but he intended to find out.

A country band with a wailing violin was playing up front near the dance floor, but Falcon had settled in one of the booths near the back, where the noise wasn't quite so loud nor the smoke so bad.

"What are you drinking?" he asked as Grant slid in across from him.

"I'll have a whiskey, neat," Grant replied.

Falcon gestured to a waitress wearing skintight jeans and a peasant blouse and ordered the drink Grant had asked for and another Pearl beer for himself.

When the drinks arrived, Grant held up his glass and said, "To pretty women."

Falcon grinned. "I'll drink to that." He took a sip of beer; Grant had finished his whiskey in a few swallows.

Grant slammed his glass onto the table and said, "That went down pretty damn smooth. I think I'll have another." Grant gestured and had the waitress bring him another whiskey.

"You need any ranch hands for that place of yours?" Grant asked after he had taken a sip of the second drink.

Falcon was startled by the question. "You need work?"

Grant shrugged. "Been laid off recently. Could use work if you've got it."

Actually, Falcon was sure he had all the help he needed. But he thought of Mara and Susannah without food on the table and said, "Sure. There's always room for another hand."

Grant's shoulders visibly relaxed. He finished off the second whiskey and called for another. "You don't know what a relief that is. Mara was beginning to think I would never… But I've got a job, after all, so everything will be fine."

It was plain from the look on Grant's face that he and his wife must have argued over the matter. Falcon was happy to change the subject to what he wanted to talk about most.

"Where did you meet Mara?"

"Her father was foreman on a ranch in west Texas where I worked right after college. I took one look at her and knew she was the one for me. It took a little convincing to get her to say yes. But she did. We've been married for eight years now."

"Where have you been living?"

Grant looked sheepish. "Here and there around Texas. We've moved every year or so. Last job I had was in Victoria. We came to Dallas because I heard some ranches around here were hiring help."

Falcon frowned. Most cowhands were footloose and fancy free—when they were single. A married man settled down in one place and raised his family. He wondered whether Grant had willingly left all those jobs, or whether there was something he had done to get himself fired. He had seemed steady enough in college, but college was ten years ago.

Had Grant Ainsworth become a thief? Was he a bully? Lazy? Incompetent? Cantankerous? Any of those faults would get him laid off in a hurry.

What had it been like for Mara to move around like that? Could she be happy with a man who was constantly losing his job? He recalled the adoring look on Mara's face when she had watched Grant with Susannah. Whatever Grant's shortcomings, Mara apparently still loved him.

"There are some houses on the property for hired hands. You're welcome to use one of them," he heard himself offer.

"I'd appreciate that," Grant said. Only he wasn't looking at Falcon when he answered.

Falcon was amazed and appalled when he realized that Grant was flirting with a pair of women sitting at a table across from them. He felt outraged on Mara's behalf. A man with a wife like her waiting for him at home had no business making eyes at other women. Suddenly Falcon didn't want to be where he was anymore.

"Look, I've got to be up early tomorrow. The drinks are on me—for old times' sake. I'll see you when you get to the ranch." Falcon threw a twenty on the table.

"There's no need—"

Falcon cut Grant off with a quick shake of his head. "Call it a celebration of your new job."

At the door to the bar Falcon glanced back and saw that the two women had already joined Grant in the booth. He scowled. Son of a bitch was cheating on his wife! Falcon felt a burning anger deep in his gut.

Falcon realized he just might have discovered why Grant had been let go from jobs so often. Suppose Grant played around with women wherever he went? That would certainly raise the hackles of the men he worked with and get him booted fast. Falcon grimaced. What kind of man had he just hired to work on the B-Bar?

Falcon thought of having Mara Ainsworth living on the B-Bar, in a house where he could see her every day. Knowing her husband didn't appreciate her. Knowing she loved the bastard anyway.

It was going to be hell.

FALCON HAD WANTED to see Mara Ainsworth again, but he had never dreamed it would be at her husband's funeral. He stood at the back of a crowd of mourners shrouded in black, waiting for a chance to speak to her, to tell her how sorry he was that Grant was dead. And he was sorry, for Grant's sake. No one deserved to die that young. Deep down, in places where honesty reigned, he felt that Mara was better off without him. But he wasn't going to voice those feelings. He owed Grant that, at least.

But he couldn't forgive Grant for the utter senselessness of his death: his friend had been killed in a one-car accident the same night Falcon had met him in the Longhorn Bar. Falcon bitterly regretted leaving Grant with money for several more drinks. Obviously Grant hadn't sobered up before he got behind the wheel. It was a tragedy that happened all too often, and Falcon could only be grateful that there had been no innocent victims in the accident.

If Falcon felt guilty at all, it was because he coveted Grant's widow. Mara was free now. He could have her if he wanted her—after a decent period of mourning, of course. Even he wasn't blackguard enough to go after a grieving widow.

But he wanted her. More than he ever had.

Dressed in black, Mara had an ethereal beauty. The deep circles under her eyes only made her look more hauntingly attractive. He knew she couldn't have gotten much sleep in the past week since Grant's death. Susannah stood beside her mother looking bewildered.

Falcon had tried to see Mara when he first heard about the accident, but realized he didn't know how to find her. He had read an announcement of the funeral services and made plans to attend. That way he could talk to her and extend his sympathy. And find out where she planned to go from here.

Because he wanted to know where he could find her when she had finished mourning Grant Ainsworth.

The graveside service had ended, and most of those gathered for the funeral had returned to their cars. Susannah had apparently gone with one of Mara's friends, because Mara was alone beside Grant's grave when Falcon approached her.

"Mara," he said.

It took her eyes a second to focus, but he knew the instant she recognized him, because her features twisted with loathing.

"How dare you show your face here!" she said in a harsh, bitter voice. "My husband is dead, and it's all your fault!"

Falcon was stunned at her accusation.

"You invited him to that bar! You got him drunk! And then you let him drive home!"

"I—"

"I hate you!" she said in a venomous voice. "I hope you rot in hell! I hope someone you loves dies a horrible death!"

She opened her mouth to speak, but all that came out was a low, ululating cry of pain. Her face crumpled in a mask of despair as she dropped to the grass beside her husband's newly dug grave. Her body shook with sobs of grief.

There was thickness in Falcon's throat that made it painful to swallow. He had never dreamed that she would blame him. How could she think he was responsible? He hadn't even been there when Grant left the bar. It wasn't his fault. She was wrong.

Not even in the farthest reaches of his mind had he planned to get Grant drunk and send him out to die in a fiery one-car crash. He had wanted Mara, it was true. But he had never wished Grant dead so that he could have her.

Small chance of his having her now. She hated his guts. She never wanted to see him again. She would as soon scratch out his eyes as look at him.

Falcon wanted to reach out to comfort her, to hold her in his arms and let her cry out her pain against his chest. He actually went so far as to touch her shoulder. "If there's ever anything I can do to help…"

The instant she realized who had touched her, she turned on him. He had never seen a woman's face contort in such fury and revulsion.

"Get away from me!" she hissed. "I don't need your kind of help. Go to hell, or go anywhere at all, but don't ever come near me again!"

He had backed away, stumbled over something, then turned and fled. He felt as though a tight band was constricting his chest. He couldn't breathe. He couldn't swallow. He felt like crying.

It was over. Mara was gone from his life before she had ever been a part of it. She hated him. She blamed him for Grant's death. He would never see her again.

But it would be a long time before he forgot the look of loathing toward him on Mara Ainsworth's face.

CHAPTER ONE

One year later

MARA HAD TRIED every other alternative, and there was only one left. She had to swallow her pride and approach Falcon Whitelaw for the help he had once offered. Although, she couldn't imagine him even giving her a chance to open her mouth before he shut the door in her face. Mara shuddered when she remembered the awful things she had said to him, even if they were true.

But Susannah was sick, very sick, and she needed treatment that would cost thousands of dollars. Mara had applied to a number of agencies for help, and it was available, but only if she and Susannah left home and traveled to another state. Life was grim enough these days without leaving behind everything that was familiar.

On Grant's death, Mara had used most of his life insurance to buy a home for herself and Susannah. She had vowed never to move again. If there was any way to stay in Dallas, where they had finally grown roots—shallow ones, but roots, nevertheless—Mara intended to pursue it. She had exhausted every other road to achieve her goal. There was only one left. She had to approach Falcon Whitelaw and ask him for money to help with Susannah's medical expenses.

Begging left a bitter taste in her mouth. But Mara was willing to humble herself in any way that was necessary to make sure Susannah got the treatment she needed. It was galling to have to approach the one man in the world she blamed for her current predicament. If Grant hadn't died in that accident, they would have had the health insurance he usually received as a part of his compensation. But Grant had been between jobs, so there was nothing. Instead Mara had been caught in every mother's nightmare. She had a sick child and no insurance to pay for medical bills.

Health insurance had been the last thing on her mind when Grant had left her widowed, and she found herself unemployed with a meager amount of life insurance and a child to raise. She had used the balance of the life insurance left after she bought the house to pay college tuition, believing that an education was the best investment for their future. It was a wise move, but had left the two of them exposed to the disaster that had occurred.

Mara hadn't even realized, at first, that Susannah was sick. In the months following Grant's death, her daughter had been tired and listless and seemed uninterested in doing the things she normally did. Mara had thought Susannah was merely grieving in her own way. Until one day Susannah didn't get out of bed at all. She had a high fever, and nothing Mara did could bring it down.

She took Susannah to the emergency room of the hospital and experienced the horror of watching her small, helpless child be hooked up to dozens of tubes and monitors. The diagnosis of Susannah's illness had come as a shock. Mara had sat stunned in the chair before Dr. Sortino's cluttered desk and listened with disbelief.

Acute lymphocytic leukemia.

"Children die of that," Mara had managed to gasp.

A pair of sympathetic brown eyes had looked out from Dr. Sortino's gaunt face. "Not as many as in the past. Nearly three-quarters of all children diagnosed with this disease today live."

"What about the rest?" Mara asked. "What about Susannah?"

"Our cure rate with chemotherapy is ninety percent. If that doesn't work, there's always a bone-marrow transplant to consider."

Mara had stared at him with unseeing eyes. Chemotherapy. She had never known anyone personally who had taken chemotherapy. But she had read enough, and seen enough on television, to know that chemotherapy made you vomit, and that your hair fell out. The thought of that happening to her precious daughter, the thought of all Susannah's long black hair falling out, made her feel faint.

"Mrs. Ainsworth? Are you all right?"

Dr. Sortino was on one knee beside her, keeping her from sliding out of the chair. She felt the sting of tears in her nose and eyes. "No, I'm not all right!" She fixed a blazing stare on the doctor who had been the messenger of such ill tidings.

"I'm angry," she spat. "I'm furious, in fact! Why Susannah? How did this happen? She's just a little girl. She's only eight years old!"

Dr. Sortino's eyes were no longer sympathetic. A look of pain and resignation had glazed his eyes after her vituperative attack. He rose and returned to his place behind the desk, putting a physical barrier between them that did little to protect him from her anger and despair.

"I'm sorry, Mrs. Ainsworth," he said. "There are as many as a dozen factors that may have been responsible for Susannah contracting the disease. We haven't done enough tests yet to make a guess on the precise reasons for her illness. But we can cure it…in most cases. You're lucky. Susannah has a tremendous chance of survival. With other diseases…"

He left her to contemplate her good fortune. But Mara didn't feel lucky. Leukemia was a serious disease. Her precious, wonderful daughter might die. "When do you start treatment?" she asked. "Will Susannah have to stay in the hospital? How will we know if it works?"

That was when kindly Dr. Sortino had started asking questions about insurance. That was when she had realized the enormity of the cost of treatment, and the hospital's inability to absorb another patient of this kind without a payment from some source.

"There are other facilities that can serve your needs better if you can't pay at least a portion of the costs up front," the doctor had said.

But those facilities were in another state.

Mara had tried buying insurance, but Susannah's illness was a preexisting condition and could not be covered.

"But I don't need insurance for anything else!" she had argued.

After the insurance companies turned a deaf ear, Mara tried the various foundations that provided assistance for children. And got the same answer. Help was available only if she was willing to go somewhere else to get it.

Mara knew she was foolish for clinging to the familiar, but she wasn't sure she could survive weeks, and maybe months, of living in a Ronald McDonald House in a strange city, all alone with only Susannah and her fears to keep her company. She needed a place that was home. She needed the support of the few friends she had made. And Susannah needed the normalcy of school and friends around her during her recuperation.

Her daughter was going to be one of the lucky seventy-three percent who were cured of the disease. Mara refused to consider any other outcome to Susannah's treatment.

But she needed money and needed it fast. Borrowing was out of the question. She had just finished her first year of college, working part-time as a cook in one of the college hangouts. She didn't qualify for the sizable loan she needed without some security, and she hadn't enough equity in the house to do the job.

On the other hand, Grant had told her before he'd gone to the bar that Falcon Whitelaw was as rich as Croesus, that he had inherited a fortune from his maternal grandfather, including the B-Bar Ranch on the outskirts of Dallas. Falcon wouldn't even miss the thousands of dollars it was going to cost for Susannah's care. Besides, she was going to offer him something in return.

Mara had grown up at her mother's side and knew everything there was to know about keeping house for a rancher. She planned to trade her services as housekeeper to Falcon in exchange for his financial assistance in paying Susannah's medical bills. She feared she would end up indentured to him for a long time. Just the initial treatment was going to cost nearly $25,000.

Which reasoning all led her to the front doorstep of Falcon Whitelaw's B-Bar Ranch. She had to admit the ranch wasn't what she had expected. The terrain was flat and grassy, but long ago someone had planted live oaks around the house. It had the look of a Spanish hacienda, with its red tile roof and thick, whitewashed adobe walls.

Her hand was poised to knock, her heart in her throat. She swallowed both heart and pride and rapped her knuckles on the arched, heavy oak panel.

No one answered.

She knocked harder, longer and louder.

At last, the door opened.

FALCON HAD BEEN out late carousing, and he had just dragged on a pair of jeans to answer the door, not even bothering to button them all the way up. They hung down on his hipbones and revealed his white briefs in the vee at the top. He scratched his belly and put one bare foot atop the other. He squinted, his eyes unable to focus in the harsh sunlight that was streaming in through the crack he had opened in the door. He thought better of trying to see and put a hand over his eyes, pressing his temples with forefinger and thumb in an attempt to stop the pounding inside his head.

"Who's there?" he muttered.

Mara stared in disbelief at the bleary-eyed, tousle-headed, unshaved face that had appeared at the door. "It's eleven o'clock," she said with asperity. "Are you just getting up?"

"Good God," Falcon said with a moan. He would

never forget that condemning voice, not in a million years. Of all the days for her to show up at the B-Bar, she had to come now. He slowly lowered his hand and squinted painfully into the sunlight until his eyes had adjusted enough to confirm what his ears had told him.

It was Mara Ainsworth, all right. She was wearing that same derisive, accusing look she had worn at Grant's funeral.

Falcon considered shutting the door in her face. He didn't owe her anything. He had offered her his help a year ago, and she had refused it in no uncertain terms.

So what is she doing here now?

From the look on her face she had come to play Puritan temperance woman. He just wasn't up for the game.

Mara's belief that Falcon was an irresponsible care-for-nobody was reaffirmed as she eyed him from head to barefoot toes. Her nose wrinkled in disgust when the smell of beer assaulted her nostrils. He was drunk! Or rather, had been. He looked hungover at the moment.

"Are you going to invite me inside?" she demanded.

Falcon was a second late responding, and Mara invited herself in, since he was obviously in no condition to do it. She pushed past Falcon and walked through the arched doorway right into the living room, leaving him standing at the open door.

The house was dark and cool. The furniture was leather and wood, large and heavy, the sort of thing the conquistadors must have brought with them from Spain. Navajo rugs were thrown on the redbrick floor, and Mara found herself facing shelves full of Hopi Indian decorations. Arches inset along the walls held ornamental vases, adding to the Spanish flavor of the room. It was beautiful. It felt like a home. Which was odd, she thought, considering a bachelor lived here.

Without turning to face Falcon she said, "I need to talk to you." Mara surreptitiously rubbed her stomach where she had brushed against him. Her belly was doing strange things. He was an animal—that was why she felt this animal magnetism toward him. She hated the man. It was absolutely ridiculous to think she could be attracted to him.

She turned to face him, willing herself not to feel anything.

But she hadn't forgotten the powerful shudders that had rippled through her when Falcon looked at her the first time they had met. Something had definitely happened that hot summer day on the street in Dallas. She despised herself for what she had felt then. And it had happened again just now.

Animal magnetism, she repeated to herself. That's all it is.

Falcon shut the door with a quiet click and leaned back against it. He folded his arms across his bare chest, crossed one bare ankle over the other and stared at her. "I didn't think you ever wanted to see me again."

She flushed. The color started at the edge of her square-necked blouse and shot right up her throat to her cheeks, where it sat in two bright pink spots. "I... I didn't."

His eyes narrowed. "But now you do?"

She swallowed hard and nodded once.

"Well." He paused. "Well." Falcon didn't know what else to say. This was certainly an astounding turn of events. Just when he had convinced himself he could live without her, the woman of his dreams had shown up at his door. Of course, she hadn't exactly picked a moment when he was at his best.

Falcon didn't ask her to sit. He didn't want her to be any more comfortable than he was. And he was downright miserable.

That didn't keep him from feeling the singular, consuming attraction for her that had struck him the first moment he saw her. And this time he knew he wasn't mistaken—she was feeling it, too. His lips curved in a self-satisfied smile. So, she was ready to admit the attraction she felt and had come to apologize for all those horrible things she had said to him.

Falcon gave free rein to the fierce sexual desire he felt for Mara Ainsworth. His groin tightened, and his blood began to hum. He refused to hide his arousal. Since she had invited herself in, she could just put up with the condition she found him in.

Mara was appalled at the blatant sensuality in Falcon's heavy-lidded stare. There was no hiding the bulge that was lovingly cupped by his butter-soft jeans. Even more appalling was her body's reaction to the prickly situation in which she found herself. She was dumbfounded by her gut response to Falcon's maleness. Her breasts felt heavy, and her belly tensed with expectation.

It was time to state her business and get out.

"I've come to get the help you offered a year ago. I need money. Lots of it."

Mara saw the shock on Falcon's face and hurried to finish before he could throw her out. "Susannah is very ill. She could die." She swallowed over the lump of pain that always arose when she said those words. "She has leukemia."

Falcon had dropped his lazy pose against the door

and was standing now on both feet with his hands balled at his sides.

"When Grant died he was between jobs and we didn't have any insurance and I don't have the money for chemotherapy and I've tried to get it other places but they want us to leave Dallas and Grant said you have lots of money so you wouldn't miss it and I think it would be better for both Susannah and me if we stayed where we are. So can you help us?"

Falcon had taken several steps toward Mara during this breathless speech. As he reached out to give her the comfort she so obviously needed, she took a step back away from him.

So. She wanted his money, but she didn't want him. That was blatantly clear.

"I'll work for you," she choked out. "I'll keep house, cook, clean, whatever you need. I know how to keep ranch books. I'll pay you back in service for every penny, I promise you that. I'm... I'm desperate. Please."

Falcon felt sick to his stomach. Mara, pretty Mara, had been reduced to begging. And she wasn't even asking him to give her the money. She was going to pay it all back. She didn't want to be beholden to him. Because she despised him.

It was there on her face every time she looked at him. She still blamed him for Grant's death. She was never going to forgive him.

So why should he give her the money?

Because there is a chance, just the slightest one, but a chance, that you might be responsible in part for her predicament. Falcon was shaken to the core by that possibility.

And that poor kid. He remembered Susannah's hazel

eyes peeping out from behind Mara's skirt on the day
he met her and the childish giggle before she hid herself completely from his sight. It was a shame for any
kid to be sick, but it caught him in the gut to imagine
that engaging little girl bedridden.

"Is Susannah…will she get well?" he asked.

"There's a good chance, a three-to-one chance, she'll
be cured by the chemotherapy. But the hospital won't
start treatments before I assure them I can pay. Can
you…will you help?"

"Give me a figure. I'll see my accountant tomorrow
and cut you a check."

"Thank you," Mara said.

He watched her take a step toward him, as though
to hug him, to share the joy and relief she was feeling.
Then she must have remembered who he was, because
she stiffened and stopped herself.

"Thank you," she said again.

But she didn't look at him. She was looking at her
hands, which were threaded together and clenched so
hard her knuckles were white.

"I can start work right away," she said.

"That won't be necessary," he said in a harsh voice.

Her head snapped up, and her brow furrowed. "I
don't understand."

"I'd go nuts with you stomping around here all self-
righteous, watching every little move I make and rak-
ing me over the coals with those big blue eyes of yours.
Thanks, but no thanks. You can have the money, but I'll
dispense with your services, if it's all the same to you."

Mara was stung by the image he had painted of her.
She wanted to fling his money back in his face, but she

had to think of Susannah. She bit her lower lip hard and kept her peace.

"Are we finished with this talk?" Falcon asked irritably. "Because I have a headache, and I'd like to get some aspirin."

"I'll pay you back," Mara said quietly. "Somehow." She hurried to the door. It meant going past Falcon. He didn't move to get out of her way, and she shivered as their bodies brushed.

"Aw, hell. You're not going to get cooties if we touch."

"I didn't—I only—" she stuttered.

"Just get the hell out of here," he said in disgust. He opened the door and held it as she rushed through, dropping a slip of paper in his hand with a breathless "My address," and then slammed it behind her.

"Women! Who the hell needs them!"

He crumpled the paper without looking at it and tossed it on the floor. He wouldn't see her to give her the check. He would have his accountant do it. There was no question, though, about his helping her. He owed it to Grant, and to the little girl who was sick. He owed Mara nothing. He hoped their paths never crossed again.

Finally, at last, he and Mara Ainsworth were quits.

CHAPTER TWO

"You don't have the money."

"What?"

"You heard me, Falcon. I said you don't have the money to be giving a blank check to some bimbo."

"Watch what you say, Aaron. Mara Ainsworth is a lady."

"My apologies. That doesn't change your situation."

"Just what, exactly, is my situation?" Falcon asked.

"To be blunt, you've damn near run through your grandfather's fortune in the past five years."

Falcon was stunned. He stopped pacing the thick carpet in his accountant's high-rise Dallas office and sank into a leather-and-chrome chair. "You're kidding, right?"

"I wish I were," Aaron said.

"Why didn't you say something sooner?" he demanded.

"I did."

Falcon remembered a conversation or two when Aaron had warned him not to make some high-risk investments. Then there were the cars. And the parties. The trips to Europe. The fancy studs and champion bulls. And the gifts he had given to his lady friends. He hadn't thought it was possible to spend a fortune in just five years.

"How much have I got left?" he asked, still a little stunned by Aaron's news.

"Enough to keep the B-Bar afloat—if you're careful and give the ranch some attention. Not enough to be loaning thousands of dollars to some woman."

"Lady," Falcon insisted. "Mara is a lady."

"Lady," Aaron conceded.

Falcon dropped his head into his hands. He could always go to his family for help; his parents and his brother and sister had assets if he really needed a loan to help Mara. And he had two uncles and an aunt. But he would be too ashamed to admit to any of them that he had squandered his inheritance. He would never live down the humiliation. And he couldn't bear to see the look on his father's face if he disappointed him. His mother would hide the pain she felt at his failure, because she knew how hard his father could be on anyone who threatened her happiness—even, or especially, her children.

Falcon was the middle child of the Three Whitelaw Brats, as they had come to be known in the vicinity around Hawk's Way, the northwest Texas ranch where he had been raised. Falcon's father, Garth, had been a hard taskmaster, demanding honesty and responsibility and accomplishment from his two sons and daughter. But Garth Whitelaw had held the leash too tight, and all three of them—his elder brother, Zachary, and his younger sister, Callen, and himself—had revolted.

They had formed a secret alliance, the Fearless Threesome, and protected each other, deftly covering one another's tracks when they were caught out in some prank. Not that they had been vicious or mean in what they had done, but they had been incorrigible, unmanageable, all three of them, daring anything and often finding themselves in desperate situations that required feats of bravado to escape.

They had been punished for their recklessness, but had remained undaunted. As a child, Falcon's behavior had been as wild and untamed as his Comanche forebearers. He hadn't improved much over the years. At thirty, he was a maverick who refused to be tied down to anything or anyone.

His siblings weren't much more settled. His sister, Callen, was a black-haired, brown-eyed rebel who had defied their father's attempts to direct her life by twice accepting marriage proposals against his wishes—and breaking both engagements when the man turned out to be the cad her father had told her he was. Zach, with his coal-black hair and dark inscrutable eyes, had become a recluse, a man who rode alone and didn't seem to need or want a woman in his life.

Thanks to the Fearless Threesome, Falcon was used to escaping the consequences of his folly. Was it any wonder he had been careless and irresponsible with his fortune? Only this time, he didn't think he could ask Zach or Callen to help him out of his trouble. Maybe it was time to grow up at last. Maybe it was time to act like the dependable, reliable, trustworthy person his parents had raised him to be.

"Isn't there something I can do to help Mara and Susannah?" Falcon asked the man sitting across the desk from him.

Aaron chewed on his pencil, a habit that was apparent from the series of teeth marks that already creased the yellow stem. "There is one thing."

Falcon waited, but when Aaron didn't speak he asked, "All right, what is it?"

"You could marry her."

"What?" Falcon leapt up and slammed his palms flat on Aaron's marble-topped desk. He leaned forward intimidatingly. "What purpose would that serve?"

"Thanks to your capable accountant, you have an excellent health-care plan. You see, the insurance company wanted your business for health coverage of employees at the B-Bar. So I was able to negotiate a special clause in the contract that allows you, as the owner, to cover your dependents—even for a preexisting condition—as soon as you acquire them, in this case, by marriage."

"That's incredible."

Aaron smiled. "I thought so myself when I wrote it into the agreement with the insurance company. You can marry Mara Ainsworth and have Susannah's medical expenses one-hundred-percent covered the next day."

"I have to think about this," Falcon said as he rose and headed for the office door. He paused with the doorknob in his hand and turned back to Aaron. "Are you sure that's the only way I can help?"

Aaron shrugged. "You could always sell the B-Bar and give her the proceeds."

Falcon grimaced. "Don't be ridiculous."

"I was being frank," Aaron retorted. "Your choices are limited, Falcon. Let me know what you decide to do."

Falcon left his accountant's office in a daze. He was dealing with a lot of emotions all at once, not the least of which was shame. What would his parents say, especially his mother, when she found out how profligate he had been with her father's bequest to him? And how was he going to face Mara Ainsworth and admit the truth? That he had managed to run through a fortune in five years of dissipated living. What would happen to Mara and Susannah if he couldn't provide her with the funds she had requested?

You could marry her.

How could he marry a woman who despised him? A woman who would never forgive him for making her a widow? A woman who shrank from his touch?

Unfortunately he had no choice. And neither did she, when it came right down to it. They would just have to make the best of it. It would be one of those marriages of convenience, where they shared the same name and the same house, but nothing else.

It would be a royal pain in the rear.

But it wouldn't last forever. Just until Susannah was out of deep water. Just until the crisis was over. He could stand being close to Mara for that long without touching.

He didn't linger and let himself come up with excuses why Aaron's suggestion wouldn't work. He jumped into his Porsche and headed for the address on the paper Mara had stuffed in his hand when she had raced away from the B-Bar yesterday.

He found her house on a shady street in an old, quiet neighborhood in Dallas. There were bicycles in the driveways and tire swings in the trees. The houses were two-story wood frame structures with picture windows and big, covered front porches. There was even one house with a white picket fence. It belonged, he discovered, to Mara Ainsworth.

He didn't see a car in the driveway, so he wasn't expecting her to be home. But he knocked anyway.

She opened the door wearing very short cutoff jeans and a Dallas Cowboys T-shirt. She was barefoot. And she wasn't wearing a bra. He knew because her nipples peaked the instant she set eyes on him.

He turned her on, but she hated his guts. It was just plain crazy. He had fought the attraction he felt, knowing it could lead nowhere. But it was clear to him, if not yet to her, that some powerful magnetism still existed between the two of them.

"Hello," he managed.

"Oh! I thought you were my neighbor Sally. But, of course, you aren't."

Of course he wasn't. He stood there on the porch for a moment, waiting for her to invite him inside. When she didn't, he took a page from her book and stepped inside on his own. He heard the door close behind him.

"Where's Susannah?" he asked when she didn't immediately appear.

"She's still in the hospital."

"Oh."

Falcon looked around with a critical eye, wanting to find something about Mara's home that he could dislike as much as she disliked him. The living room was done in quiet colors and simple Western patterns that were easy on the eye. She had a green thumb, because there were lush plants everywhere, bringing the outdoors inside. Plump pillows decorated the couch, and a cozy, overstuffed chair invited him to sit down.

Only, he knew better than to make himself comfortable. Once she heard what he had to say, she might very well throw him out. He turned to face Mara.

She was leaning against the door in much the same way he had done, but there was nothing relaxed about the pose.

"I didn't bring a check," he said.

She caught her lower lip with her teeth. "You changed your mind about helping us?"

"No, I didn't change my mind," he retorted irritably. "I don't have the money."

She snorted in disbelief. "You mean you choose not to loan it to me."

He began to pace, like a tiger in a cage. "No, I mean exactly what I said. I don't have the money." He paused in front of a natural-rock fireplace and leaned both palms against the mantel with his back to her. "It seems I've already spent most of my fortune. I only have enough left to keep the B-Bar in business."

"I'm sorry," she said.

He whirled, his eyes blazing. "I don't need your pity."

"I don't pity you," she said.

No, it wasn't pity he saw in her eyes. It was disappointment. And disgust. He felt a burning rage deep inside that he should be subjected to all this.

It wasn't my fault. I wasn't the one who killed Grant Ainsworth. Why should I feel responsible for rescuing Grant's wife and child?

If not for the situation he found himself in, it wouldn't have been anyone's business but his own whether he squandered his fortune.

"You could have told me all this in a phone call," Mara said. "Why did you bother coming here?"

"Because even though I can't give you the money I promised, there is a way I can help you."

He saw hope blossom bright and beautiful in her

eyes. And dreaded the moment of disillusionment when he told her what he had to say.

"If you marry me," he announced, "Susannah will be covered by my insurance the day after we tie the knot."

"What?"

He thought she was going to faint, so he went to her, to help her. He stopped in his tracks when she backed away from him.

"I don't understand," she said.

"I thought I was very clear," he said in a harsh voice. "My insurance policy will cover any dependents of mine, even for a preexisting condition, the day after I acquire them. If you marry me, my insurance will cover Susannah's treatment."

"Marry you?"

"Yes, dammit, marry me! You don't have to sound so appalled at the idea."

"I'm not…appalled. I'm just…surprised."

Mara crossed to the overstuffed chair and sank into it. "I hadn't thought of getting married again."

"Especially not to the likes of me," Falcon finished for her.

Her brow furrowed. "I don't know what to say."

"Say yes."

She sought out his eyes with her own, and he could see the turmoil there. He knew he ought to let her refuse. Then he would be out of it, and the problem would be hers again. But the truth was, he wanted to be the one to rescue her. He wanted to redeem himself in her eyes. He wanted to earn her respect. He wanted a chance to prove he wasn't the good-for-nothing she thought he was.

"It doesn't have to be a real marriage," he said. "We'll

have to live together, of course. But that shouldn't be a problem."

"I don't want to leave my house."

"It's just a house," Falcon argued.

"It's more than that," Mara said, eyes flashing indignantly. "It's a place where I belong, where I have friends. I can't give that up, too."

She bit her lip to keep from letting the whole of her tragedy spill out at him—namely, her fear that she might soon lose Susannah, as well.

He saw the tears that filled her eyes, ready to brim over. He knew she was going to reject him again, but he had to make the effort to comfort her anyway. He pulled her up out of the chair and into his arms.

To his amazement, she clutched him around the waist and pressed her forehead against his chest and began to sob. He tightened his arms around her and crooned words of solace. He didn't know how long they stood there, but when she finally stopped crying, one of his hands was tangled in her hair and the other pressed her tightly against him.

His throat felt thick. His chest ached. He would have given anything to be worthy of her. But it was too late. He had lived a profligate, self-indulgent existence. Now, without the other two-thirds of the Fearless Threesome to rescue him, he was finally going to have to face the consequences of his behavior.

He knew when she was herself again, because she stiffened in his arms. She didn't struggle to be free, but he knew that if he didn't let her go soon, she would.

"Marry me," he whispered. "I promise I won't do anything to make you uncomfortable in my home. For Susannah's sake. Marry me."

She heaved a ragged sigh that ended in a sob that she quickly caught with her fist. She lowered her hand and raised her tear-drenched face to his. "All right," she said in a hoarse voice. "I'll marry you."

She took a step backward, and he was forced to release her.

"I'll take care of getting the license," he said. "You'll have to get a blood test—"

"I'll take care of that on my own. When?" she asked.

"As soon as possible, don't you think?"

Her face looked ravaged. Her eyes were red-rimmed. But she faced him without flinching this time. "You tell me when and where, and I'll be there."

"I'll help you move your things—"

"I'll leave the house exactly as it is," she said fiercely. "It's my home, mine and Susannah's. When this travesty of a marriage is over—" she choked back a sob "—when Susannah is well, we'll be coming back here to live. Now get out! I can't stand to look at you anymore."

Falcon backed away to the door, unable to take his eyes off her. Mara hated him. And he was going to marry her. He told himself it was a sacrifice that he owed her.

But as he closed her door behind him, he couldn't help feeling regret, and even despair.

How the hell were they going to get through the next year together?

CHAPTER THREE

IT WAS HER wedding day, and Mara felt trapped. This was not the perfect solution she had been searching for, not at all. But at least she didn't have to leave Dallas. She would find some way to keep Susannah in the same school, and she would be able to keep an eye on her house. But she had paid a high price for those small victories. She had to marry the man responsible for Grant's death.

Falcon had promised her it would be a marriage in name only, but in the same breath he had insisted they live together. She supposed there was some danger the insurance company could refuse to pay if they discovered it was a sham marriage, so it had to look real.

But it was a sham. A farce. A pretense. A mockery. She would be Mrs. Falcon Whitelaw. She would be married to a man she despised, a man so irresponsible he had run through a fortune in five years. She had to live in his house, make his meals, iron his clothes. Be his wife.

But she would never forgive him. What he had done was unforgivable. And yet, she owed him something for the help he had given her.

Mara felt torn in half. Because there were other feelings she had for Falcon Whitelaw that had nothing at all to do with hate and scorn. She felt drawn to him in a way that was disturbing, to say the least. She had tried to deceive herself, to say that there was no substance to her attraction to the handsome rogue. But her body made a liar out of her every time she got near him.

So how was she going to survive living in the same house with him, seeing him every day?

"Are you ready?"

Mara was jerked from her thoughts by the words Falcon had murmured in her ear.

"It's time," he said.

"I'm ready." She turned to Falcon. He looked as grim as she felt. "Isn't there anybody you wanted to have here? Some family?" she asked him.

"No. You?"

"No. My parents are gone, and I haven't any brothers or sisters." But she knew Falcon had family. Grant had told her about the Fearless Threesome. Falcon must be missing his brother and sister about now. She wondered how he was going to explain all this to them.

As Falcon listened to the judge reading the words legally binding him to Mara Ainsworth, he was wondering the same thing. How was he going to explain a wife and child to his family? How was he going to explain this slapdash wedding, to which none of them had been invited?

He couldn't tell them the truth. But he didn't want to lie. Better to tell them half the truth. That he had met a very special woman, and that he and Mara hadn't wanted to wait to get married. He would promise to bring his wife to meet the family soon but explain that they had to stay in Dallas for the moment because Mara's daughter was sick and needed treatment at the hospital here. That ought to keep them at bay for a little while.

Then what?

He would worry about the future when it got here, Falcon decided. Right now he had his hands full dealing with the present.

He answered "I will" at the proper moment and watched Mara's face as she said the same vow. Her complexion was pale, and she had been chewing on her lower lip so it pouted out a little. He wanted to soothe the hurt. Before the thought got much further than that, the judge was telling him he could kiss the bride.

Falcon put his hands on Mara's shoulders, because he suspected she would retreat if he gave her the chance. He was watching her face as he lowered his mouth toward hers, so he saw the moment her eyelashes fluttered down. Her body was rigid beneath his hands, but her mouth…her mouth was soft and pliant beneath his.

Falcon had kissed a lot of women, but there was no time when he had ever felt like this. It was a reverent meeting of lips, and he cherished Mara, giving himself to her and imploring her to take what he offered.

For a moment, she did.

He felt, as much as heard, her tremulous sigh. She gave herself up to the kiss, her trembling body melting into his, her mouth clinging so sweetly that he thought his heart was going to burst with the joy of it.

Then she jerked away with a cry of distress that she quickly stifled. Her eyes, wide and wounded, stared at him accusingly, as though her surrender was all his fault.

Then he was turning away to smile at the judge—or at least to bare his teeth in a semblance of one—and shake the man's hand and receive congratulations. Falcon didn't risk putting his arm around Mara to lead her from the judge's chambers, but he walked as close behind her as he dared.

The judge knew his father, but had promised to let Falcon break the news of his wedding. Even so, Falcon kept up the facade of wedded bliss until the door was closed behind him, because he didn't want any stories about the real state of his marriage getting back to his family. At least not before he had figured out how to explain things that didn't leave him in such a bad light.

Falcon opened the door of his Porsche and made sure Mara's calf-length ivory dress was inside before he closed it after her. They were on their way now to pick up Susannah, who was well enough to come home from the hospital until her induction therapy began. Funny name for it, Falcon thought, induction therapy, but that was what the hospital called chemotherapy used to induce remission. Susannah needed six to twelve weeks of treatment, which was scheduled to begin on Monday. With her condition stabilized, she was being allowed to spend the weekend with her family.

"How have you explained our wedding to Susannah?" he asked Mara.

A flush of color appeared on her ashen cheeks. "I told her we met and liked each other very much, so we decided to get married."

Falcon hit the brakes and almost caused an accident. "You told her what?"

"What did you expect me to tell her," Mara retorted. "That I was marrying you to get the money for her treatments? She's an impressionable child. I want to leave her some illusions about life."

"What's going to happen the first time she sees you cringe when I touch you?" Falcon demanded. "Or didn't you think she was going to notice?" he asked sarcastically.

"I…" Mara hadn't, in fact, thought any further than the wedding. She glared at Falcon. "I suppose I'll have to stop cringing," she announced.

"Great," Falcon muttered. "That's just great. What about our sleeping arrangements? How are you going to explain separate bedrooms to this precocious child of yours?"

"I'll be staying in a room next to Susannah," Mara said. "You'll be the understanding husband who wants me to be near my sick child."

Falcon snorted. "You've thought of everything, haven't you?"

"I wasn't able to think of a way to get out of marrying you!" she snapped.

Falcon slid the car into a parking place at Children's Hospital and cranked off the ignition. He turned to face Mara. "All right," he said, "let's get a few things straight before we go in to see Susannah."

Mara crossed her arms over her chest. "I'm listening."

Big concession, Falcon thought. "You're the one who wants Susannah to believe this marriage is real. I'm willing to go along with you."

This time Mara snorted.

Falcon ignored her and continued, "So I think we better set some ground rules. First, no more cringing, flinching or stiffening up like a board when I get near you. Can you handle that?"

Mara nodded curtly.

"Second, no more mudslinging, in either direction. Agreed?"

"That's fine with me."

He took a deep breath. "Third, you're going to have to allow me to show you some signs of affection."

"What? No! Absolutely not!"

"You're not thinking this through," Falcon said. "Won't Susannah be sure to make comparisons between the way you act toward me and the way you acted toward Grant? She'll know right away that there's something wrong if I never kiss you, if I never lay a hand on you."

Falcon watched Mara's face. He could see the struggle going on, the war she was waging. He saw the moment she conceded the battle. Her chin came up pugnaciously, and her hands balled into tight little fists.

"All right," she said through gritted teeth. "We'll do this your way." She turned to face him, eyes bright with unshed tears. "But don't push me, Falcon. Because I won't stand for it!"

There were things she had put up with in her marriage with Grant that she had decided in the year since his death she should never have tolerated. She wasn't going to make the same mistake twice. Better to lay down rules with Falcon now that would protect her later.

Falcon could have wished for more cooperation from Mara. At least she had been forced to put a door in the high walls that kept her separated from him. Falcon felt the first signs of hope he had known since he had agreed to this untenable situation. He would be able to hold Mara, to kiss her. Maybe, as she got to know him better, as he earned her respect, she would allow him to do more.

He would have a year to prove himself. Mara had told him that after Susannah had the chemotherapy treatments, her leukemia had to stay in remission for a year in order for her to be deemed past the first hurdle toward a cure. Mara and Susannah would be with him at least that long. And a year was a long time.

"I won't go beyond what I think is necessary to convince Susannah we have a normal relationship," Falcon said at last. He knew his idea of "necessary" signs of affection and hers were likely poles apart. But he wasn't about to make promises he couldn't keep. "Shall we go inside now and get Susannah?"

Falcon had forgotten how much Susannah looked like her mother. Her face had the same oval shape, the same strong cheekbones and short, straight nose. Her eyes were large and wide-set like Mara's. But he was shocked at the toll her serious illness had taken on Susannah. It was like seeing Mara pale and thin. His heart went out to the little girl the instant her eyes met his.

"How are you, Susannah?" he asked with a cheerful smile. "Do you remember me?"

Mara was sitting on the bed next to her daughter, and Susannah retreated behind her mother, peeping out at him shyly around Mara's shoulder.

"Your mother has some news for you," Falcon said.

Mara shot him a perturbed look, then smiled down at her daughter. "Yes, sweetheart. Falcon and I got married this morning."

Susannah looked curiously at Falcon. "Are you my daddy now?"

Falcon felt the floor fall out from under him. He obviously hadn't focused on all the responsibilities he was taking on. "I...suppose I am."

"Will you buy me a pony?"

"Susannah!" Mara exclaimed. "You shouldn't be asking Mr. Whitelaw to buy you things."

"Why not, if he's my daddy?" Susannah demanded. "Will you buy me a pony?"

Mara looked helplessly at Falcon, who shrugged helplessly back. Then he turned his attention to Susannah.

"Sure I will, pumpkin. What color pony did you want?"

Mara's lips pursed. "You're going to spoil her rotten."

"That's what fathers are for," Falcon replied. "Right, Susannah?" He grinned and tousled the little girl's hair affectionately.

Susannah beamed. "Right."

Falcon stopped what he was doing when it dawned on him Susannah's hair was all going to fall out when the little girl had chemotherapy. He kept the smile on his face for Susannah's sake, but he felt sick inside.

Mara saw Susannah's smile, the first one she had seen in weeks, and forgave Falcon for catering to her daughter. Nevertheless, she couldn't help resenting the fact that Falcon was able to give Susannah something that Grant wouldn't have been able to afford. She and Grant had barely been making ends meet, in fact. But she kept her mouth shut about how she felt. She had promised to curb her tongue for Susannah's sake.

Susannah had to ride a wheelchair downstairs, but the moment they reached the hospital exit, Falcon swept the little girl up into his arms. Mara didn't have time to feel left out, because Falcon slipped his other arm around her waist and pulled her close. A quick, warning glance kept her from pulling free.

Mara was glad she hadn't when Susannah reached out and grabbed her hand, so the three of them were completely connected. "Let's go home, Mommy," the little girl said.

"We're going to my house, if that's all right with you," Falcon said.

Susannah frowned.

"I live on a ranch," Falcon added.

Susannah's face brightened. "Will my pony be able to live with us?"

"Yes, he will."

"Is Mommy coming, too?"

"Wouldn't go without her," Falcon confirmed.

"All right. Let's go," Susannah said.

Mara marveled at how little effort it had taken for Falcon to convince Susannah that his ranch was a better destination than the home she had worked so hard to create for her daughter over the past year. But other than the doll Susannah had grasped tightly in her arms, and Mara herself, her daughter apparently had no attachments to the house in Dallas.

To Mara's amazement, Falcon turned out to be a totally charming companion on the trip to the B-Bar Ranch. He kept Susannah entertained with outrageous stories about himself and his siblings. The Porsche plainly needed to be replaced with a family car. Mara didn't relish confronting Falcon on the issue. Maybe he would realize the problem himself.

Falcon had just finished an anecdote when Susannah sighed and said wistfully, "I wish I had a sister. Can you and Mommy get one for me?"

Mara exchanged a horrified look with Falcon, whose lips twisted in a wry smile.

"That's entirely up to your mother," he said, throwing the ball back into her court.

"Will you, Mommy?"

"It's not quite as simple as buying a pony," Mara said as she sent a cutting glance toward Falcon. "Why don't we wait awhile, until you're well. Then we'll see."

Mara saw Falcon's eyebrow arch at the way she had caviled. But she refused to take away any of Susannah's dreams, no matter how far-fetched. Especially since there was no telling how much longer Susannah had to dream dreams.

That awful lump was back in Mara's throat, and she swallowed it down and forced a smile to her face. "Besides, you'll be too busy with your new pony to have time for a little sister right away."

"We're here," Falcon announced.

He unbuckled Susannah's seat belt and lifted her into his arms. "Come on," he said. "I want to show you your new home."

Mara followed, feeling forgotten, and though she wouldn't have admitted it, a little jealous of her daughter. Just when she thought Falcon was going to leave her behind, he stopped and set Susannah on her feet in the arch of the Spanish tiled entryway.

"There's a ritual that has to be observed," he said with a wink to Susannah.

Without warning, he swept Mara off her feet and into his arms. "I have to carry my bride over the threshold."

Susannah laughed. "Falcon picked you up, Mommy."

"He sure did!"

Mara was glad Susannah had bowed to Falcon's request in the car and was calling him by his name. It would have been sad to see Grant displaced so quickly by Falcon in her daughter's affections. But children, thank God, were resilient creatures, and Mara was glad Grant's death hadn't devastated her daughter.

"Can you get the door, Susannah?" Mara asked. "If Falcon stands here too long, he just might get tired and drop me."

Susannah laughed at the idea. "Silly Mommy," she said.

Falcon was surprised to hear the teasing quality in Mara's voice. He was enjoying holding her, and he wished he didn't have to set her down until he got her upstairs to his bed. Only it wasn't his bed anymore. He had ceded it to Mara.

Susannah pushed the door open, and he followed her inside. He managed to plant a quick, searing kiss on Mara's lips before he set her down. She shot him a warning look, but with Susannah present, there wasn't much else she could do. Falcon figured all was fair in love and war, and this marriage was sure to have a good deal of the latter.

"Welcome to your new home, Mrs. Whitelaw," he said.

The stricken look on Mara's face came and went so quickly he might have missed it if he hadn't been watching her so intently. But he did see it. He set his back teeth. So she didn't want his name, either.

Falcon had never really desired anything badly that he couldn't buy with money or have for the asking. Now he was finding out what it was like to want something that was beyond his reach. What he hadn't known about himself until this moment was how hard he was willing to strive to achieve his wants. And, though it irked him to admit it, he wanted Mara to want him with the same aching desire he felt for her.

It might take some time for him to find the right methods to win her over, but he was determined to seek them out. However, he was starting at the bottom of a very tall mountain and he didn't think he was in for an easy climb. Still, when he thought of the rewards to be had at the top, he was willing to take the first step.

If he could only figure out what it was.

Right now he had to concentrate on getting the three of them situated in his house. He took Mara and Susannah upstairs to show them the master bedroom and the guest bedroom next door to it.

"I'm in the bedroom downstairs," he said. "That way we won't get in each other's way."

Mara had moved in her and Susannah's things the previous day and had worried about whether Falcon would take one of the other two upstairs bedrooms. She managed not to sigh aloud in relief that he had relegated himself to the downstairs area.

"We'll join you in a little while," Mara said. "I want to change clothes before I start lunch."

Falcon had been dismissed. He took one last look at his wife and new daughter before heading down the stairs.

They joined him an hour later in the kitchen. Falcon took a moment to admire his wife. She was wearing jeans that molded her hips and long slender legs and a plaid Western blouse that had the first two buttons undone so he saw a hint of her rounded breasts. She had rolled up her sleeves and had tied her hair in a ponytail that made her look like a girl again. He wanted to be the teenage boy that got her alone in the backseat of an old convertible and taught her all about the birds and the bees.

"I would have been glad to fix lunch," Mara said when she saw the table set and food waiting to be served.

"It was my pleasure," Falcon said. "It's just steak and baked potatoes and a salad." He grinned roguishly. "I'm afraid that's my entire repertoire."

Mara sat down in the chair he held out for her and watched with raised brows as he poured decanted red wine into a crystal glass.

"Wine?" she said. "At lunch?"

"It's a late lunch," he quipped. "And we did just get married," he pointed out.

Mara flushed and wasn't sure whether it was chagrin or pleasure she was feeling. Maybe it was both. She could be excused for her confusion. This was, after all, a somewhat muddled situation.

Falcon poured some milk into a wineglass for Susannah. "So you can join in our toast to a happy life," he said.

Mara saw how pleased her daughter was to be included in the grown-up ritual. It appeared Falcon Whitelaw had a knack for pleasing females that she hadn't imagined.

Once they were served and Falcon had seated himself, he raised his glass for the toast he had promised. "To a long and happy life," he said.

Mara stared at him aghast. Such a toast might be appropriate for a newly wedded couple, but with Susannah sitting there, her life in the balance, it seemed particularly cruel. Falcon held his glass aloft, ignoring her wordless censure, demanding that she join him.

At last she did. "To a long and happy life," she echoed, clinking her glass against his and against Susannah's.

"To a long and happy life," her daughter said. Susannah grinned and drank some of her milk. "I'm hungry, Mommy. Let's eat."

That was a good sign. Susannah had been nauseous after the interim treatment she had received, and the doctor had given her a Benadryl injection to help counter the sickness. Apparently it was working.

"I was thinking that you might like to come see the horses in my stable after lunch," Falcon said to Susannah.

"Is my pony there?"

Falcon laughed. "Not yet. But I have a few colts and fillies that you might like to pet."

Susannah was beaming again. How did he do it? Mara wondered. Maybe the reason she was unable to make Susannah laugh was because she didn't feel much like laughing herself. So perhaps some good would come of staying with Falcon, after all.

"Do you want to come with us?" Falcon asked as he headed out the back door with Susannah after lunch.

Mara felt anxious letting Susannah out of her sight. But she didn't want to spend any more time with Falcon than she had to.

Misreading her indecision, Falcon said, "I'll take good care of her. I won't let her get hurt."

"Susannah's spent a lot of time around horses. She knows how to act." Her words came out sounding sharp and reproachful, and she wished them back. But it was too late. Falcon frowned and turned his back on her.

"We won't be gone long," he said as he let the screen door slam behind them.

Mara looked around at the mess in the kitchen and realized this was a way she could repay Falcon in part for the service he had rendered when he married her. There was more to be done in the kitchen than simply cleaning up after the meal. Falcon obviously hadn't had a housekeeper in a while. The floor needed scrubbing, and the cabinets were disorganized. There were other things she would be able to do when she had more time: curtains for the windows, flowers on the sill, cleaning the refrigerator and the stove. She would settle now for washing dishes and putting away leftovers.

Mara was just wiping down the front of the refrigerator when Falcon returned with Susannah. He had been gone, she suddenly realized, for most of the afternoon. Where had the time gone? She looked around her and saw a kitchen that sparkled. Her eyes shifted back to Falcon.

Mara sensed from the worried look on his face that something was wrong. Susannah had her head on his shoulder, and her arms were wrapped around his neck.

"I didn't mean to keep Susannah out so long," Falcon said. "She got a little tired. I'll take her upstairs for you."

But his eyes said, Please don't leave me alone with her.

In fact, Falcon was terrified. Without warning, Susannah had deflated like a balloon with a pinhole in it. One second she was patting the forehead of a pretty bay filly with four white stockings, the next she was hanging on to the leg of his jeans as though that was all that was holding her upright. Susannah had sagged into his arms when he picked her up, almost like deadweight.

He could feel her erratic breaths against his neck, and she had become unusually quiet. He was even more afraid of what Mara would say about Susannah's condition.

"We didn't do anything strenuous," he found himself saying to Mara. He waited for her to pull down the covers so he could lay Susannah on her bed. "One minute she was fine, and the next minute she was practically asleep on her feet."

"It wasn't anything you did," Mara said. "It's the disease. It saps her strength."

She took off Susannah's tennis shoes and covered her with the sheets and a quilt. The little girl was already asleep.

Mara turned to face Falcon and found herself wanting to smooth the furrow of worry from his brow. "She'll be all right again once she's rested."

When the shadows didn't leave his blue eyes, she reached out a hand to him. "It isn't your fault," she said in a quiet voice. "You didn't do anything wrong."

He seemed to notice suddenly that she was touching him. He stared at her hand, then turned his hand to thread his fingers with hers. "Come downstairs with me," he said. "We need to talk."

Mara felt the calluses on his hand, felt the strength of it and felt all kinds of other things that she had no business feeling. For a moment she resisted his gentle tug. Then she was on her feet and he was leading her downstairs.

He sat on the heavy Mediterranean couch of deep wine leather and dark wood and urged her down beside him. He slipped his arm around her and pulled her close.

Mara nestled her head under Falcon's chin and felt

the lickety-split beat of his heart and the grip of his hand on hers. She didn't try to free herself or chastise Falcon for his presumptuousness. She knew he needed comfort, and she needed it too much herself to refuse it to him. They sat there for a long time in silence.

Without fanfare, without warning, dusk fell. The light coming in through the arched windows turned pale yellow and pink and orange. It wouldn't be long before it was full dark. "I thought we were going to talk," Mara said.

"We are," he said. "I just needed this first."

"Me, too," Mara admitted.

"Is she going to die?" Falcon asked.

Mara felt the tears sting her eyes. "No."

Falcon tightened his hold on her. "Is that wishing? Or is that the truth?"

Mara told him everything she knew about acute lymphocytic leukemia. About the six to twelve weeks of chemotherapy to induce remission. About the ninety-percent cure rate for the chemotherapy. About the possibility of relapse, which could happen at any time, and which would require the entire chemotherapy treatment all over again.

"If she makes it for a year without a relapse, there's a good chance she'll be home free."

"And if the chemotherapy doesn't work?"

"There's always a bone-marrow transplant."

"And if that doesn't work?"

Mara tore herself from Falcon's embrace; it was no longer comforting. She rose and turned to face him with her hands on her hips, her feet widespread in a fighting stance. "What do you want me to say? That

Susannah may die? The possibility exists," she said. "Are you happy now?"

He rose and faced her in an equally belligerent stance. "No, I'm not. How can you stand it, knowing what may happen?"

Suddenly all the fight went out of her. "I don't have much choice," she said, her eyes bleak.

"Mara, I—"

Falcon reached for Mara, to comfort her, but she whirled and ran. He didn't go after her. He wished he hadn't let himself get involved. He wished he had borrowed the money from someone to pay for the treatments Susannah needed. Because he didn't think he could stand by and watch Susannah Ainsworth die. Most of all, he didn't think he could bear to watch Mara suffer if her daughter didn't survive.

It was too late to back out now. He wanted Mara. And he had already given a piece of his soul to Susannah. He was bound to both of them by ties he hadn't even begun to imagine existed before they came into his life.

He would make sure Susannah had the best care possible, no matter what it cost. Even if he had to humble himself before his family to get more money to pay for it.

CHAPTER FOUR

FALCON HAD BEEN married for two weeks, during which time Susannah had begun induction therapy in earnest. He made it a point to be at the house whenever Mara returned from the hospital with her daughter. He carried the child up to her bedroom from the van he had recently bought to replace his Porsche, holding her limp form in his arms while Mara arranged the bed. Then he settled her under the covers.

It was getting harder and harder to smile for the little girl. But Falcon forced himself to be cheerful. Mara's face was stark, her eyes bleak and worried. He didn't think so much solemnity could be good for Susannah.

"How are you feeling?" Falcon asked Susannah. He immediately regretted the words, but to his surprise Susannah lifted a flattened hand and tipped it back and forth like airplane wings.

"So-so," she said.

"Why ask when you know she's feeling sick?" Mara rebuked him.

"There's sick, and then there's sick," Falcon said. "Isn't that so, Susannah?" He brush her bangs away from her forehead and a hank of hair came out in his hand.

He turned stricken eyes to Mara, but found no comfort there. She looked as stunned as he felt.

Falcon sought a way to hide the scrap of hair from Susannah, but she saw it and took it from him, inspecting it carefully.

"My hair is falling out," she said matter-of-factly.

"It appears so," Falcon replied cautiously.

"Dr. Sortino says that's a good sign," she explained to Falcon. "He says that means the medicine is working. I want to get a red hat, like my new friend Patsy wears. Is that okay?"

"That's fine, pumpkin," Falcon said. "Your mom and I will see if we can find one." He started to playfully tug a curl that lay on Susannah's cheek and barely managed to stop himself in time. What if it came away in his hand? Susannah's disappearing tresses didn't seem to worry her, but he was still shaken by his recent experience.

Falcon tucked Susannah in and leaned over to kiss her on the forehead. As he did so he realized he was going to be devastated if chemotherapy didn't stop the disease. He had already started reading about bone-marrow transplants. They were horribly painful, and it was difficult to find donors. And they didn't always effect a cure. The statistics weren't encouraging. He couldn't imagine putting Susannah through it, knowing how much she suffered from the induction therapy.

When he stood up, he realized Mara had already left the room. That wasn't like her. Usually she stayed to read to Susannah after he was gone.

"I wonder what happened to your mom," he said.

"She left a minute ago," Susannah informed him. "She was crying again."

"Again?"

"She doesn't think I know, but I've seen her cry lots

of times," Susannah confided. "She thinks I'm going to die. Am I?"

Falcon was startled by such frank speaking. He wanted to reply "Of course not!" But that wouldn't have been honest. On the other hand, did an eight-year-old child deserve to hear an honest evaluation of her chances of survival?

Mara should be answering these questions, he thought.

Before he could answer Susannah, she asked, "What is it like to die?"

Falcon grinned ruefully. "You've got me there, pumpkin. I can't answer that. My suggestion is that you concentrate on getting well."

Susannah wrinkled her nose. "You never answered my first question. Am I going to die?"

Falcon didn't care if it was a lie. It was the only answer he was willing to give her. "No, pumpkin. You're going to be fine. But you have to rest and take care of yourself."

Falcon was amazed that Susannah accepted his dictum as truth. She closed her eyes and settled back against her pillow.

"Tell Mommy it's okay if she cries. I understand."

Falcon felt his throat swell with emotion. "I'll do that," he managed to say.

He got out of the room as quickly as he could, closing the door behind him.

He didn't have to search far for Mara. She was standing right there with her back against the wall, her chin on her chest, her arms crossed protectively over her breasts.

"Did you hear?" he asked quietly.

She looked up at him and nodded. Her eyes welled with tears. As he watched, one slid onto her cheek.

"I didn't know what to say," he confessed.

"You said exactly the right thing."

"I lied."

"It was not a lie! She's going to live!" Mara said fiercely.

Falcon slipped an arm around her shoulders and led her toward the master bedroom. "Susannah's liable to hear us," he warned.

Mara jerked herself free, and instead of going the rest of the way to her bedroom, headed downstairs. "Let's go where we can talk freely."

Falcon followed after her. It hadn't been an easy two weeks of marriage, but he and Mara had managed to remain civil to each other. He had a feeling their truce was about to end.

Mara marched all the way to the kitchen, where she found a glass and some ice and poured herself some tea. She drank half the glass and wiped her mouth with the back of her hand. "All right, let's get this over with."

"I don't want to fight with you," Falcon said.

Mara was filled with pent-up anxiety. If she didn't release it, she was going to burst. She slammed her tea glass down on the table. "You must be missing all those parties about now," she said. "All that late-night carousing…all those women—"

"Don't start," Falcon warned, grabbing her shoulders and giving her a shake. "I'll accept that you're over-wrought because of Susannah's condition. That's no reason to take out your frustration on me."

Mara stared at Falcon, stunned at the accuracy of his statement. Dread and fear crowded her every waking moment, making it impossible to act normally. She shuddered at the thought of how she was behaving toward Falcon. True, she despised his irresponsible, devil-may-care attitudes. But if it hadn't been for his lighthearted teasing, his smiles and cajolery, she didn't think she could have survived the past two weeks. And there were so many more weeks to be endured!

She looked up at Falcon and let him see the remorse she felt. "I'm sorry," she whispered.

Her lips were trembling, her eyes liquid with feeling. Falcon didn't think, he acted on impulse. His mouth slanted across hers, and he thrust his tongue inside, meeting hers in a passionate duel. His hands slid from her shoulders across her breasts, and he heard her moan as he cupped their fullness.

Mara's hands slid around Falcon's waist and up his back, as she sought solace for the ache deep inside. She wanted to disappear inside him, to be absorbed into his being so there was no more Mara and Falcon, only one stronger being, more capable of surviving the awful uncertainty of the future.

"Falcon," she whispered in a ragged voice. "Please. Please."

Falcon picked her up and carried her to his bedroom. He kicked the door closed behind them and captured her mouth as he lowered her to the bed.

"Are you protected?" he asked. There was no sense bringing an innocent child into this convoluted situation. Later, if things worked out... But not now.

"Are you?" he demanded in a voice harsh with the need he was striving to control.

Mara nodded jerkily. "Hurry," she said. "Please hurry." It was a strange thing for a woman to ask a man who was about to make love to her. But Mara didn't want time to think about what she was doing. Nor did she want to give Falcon time to change his mind.

Mara wanted to touch his skin, to feel the warmth, the strength of him. She yanked the snaps free on his shirt and shoved it off his shoulders. She tested bone and sinew with her hands, then tasted with her mouth. She heard the zipper slide down on her jeans and felt Falcon pushing them down along with her panties.

Then she was naked to his touch and his hand was caressing her. His fingers slid inside her, first one and then another. She arched beneath him and bucked a little as the pleasure became too intense to bear. She bit his shoulder, hardly aware of what she was doing, only knowing that she wanted him, needed him. Now.

She reached for him and felt the hard bulge that threatened the seams of his jeans. He groaned as she cupped him in her hand and then stroked up and down. He unsnapped his jeans and shoved them down along with his briefs.

An instant later he was inside her. She moaned deep in her throat as she felt the hot, hard length of him thrust once into the welcoming warmth, then retreat and thrust again.

She lifted her hips in a primitive response to him, then reached for his mouth to mimic with her tongue his intrusion below. She gasped as she felt her body begin to convulse. Her fingernails left crescents on his flanks as she urged him deeper. She wrapped her legs around him and held him captive as he released his seed.

It was over too soon.

Mara felt the tears squeezing between her tightly

closed lids. She was panting, trying to catch her breath, and failing. She felt totally enervated. And exultant.

And horrified.

What had she done? She shoved frantically at Falcon's broad shoulders, and he rolled over onto his back. He exhaled a deep sigh of contentment. Mara scrambled to her knees, pulling up her underwear and her jeans, which she realized had caught around her ankles. She searched for her shirt, meanwhile crossing one arm across her breasts.

"Where are you going in such a hurry?" Falcon asked.

"I…I have to get out of here," Mara said.

Falcon kicked his jeans the rest of the way off. Mara was appalled to realize that they hadn't even been able to wait long enough to get their clothes off! She chanced a glance at Falcon and was sorry she had looked. He looked smugly satisfied. As well he should be. She had practically fallen on him and dragged him to the ground. What on earth had she been thinking? She had just made love—no, no—she had just had sex with a man she despised!

She had been seeking comfort, and he had willingly offered it. The cad. The rogue. The cur.

"Don't bother seeing me out," she snapped, shrugging her way into her shirt.

He laughed.

She glared at him. "What's so funny?"

"You are. You can't pretend nothing happened, Mara."

"Oh, yes I can!" She turned and marched out the door. At the last instant she was careful not to slam it. She didn't want to take the chance of waking Susannah.

All the way up the stairs Mara pounded her fist against the banister. "How on earth did I let that happen? I'm an idiot. I have to be out of my mind," she muttered.

But the truth was, she had never had such a devastating sexual experience with a man. She wasn't sure exactly what had happened, but she was terrified that she wouldn't be able to resist Falcon if he offered her a chance to repeat the encounter.

How the mighty had fallen.

It was time she reevaluated her relationship with Falcon Whitelaw. Maybe, if she looked hard enough, she could find enough redeeming features in him to justify a second look at the man.

IT HAD BEEN three long weeks since Falcon had made love to his wife—and he had been making love, even if she hadn't. Lately she looked sideways at him every time he got near her, as though she expected him to pounce on her and carry her off to his bedroom again. He wouldn't have minded one bit. But it was as clear as a pane of glass that she would fight him if he made the attempt. So he bided his time, waiting for the moment when she came to him.

Falcon needed to talk to someone about his feelings for Mara. Could he really want a woman this bad who went out of her way to avoid him? Was it asking for heartache to keep hoping she would forgive him— and herself—and work with him to make theirs a real marriage? Falcon had mulled the subject until he was nearly crazy but found no answers. Which was when he decided to approach his brother for advice.

Zach was the person closest to him, the person he

had always turned to in the past when he needed a sounding board. He didn't want to leave Mara and Susannah for even the couple of days it would take him to visit his brother at Hawk's Way. So he called Zach and asked him to come to Dallas.

"What's going on?" Zach asked.

"I got married," Falcon confessed.

There was silence on the other end of the line. "Who's the woman?"

"You don't know her," he said. "She has a daughter who's very ill. There were reasons… Look, I don't want to have to explain all this on the phone. Will you come?"

"I'll be there tonight," Zach said.

Zach piloted his own jet, so airline connections weren't a problem for him. Falcon made arrangements to pick him up at Dallas/Fort Worth International Airport.

Falcon realized he would just as soon not introduce his wife to his brother, or his brother to his wife. So he took Zach to a restaurant in town for dinner.

"Where does your wife think you are tonight?" Zach inquired as he folded the menu and set it beside his plate.

"Mara and I aren't accountable to each other."

Zach's brow arched in disbelief. "That's some marriage you have, baby brother."

"There are…complications," Falcon conceded.

"And?"

Falcon found it difficult to explain his marriage of convenience to his brother. Especially when Zach interrupted him to say, "I've never heard of such an idiotic reason to get married. You should have come to me for the money. Or gotten it from Dad."

His eyes narrowed and Falcon felt his brother's sharp perusal. "Unless you didn't really marry the woman just to help her out of her financial troubles. Is that it? Are you in love with her?"

Falcon flushed. Trust Zach to put his finger on the pulse of the problem. "I have feelings for her," Falcon conceded. He wasn't going to label them love, although they felt suspiciously like it. But only a fool would admit to love under the circumstance. "Unfortunately she hates my guts," he told Zach.

Zach hissed in a breath of air. "That's too bad. Any hope she'll change her mind?"

Falcon flashed his brother a devil-may-care grin that was tremendously hard-won. "I have some hope of it."

"So why did you call me?" he asked bluntly.

"I guess I wanted someone to tell me I wasn't an idiot to marry her," Falcon muttered.

Zach laughed. "Sorry I couldn't oblige you. Look, once the kid is well, you can get a divorce and forget all about the woman."

Falcon's lips flattened. "I don't want to forget about her. And the kid's name is Susannah."

"Well, well. Baby brother has grown some sharp teeth. If you feel so strongly, why don't you act on your convictions?"

"And do what?" Falcon demanded.

"Woo her. Win her love. Make it a real marriage."

"How?" Falcon asked in an agonized voice.

Zach took a sip of his whiskey. "I have a suggestion. I don't know if you're going to like it."

"I'm desperate. What have you got in mind?"

"Give her an ultimatum."

"What?"

"Tell her you can't be expected to live like a eunuch for the next year, and if she doesn't want you looking cross-eyed at other women, she can fulfill her marital duties."

Falcon flushed. "I couldn't put her in that position."

"Why not?"

"That wasn't part of the original bargain."

"So what?"

"You can be a ruthless, coldhearted bastard, Zach." He pitied the poor woman who ever fell in love with his brother.

Zach shrugged. "You asked for my advice. I've given it. You're welcome to come up with your own solution to the problem."

Maybe it wasn't fair to demand conjugal relations, Falcon thought, but perhaps he could merely suggest they start sleeping together. He knew from their one experience together that he and Mara were completely compatible in bed. It wasn't much on which to base a relationship. But it was a start.

"Thanks for coming, Zach," Falcon said.

"Don't mention it. When am I going to meet this paragon?"

"Not this trip," Falcon said. He didn't think he could stand to have Zach see the way Mara flinched when he got near her. It was one thing to admit to his big brother that he had problems, it was another to allow him to witness them in person. "If Susannah's induction therapy is successful we might be able to come for the family Labor Day picnic."

"I'll count on seeing you there." Zach threw his napkin down on his clean, empty plate. "If we're finished," he said wryly, "I think I'd just as soon fly back to Hawk's Way tonight. I can catch a cab back to the airport. I think you should go home."

Falcon rose and shook his brother's hand. "Goodbye, Zach. I think I'll take you up on that."

It wasn't that he thought Mara would be worried about him. She didn't like him enough to worry about him. But he wanted to be there to say good-night to Susannah before she went to bed.

"Think about what I said," Zach called to his retreating back.

Hell, Falcon thought, it wasn't likely he was going to be thinking about much else.

CHAPTER FIVE

"Is Falcon there?"

Mara tensed at the sultry sound of the female voice on the other end of the line. "Yes, he is," she answered.

"Who's this?" the female asked.

"This is his wife," Mara said with relish.

"Oh. Then I don't suppose he's free to fly to New York this weekend."

"That's entirely up to him," Mara said.

"Ooooohh."

Mara could tell she had created confusion at the other end of the line. But really, did she have the right to dictate when and where Falcon went? She was his wife, but it was a marriage in name only. If he wanted to go traipsing off to New York with some sexy Southern belle, who was she to say nay. "I'll get him for you," she said as she set the phone down on the desk in Falcon's office.

She found Falcon in the kitchen with Susannah. "There's a call for you," she said.

Falcon picked up the wall phone extension in the kitchen. Mara stood there listening, her arms crossed defensively over her chest. She knew Falcon must have a lot of old girlfriends, and she wanted to know how he was going to handle this situation.

"Oh, it's you, Felicia." Falcon turned his back on Mara and lowered his voice.

"Yes, I am married," he said. "Over two months ago. It was a very small wedding, Felicia. I didn't even invite my family!" he said in exasperation. "New York? This weekend?" He turned to face Mara, an incredulous look on his face. "My wife has no objection to my going? How do you know that?"

Falcon frowned. "She told you so?"

Mara shrugged with great indifference.

"No, I can't go, Felicia. I have responsibilities here."

Even from across the room Mara could hear the other woman's laughter and see Falcon's embarrassed flush.

"I know that's never stopped me before," Falcon hissed into the phone. "Things have changed since I got myself a family.

"I have a daughter, too," Falcon said. "She's eight. As a matter of fact, we have plans of our own this weekend. We're going shopping for a pony. So, I'm afraid I can't meet you in New York. Have a good time, Felicia. Goodbye."

Falcon slammed the phone down and had rounded on Mara in a fury when he noticed Susannah's wide-eyed interest. "You finish your lunch," he said to the little girl. "I want to talk to your mother in private."

He dragged Mara all the way to his office, which was across the hall from his bedroom, and shut the door with an ominous click behind him. Then he turned to face Mara with his legs spread and his hands fisted on his hips.

"How could you dare to suggest to Felicia that I'd be willing to trot off to New York? I'm a married man!" he snarled. "I take those vows seriously."

"It's a marriage of convenience," Mara corrected. "Plain and simple."

"Have I gone out once without you in the two months we've been married?" he demanded. "Well, once," he conceded, recalling his meeting with Zach. "But have I spent even one night away from home?"

"No."

"Then what makes you think I'd be willing to go carousing with another woman in New York? Did you want me to go?"

"No," Mara admitted in a small voice. She lifted her chin and said, "I... =I thought you might need to be with a woman."

"And better anyone else than you," he said in a harsh voice. "Is that it?"

Mara dropped her chin to her chest. "I thought..."

"You didn't think!" Falcon accused. "Or you would have realized there isn't any woman I want except you!"

Her head snapped up, and her eyes widened in astonishment.

Falcon let her see the desire he felt for her, let his eyes roam her body voraciously. He should have done what Zach recommended. He should have come right home and demanded his husbandly rights.

But when he had returned from meeting Zach he had found Mara with Susannah in the upstairs bathroom. The little girl had her head bent over the toilet, where it had been for an hour. He had sat down beside Mara, and the two of them had stayed with Susannah until she had finally lain her head down in Mara's lap, exhausted. Falcon had carried Susannah back to bed and told her funny stories about his childhood until she had fallen asleep at last.

He had taken one look at Mara's face, at the terror and exhaustion, and known he couldn't ask anything from her that night. Nor had an opportunity arisen over the succeeding days and weeks. Falcon had faced the fact that his needs would have to wait. It was one of the first truly unselfish acts of his life.

Now he saw that his self-sacrifice had earned him nothing in Mara's eyes. She believed he was capable of abandoning her and Susannah for a weekend on the town.

"You must not think very much of me," he said, his brow furrowed with the distress he felt.

Mara realized now the mistake she had made. And why she had made it. She had heard that other woman's voice on the phone, and she had been jealous of her, and of every woman who had ever enjoyed Falcon's attention. Because she wanted that attention for herself.

Unfortunately, for both her sake and Falcon's, she had been too much of a coward to ask for it. He had not made one move toward her since the night they had made love, had not hinted by so much as a look that he wanted to repeat the experience. Meanwhile, she ached whenever she looked at him. Her body coiled with excitement when he merely touched her hand. She couldn't look him in the face for fear her feelings, which she was certain he didn't return, would be blatantly apparent to him. Obviously she had put him in an awkward position when she sought oblivion in his arms. Obviously he hadn't enjoyed it as much as she had. Obviously he hadn't wanted to repeat the experience.

It was easy to believe that he might have contacted Felicia, or that he might have planned to have Felicia call so Mara would let him go. Now he was telling her that she had been wrong. That he would prefer a weekend with her and Susannah to a weekend with a luscious femme fatale in New York.

"I'm sorry," she said. "I mistook the matter. I'll understand if you want to change your mind about spending time with me and Susannah—"

"Sometimes I could just shake you," Falcon said. He suited word to deed and grabbed her by the shoulders. "I burn for you, woman! Can you understand what that means? I want to be inside you. There isn't a moment when I don't remember what you taste like, what you feel like. I don't want another woman. I want you!"

His mouth slanted over hers, and he told her of his desperate need with his lips and his hands. It took a moment for him to realize that she was crying.

He let her go and stepped back, tunneling all ten fingers through his hair. "Hell, Mara. I'm sorry."

She closed her eyes and pressed the back of her hand over her mouth.

"You don't have to worry about that happening again. I can control myself. I'm not an animal."

He turned on booted heel and left the room, closing the door quietly behind him.

Mara let out a tremulous sob. "Oh, my God. What have I done? And what am I supposed to do now?" she said to the empty room.

How could she want to make love to the man responsible for Grant's death? How could she let him hold her, love her, when she could not forgive what he had done?

More to the point, why was she finding it so impossible to let go of the anger she felt over Grant's death? It had been more than a year. Her feelings of bubbling hostility should have dissipated by now. But whenever she thought of Grant, feelings of vexation, of frustration and annoyance simmered to the surface. Until she could manage to quell those feelings, she would be better off keeping Falcon at arm's distance. For his sake, as much as hers.

DESPITE THEIR ALTERCATION, Falcon was true to his word. He announced to Mara the next time he saw her, that the trip to the auction to find a pony for Susannah was all planned.

"We'll be getting there just in time to see the ponies auctioned, so Susannah shouldn't get too tired," he said.

"Come on, Mommy!" Susannah said excitedly. "Hurry up and get ready. It's time to go!"

Mara felt her spirits lift when she saw how happy and excited her daughter was. She quickly dressed in a Western blouse, jeans and boots and joined Falcon and Susannah outside.

Falcon was sitting on the edge of a tile fountain that graced the courtyard in back of the house, with Susannah in his lap. As Mara came up behind them she saw that Falcon had given Susannah a penny and was telling her to make a wish and toss the coin into the fountain.

"Will my wish come true?" Susannah asked.

"Who knows?" Falcon said. "This may be a magical fountain."

Susannah squeezed her eyes closed and tossed the penny. It landed with a plop that sent water back up onto her face. She opened her eyes and laughed as Falcon brushed the crystal droplets away with his fingertips.

Mara was moved by his gentleness with the little girl. "I'm ready," she announced. But a moment later

she realized she wasn't the least bit ready to deal with
the things Falcon made her feel.

She stood frozen as his eyes roamed her body. She
felt warm everywhere his eyes touched her. She wanted
to surrender to him heart and soul. She gritted her teeth
against her wayward feelings.

Remember Grant, she admonished herself.

But the hate wouldn't rise the way it had so easily
in the past.

That's because you know who's really to blame for
Grant's death, don't you, Mara? And it isn't Falcon
Whitelaw. Admit it, Mara. You're to blame! You knew
what would happen, and you let Grant go anyway. It's
all your fault! Your fault! Your fault!

"Mara? Is something wrong?"

Falcon's interruption silenced the accusing voice in
Mara's head. She pressed a hand to her temple where
her pulse pounded. "I'm fine," she said. "Shall we go?"

Falcon gathered Susannah in his arms and walked
toward Mara. When he reached her, he slipped an arm
around her waist and guided her toward the van. Their
hips bumped, and she tried to free herself, but his hold
tightened. She was aware of the warmth of his hand at
her ribs, of a desire to be alone with him, when he could
let that hand ramble at will.

You're crazy, Mara. You're out of your mind. How
can you even think about making love to Falcon
Whitelaw? He killed Grant!

No, you killed Grant.

Mara chewed on her lower lip, wishing the awful
voice would go away and leave her alone.

Falcon saw the furrow on Mara's brow and wondered
what was troubling her now. Maybe he shouldn't have

let her know how he felt about her. Maybe she was concerned he would try to take advantage of their situation.

It perturbed him that Mara could think he might take by force what she did not willingly offer him. He had never forced a woman into his bed. Despite Zach's advice, he wasn't about to start now. But he didn't think there was anything he could say that would ease her mind. Every time he opened his mouth he ended up with his foot in it. Better to just let sleeping dogs lie.

At the auction Falcon nodded and tipped his hat to the several ranchers he knew, but he didn't approach them as he would have if Mara and Susannah hadn't been with him. He didn't want to have to explain a year from now about his absent wife and daughter. Instead he concentrated all his attention on finding just the right pony for Susannah.

It was quickly apparent that Susannah wanted a pinto.

"I like the ones with patches," she said.

It was up to him to find an animal she liked that also had both excellent conformation and a good disposition. It wasn't until near the end of the auction that he was satisfied with an animal that Susannah also liked.

"That one!" Susannah breathed with a sigh of awe. "Oh, please, Falcon, that one!"

The pony had a white face, with a black patch that ran across his eyes. Falcon was having trouble deciding if the gelding was black with white patches, or white with black, it was so evenly divided by the two colors.

"I'm going to call him Patches," Susannah announced as she hugged the pony's neck after the auction. "You like that name, don't you, Patches?"

They were approached by one of the ranchers Falcon had seen earlier, Sam Longstreet.

"Howdy, Falcon," the tall, rangy man said, tipping his hat. "Are you going to introduce me to this little lady?"

He said "little lady," but his eyes were on Mara when he spoke, so Falcon knew it wasn't Susannah who had caught his interest.

Sam Longstreet and his father had a cattle ranch that bordered Hawk's Way. Sam was a little older than Falcon, maybe two or three years, but his face had more lines and his body was leaner, toughened by long days spent on the range. His sun-bleached chestnut hair was shaggy and needed a cut, and he hadn't shaved in the past day or so. Sam's boots were worn and his jeans frayed. Falcon wasn't sure whether that was because Sam didn't worry about appearances, or whether it meant hard times for the Longstreet ranch. Sam's father, E.J., had some business dealings with Falcon's father, although Falcon wasn't up on the exact details.

"How are you, Sam?" Falcon said. "I'd like to introduce my wife, Mara, and my daughter, Susannah. Mara, this is Sam Longstreet. Our families have been neighbors for generations."

Sam grinned. "It's a mighty big pleasure to meet you, ma'am. You're a sly one," he said to Falcon. "Haven't heard a peep out of your folks about you getting hitched."

"They don't know."

"I won't breathe a word to them," Sam said. "If that's how you want it."

"It's not a secret," Falcon said. "I just haven't found the right moment to tell them the news."

Sam grinned again. "Can I tell E.J.?"

That was sure to put the fat in the fire. Word would get back to his father through E.J. that he had gotten married. "Give me a day to call my folks, then be my guest."

So, the moment of reckoning had come. He would have to tell his parents what he had done, and try to keep them from visiting the newlyweds before he had resolved his relationship with Mara.

Sam turned his attention back to Mara. "How did you hook up with this maverick?" he asked.

Falcon saw the consternation on Mara's face and knew she was trying to decide the best way to explain things to Sam.

"We met through an old friend of mine, a former football teammate at Tech," Falcon said. That was the absolute truth, and so much less than the whole story.

"Makes me wish I'd gone to Tech," Sam said, with an admiring glance at Mara. "Didn't make it to college myself." He turned his attention to Susannah, who was rubbing her own nose against the velvety soft nose of her new pony.

He squatted down so his green eyes would be at a level with her hazel ones. "My name's Sam," he said. "What's yours?"

To Falcon's amazement, Susannah didn't run and hide behind her mother. She answered Sam with a girlish, "My name's Susannah. This is my pony. His name is Patches."

Sam reached out to run a big, work-worn hand along the pony's jaw. "He's a mighty fine-looking pony," Sam agreed.

Susannah was wearing her red hat, but it was plain

to anyone who looked closely that she was bald underneath it. Sam wasn't the kind of man to miss a detail like that. He exchanged a surprised look of sympathy with Falcon before he set his hands on his thighs and pushed himself back onto his feet.

He didn't ask questions about Susannah. Things hadn't changed so much in the West that a man could ask another man's business uninvited.

"Guess I'd better be getting along," Sam said. "I've got a new bull to get loaded up, and then I'm headed home."

"Be seeing you," Falcon said.

"Hope so," Sam said with a smile aimed at Mara. "Ma'am." He touched the tip of one callused finger to his battered Stetson, a mark of respect to Falcon's wife.

"What a strange man," Mara said.

"How so?" Falcon asked.

"He looks so…dangerous…and yet his eyes are so… kind. Which is the real Sam Longstreet?" she asked.

Falcon shrugged. "I don't know him very well, even though we lived close. He's older than me or Zach, and his father needed him to work on the ranch, so he never socialized much."

"Will he tell your family about us?"

"He'll tell his father, which is the same thing. But not before tomorrow. Which means I need to call them tonight."

"What do you think they'll say?"

Falcon had a pretty good idea, but he didn't want to burn Mara's tender ears. "They'll be happy for us," he lied.

"Come on," he said. "Let's get this pony home where Susannah can ride him."

But by the time they got home, Susannah's good day had gone bad. She was feeling sick and so tired that she could hardly keep her eyes open. Mara and Falcon put her to bed together with promises that she could ride Patches the moment she was feeling better.

"Are you sure the day wasn't too much for her?" Falcon asked as he and Mara left the room.

"The trip was a wonderful idea. It was only to be expected she would get tired," Mara said. "I don't think she would have missed it for anything," she said in an effort to take the guilty look off Falcon's face.

Falcon allowed himself to be assuaged by Mara's absolution. He didn't want to be responsible for making Susannah any sicker than she already was, and if Mara believed the day hadn't been too taxing for her daughter, he was willing to take her word for it.

"I'd like you with me when I make the call to my parents," Falcon said.

Mara followed him into his office and sat on the bench that ran parallel to his desk. Falcon sat down in the swivel chair in front of the oak rolltop.

"What are you going to tell them?" Mara asked.

"That I met a woman, and we got married."

"Won't they ask questions?"

"Probably."

"How will you explain...everything?"

Falcon grinned ruefully. "It depends on what they ask."

"You know what I mean," Mara said. "What will you tell them about why we got married?"

Falcon fiddled with his computer keyboard. "I don't know."

"Will you tell them the truth?"

"Not all of it," Falcon said. "They wouldn't understand."

"Why do you need me here?" Mara asked.

"They may want to say hello to you, to offer their best wishes," he said. They would want to do more than that, Falcon feared. They would want to know every last detail about Mara Ainsworth Whitelaw.

He dialed the phone number. It was answered on the second ring. His mother was breathless. She had apparently run to answer the phone. "Hi, Mom," he said.

"Falcon! We've been wondering what you've been up to. You haven't been in touch for months!"

"I've been busy," Falcon said.

"Surely not too busy to write or call your parents and reassure them you aren't lying dead in a gully somewhere," Candy Whitelaw chastised. "Now, tell me what prompted this call?"

His mother had never been one to shilly-shally around, Falcon thought. "I wanted to let you and Dad know that I got married."

"You what?" His mother called into the other room, "Garth, pick up the phone in there. It's Falcon. He's gotten married!"

Falcon heard his father's deep voice asking, "When did this happen? Do we know the bride? When are you bringing her here to meet us?"

"Is she there?" his mother asked. "Can we talk to her? What's her name?"

"Her name is Mara Ainsworth. She's standing right here. I'll put her on so you can say hello." Falcon handed the receiver to Mara, who looked at it as though it had grown fangs. At last she took it from him and held it to her ear.

"Hello?" she said tentatively.

"Hello, dear," Candy said. "I'm Falcon's mother. We're so delighted to hear the news. When did you and Falcon meet? When was the wedding? Oh, I'm so sorry we missed it!"

"Hello, Mara," Garth said. "Welcome to the family. When are we going to get to meet you?"

Mara wrinkled her nose at Falcon. She held her hand over the mouthpiece and said, "You rat! They're full of questions I think you should answer."

"It's nice 'meeting' you at last, Mr. and Mrs. Whitelaw. I—"

"Call me Candy, please," Falcon's mother said. "And Falcon's father is Garth. Now, tell us everything."

"Thank you, Mrs.—Candy," Mara said. "I don't know where to start."

"Where did you two meet?" Garth asked.

"In downtown Dallas. I was there with my husband and daughter and—"

Mara cut herself off when she heard a gasp on the other end of the line. She looked up at Falcon and saw his eyes were squeezed closed. He was shaking his head in disbelief.

"I'm a widow now," she blurted into the phone.

There was a silence and then a relieved sigh at the other end of the line.

"I'm sorry to hear that," Candy said. "Oh, this is so awkward, isn't it, because if you weren't a widow you wouldn't be married to Falcon, and of course I'm glad Falcon found you, but not under such sad circumstances."

"I feel the same way, Mrs.—Candy," Mara said in a soft voice.

"Tell us about your daughter," Garth said.

"Her name is Susannah, and she's eight years old. She's been very ill lately, but we're hoping she'll be well soon."

"Is there anything we can do?" Candy asked.

"Pray," Mara said in a quiet voice.

"It must be very serious," Candy said. "Are you sure—"

"Susannah has leukemia. She's in treatment right now. We'll know more when the therapy is completed."

Again that silence on the other end of the line, while Falcon's parents digested the newest bomb dropped in their laps.

"Let me speak to Falcon," Garth said.

Mara handed the phone to Falcon. "Your father wants to talk to you."

"Dad?"

"What the hell is going on, Falcon?" Garth demanded in a harsh voice. "What kind of trouble have you gotten yourself into this time?"

"No trouble, Dad," Falcon answered in an equally harsh voice. "Mara is a widow and Susannah is sick, it's as simple as that. I'm not asking your approval of my marriage, Dad. I was only offering you the courtesy of telling you about it."

"We want to visit," Candy said.

"No, Mom. That wouldn't be a good idea right now."

"Why the hell not?" Garth said.

"Because I said so!" Falcon retorted, resorting to the words his father had always used to justify every order to his children. "We'll try to be there for the Labor Day picnic." It wasn't much as peace offerings went, but it was all they were going to get. "Goodbye, Mom, Dad."

"Falcon—" Garth roared.

"Falcon—" Candy cried.

Falcon gently hung up the phone. "Well, that's taken care of."

"They didn't sound too happy," Mara ventured.

Falcon tipped Mara's chin up with his forefinger. "It's not their life, it's mine. If I'm happy, it doesn't matter what they think."

"Are you happy?" Mara asked, searching his face for the truth.

His thumb traced her lower lip. It was rosy and plump because she had been chewing on it again. "I'm not sorry I married you, if that's what you're asking."

She lowered her eyes, unable to meet his lambent gaze. But she didn't move away from him. Mara felt rooted to the spot. "You should have told them the truth," she murmured.

"Who knows what the truth is," Falcon said enigmatically.

Mara knew he was going to kiss her. She didn't try to escape the caress. Because she needed it as much as she believed he did. His mouth was gentle on hers, his lips seeking solace, not passion. She kept her mouth pliant under his, giving him the succor, the sustenance he sought.

When the kiss ended, she opened her eyes and was moved by what she saw in his.

He cared for her. He wanted her. And he despaired of having her. It was all there on his face.

Mara wished she could give him ease. But the past intruded and would not be silenced.

It had been easy to blame Falcon for Grant's death, even though she was more at fault than he was. Nevertheless, it was hard to let go of her feelings of rage and hate toward Falcon, however undeserved they were. Grant was still dead, and because of Susannah's illness—which was no one's fault at all—her life had been turned upside down.

There's a great deal of good to be said about Falcon Whitelaw, a voice inside her argued. He's not a bad man, he just had a little growing up to do. He's wonderful with Susannah. And he makes your blood sizzle. Would it be so awful to give him what he wants from you?

Falcon saw the conflict raging within her. She hated him. He tempted her.

He was the one who stepped back.

"Good night, Mara," he said.

"Good night, Falcon," she replied.

She didn't want him to go. She wanted him to stay.

Afraid she might do or say something she would regret later, Mara whirled and fled the room.

CHAPTER SIX

"WHERE HAVE YOU BEEN?" Mara demanded.

Falcon was astounded to find Mara waiting for him in the kitchen. She had a cup of coffee sitting in front of her. He could tell it was cold, which meant she had been there awhile. He hadn't come home for supper, unable to face the thought of being near her and knowing he couldn't touch. He hadn't been far away, just in the barn, where he had worked soaping saddles that were in better shape than they had ever been, thanks to his restlessness. Was it possible she had been worried about him?

"I was in the barn," he said. "Working on my saddle."

"I thought something had happened to you. It's so late. You're usually in by dark."

"You were worried about me," Falcon murmured. "I'm sorry, Mara. I'll let you know where I am next time."

If anyone had told Falcon three months ago that he would have been willing to be accountable to anyone, let alone a woman, he would have slapped his knee at the jest and hurt his ribs laughing.

How the mighty had fallen.

Mara rose and crossed to the sink. "Susannah asked about you," she said, as though to deny her own concern.

"Is she all right?" Falcon asked anxiously.

Mara left the cup in the sink and turned to face Falcon. "The doctor thinks she may be in remission."

Falcon stared at her, stunned. Then he whooped and grabbed her around the waist and swung her in a circle. "This is fantastic!"

Mara held on so he wouldn't drop her. "Let me down."

Falcon set her down, but he kept his hands on her waist. He needed to hold on to someone, or he just might float off into space. "I can't believe this is happening. It's too soon. She's only been in therapy ten weeks."

"I know," she said. "It's…a miracle."

Falcon looked at Mara and wondered why she wasn't more excited. "You said may be in remission. Is there something you aren't telling me? When will we know for sure?"

"Dr. Sortino wants to do a spinal tap tomorrow. We'll know as soon as he gets the results from the test."

"Susannah hates those back-sticks," Falcon said. His hands tightened at Mara's waist. "They hurt."

"I know," Mara said. "Will you come with us tomorrow?"

It was the first time she had asked him to join her. The first sign at all that she needed him for anything other than his money. "I'll be glad to come with you."

She smiled for the first time since he had come into the house. "I'm glad you'll be there. Susannah has been asking when you're going to come to the hospital with us."

"She has?"

Mara stepped back, and Falcon let his hands drop. "She's very attached to you," she said.

"I'm attached to her, too," Falcon said.

"Well, that's what I waited up to tell you. Good night, Falcon."

"Mara, wait." Falcon didn't want her to leave. He wanted to hold her. He wanted to sleep with her in his arms. He thought of the ultimatum Zach had wanted him to give her—how many weeks ago had that been?—and knew he still couldn't do it. Not now. Not yet. Maybe if—when—they found out Susannah was in remission he could start making husbandly demands of his wife.

"What is it?" she asked.

"What would you think, if Susannah's feeling well enough, about going to Hawk's Way over Labor Day?"

Mara leaned back against the refrigerator and crossed her arms protectively around her. "Do you really think that's a good idea, for me and Susannah to meet your family?"

"You're my wife," he said. "And Susannah is my daughter."

Not for much longer.

The words hung in the silence between them. If Susannah was truly in remission, it would change everything. Mara wouldn't need him anymore. She would be able to move back to her house in Dallas with its covered porch and its white picket fence.

"I want them to meet you, Mara. Even…even if things don't work out between us. I think you're a very special woman. I've felt that way since the first moment I laid eyes on you."

Mara flushed and shot a quick look at Falcon. "I was a married woman when you first met me," she reminded him.

Falcon's lips flattened, and Mara was sorry she had
spoken. She had only meant that he shouldn't have been
looking at a married woman that way. She hadn't meant
to remind him of the catastrophe that had made her a
widow. Falcon turned on his heel, and she knew he
would leave the house again if she didn't do something
to stop him.

"I've been doing some work in your office," she said
as his hand reached the kitchen doorknob.

Falcon turned and glanced at Mara over his shoulder. "What kind of work?"

She gave him a lopsided smile. "Your desk was a
little disorganized, and so was your computer filing
system."

"You've been working on my computer?" He turned
completely around and assumed a pose Mara was coming to recognize as his "I'm King of the Roost and Don't
Give Me Any Backtalk" stance, his legs widespread and
his hands fisted on his hips.

"I've been organizing," she said.

Falcon raised a skeptical black brow. "Organizing?"
Lord help a man when a woman started organizing.

"Come with me, and I'll show you some of what
I've done."

Falcon knew an olive branch when he saw one. He
willingly reached out to take it. "All right. Lead the
way."

Falcon had noticed little improvements around the
house since Mara had moved in. Certainly her green
thumb was much in evidence. There were potted flowers in the kitchen and trees in planters in the living
room.

She had stuck patterned pillows on the leather couch

to break up the somber expanse and rearranged nearly every vase into a different arched cubbyhole. The heavy curtains in the living room had been removed so the sunshine filtered in during the day, and gingham curtains had been added for color in the kitchen.

The whole house sparkled with cleanliness. She hadn't been kidding about her ability as a housekeeper. Which should have made him less nervous about her bookkeeping talents, but somehow didn't.

Mara hadn't completely rearranged his office. He could—and would—have complained if she had. She had been more subtle than that, making small changes, a book moved here, a file moved there. Of course, the spurs and halter he had been repairing had been relegated to a worktable in the pantry off the kitchen.

It wasn't until he sat down next to Mara at the computer that he realized what significant changes she had made in his bookkeeping system. She showed him how she had organized his files so he could see which stud had covered which mare, which cows had been inseminated by which bull. Amounts of grain that had been fed, and increase in weight on the hoof, were also calculated for his beef cattle.

"This is incredible! How did you learn to do this?" he asked.

"I told you I grew up at my mother's knee. I spent a lot of time looking over my father's shoulder, too," she said with a cheeky grin.

"I'm impressed. Why haven't you ever gotten a job doing this for some rancher?"

"I don't have a college degree," she admitted. "I had just finished my first year of school when I found out Susannah was sick."

Falcon was thinking she didn't need a degree to do his bookkeeping. But he could see that if something ever happened to him, she might need an education. "You should go back and finish," he said.

"I can't until I know Susannah is well."

"With any luck, we'll get good news tomorrow. I think you should plan to go back this fall, Mara. I can hire someone to take care of Susannah while you're in class."

"I already owe you too much."

"You don't owe me anything," Falcon said. "I've done what I've done because I wanted to do it. I wish you'd get it out of your head that you have to pay me back."

Falcon didn't breathe, he didn't move. On second thought, there was something she could do for him. She had presented him with the perfect opportunity to ask for what he wanted from her without giving her an ultimatum.

"There is something you can do for me," he said.

"What?" Mara asked.

He hesitated, then took the plunge. "I need a woman, Mara. You're my wife. I want to sleep with you."

She hissed out a breath, but didn't say anything right away.

He reached out and caressed her cheek with the back of his hand. Her eyelids slid closed. Her teeth caught her lower lip and began to worry it.

"I want to give you what you want," she said. "I know I owe you—"

Falcon jerked his hand away, and Mara's eyes flashed open. He rose to his feet and towered over her. The muscles in his jaw worked as he gritted his teeth. "If that's the best you can do, forget it."

She leapt to her feet and grabbed his arm to keep him from leaving. "I'm trying! I have needs, too," she admitted in a choked voice. "But I can't forget who you are. Don't you understand? I loved Grant. And because of you, he's dead."

"Grant was a drunk who killed himself in a car wreck!" Falcon snarled.

All the blood left Mara's face. "Who told you Grant was a drunk?"

Falcon stared at her, not sure what had upset her so much.

"Who told you Grant was an alcoholic?" she insisted.

"An alcoholic? Was he?" Falcon asked, dumbfounded.

Mara covered her mouth with her hand. She hadn't ever said the words aloud. Not to anyone. She had lived with Grant, realized he had a weakness, and tried to pretend it didn't exist.

Falcon grabbed her by the arms. "Are you telling me that you've blamed me for Grant's death all this time when you knew he had a drinking problem?"

"He didn't have a problem—"

"Tell me the truth!"

"Yes! Yes, I blame you. He was going to AA meetings. He had quit for almost six months before he ran into you."

"Is that why he lost all those jobs?" Falcon asked. "Was he drinking on the job?"

"I don't know," Mara admitted miserably. "He gave different reasons for why he was let go."

"And you never checked?" Falcon demanded.

"I trusted him!" she said fiercely. There were tears in her eyes that betrayed the truth. The first time, or maybe the second, Grant had been able to fool her. But by the sixth or seventh time he was fired, she'd had no illusions left.

"How could you love a man like that?" Falcon asked, truly puzzled by her devotion to someone who must have caused her untold pain.

She shrugged helplessly. "He was a good father." When he wasn't drinking. "And a good husband." When he wasn't drunk and chasing other women.

Mara couldn't meet Falcon's intent stare and lie anymore. To him or to herself. It had been easier to blame Falcon than to admit Grant's weakness. Easier to blame Falcon than to admit her own culpability. Because, when all was said and done, she was responsible for Grant's death.

She had known he had a drinking problem. She should have watched him more closely. She should have gone with him.

Mara knew that sort of thinking was irrational. She had read enough since Grant's death, and learned enough in college psychology and sociology classes she had taken, to understand that Grant was responsible for his own behavior. But she couldn't shake her feelings of guilt. She should have been able to save Grant. And she had failed.

"It wasn't your fault," Falcon said in a quiet voice.

Mara's head jerked up, and she sought Falcon's eyes.

"He was an alcoholic. It was his problem. You aren't to blame."

"How did you know..."

"That you blame yourself?"

She nodded.

"Because I couldn't help thinking there was something I could have done to prevent Grant's death. Maybe if I'd noticed how much he was drinking…" Falcon thrust a hand through his hair. "Maybe if I hadn't left that twenty on the table… Maybe if I had stayed with him and made sure he didn't drive home drunk…."

"That's a lot of 'maybe's,'" Mara said.

"Don't I know it!"

"I feel the same way," Mara admitted. "I was his wife. I should have known better.

"After we left you that day, I begged him to call you up and meet somewhere, anywhere besides a bar. He said it was too late for that. He didn't know where to find you to make other arrangements. And he swore he wouldn't be tempted. He swore he wouldn't drink anything stronger than club soda. He had been sober for months before that night, so I believed him. I should have known he wouldn't be able to resist a drink when it was offered to him, especially since he wanted to keep his alcoholism a secret from you. I should have made arrangements to pick him up."

"What about Grant? Doesn't he deserve some of the blame for what happened?" Falcon asked. "Maybe more than some," he amended.

Mara thought of all the ugly things she had said to Falcon, all the accusations she had heaped on his shoulders. "I owe you an apology," she said. "Some of the things I said…"

"Apology accepted," Falcon said.

Mara felt awkward. All her animosity toward Falcon had been based on his irresponsible behavior at the bar that had resulted in Grant's death. Bereft of antagonism, she wasn't sure how to interact with him.

"Can we start over from here?" Falcon asked.

"Can you ever forgive me—"

"Can you forgive me?"

Mara exhaled a ragged sigh. "I'm so sorry, Falcon. For everything I said. I was horrible."

"You were," Falcon agreed.

When her eyes widened in surprise, his lips curled in a roguish grin.

"Sorry," he said. "I couldn't resist."

"Behave yourself," she chided.

They were teasing each other, Mara realized. It was a start. A very good start.

Mara knew there was one way she could show Falcon he was truly forgiven. He had told her what he wanted from her. And if she was going to be honest, she wanted it, too. She reached out, her hand palm up.

"I'm tired," she said. "Let's go to bed."

Falcon arched a brow, but threaded his fingers through hers. "My room?"

She nodded. She didn't want to take a chance on disturbing Susannah. Or on having to explain to Susannah why she was suddenly sleeping with Falcon.

Mara felt unaccountably shy. "This feels strange," she admitted.

"I know what you mean," Falcon said with a rueful twist of his mouth. "I've been wanting to make love to you for weeks. Ever since—"

"Don't remind me," she said, putting a hand to one rosy cheek. "I was an absolute wanton."

"I didn't have any complaints," Falcon said with a grin. When they got to the living room, he tugged on

Mara's hand and she followed him around to the couch. He pulled her into his lap and sat there holding her.

She laid her head on his shoulder and let her hand slide around his waist.

"I've been needing this," Falcon said.

"And not the other?" Mara teased.

"Oh, I want that, too. But it can wait."

Mara felt a pleasant sense of expectation. She had been afraid, when she had agreed to give Falcon what he wanted, that he would rush her into bed. She was glad to see he was willing to take his time. She sighed.

"What was that for?" Falcon asked.

"I was just thinking about how badly I've misjudged you."

"So I'm not an irresponsible ne'er-do-well?"

"You did fritter away your fortune," she said.

Falcon stiffened. There was that. He might not have murdered her husband, but he still was not the sort of solid person she might have chosen for a husband. Especially after the bad experience she'd apparently had with Grant. His arms tightened around her. He had done nothing over the past ten weeks to prove he would be a better husband to her than Grant.

Except he had stopped drinking and carousing and spending money like it was water. That had to count for something. He hadn't missed any of those things, either, Falcon realized. Nothing mattered as much to him as Mara. And Susannah. There had to be a way to convince her they belonged together as a family.

"I hadn't planned ever to marry again," Mara admitted.

He didn't want to hear this.

Falcon pressed a kiss to Mara's nape to distract her

and felt her shiver. He kissed his way up her throat to her ear and teased the delicate shell with his tongue.

Her hand slid down to the hard bulge in his jeans. She traced the length of him through the denim with her fingertips. He drew in a breath of air and held it.

"Mara," he whispered in her ear.

"Yes, Falcon."

"Sweetheart, let's go to bed."

She didn't answer with words, just rose and headed for his bedroom, leaving him to follow behind her.

Mara knew she was asking for heartache. The more attached she let herself get to Falcon, the harder it was going to be to leave him when Susannah was well. The truth was, she was terrified of getting involved with another man. Falcon hadn't gotten drunk during the past couple of months, but that didn't mean he wouldn't revert to his former behavior sometime in the future. Grant had been sober for months at a time during their eight-year marriage. She didn't yet trust Falcon not to become another Grant.

There was still the awful uncertainty about whether Susannah would survive. And there were no guarantees Falcon wouldn't be claimed by an accident working on the ranch, or driving in his car. How could she dare make any kind of commitment to another human being who might be taken from her?

But, oh, how she was tempted to throw caution to the winds. The more time she spent with Falcon, the more feelings she had for him. He was funny and generous and gave of himself wholeheartedly. He was compassionate and caring. He was a scintillating lover. Such a man would make some woman a very good husband. He just happened to be hers at the moment.

She knew it had been unfair to expect Falcon to remain celibate during their marriage. She owed him tonight, at least. But she wasn't promising more. She couldn't promise more.

Mara stood at the foot of Falcon's bed feeling awkward, uncertain what to do next. Their previous coupling had been a frenzied thing, more an act of desperation than anything else. She had needed solace and forgetfulness, and Falcon had provided those things in lovemaking that was so passionate it had taken away all thought and left only feeling.

Mara didn't know what to expect now.

Falcon was also aware of how different their joining together was this time. He wanted to show Mara the tenderness he felt, as well as the ardent passion.

"May I undress you?" he asked.

Mara nodded, suddenly shy. Although she didn't know why that should be. He had seen everything before. But she realized, as Falcon slowly undressed her, admiring her with his eyes and his hands and his mouth, that there had been no time before to truly appreciate each other's bodies.

"I want to touch you, too," she told him.

He shook his head. "It would be too distracting. I wouldn't be able to enjoy what I'm doing."

As his mouth closed around a nipple and he suckled, she surrendered to his ministrations. His hands caressed her skin, and the roughness of his callused fingertips raised frissons of sensation wherever they coursed.

Falcon tried to tell Mara with his hands and his mouth how much he adored her, how much she meant to him, how necessary she was to his very life. He wished he was better with words so he could tell her how he felt. Of course the word love never entered his head. He couldn't think such thoughts when he knew she hated him. But she had forgiven him. She had no reason to hate him anymore.

Mara was amazed at how her body responded to the touch of Falcon's hands, the feel of his lips on her skin. She experienced things Grant had never made her feel in eight years of marriage. How was she able to find so much pleasure in the arms of another man?

Mara stiffened imperceptibly, but Falcon was sensitive enough to her response to know something had gone wrong. She was no longer giving herself up to his caresses as she had been a moment before.

"Mara?" he murmured in her ear.

She gripped his waist tightly with both hands and for a moment he wasn't sure whether she was going to pull him close or shove him away. Then her arms slid around him.

"Hold me, Falcon," she said. "Make love to me."

"I will, darling. I am."

Falcon meant what he said. He was making love to Mara. But when he had her under him, and when he had brought her to satisfaction, he did not feel like shouting with joy. He felt like crying instead. Because he knew that what he was feeling for her was all one-sided. He had made love to her. She had submitted to having sex with him.

He tried not to let the despair overwhelm him. There was still time to win her love. There was still time for a happy ending.

He was torn, because as much as he wanted Susannah to be well, he knew her recovery heralded the end of his time with Mara. He would have to find a way, and soon, to convince Mara that she couldn't live without him.

Because he knew now he couldn't live without her.

CHAPTER SEVEN

OVER THE MONTHS he had been forced to stay close to the B-Bar because of his responsibilities toward Mara and Susannah, Falcon had made an astounding discovery.

He liked being a rancher.

His skin had browned in the Texas sunshine, and a fine spray of sun lines edged his blue eyes. His hands had been callused before, but now they were work-hardened. His body had been honed by hard physical labor until he was a creature of muscle and bone and sinew.

He had made hard decisions, and most of them had turned out right. A recent visit to his accountant had confirmed what he already knew. His attention to the details of running the B-Bar was making a difference. Things functioned more smoothly. There was less waste. And the profit margin on the sale of his cattle and horses was higher. To add sugar to the pie, one of the risky investments Aaron had advised him against making had started paying huge dividends.

"If you keep this up, you're going to be rich again," Aaron teased.

Only, it looked like he wasn't going to need any of his reacquired wealth to pay medical bills.

Susannah was in remission.

The induction therapy had worked more quickly and

efficiently than even Dr. Sortino had hoped. It had only taken ten weeks for Susannah's white blood cells to register normal.

Falcon was amazed at what a difference good health made to Susannah's behavior. She sparkled, she fizzed, she had an absolutely effervescent personality. She was tremendous fun to be with. Falcon teased Susannah that she was so bouncy she was liable to take off someday and go right through the ceiling.

"I don't want to sit still ever again," Susannah said.

"Not even to eat supper?" Falcon had asked.

"Well, maybe for that," she conceded, stuffing a man-sized spoonful of mashed potatoes into her mouth.

When Falcon looked to Mara, to share the humor of the situation, he found her brow furrowed, her eyes dark and despairing. Despite Susannah's good health, Mara didn't appear happy. Falcon dragged her away to the living room after supper to find out what was bothering her. He settled her on the couch and sat down on the coffee table across from her.

"What's wrong?" he asked.

"I want to expect the best, that Susannah is out of deep water," Mara said. "But I can't help dreading the worst, that her good health is a mirage that's going to disappear if I take my eyes off her."

"You have to live for today," Falcon chided.

"I might have expected you to say something like that," Mara snapped.

Falcon flushed. "Once upon a time, I might have deserved that comment," he said. "Not anymore. I'm as anxious as you are to plan for the future." With you. "But there's no planning ahead in Susannah's case. She's either going to stay well, or she isn't. There's nothing you, or I, or all the worrying in the world can do to change that."

Mara's eyes were bleak. "You're right," she said. "I know you are. I just can't seem to shake this feeling…"

"Then Susannah and I will just have to do it for you." Falcon set out then and there to put a smile on Mara's face. He enlisted Susannah's aid. "Hey, Susannah," he called to the little girl.

Susannah popped up in the living room like a jack-in-the-box. "What is it, Falcon?"

"I say your mom is more ticklish than you are. What do you think?"

"Ticklish?" Mara said warily. "Who said anything about ticklish?"

Falcon grinned and approached her, hands outstretched, ready for serious tickling.

Mara jumped up and ran.

Falcon chased her.

When he caught her, he wrestled her to the floor and hog-tied her with his hands, like she was a newborn calf.

Mara was breathless, she was laughing so hard. "Falcon, stop! I just ate supper."

He leered at her like the villain in a melodrama. "She's all yours, Susannah. Have at her."

Susannah tickled her mother in the ribs and under the arms and behind her ears and on the soles of her feet.

Mara laughed so hard she howled. "Oh, stop," she cried through her giggles. "Oh, please, stop."

"What do you think, Susannah?" Falcon said. "Should we let her up?"

"I guess so."

"Of course, this experiment is only half over," Falcon

said, perusing Susannah with a speculative eye. "We haven't seen yet how ticklish you are."

Susannah screeched, "Help, Mommy!" but Falcon caught her before she had taken two steps and pulled her into his lap, where he began to tickle her mercilessly.

By that time Mara had recovered slightly, and she rescued her daughter. "I think there's someone here who needs a little of his own medicine," she said to Susannah.

"Yeah!" Susannah said as she launched herself against Falcon's chest.

Her attack knocked Falcon onto his back on the floor, and before he could recover, Mara had joined her daughter tickling his ribs.

Falcon was very ticklish.

He howled, he begged, he pleaded. "Please, no more!"

He could easily have escaped their attack at any time. He was bigger and stronger than both of them combined. But Falcon didn't want to escape. He loved being tickled by the two women in his life. He loved seeing their smiling faces and their eyes crinkled with laughter. Their chuckles and giggles and guffaws made him feel warm deep inside.

He let them tickle him until they were exhausted, until they fell onto the Navajo rug on either side of him and sighed with happy fatigue. He smoothed his fingers across the prickly crew cut that was all the hair Susannah had grown back so far. His other hand tangled in Mara's silky black tresses. He pulled them close on either side of him and closed his eyes and wished to be this happy the rest of his life.

But it was only a moment in time and not to be captured or held except in memory.

AFTER THAT NIGHT, however, Mara seemed to let go of some of her fear. She didn't offer a smile often, but Falcon treasured every one. As Susannah regained her strength, she and Mara began riding out to meet him when he was working on the range.

The first time it happened, Falcon reached for his shirt and dragged it on over his sweat-slick body. But Mara seemed to find the dark hair in the center of his bronzed chest, and the droplets of moisture that slid down his breastbone, absolutely mesmerizing. So the next time he just left his shirt off and basked in the pleasure of knowing she found pleasure in looking at him.

Not that either one of them would have acknowledged the sexual tension that sparked between them.

Mara was more determined than ever that she and Susannah were going to return to her house in Dallas. It was safer not to get any more involved with Falcon than she already was. The sooner she escaped his home—and the temptation to succumb to his charm—the better. Now that Susannah was in remission, it was just a matter of marking time, to make sure the cure had taken.

On the other hand, Falcon was encouraged by the fact Mara sought him out when he was working—even though she carted Susannah along as a chaperon whenever she visited him.

Today, Mara had brought along a picnic lunch. They headed for the trees at one of the stock ponds and fought the cattle for enough space to settle down on a blanket and eat.

Falcon knew he would never get a better chance to

broach a subject that had been on his mind since his parents had asked when they were going to meet Mara and Susannah. After they had eaten, and while they were lazing around on the blanket in the shade, he casually mentioned his family's annual Labor Day picnic.

"Ever since we've been grown and out on our own, it's been a way for us to get together once a year and exchange news. I've never missed one."

"Can we come, too?" Susannah asked.

Falcon blessed the child for her eagerness. "I'd like it if you did," he said. "I know my mom and dad would like to meet you," he said to Susannah.

"They would?" Susannah said, eyes wide. "Why would they want to meet me?"

"Because you're their first granddaughter." Falcon glanced at Mara from the corner of his eye to see how she was reacting to his discussion with Susannah. Her lips were pursed, and she looked thoughtful.

"Can we go, Mommy?" Susannah asked.

"I don't know, sweetheart," Mara hedged.

"Please," Falcon said.

"Please," Susannah said.

"I suppose we can go—"

"Great!" Falcon said, cutting her off and preventing the qualifications he could see were coming.

"Great!" Susannah echoed, straddling Falcon's belly and jumping up and down.

Falcon rolled her off him so she was caught between him and Mara on the blanket. He had turned on his side, so he could see Mara's worried eyes.

"I'm not really your— And Susannah isn't actually your parents'—"

"Don't sweat it," Falcon said with a grin. "They'll love you. And they'll adore Susannah."

"Falcon, are you sure?"

"Do this one thing for me, please, Mara," he said.

"All right, Falcon," she agreed.

But he could see from the look on her face that she was anticipating disaster. He wasn't so sure she might not be right.

FALCON COULD FEEL his stomach knotting as they turned onto the road that led to Hawk's Way. The house he had grown up in was as impressive as ever, with its two-story antebellum facade, its railed porches and four towering white columns. The drive up to the house was lined with gorgeous magnolias, while the house itself was draped with majestic, moss-laden live oaks. It wasn't until he had returned home after leaving for the first time that he realized the house had been built more in the architectural style of the Deep South than the typical Texas dogtrot home.

"It's beautiful," Mara said. She turned to meet Falcon's gaze and said, "I envy you growing up here."

"It's just a house," Falcon said. But he had a lot of happy memories here.

When they stopped the car in front of the house, they were greeted by an ancient man with long gray braids who was wearing a buckskin vest decorated with feathers and beads. His copper skin was deeply etched with wrinkles.

"Is that a real Indian?" Susannah asked, awed and somewhat intimidated.

"That's Charlie One Horse. He's got a bit of Comanche blood running through his veins. But I promise he's friendly."

Charlie One Horse, the housekeeper who had brought up the Whitelaw kids—Falcon's father and his aunt and uncles—after Falcon's grandfather had died, raised his hand, palm outward, with great solemnity toward Susannah and said, "How."

"Cut it out, Charlie," Falcon said with a grin. "You're scaring my wife and daughter." Falcon was aware of the pride in his voice when he introduced his family to the man who had been like another grandfather to him.

The old man grinned, exposing a missing eyetooth. "Howdy," he said, nodding to Mara. He turned to face Susannah who had retreated behind Falcon. "Sorry if I scared you, Susannah. My name's Charlie. I've got some chocolate chip cookies in the kitchen that I baked myself."

"You can make cookies?" Susannah said with a startled laugh.

"Best damn—" he caught Falcon's warning look and quickly amended "—darn cookies you ever ate. Come on and I'll let you taste one."

Susannah looked up at Falcon for permission and reassurance, which he gave. "I can vouch for Charlie's cooking."

"Only one, Susannah. You don't want to spoil your supper," Mara admonished as Charlie whisked her daughter away.

She turned to Falcon and said, "I didn't think she'd go anywhere with a stranger."

"Charlie doesn't allow strangers in the house. Before he's through she'll be wearing feathers in her hair and war paint on her cheeks.

"Shall we go on inside?" Falcon said. "I'll come back for the luggage later."

To Mara's surprise, there was no greeting party waiting for them in the foyer of the house, nor even in the parlor where Falcon led her.

"This is beautiful," she said as she observed the scarred antiques of pine and oak—all polished to a bright shine—in the parlor. An ancient map was framed over the mantel. "Is this Hawk's Way?"

"Uh-huh." Falcon followed her to the stone fireplace so they could look at the map more closely. "It shows all the various borders of Hawk's Way from the time my ancestors settled here more than a hundred years ago until today."

"It's huge," Mara said.

"It's not as big as it once was," Falcon said. "When my elder brother, Zach, reached his majority, my father carved off a piece of the place and gave it to him for his own. Zach calls his portion Hawk's Pride." Falcon showed the lines that indicated the borders of Zach's ranch. "You can see there's still plenty left for my father."

Mara took several steps away from Falcon. She had been much too aware of the way his shoulder brushed against her back, aware of the feel of his moist breath on her neck, aware of him. "Where is everybody?" she asked.

Falcon grinned sheepishly. "We're hours earlier than I told my folks we'd be here. I wanted to avoid exactly the sort of crowd at the door you were expecting."

Mara smiled gratefully. "Thank you."

"Then you don't mind them not being here to greet you?"

"I'd give anything for a shower and a change of clothes before I have to meet anybody," she said earnestly.

"Your wish is my command." Falcon quickly retrieved Mara's suitcase, then returned and led her up an elegant winding staircase that ended in a hall with a row of doors on either side. "This is where the family usually stays when they come to visit. This will be our room."

Mara stopped in her tracks. "Our room? I thought…" Mara realized she hadn't been thinking at all. She had slept with Falcon in his room at the ranch, even though her clothes had remained upstairs in the room next to Susannah's. Obviously that facade of separation was not going to be maintained under his parents' roof. "We're staying in the same room?"

Falcon looked at Mara from beneath hooded eyes. "I have no intention of telling my parents the true facts of our marriage. They wouldn't understand. There's a king-size bed in this room, which is plenty big enough for both of us to sleep in without running into each other, if that's what you're worried about."

"Wouldn't it be better just to tell them the truth?" Mara asked.

"Why? What purpose would it serve? My mother would be hurt, and my father would be angry and disappointed. I haven't asked much from you, Mara. I'm asking for this."

For a man who didn't ask much, he had asked quite a lot lately. Mara had known there were pitfalls to this trip, she just hadn't known what form they would take. Now she did. Mara gave a gusty sigh. She supposed she should have expected something like this.

"All right," she said. "I'll play along with your charade." Some imp forced her to add, "But I expect you to stay on your own side of the bed."

Falcon grinned. "You can draw a line down the middle, if it'll make you feel any better. Come on in. This room has an adjoining bathroom, with a great shower."

Mara let him show her around the room, which she learned he had shared with Zach when the two boys were growing up. "His ranch is so close, he doesn't stay here overnight anymore," Falcon explained. "So I inherited the room."

"It's mine now," she said with a teasing smile. "Go away and let me get cleaned up."

"Are you sure you want me to leave?" Falcon asked with a lecherous grin, as he let her push him out the door.

"Absolutely," she said as she shut the door in his face.

Mara turned to peruse the room where Falcon had slept as a boy. The head and footboard of the huge bed were oak. There was an antique wardrobe along one wall and a copper-plated dry sink topped by a patterned pitcher and washbowl on another. An overstuffed corduroy chair with a rawhide footstool at its base was angled in the corner with an old brass standing lamp to provide light to read by. A small, round table held a selection of books secured between two bookends which, she was delighted to discover, were two pairs of pewter-dipped baby shoes. Falcon's and Zach's, perhaps?

The large, sheer-curtained window looked out over the front of the house, toward the long, magnolia-lined drive. There was no lawn to speak of. The prairie had been allowed to run wild.

Like the Three Whitelaw Brats, Mara thought.

It had never crossed her mind to consider how her marriage to Falcon would affect his family. Her mother had died when she was fifteen, and her father had been stomped by a bull he was trying to move from one pasture to another only a year after she married Grant. She had no brothers and sisters, no aunts and uncles.

Falcon, she was discovering, had more family than he could shake a stick at. Mother, father, sister and brother, aunt and uncles. That wasn't all. She had discovered on the drive here that he had numerous cousins who would all be arriving shortly.

Mara took a deep breath and let it out. Could she play the loving wife to Falcon in front of his family? She thought of everything Falcon had done for her and Susannah and knew she could. She need only remind herself of the laughter and joy Falcon had brought to a household that would otherwise have been mired in the somber reality of a life-threatening disease. Oh, yes, she could easily play the loving wife for him.

It occurred to Mara to wonder how much of the adoration in her eyes when she looked at Falcon would be an act.

CHAPTER EIGHT

MARA HAD JUST stepped out of the shower and wrapped a towel around herself when the bathroom door opened without a knock.

"Who—"

"Omigosh! I didn't know anyone was in here!"

Mara stared at the young woman frozen in the bathroom doorway. She had wide-set dark brown eyes that danced with mischief and long black hair tied up in a ponytail with a ruffle of bangs across her forehead. She looked about seventeen. But if what Mara suspected was true, this was Falcon's twice-engaged and never-married twenty-eight-year-old sister.

"I'm Callen, Falcon's sister," the young woman confirmed with a welcoming smile. "You must be Mara."

"I am," Mara said.

Mara didn't know where to go from there. Callen didn't look like she was planning to leave anytime soon, and Mara was too modest to continue drying off in front of her.

Mara realized Callen was giving her a very thorough perusal. "Were you looking for something in particular?" she asked archly.

Callen laughed. "I'm afraid I'm too nosy for my own good," she admitted. "You're not at all what I expected."

"Oh?"

"Falcon's women in the past were...different," she said diplomatically.

Mara knew she should leave it at that. But her curiosity was killing her. "How so?"

"You're very pretty, but Falcon always had an eye for truly beautiful women."

Mara swallowed hard. "I see."

"Obviously Falcon found other things to admire in you besides your looks." Her brown eyes twinkled and she said, "You must have a very fine mind."

Mara saw the teasing smile spread on Callen's face and felt the startled laughter spill from her own throat. It was the first genuine, spontaneous laugh she could remember in months and months. "You are incorrigible," she said when she could speak again. "I like you, Callen. Now, what was it that brought you in here?"

"Oh. I was looking for a razor to use on my legs."

"In Falcon's bathroom?"

She shrugged impishly. "He keeps a package of disposable razors in here somewhere."

Mara gestured the other woman into the bathroom. "Be my guest. While you're hunting, I'll just dry off and get dressed."

She closed Callen inside the bathroom and quickly toweled herself off and grabbed clean clothes from the suitcase Falcon had left by the bed. She was wearing no more than a bra and underwear when Callen reappeared.

Callen was holding up a blue plastic razor and had a smug look on her face. "See? What did I tell you?"

"That's great." Mara reached for a turquoise skirt and pulled it on, then added a white peasant blouse and a concha belt. Finally she pulled on stockings and added a pair of short leather Western boots. She shoved her hand through her hair in an effort to shake out some of the wetness.

"Do you need a hair dryer?" Callen said.

"Oh, are you still here?"

Callen sat down on the bed. "I was just wondering."

"What?" Mara said resignedly. Evidently Callen wasn't leaving until she was good and ready.

"What do you see in my brother? I mean, what was it about him that made you decide to marry him?"

His health insurance, Mara thought. There was no way she was going to tell Callen that. "You are nosy, aren't you?" she said instead.

"Uh-huh. You're avoiding the question."

Mara searched quickly for some attributes that would make Falcon seem good husband material. "He's fun to be with. He's good with my daughter. He's patient. He's—"

"Falcon?" Callen interrupted. "Patient?"

Mara nodded. "Infinitely. He's gentle and—"

"Gentle?" Callen interrupted again.

"Gentle," Mara repeated firmly. "And of course," she said with a look of mischief, "he has a very fine mind."

Callen laughed.

Mara watched as Callen's glance slid to the bedroom doorway. "Oh, hi, Falcon. How long have you been there?" she asked.

"Long enough," he said with a grin.

Mara turned beet-red. She fluffed her hair over her face and eyes to hide her embarrassment.

"I can see I'm de trop," Callen said as she looked from Falcon to Mara and back again. "See you at supper tonight, Mara." She gave Falcon a sucker punch in the stomach as she scooted past him. "You too, Falcon."

A moment later she was gone.

Falcon closed the door, shutting himself inside with Mara. "Well, well," he said. "I had no idea I was such a good husband."

"I had to tell her something," Mara said as she flung her hair back off her face. Her eyes flashed dangerously. "I thought you wanted us to appear a happily married couple to your family."

"I did. I do," he said soothingly. "It's all right, Mara. You lied in a good cause."

"I wasn't lying," she said quietly.

"What?"

"You heard me," she said, meeting his gaze. "You are gentle and patient and kinder than Susannah and I have any right to expect."

He noticed she didn't repeat her boast about his "fine mind," which he had easily recognized for the euphemism it was. The proof was in the way her breasts stood peaked beneath her blouse, the way her cheeks flushed, the way her eyes observed him, dilated with passion.

He didn't wait for an invitation. He took the several steps that separated them and pulled her onto her feet. He slid one arm around and cupped her buttocks, pulling her tight against him. The other hand he tangled in her wet hair, drawing her close for his kiss.

He was gentle. Achingly gentle, even though what he wanted to do was ravage her mouth. And she responded, reluctantly at first, and then ardently, so he started to lose control. He thrust against her, letting her feel his need. He was having trouble drawing breath, but he didn't want the kiss to end.

There was one sharp knock and the door opened.

"Falcon, I—"

"Dad," Falcon managed to gasp. He kept Mara close, to hide the state of arousal they were both in.

"Doesn't anybody in this house believe in privacy?" Mara muttered with asperity.

Falcon saw the rueful twist of his father's lips. "Sorry for interrupting. Your mother wants to meet Mara. And Susannah is asking where her mother is."

"Is she all right?" Mara asked anxiously, meeting her father-in-law's eyes for the first time.

She would have pulled from Falcon's embrace, but he kept her where she was with the slight pressure of his hand on her spine.

"She's fine," Garth reassured Mara. He focused on Falcon when he said, "We'll be waiting for you downstairs when you're finished with what you're doing."

Falcon flushed. He felt like a teenager caught necking on the front porch. "We'll be down in a minute, Dad."

When his father closed the door, he released Mara. She closed her eyes and groaned. "I have never been so embarrassed in my entire life. What must your father be thinking?"

"Exactly what we want him to think," Falcon said. "That we're a happily married couple."

"When you kissed me, did you know he was coming up here to get us?" Mara asked.

"Would it matter if I did?" Falcon said.

Mara sighed. "No, I suppose not." She had wanted to believe he found her desirable. But after what Callen had told her about his taste in women, she must be a very poor second choice. However, she had known for a long time she couldn't hold a man's attention for long. Hadn't Grant taught her that lesson? They had been married only six months when he started flirting with other women. It had been all of a year before she saw signs that he had taken another woman to bed.

Mara hissed in a breath of air. She hadn't thought for a long time about that night. About the humiliation she had felt when she had confronted Grant, expecting denial and getting none.

"A man needs a woman now and then," Grant had said.

"And what am I?" she had cried, her heart breaking in two.

"You're my wife," he said. "You don't have to worry about me leaving you, sweetheart. But there are itches I have that you can't scratch."

Mara's face had bleached white at the insult. She wasn't enough woman for the man in her life.

She had hidden her shame deep. She had been a good wife and mother, and Grant had praised her for those attributes. And he had come to her bed. But that hadn't stopped his trysts with other women. She had known the fault was somehow hers, not his. That if she was just more of a woman, he wouldn't be straying from her side.

Suddenly all those feelings of inadequacy came flooding back. All because her relationship with Falcon was changing.

When she had first married Falcon, she hadn't been worried about the issues that had caused such trouble in her marriage with Grant, because nothing about her marriage to Falcon was real. The normal expectations in such a relationship hadn't existed. Now she feared that history was going to repeat itself. Not that she had seen any signs of Falcon flirting, but if her experience with Grant was any guide, it was bound to happen eventually.

Only, it shouldn't matter to her what Falcon did, because their marriage was only a matter of convenience. Even if her feelings toward him were not as nonexistent as she could wish.

"Mara?"

Falcon had noticed Mara's pale features, the tense set of her shoulders, the way she worried her lower lip with her teeth.

"It's going to be all right. My parents won't eat you," he teased. "I promise they're going to like you."

"Even though I'm not like the women you've brought home before?"

"I've never brought a woman here before," Falcon said.

"Oh. But Callen told me about the kind of women you're usually attracted to," Mara said. "I'm not anything like them."

"Callen's too outspoken for her own good."

"I'm glad she told me. At least now I have no illusions about our relationship."

Falcon's eyes narrowed suspiciously. "What does that mean?"

"It means I know I'm not the kind of woman you would have freely chosen for a wife, and that as soon as it's possible, I'm going to release you from this marriage."

"Aw, hell," Falcon said, tunneling all ten fingers into his hair. "Look, Mara, the kind of woman a man carouses with and the kind of woman he marries are two different animals."

"You don't have to tell me that," Mara said quietly. "Grant explained the situation very thoroughly."

"What do you mean?"

Mara lowered her eyes so Falcon couldn't see what she was feeling. "I mean he explained how I was a good wife and mother, but he needed other women for...for his other needs."

"That bastard."

Falcon crossed to Mara and grabbed her by the shoulders and gave her a little shake. "Look at me," he commanded. When she had lifted her lids to reveal dark, wounded blue eyes he said, "I'm not Grant."

"You could be like him," she whispered. "I've seen you drunk. And that woman who called you—"

"Is that what you've been afraid of? That I'll turn out to be an alcoholic like Grant? Or a womanizer? I'm nothing like Grant! Haven't you learned that by now?"

"You drink—"

"A whiskey now and then," he interrupted. "Alcoholism is a disease," he told Mara furiously. "And I don't have it!"

"What about Felicia?"

"What about her?"

"Why would she think she could call and invite you for a weekend on the town if you hadn't encouraged her?"

"Felicia was a flirt of mine," he conceded, "when I was single. I haven't even looked cross-eyed at another woman since I married you."

"But you must have needs—I haven't— Grant always said—"

"I'm not Grant!" Falcon interrupted in a voice hoarse with rage. "You're the woman I want in my bed, the only woman!"

"But—"

"Don't say any more, Mara," he warned. "I'm leaving. Come down when you're ready. I'd give the whole game away if my parents saw us together right now." He turned and marched to the door, closing it with a heavy thunk behind him.

Mara was stunned by Falcon's outburst. Did she dare believe him? But what reason would he have to lie? And if he wasn't lying, what was she going to do about it? Did she dare trust him not to hurt her as Grant had? Did she dare let herself begin to love him?

She had to put such thoughts aside, at least for the moment. There was a job to do. She had to go downstairs and play the role of loving and contented wife for Falcon's family.

It was easier than she had expected it to be.

In the first place, Falcon's mother, Candy, was a dear. Mara could see how the Three Whitelaw Brats had gotten so spoiled. Candy was an indulgent and adoring mother, and she had her husband twisted around her little finger. Mara was amused at the solicitous treatment the tall, rugged cowboy gave his wife.

She had trouble keeping all Falcon's relatives straight. Honey and Jesse Whitelaw were there with Honey's two older boys from a previous marriage, Jack and Jonathan, and their daughter, Tess. Falcon's Aunt Tate was there with her husband, Adam Philips, and their two grown daughters, Victoria and Elizabeth. His uncle Faron Whitelaw and his uncle's wife, Belinda, had come with their two adopted teenage sons, Rock and Drew. It was a boisterous, motley and exceedingly noisy crowd.

Mara's main concern was that Susannah not get tired out. She watched her daughter carefully, but Susannah basked in all the attention she got from her cousins-by-marriage. Toward the end of the evening, after a supper that culminated in a food fight in the kitchen while the dishes were being washed, Mara separated her daughter from Rock and Drew and started upstairs with her.

"Come back when you've gotten her settled," Falcon's mother said. "We'll be gathered in the parlor in front of the fire."

Mara couldn't find a polite way to refuse. "All right."

Susannah was so keyed up, Mara wasn't sure she would ever get her settled. Her daughter's hazel eyes were feverishly bright and her cheeks were flushed. Mara pressed her hand against Susannah's forehead, fearing the worst.

Susannah shoved it away. "I'm fine, Mommy. Don't worry about me."

Mara forced herself to smile. "That's what mothers do best," she quipped.

Susannah bounced onto the bed and shoved her feet under the covers. "I can't wait until tomorrow," she said. "Drew said he'll take me riding. They have lots of ponies here! Can you believe it?"

"Now, Susannah, I don't know—"

"Please, Mommy. You have to let me go! Everyone's going!"

"I haven't been invited."

"It's just for kids. No grown-ups allowed."

At that moment Falcon stuck his head in the door. Susannah's room was across the hall from theirs, and would eventually be occupied by several other children. "Everything all right in here?"

"Falcon, tell Mommy it's all right for me to go riding tomorrow."

Falcon turned to Mara and solemnly repeated, "It's all right for me to go riding tomorrow."

"Not you!" Susannah said with a laugh. "Me!"

"Wasn't that what I said?" Falcon asked.

Susannah snorted in disgust. "Mommmmy! I want to go!"

"It really will be safe," Falcon reassured Mara. "The older boys and girls will take care of the younger ones."

Mara didn't have the heart to refuse Susannah. She pursed her lips ruefully. She had no business judging Candy's indulgent behavior toward her children. Look how lenient she was with her daughter!

"All right," Mara conceded. "You can go."

"Yippeee!"

"If you get a good night's sleep," Mara qualified.

Susannah pulled the covers up under her arms. "Turn out the light, Mommy, quick. I'm ready to go to sleep now."

Mara kissed her daughter on the forehead, using the opportunity to reassure herself that Susannah didn't have a fever. To her surprise, Susannah felt a little warm. "Susannah, are you feeling all right?" Mara asked.

"I'm fine, Mommy. Really, truly I am!"

Falcon crossed past Mara and pressed his own kiss to Susannah's brow. "Good night, pumpkin," he said as he turned out the lamp beside the bed.

He had left the door open, and he and Mara headed for the stream of light from the hallway. He closed the door behind them.

"I hope the other kids don't wake her up when they come to bed," Mara said. "She needs her rest."

"I'm sure they'll be quiet," Falcon said.

"As a herd of buffalo," Mara said with a sideways glance at Falcon.

He grinned. "You're probably right, but the only other choice was to put Mara in with us. I thought she would have more fun with the other kids."

And they would have the privacy that a newly wedded couple should want. He didn't mention that to Mara. She had already coped with enough friendly badgering from his family this evening to know he was right.

"How are you holding up?" he asked her as they headed back down the stairs. "My family can be a little overwhelming."

Mara shot him an arch look. "A little overwhelming?"

He grinned. "All right. They're a riot looking for a place to happen." He put a hand on the back of her neck and kneaded muscles that were tight with strain.

Mara groaned. "Lord, that feels so good!"

"Want to come back upstairs with me now? I give a killer back rub." And he was dying to give her one.

Mara hesitated, then shook her head. "I promised your mother I'd come back downstairs."

Falcon turned her to face him. He settled both hands on her shoulders and began to massage the tenseness he found there. He had the satisfaction of hearing Mara moan and watched as her eyes drifted closed in pleasure. "She'll understand if we both disappear," he murmured in her ear.

Excitement shivered down Mara's spine at Falcon's invitation. She was tempted! So tempted. She opened her eyes and saw him looking down at her, his eyes hooded, his nostrils flared. She knew what they would end up doing if she followed him up the stairs. In his parents' house. With his whole family waiting for them in the parlor.

"I don't want everyone leering at me tomorrow morning."

"They wouldn't dare—" Falcon grimaced. They would. He and Mara would be teased mercilessly. "You're right," he said, starting her back down the stairs. "Let's go join the multitudes."

Falcon seated Mara on the floor in front of the fire and settled himself behind her. His arms slid around her hips, and he pulled her close. They had arrived just in time to hear Candy finishing the story of how she and Garth had met and fallen in love, complete with fairy-tale ending.

"That's the most outrageous pack of bullsh—"

"Zach!" Candy admonished. "Keep your cynicism to yourself."

"I want to hear the story of how Falcon and Mara met," Callen said.

Mara stiffened. She hadn't expected this. She shot a frightened look over her shoulder at Falcon, who shook his head once, very slightly, to let her know there was no escape. To her relief, he was the one who undertook the task.

"It's really very simple," he said. "I was walking down the street in Dallas when I spied this absolutely stunning woman on the corner."

"You're kidding, right?" Callen challenged.

Falcon shook his head. "That's exactly the way it happened. Only, the next thing I saw was her daughter, and then a man joined her," he recalled.

A hush had fallen on the crowd.

"Who was the man?" Callen asked.

"He was an old friend of mine, a football teammate from Tech," Falcon said. "He was Mara's husband, Grant Ainsworth."

"I remember him," Garth said. "I met him in the locker room after one of your games."

What happened to him?

The silence was pregnant. Falcon said very matter-of-factly, "Grant was killed in a car accident. It was a year later before I saw Mara again, but I knew I couldn't let her walk out of my life again. I asked her to marry me, and she said yes."

"How romantic," Candy said with a sigh. "True love conquers all."

Falcon realized Mara was squeezing his hand so tightly her fingernails were cutting into his skin. He made himself smile at her. "I've been doubly blessed," he continued. "I got a daughter in the bargain."

"And a pretty little minx she is," Charlie One Horse contributed.

"Falcon told us Susannah has been sick," Candy said to Mara. "But she seems so well now."

"She has—had—leukemia. It's in remission."

"Thank God for that," Candy said.

The discussion shifted to Callen, and the fact that for the first time in years she didn't have a man at her side.

"And thank God for that!" Mara heard Garth mutter.

Mara watched Candy put her fingers over his mouth to shut him up and hiss, "Garth! Be good."

The evening wound to a pleasant close, as couples settled back together to watch the fire burn and to drink a glass of whiskey or brandy or some sweet liqueur. No wine drinkers here, Mara thought with an inner smile. But then, this was the frontier, where things were harder, the elements harsher and life was lived to the fullest.

She caught herself yawning and looked quickly to see if anyone had noticed. To her chagrin, Falcon's father was staring right at her.

"Time for bed," he announced.

She started to say, "I'm not tired" and realized she was. Falcon had to haul her to her feet. Her knees felt like jelly.

"Come on, sleepyhead," he said. "We've got a big day tomorrow."

"We do?" Mara said. This day had seemed quite big enough.

"Picnic. Football. Frisbee. Croquet. We've got games to play."

Mara snickered softly. "That we have, Mr. Whitelaw. Games no one else even knows about."

Falcon swatted her on the fanny. "Save the cynicism," he said. "I get enough of that when Zach's around."

Mara undressed in the bathroom and put on a thick terry-cloth robe before she ventured into the bedroom. To her relief, Falcon was already under the covers. To her chagrin, his bronzed shoulders were bare.

She narrowed her eyes suspiciously. "Are you wearing anything under those sheets?" she asked.

"Pajama bottoms," he said.

"Oh. Well. That's okay."

"I'll be glad to take them off," he volunteered.

"Thanks, but no thanks." Mara turned off the light before dropping her robe beside the bed and slipping under the covers. She was aware that she wasn't alone in the king-size bed. It seemed to have shrunk. She could hear Falcon breathing, even believed she could feel the heat of his body.

"Good night, Mara."

"Good night, Falcon."

Mara stared at the ceiling, not the least bit tired.

Ten minutes later she said, "Falcon? Are you awake?"

"I am now."

"I like your family."

"They like you, too."

Mara shivered. But she wasn't the least bit cold. "Falcon?" she whispered.

"Why are you whispering?" he whispered back.

"I don't know," Mara whispered. "I don't want to wake anyone."

"I'm the only one in here," Falcon said, "and I'm already awake. Is there something you wanted to say to me, Mara?"

Mara heard the irritation in his voice and wondered what had caused it. "I guess not."

Falcon flipped the light on. He sat up and the sheet dropped to his hips. Mara's eyes shot to the expanse of bare flesh he revealed.

"What is it?" he demanded. "I'm awake, and you have my full attention."

"I was just wondering if you'd still be willing to give me that back rub."

"Why didn't you just say so? I'd be glad to." Falcon scooted over and ordered, "Turn over onto your stomach."

Mara did as she was told. Falcon quickly straddled her at the waist and his hands came down firm and sure across her shoulders and began to massage the sore muscles there.

"How's that?" he asked.

"Mmmm," she murmured.

"How about getting this nightgown out of the way?" He pulled the thin straps of her silk gown off her shoulders and shoved the garment down below her waist, freeing her arms. "There," he said with satisfaction.

Mara had a sudden realization of what she had done. What she didn't understand was why she had done it. She knew where this encounter was heading, and she had to make up her mind quickly whether she was going to let Falcon make love to her.

There was no doubt he was ready and willing.

His hands caressed as well as massaged, and as her languor increased she knew her resistance was decreasing.

"Falcon?"

"Yes, love?"

Mara shivered again as he murmured the endearment against her ear.

"Would you like a massage when you're finished doing me?"

Falcon chuckled. "I would love one," he said. "Just as soon as I finish doing you."

She gasped as he slid his hands beneath her and cupped her breasts, teasing the nipples into tight buds with his fingers. "Falcon?" she whispered.

"Why are you whispering again?" he whispered.

"Because I haven't got the breath to talk," she admitted.

For a long time, neither of them said anything. They spoke with their hands, with their mouths and with their eyes.

When Mara drifted to sleep, she was snuggled tightly in Falcon's embrace. She refused to question the right or wrong of what she had done. For now, he was her husband, and he wanted her. And she loved being with him. Maybe she had heard one too many fairy tales this evening.

Tomorrow was soon enough to let reality creep back in.

CHAPTER NINE

A SINGLE RIDER galloped hell-bent-for-leather toward the Whitelaw mansion. He leapt from his horse before it had even stopped on its haunches and raced toward the crowd gathered under the live oaks in back of the house.

"Falcon!" Drew called. "Falcon!"

"I'm here, Drew," Falcon said, racing toward the teenager. "What's wrong?"

Mara was sitting at a picnic table with several of the other wives. When she heard Drew's cry she jumped up and ran toward him. "What's wrong?" she repeated only a moment after Falcon.

"It's Susannah," Drew said, his eyes huge and worried. "She's hurt. She fell off her horse."

"Oh, no!" Mara cried. "How bad is it?"

Falcon clutched Mara hard around the shoulders to keep her from seizing Drew's shirt and shaking him. "How is she?" he asked Drew.

"I couldn't tell," Drew confessed. "I left her with the others and rode back to get help. She seemed fine when we started out. We asked her if she could lope, and she said yes."

"She's a good rider," Falcon confirmed.

"But she fell off!" Drew said. "We weren't even going very fast."

"I'm sure you weren't," Falcon consoled the inconsolable boy. Falcon gave Mara a push toward his mother's already-outstretched arms and said, "Keep her here."

"I want to go with you!" Mara said fiercely.

"Wait here," Falcon replied, his voice like granite. "I'll bring her back to you. Call the family doctor and make sure he's here when I get back," Falcon told his father.

Garth nodded.

Mara let Candy lead her into the house. To her relief, Falcon's mother didn't ply her with platitudes like, "I'm sure she'll be all right." They sat together in silence in the kitchen, each with a cup of hot coffee in front of her that neither touched.

It seemed ages before Falcon returned. He had Susannah in his arms.

"She wasn't hurt by the fall," he said quickly, before Mara had a chance to be frightened by her daughter's ashen complexion. "At least, not more than a few scratches."

"Then what's wrong with her?" Mara demanded.

Falcon's blue eyes were bleak as a winter day. "She has a fever. And her lymph nodes are swollen."

Mara felt a chill slide down her arms. "No. No!"

"I think she must have fainted. That's why she fell from her horse."

"This can't be happening," Mara pleaded. "Please, God, nooooo!" she wailed.

"What is it?" Candy asked her son.

Falcon's lips were pressed flat to keep them from trembling. He wasn't sure he could speak past the constriction in his throat. "I think the leukemia is back."

Falcon could say one thing for his family, they rallied around in times of trouble. Zach flew the three of them back to Dallas in his private jet, while Callen promised to drive their car home for them. Garth phoned Children's Hospital to tell them to expect Susannah. Candy volunteered to pack their clothes and send them along with Callen.

The rest of Falcon's cousins and aunt and uncles promised to pray.

Falcon only managed to keep Zach from staying with them at the hospital by turning on his brother like a rabid dog. He bared his teeth ferociously. "Leave us be. We can handle this better alone."

What he really meant was I don't want you to see me fall to pieces. He felt like he was already in pieces. Mara wasn't in much better shape. He wanted to be alone with her somewhere in a dark place and put his arms around her and lay his head on her shoulder and comfort her and be comforted.

Zach settled a succoring hand on Falcon's shoulder, which was tensed hard as stone. "You don't have to go through this alone."

"Don't stay," Falcon said starkly. His eyes glittered with unshed tears. His throat had a huge lump in it. If his brother was there, if he had someone to lean on, he might break down completely. If he was alone with Mara, he would have to be strong for her. He would be able to stay in control.

Zach tightened his grip momentarily, then let go. "Call us," he said. "We want to know how Susannah is doing."

Falcon nodded. He couldn't manage any more speech.

Zach swept Mara up in a tight embrace, as though to

lend her strength, then let her go. "She'll be all right," he whispered in her ear.

Mara whimpered, the sound of a suffering animal. "Thank you, Zach," she grated out. "I needed to hear that."

Even if she knew it wasn't necessarily true.

When they were alone together, neither Mara nor Falcon seemed to be able to reach out to the other. They sat down in chairs next to each other in the hospital waiting room, but they didn't touch.

At long last, Falcon broke the silence. "Even if it is the leukemia back again, that doesn't mean she won't eventually get well," he said, as though to convince himself.

"But she'll have to start all over with those awful treatments," Mara said in a low voice. "She'll be sick again. And lose the hair she was so pleased to be growing back."

Mara reached out a hand, and Falcon grasped it. They clung to each other in a way people do when they know there is strength and fortitude to be found in the other's grasp. Mara raised her eyes and met Falcon's steady gaze. It gave her courage to face whatever was to come.

He isn't like Grant. He's nothing at all like Grant.

The revelation came to Mara in those few seconds like a star bursting and shedding great light. Grant had never been there for her when she needed him. He had never offered her strength. He had never been a rock to which she could cling in times of trouble.

Falcon hadn't reached for a bottle in times of trouble, nor sought out another woman. He had reached for her. He had come to her.

That wasn't the end of her epiphany.

Why, I love him, she marveled. Mara stared at Falcon as though seeing him for the first time. How had he come to mean so much to her? When had she started caring more for his pain than for her own? When had she started wanting him to love her back?

Her thoughts were cut off by the arrival of Dr. Sortino. Mara knew before he said a word that the prognosis was not good. She rose to her feet, still gripping Falcon's hand, and waited to hear what the doctor had to say.

"The leukemia is back."

Four words. Four frightening words.

Mara bit her lip to keep from crying. She pressed her face to Falcon's chest as though to escape what was happening.

There was no escape.

"We've got her stabilized," Dr. Sortino said. "We'll start the therapy again within the next few days. Don't despair," he said. "Children often have a relapse and then recover completely."

Mara lifted her head and stared at him with liquid eyes. "But some don't," she challenged.

"Some don't," he conceded reluctantly. "We'll have to wait and see."

"Can we see her?" Falcon asked.

"You can look in on her. She's sleeping now. The nurse will show you to her room."

He left then, without saying more. But Mara had heard quite enough.

"Hold me," she said to Falcon. "Hold me."

Falcon needed to feel the warmth of Mara in his arms. Because he was cold. So cold.

"She'll be all right," he told Mara. "She has to be."

But when they saw Susannah lying in the hospital bed, her face almost as white as the sheets, neither could manage an optimistic word. They grasped hands and held on.

"Your pony is waiting for you to get well," Falcon whispered to the sleeping girl. "And your mommy needs some more tickling," he said. "And I need you home to bounce around the house," he said in a choked voice.

He turned to Mara, and this time she took him in her arms and comforted him. His powerful body shook with silent sobs that were all the more intense because he fought them, even as they escaped.

Mara reached out a hand and touched her daughter's cheek. "Good night, Susannah," she whispered. Then, to Falcon, "Let's go home."

There was no question of staying in separate bedrooms. Falcon never let go of Mara's hand. He led her to his room and silently undressed her then undressed himself. He laid her on the bed and joined her there, twining their bodies together.

"I need you," he said.

Mara knew what he was asking. She gave herself to him, gave him the comfort and reassurance and love he needed, and took it in return. It was a gentle joining of two bruised souls who sought solace in each other's bodies.

Mara's heart swelled with love, and she gave Falcon a part of herself that she had kept hidden somewhere deep inside for long years—ever since Grant had told her she was not enough woman for him. For Falcon she could be more, was more, because he sought more from her.

Falcon lay beside Mara and realized that he felt far more than physical satisfaction. There had been a difference in their lovemaking this time, subtle but detectable.

Mara had held nothing back. She had been lightning and fire in his arms, and he had found himself burning in her embrace. He knew now that what he felt for her was more than lust, or mere affection, or even admiration. He loved her, body and heart and soul.

He wanted to say the words. He needed to say them.

I love you, Mara. I want to spend my life loving you. I want you to have my children. Susannah needs brothers and sisters to play with. I'll make you both happy. I promise it.

But he didn't say any of those things.

She was already asleep.

DURING SUSANNAH'S SECOND bout of induction therapy, any discussion of Falcon's and Mara's life together, their future, was held in abeyance. It was as though Susannah was the glue that held them together. Neither was willing to contemplate what form their relationship would take if something should happen and she should disappear from their lives. It might be too painful to remain together as a couple, because each would see in the other's anguished eyes a constant reminder of what they had lost.

In spite of that, their love grew. It happened in small ways, over many days.

They shared duties taking care of Susannah, relieving each other when one had reached the end of his patience with the sick child's petulant whining on the one hand, or was unable to endure another moment of the little girl's tremendous persistence in the face of her debilitating illness on the other.

They spent their nights together making love. Neither spoke the words each privately thought. They told each other of their love in the only way they were allowed. Because there was no question of committing themselves to each other until—unless—Susannah recovered.

Mara made a point of getting up each morning with the sunrise, as Falcon did, and making him breakfast.

"I can do this myself," he said. "I know you're tired."

She traced the shadows under his eyes with a gentle hand. "And you're not?"

"Some sex goddess keeps me up half the night with her demands on my body," he teased.

"Remind the sex goddess you have to work in the morning, and I'm sure she'll leave you alone," Mara replied pertly.

Falcon pulled her into his arms and showered her face with kisses. "I'd rather miss the sleep," he said, snuggling his face against her hair.

Mara felt loved and cherished and appreciated.

"Get going, you've got work to do," she said as she shoved him out the kitchen door.

Sometimes, late at night, after he had made sweet love to Mara and she had fallen asleep, Falcon returned to his office. He wanted Mara to know she would be getting a husband who was financially responsible if she agreed to extend their marriage beyond its current artificial structure. He was planning for the future, something that hadn't interested or concerned him before Mara came into his life.

One night Mara awoke and found herself alone. She sought Falcon out and found him in his office.

"What are you doing here in the middle of the night?" she chided. "You need your sleep."

He was sitting in the swivel chair in front of his desk,

and he circled it to face her. Because it had become second nature to find comfort in his arms, she settled herself in his lap and twined her fingers in his hair, pulling
his face down to hers for a tender kiss.

"Now," she murmured against lips that were warm
and wet against her own, "tell me what's going on. Are
we in financial trouble? Do I need to go back to work
as a short-order cook?"

"No," he said, perhaps too emphatically. "The whole
reason I'm spending time at this desk is to secure our
future together in a way that will leave you free to be
home with Susannah." And any other children we have.

Falcon hesitated, aware he had crossed an invisible line. When Mara gave him no encouragement, he
backed up again, into neutral ground. "I'm just making
sure the ranch is run well and reinvesting what money
I have in less risky ventures."

"You're a man who needs risk in his life," Mara said
in a quiet voice.

"Not this kind," Falcon objected.

"Then let me see if I can provide another kind," Mara
said, as she bit the lobe of his ear. Her hand slid across
his naked chest and down toward the pajama bottoms
he wore in case he had to check on Susannah during
the night. He was already hard by the time her hand
got to him.

"Mara," he warned. "It's nearly dawn. I have to get
dressed and go to work in an hour."

"We've got a whole hour? That should be enough
time for what I have in mind."

A moment later she was on her back on the floor
of his office, and he was inside her. Their loving was
stormy and tempestuous, full of risk, and she climaxed

twice before he was finished and lowered himself, chest heaving, to the carpet beside her.

Falcon groaned. "I'm sorry, Mara. I didn't mean to be so rough."

She took one look at the love bite she had left on his shoulder and laughed. "I'm sorry, Falcon. I didn't mean to be so rough, either."

ONCE, DURING THOSE weeks and months while their lives were on hold, Mara took herself back to the house she had bought because of its location on a quiet, tree-lined street where children played. She was amazed to see it was just an ordinary house. There was nothing particularly special about it. Yet, keeping this home was one of the reasons she had been willing to marry Falcon Whitelaw.

She let herself in and wandered through the house. It felt empty, despite the furnished rooms. She wondered what it was that had made this place seem so much a necessary part of her life. And realized it wasn't the house, but what it had represented. Permanence. A place of belonging where memories could be made.

This house wasn't a home. A home was where people lived and loved. Home was where Falcon and Susannah were. Home was the B-Bar Ranch.

Mara threw herself on the bed in her room and wept. For all the might-have-beens with Grant. What would their life have been like if only…? There, in the house where she had sought the happiness she had been denied in her marriage with Grant, she let go of the past. Her first love was dead and buried. He no longer had the power to hurt her.

The only question now was whether she had the

courage to put aside her past fears and reach out and grasp what she wanted. It meant taking risks. She might be hurt again. She might not live happily ever after. It all came down to a matter of trust.

Did she trust Falcon Whitelaw—who less than a year past had been an irresponsible, carousing, ne'er-do-well—to offer her a future filled with happiness? Or would a lifetime with him be filled with trials and tribulation? Had he merely been on his best behavior for the months they had spent together? Would he revert to form once Susannah was well?

Mara sat herself down on the edge of the bed and dropped her head into her hands. There were no guarantees. She was going to have to take a chance. She was going to have to make up her mind one way or the other. Because she knew that the moment Susannah was out of danger—and she would be someday soon—Falcon was going to start asking questions and demanding answers about their relationship.

And she would have to answer yes or no.

CHAPTER TEN

"HI, MOM. I'M AT the hospital."

"Falcon? What is it? Is it bad news?"

"She's in remission."

"That's wonderful, Falcon!" his mother said. "Oh, I'm so glad for all of you!"

"Tell Dad for me, and Zach and Callen." Falcon didn't think he could handle talking to all of them. He was having trouble keeping his voice steady as it was.

"How's Mara?" Candy asked.

"She's fine."

"When will we see you again?" Candy asked.

"I don't know, Mom. Everything is pretty hectic right now. I'll call you again when things are more settled. Okay? I've got to go now."

"Goodbye, Falcon. Take care of yourself. Give our love to Mara and Susannah."

When things are more settled. Falcon wasn't sure how soon that would be. Certainly not until he had an answer from Mara about whether or not she was willing to end their sham marriage and start a real one. Although, since the day of Susannah's relapse, there had been nothing halfway about Falcon's commitment to his wife. Mara had given him hope that she felt the same way he did, but until the words were spoken, nothing was settled.

It had taken the full amount of time—Christmas had come and gone—for the induction therapy to work a second time. Even Susannah welcomed the "backstick" that had resulted in the news that she was in remission again.

"We're going to take things a little slower this time," Mara gently admonished her daughter as they rode home from the hospital. "No more bouncing off the walls."

Falcon winked at the little girl. "You'll have to settle for bouncing on the beds," he teased.

Mara shot Falcon a warning look. She had almost lost Susannah the last time. She wasn't taking any chances with her daughter's health now that she had been given a second lease on life.

Falcon had different ideas about what was appropriate behavior for Susannah's present state of health, and during the next few weeks, the two adults were constantly at loggerheads over what Susannah could and could not do.

"You can't keep Susannah wrapped up in cotton batting," Falcon argued.

"I can, and I will!" Mara retorted.

"She's a little girl. She needs to run and play."

"What if she gets sick again?" Mara said, her heart in throat.

Falcon pulled her into his arms and rocked her back and forth. "We'll make sure she rests, but she has to be allowed to live as normal a life as she can, Mara."

Mara knew Falcon was right. She was being overprotective. "But I'm so scared," she admitted in a small voice.

"I'm here," he said. "I'll watch over you both," he promised.

It was as close to a declaration of love as he had ever come. He wanted to go further. He wanted to say the rest. But Mara stopped him.

"I know you'll take care of us," she said. "But I wonder sometimes if it's fair of me to ask it of you. This isn't what you bargained for when you married me," she reminded him.

"But I—"

Again, she cut him off. "I don't want to think about the future. I want to do what you advised me once before. I want to enjoy today for what it brings and forget about tomorrow. Maybe when I know Susannah is going to get well, I'll think differently. But now…now life is too uncertain."

When she said things like that, how could he talk to her about their future together? But neither could he let what she had said pass without challenging it.

"Do you really mean to put your life on hold for however long it takes Susannah to get well? She won't be truly in the clear unless she stays in remission beyond the five-year mark. Five years, Mara. That's a long time."

"I know," she conceded. "When you put it that way, I know I'm being ridiculous. But I need a little time to start believing there will be a future for us—for me and Susannah."

He was achingly aware he was not included in her picture of the future.

"A year," she said. "If Susannah stays in remission a year, I'll let myself hope again. But it's too dangerous to believe in the future before then. You do understand, don't you, Falcon?"

He did. All too well. Mara wasn't going to make promises to him or to herself that she wasn't sure she would be able to keep. He wanted to say they could have a life together even if the worst happened, and Susannah died. But he discovered he couldn't voice even the possibility that the world might lose a free spirit like Susannah. She had become as dear to him as though she were his own flesh and blood.

To anyone watching from the outside, they appeared a perfectly normal, happy family over the months of winter that led into spring. In fact, Susannah quickly got well enough to misbehave. That created a whole new set of problems for Mara and Falcon. They were no longer merely caretakers for a youthful invalid, they were parents trying to raise a responsible, honest and self-sufficient child.

Falcon found himself sympathizing with what his own parents must have gone through with him and his siblings. Susannah had gotten used to being waited on and catered to during her illness. The first time Falcon insisted she pick up her damp towel and put it back on the bathroom rack, she responded as the spoiled child she had become.

"You do it," she said.

Falcon wasn't sure what to do next, but he wasn't about to let an eight-year-old order him around. "Pick it up, Susannah. Otherwise, you can go to your room and spend the rest of the morning thinking about ways you can help do your share in this family."

"You're not my father," Susannah shouted back. "You can't tell me what to do!"

Falcon stood stunned, appalled at the child's apparent dismissal of the role he had played in her life over the past nine months. Surely no real father could have been more kind or considerate, more loving or caring during her illness. But children, he was learning, can have short, selfish memories.

"Susannah Ainsworth! You apologize to Falcon this instant!"

Mara had overheard the entire conversation and was appalled at her daughter's devilish behavior. "You will pick up that towel and hang it back on the rack. Then you can go to your room and stay there the rest of the morning!"

"I'm sorry, Falcon," Susannah said in a petulant voice. Then she turned to her mother. "If I've picked up the towel," Susannah reasoned as she sullenly hung the damp towel on the rack, "why do I still have to go to my room?"

"Because you were rude and disobedient," Mara said.

"Why do I have to do what Falcon says?" Susannah complained. "He's not my real father."

Mara looked quickly at Falcon's face, which had hardened like stone, then back to her daughter. She was the one who had forced Falcon to remain on the fringes of her and Susannah's life. She was the one who wanted everything on hold until she was good and ready to move forward. She had created this situation, and the time had come for her to resolve it.

"Falcon is your father in every way that matters," Mara said. "He has the right to tell you what to do. And you have the duty to obey him and to treat him with respect."

Susannah turned wide, hazel eyes on Falcon. "Are

you really going to be my real father?" she asked, her
tone more curious now than belligerent. "Forever and
ever?"

Falcon shot one desperate look at Mara, wanting to
be able to say yes, and knowing that he hadn't the right.

Mara knew she had to make a decision. "Yes, he is,"
she answered for Falcon. It was easy, she realized, so
easy to say yes to a lifetime with Falcon.

Their glances caught and clung for a moment. Mara
almost gasped at the powerful emotions she saw in Falcon's eyes. She knew then she had done the right thing.
She was committed to this man. For better or worse.
For richer—and he was beginning to spend money
like Croesus again—or poorer. In sickness—and there
might be more of it for Susannah—and in health. It only
remained for the words to be spoken between them.

Only, now that she had taken a step off the edge
of a treacherous cliff, Mara was terrified that Falcon
wouldn't be there to catch her.

"All right, you can be my father," Susannah said in
the way children have of accepting momentous occa-
sions with aplomb. "I'm sorry, Falcon," she said, this
time with more contrition in her voice. She crossed to
him and put her arms around his waist and said, "Actually, I'm glad you're going to be my father for real and
always. I guess I sorta like you a lot." Then she looked
up at him with an innocent, angelic face and said, "Do
I still have to go to my room?"

Falcon swept the little girl into his arms and gave her
a tremendous hug. "God, I love you, Susannah. I'm so
glad you're my daughter for real and always." Then he
set her on her feet and said, "And yes, you still have to
go to your room."

Susannah grimaced. "All right, but if I stay in my room this morning, can we go riding this afternoon?"

Falcon shook his head at her persistence. He sent a questioning look to Mara as if to say, "All right?" When she nodded, he said to Susannah, "Sure. You use the morning to think, and we'll go riding this afternoon."

"Yippee!" Susannah said as she hopped, skipped and bounced away.

In an exaggerated motion, Falcon wiped his brow with his sleeve. "I have great respect for my parents when I see what they coped with from the other side of the fence."

"It isn't easy knowing the right thing to do or say," Mara conceded.

"Did you mean it, Mara? That I'll be Susannah's father for now and forever?"

Mara flushed. "Yes," she said in a whisper. "If you want to be."

"If I want to be? How can you even ask? I love Susannah." It would only take another breath to say And I love you.

Mara never gave him the chance. "I've got a lot to do this morning if I want to be free to ride with you and Susannah this afternoon," she said.

She backed up a few steps, then turned and almost ran for his office. She was like a skittish filly that had walked up to his hand to take the sugar he held out to her, but at the last moment had taken fright and run. Like the filly, he knew she would be back. Because once a creature had developed a taste for sugar, it was an irresistible lure.

It wouldn't be a bad thing to wait a little while and give his jumbled feelings time to sort themselves out.

And give Mara time to realize that he would be there, waiting with his hand outstretched, whenever she was ready to move forward in their relationship.

At least the suspended animation in which they had lived for the past nine months was coming to an end. But Falcon wasn't taking anything for granted. He wanted the words spoken. He wanted things decided once and for all. And if he moved slowly and carefully enough, there was just the chance she would come to him today.

Just before lunchtime, Susannah came running into the kitchen. "Can we go riding now?" she asked. "Patches needs some exercise."

"What do you say, Mara?" Falcon asked. "Shall we go riding now, or after lunch?"

Mara finished wrapping the last of the sandwiches she had been preparing. "I've put together a picnic to take to the stock pond," Mara said. "But mind you, no racing!"

Falcon and Susannah raced the last few hundred yards to the stock pond, with Mara flying close behind.

"Whew! I have to admit that was exhilarating," Mara said with a laugh as she slid off her horse.

"I'm hungry," Susannah said. "Can we eat lunch now?"

"Sure. Untie the blanket from behind your saddle and I'll get the food." Mara began untying the saddle-bags on her horse.

Falcon quickly relieved her. "I'll do this. You can help Susannah spread out the blanket."

All of them ate like they were never going to see food again. Replete, they settled back lazily on the blanket and watched the shapes on the ground made by the broken shadows of the leaves.

In a very short while, Mara and Falcon were treated to the sight of Susannah sound asleep on the blanket between them.

"She seems to tire so easily," Mara said as she chewed worriedly on her lower lip.

"Most kids her age take a nap, don't they? Or would if their parents could get them to slow down long enough. She's fine, Mara. Try not to worry so much."

"I do try!" Mara said. She rose from the blanket and walked a few steps away, where they wouldn't disturb Susannah's slumber.

When Falcon came up behind her and circled her waist, she leaned her head back against his shoulder. This felt good. This felt right. She wanted to stay married to Falcon. She wanted them to be husband and wife. But was that fair to him? What if she had trapped him by the things she had said this morning. What if he didn't want to stay with her and Susannah after all? She had to know the truth.

"I took advantage of the situation this morning," she said. "If you want out of this marriage, all you have to do is say so."

"Oh?"

Mara couldn't tell from that one quiet word whether Falcon was relieved or infuriated by what she said. But his hands had tightened uncomfortably around her.

"I can't breathe," she protested.

His hold loosened, but he didn't let her go. Neither did he speak. Maybe he did want out.

She continued, "When Susannah asked if you were going to be her father forever and ever, I said you would.

But we've never talked about forever, Falcon. I made
the choice for you. I know that's unfair, and if you want
to be free of us, of both of us—"

He whirled her around and clutched her tightly at the
waist. "Look at me, Mara."

But she couldn't. She was afraid.

He caught her chin between his fingers and forced it
upward. He tightened his grasp and demanded, "Look
at me."

He waited until she looked up at him before speaking again. His eyes were narrowed, his gaze fierce. A
muscle worked in his jaw. This was not a weak man.
This was not a man who would let her fall from a cliff.
He would be there to catch her.

"I want to be Susannah's father," he said in a harsh,
grating voice. "Very much."

"That means you'll also be stuck with me," Mara
said with a breezy laugh that somehow got caught in
her throat.

Falcon let go of Mara's chin and caught her by the
shoulders. "I love you, Mara. I want you to be my wife,
forever and ever."

Mara's heart soared when she heard Falcon's declaration of love. But she had to make sure he knew what
he was getting into. "Are you sure?"

There was a silence that sent Mara's heart to her
throat.

Falcon was shaken by Mara's third attempt to set
him free. Didn't she hear what he was saying? Didn't
she realize how much he loved her? There was only one
thing that could possibly change his mind about staying married to her, and that was if she didn't want him.
He needed to know that Mara loved him. He needed

o hear the words. But he didn't dare ask her outright. What if she said no?

For the first and most important time in his life, Falcon found himself at a loss for words with a woman. 'Mara, do you— Is there a chance that— Is it possible—"

"What are you trying to say, Falcon?"

From the blanket behind them a little voice piped up, "Falcon wants to know if you love him, Mommy."

"What?"

Both adults shot startled looks at the little girl, who was lying on her stomach with her head perched on her hands and her legs waving in the air.

"I thought you were asleep," Mara said.

"Well, I'm not," Susannah replied. "Do you love him, Mommy?" she demanded.

Mara flushed, and Falcon feared the worst. He tried to get the words past a constricted throat, tried to offer her the divorce she so obviously wanted. Fortunately he was too distressed to speak.

Because the next words out of Mara's mouth were, "Yes, Susannah, I love him very much."

Mara and Falcon exchanged glances that shouted hosanna and hallelujah, before Falcon pulled Mara into his arms for a possessive kiss. A moment later, Susannah was tugging on his shirt, demanding to be included in the family embrace.

"Love me, too, Daddy," she said. "Me, too."

"You, too, Susannah," Falcon assured the little girl. "I'll love you and your mommy both, forever and ever."

Falcon met Mara's eyes and they spoke without words. They might not have forever with Susannah. There were no guarantees of long life and happiness.

But whatever time they had together, they silently vowed to live to the fullest.

"Let's go home," Falcon said. "I want to make love to my wife," he whispered in her ear.

"Yes," Mara replied in a soft voice. "Let's take our daughter and go home."

* * * * *

She looked up at him, her expression stricken. "You don't
believe me either, do you? You don't think I can prove
that Russell was on to something real."

"I'm reserving judgment," he said, keeping his word
as steady as he could, "until I see more evidence. And
you might want to consider holding back on any more
accusations until you've recovered from this shock—and
you have that proof in hand."

"Oh, I'll find the proof. I have a good idea where, too.
All I have to do is get back to the turbines as soon as
possible and find the—"

"No way," he said sharply. "You're not going out
there. You saw the email, right? About Green Horizons'
safety review?"

She gave him a disgusted look. "Of course they want to
keep everyone away. If they're somehow involved in a

his, they'll drag out their review forever. And leave any
vidence cleaned and sanitized for their own protection."

"Or they're trying to keep from being on the hook
or any further accidents. Either way, I said no, Emma. I
on't want you or your students taking any unnecessary
hances."

"I'd never involve them. Never. After Russell, there's
o way I would chance that." She shook her head, tears
lling her eyes. "I was—I was the one to call Russell's
arents. I insisted on it. It nearly killed me, breaking that
ews to them."

"Then you'll understand how I feel," Beau said, "when
tell you I'm not making that call to your folks, your boss
r anyone else when you go getting yourself hurt again.
r worse."

She made a scoffing sound. "You've helped me
ut a couple times, sure. That doesn't make me your
esponsibility."

"That's where you're wrong, Dr. Copley. I take
veryone who lives on, works on or sets foot on my
pread as my responsibility," he said, sincerity ringing in
is every word, "which is why, from this point forward,
'm barring you from Kingston property."

Don't miss
Deadly Texas Summer
by Colleen Thompson

Available March 2020 wherever
Harlequin Romantic Suspense
books and ebooks are sold.

Harlequin.com

**IF YOU ENJOYED THIS BOOK
WE THINK YOU WILL ALSO LOVE**

HARLEQUIN
INTRIGUE

Seek thrills. Solve crimes. Justice served.

Dive into action-packed stories that will keep you
on the edge of your seat. Solve the crime
and deliver justice at all costs.

6 NEW BOOKS AVAILABLE EVERY MONTH!

SPECIAL EXCERPT FROM

⊕ HARLEQUIN
INTRIGUE

*Sheriff Jamison Wyatt has never forgotten Liza Dean,
the one who got away. But now she's back, and she needs
his help to find her sister. They'll have to infiltrate a crime
syndicate, but once they're on the inside, will they
be able to get back out?*

Read on for a sneak preview of
South Dakota Showdown *by Nicole Helm.*

Chapter One

Bonesteel, South Dakota, wasn't even a dot on most maps, which
was precisely why Jamison Wyatt enjoyed being its attached
officer. Though he was officially a deputy with the Valiant County
Sheriff's Department, as attached officer his patrol focused on
Bonesteel and its small number of residents.

One of six brothers, he wasn't the only Wyatt who acted as an
officer of the law—but he was the only man who'd signed up for
the job of protecting Bonesteel.

He'd grown up in the dangerous, unforgiving world of a biker
gang run by his father. The Sons of the Badlands were a cutthroat
group who'd been wreaking havoc on the small communities of
South Dakota—just like this one—for decades.

Luckily, Jamison had spent the first five years of his life on his
grandmother's ranch before his mother had fully given in to Ace
Wyatt and moved them into the fold of the nomadic biker gang.

Through tenacity and grit Jamison had held on to a belief in
right and wrong that his grandmother had instilled in him in those
early years. When his mother had given birth to son after son on the
inside of the Sons, Jamison had known he would get them out—
and he had, one by one—and escape to their grandmother's ranch
situated at the very edge of Valiant County.

It was Jamison's rough childhood in the gang and the immen
responsibility he'd placed on himself to get his brothers away fro
it that had shaped him into a man who took everything perhaps
shade too seriously. Or so his brothers said.

Jamison had no regrets on that score. Seriousness kept peop
safe. He was old enough now to enjoy the relative quiet of patrolli
a small town like Bonesteel. He had no desire to see lawbreakin
He'd seen enough. But he had a deep, abiding desire to make su
everything was right.

So it was odd to be faced with a clear B and E just a quarter pa
nine at night on the nearly deserted streets. Maybe if it had be
the general store or gas station, he might have understood. But t
figure was trying to break into his small office attached to city ha

It was bold and ridiculous enough to be moderately amusin
Probably a drunk, he thought. Maybe the…woman—yes,
appeared to be a woman—was drunk and looking to sleep it off.

When he did get calls, they were often alcohol related a
mostly harmless, as this appeared to be.

Since Jamison was finishing up his normal last patrol for th
night, he was on foot. He walked slowly over, keeping his ste
light and his body in the shadows. The streets were quiet, havir
long since been rolled up for the night.

Still, the woman worked on his doorknob. If she was drun
she was awfully steady for one. Either way, she didn't look to po
much of a threat.

He stepped out of the shadow. "Typically people who break a
enter are better at picking a lock."

The woman stopped what she was doing—but she hadr
jumped or shrieked or even stumbled. She just stilled.

Don't miss
South Dakota Showdown *by Nicole Helm,*
available March 2020 wherever
Harlequin Intrigue books and ebooks are sold.

Harlequin.com

HARLEQUIN

Heartfelt or suspenseful, inspiring or passionate, Harlequin has your happily-ever-after.

With new books published
every month, you are sure to find the
satisfying escape you know you deserve.

SIGN UP FOR THE HARLEQUIN NEWSLETTER

Be the first to hear about great new
reads and exciting offers!

Harlequin.com/newsletters

Love Harlequin romance?

DISCOVER.

Be the first to find out about promotions, news and exclusive content!

Facebook.com/HarlequinBooks

Twitter.com/HarlequinBooks

Instagram.com/HarlequinBooks

Pinterest.com/HarlequinBooks

ReaderService.com

EXPLORE.

Sign up for the Harlequin e-newsletter and download a free book from any series at **TryHarlequin.com**

CONNECT.

Join our Harlequin community to share your thoughts and connect with other romance readers!
Facebook.com/groups/HarlequinConnection